Thirty Years Passed among the Players

An Archon Book on Popular Entertainments

A. H. Saxon, General Editor

THIRTY YEARS
PASSED AMONG THE PLAYERS
IN
ENGLAND AND AMERICA

By

Joe Cowell

(A facsimile edition)

ARCHON BOOKS   1979   Hamden, Connecticut

Library of Congress Cataloging in Publication Data

Cowell, Joseph, 1792-1863.
Thirty years passed among the players in England and America.

(An Archon book on popular entertainments)
Reprint of the 1844 ed. published by Harper,
New York.
1.   Cowell, Joseph, 1792-1863.   2.   Actors —
Great Britain — Biography.   3.   Theater — History —
19th century.   I. Title.   II. Series.
PN2598.C8A3   1979   792'.028'0924   [B]   78-26796
ISBN   0-208-01778-X

First published 1844 in New York

by Harper & Brothers, 82 Cliff-Street.

This facsimile edition published 1979

as an Archon book, an imprint of

The Shoe String Press, Inc.,

Hamden, Connecticut 06514

Contents

Foreword

The author of these memoirs, the popular actor Joe Cowell, was born Joseph Leathley Witchett in the Devonshire village of Torquay on 7 August 1792. After an abortive career in the navy, which he joined at the age of thirteen (the author is understandably reticent on the cause of his leaving the service, which was necessitated, in fact, by his striking an officer — an impetuous action that might well have resulted in a sentence of death, had it not been for young Joe's shortly afterward distinguishing himself in battle and receiving an antedated discharge for his bravery), he entered upon the life of an itinerant actor, adding to his meagre income by painting portraits and stage scenery. For the next several years he experienced the vicissitudes of a strolling player, performing in provincial theatres and traveling the English circuits, while establishing his reputation as a low comedian in such roles as Crack in *The Turnpike Gate* and Bob Acres in *The Rivals*. Eventually he made his way to London and Drury Lane Theatre, where he encountered such luminaries as Edmund Kean and served under that "best of cut-throats," Robert William Elliston. In the summer of 1821, while performing the role of Gil Blas at Astley's Amphitheatre, he was introduced to the American manager Stephen Price, who promptly engaged him for his own theatre, the Park, in New York City. Taking French leave of his colleagues at Astley's, he arrived on these shores in the fall of that year, and had the pleasure — as has many a traveler since — of being robbed during his first night in Gotham.

In subsequent years Joe Cowell was a well-known figure in the American theatre, not only as an actor but frequently as a manager. His original employers, Price and his partner Edmund Simpson, after purchasing the circus company of the English manager James West, had no hesitation in entrusting him with the direction of this valuable acquisition, and for several years he was what was known in the profession as a "horse shit and sawdust" manager. At other times he was in theatrical and circus management in such far-flung cities as Philadelphia, Charleston, and Nashville, always continuing to exercise his original vocation as an actor, however, and in this latter capacity often striking out on his own. For a time he was accompanied on his travels by his son Sam (1820-64), who made his stage debut, mimicking his father, at the age of nine and later became a star of the English music hall.

Although he was hardly present at the birth of the American theatre, Cowell was in a position to observe that institution in its infancy, and his descriptions of and candid comments on what he saw — whether the theatres themselves, the performers who appeared in them, or the makeshift arrangements actors were often forced to resort to when touring the frontier — are of particular interest to the historian. Throughout his narrative he expresses a lively sympathy for the young country and its people and institutions, in refreshing contrast to his compatriot Mrs. Trollope, whose ridiculous pretensions to fashion in Cincinnati he observed firsthand (and was glad to escape) and whose own publication, *Domestic Manners of the Americans*, he dismisses with the statement "Poor old lady, what a mess she made of it!" At the time of the appearance of his memoirs in 1844, Cowell's popularity with American audiences was still undiminished, and he continued to perform in provincial and metropolitan theatres for many years afterward. Toward the end of his life he returned to England and retired to Putney, where he died on 13 November 1863.

A. H. Saxon
General Editor

Thirty Years Passed among the Players

THIRTY YEARS

PASSED AMONG THE PLAYERS

IN

ENGLAND AND AMERICA:

INTERSPERSED WITH

ANECDOTES AND REMINISCENCES

OF A VARIETY OF PERSONS,

DIRECTLY OR INDIRECTLY CONNECTED WITH THE DRAMA DURING THE

THEATRICAL LIFE OF

JOE COWELL, COMEDIAN.

WRITTEN BY HIMSELF.

IN TWO PARTS.

PART I.—ENGLAND.

"No author who understands the boundaries of decorum and good breeding, would presume to think all: the truest respect which you can pay to the reader's understanding is to halve this matter amicably, and leave him something to imagine in his turn, as well as yourself."—STERNE.

NEW-YORK:

HARPER & BROTHERS, 82 CLIFF-STREET.

1844.

ADVERTISEMENT

TO THE WICKED READER.

In addressing for the first time a person—or body corporate or incorporate—some embarrassment often arises as to "the eftest way" of commencing your request or apology; but as I intend making neither the one nor the other, I feel no hesitation in adopting the above, as being most likely to suit the character of the class of persons into whose hands this work may fall. I have "turned over many books," and have found "Gentle Reader," and "Kind Reader," and all sorts of amiable "Readers" by dozens, but the "Wicked Reader" I think I have got all to myself. And if we only take notice of all that occurs to us every day in the week, and believe half what is said to us every Sunday, this book will certainly be perused by a very large majority who fully deserve the title I have selected for them.

Depending solely on memory for material, the incidents in the following pages are told without any strict regard to chronological order, but as they naturally connected themselves by "relative suggestion," as far as possible, with the impressions they made at the time. In fact, encumbering a book of this kind with dates, and heights, and distances, is like throwing a man overboard, to swim for his life, buttoned up in buckskin breeches and boots, when, by "*going it with a perfect looseness,*" he might have a small chance to escape.

The way I came to undertake this task at all was simply this. In the winter of 1841, my esteemed friend F. W. Thomas, Esq., the successful novelist, requested me to give him some anecdotical sketches of my life, to be prepared by his practical pen, as matter for a periodical he was then providing with suchlike insufficient food; and I wrote for that purpose the beginning of this very book. Faults are beauties to the eye of friendship; he declined accepting it, deeming it of higher value; and so strongly urged me to proceed with my recollections, that, having the luxury of leisure during the following summer, I wrote at random the first volume. But since then till now, having had to get my living by putting the nonsense of others into my head, I have had no time to spare to put my own upon paper. This long *wait between the acts* will, therefore, account for my speaking of my old friend Barnes and others as if they were still alive, when they have been foolish enough to die in the interim.

In the second volume, as I wrote carelessly along, I found I was recollecting too much, and was therefore compelled to take shelter in an abruptness which I had not at first contemplated. A smile of approbation from my old associates is the chief reward I look for from this truth-telling gossip; but if I told the *whole truth,* it might cause a *laugh on the wrong side of the mouth.* And even you, wicked reader, wouldn't wish me, though in joke, to wound the feelings of a class of persons the canting world has for ages made most sensitive to wrong, because it has never done them right.

And now, to borrow the extemporaneous language of the members of my profession, when "*respectfully*" informing an audience that some villanous tyro will be substituted instead of the sterling performer they have walked a mile and paid their dollar to see,

Most Wicked Reader,
"*I rely on your usual indulgence.*"
JOE COWELL.

Baltimore, August 1, 1843.

THIRTY YEARS

PASSED AMONG THE PLAYERS.

CHAPTER I.

"But what's his name, and where's his hame,
I dinna choose to tell."—Coming through the Rye.

" But whence his name
And lineage long, it suits me not to say."
Childe Harold.

On the seventh day of August, Anno Domini one thousand seven hundred and ninety-two, I came "into this breathing world."

CHAPTER II.

"I have neither the scholar's melancholy, which is emulation; nor the musician's, which is fantastical; nor the courtier's, which is proud; nor the soldier's, which is ambitious; nor the lawyer's, which is politic; nor the lady's, which is nice; nor the lover's, which is all these; but it is a melancholy of my own, compounded of many simples, extracted from many objects: and, indeed, the sundry contemplation of my travels, in which my often rumination wraps me, is a most humorous sadness."—SHAKSPEARE.

THE only spot on earth to which my memory turns with that peculiar feeling which they alone can appreciate who can remember the cot where they were born, is the little village of Tor-Quay, in Devonshire. But it was not where I was born: all I can recollect of the place of my nativity is, a very large, dark-looking room, and a very large, black-looking chimneypiece. Children always imagine every object much larger than it really is, and generally much brighter: it appears I was an exception to the latter supposition. I remember no little window

" Where the sun came peeping in at morn;"
Nor

" Fir-trees close against the sky,"

as Hood says so prettily; nothing but the large, dark room, and large, black chimneypiece: perhaps a sad prognostic of my future fortunes.

The local inhabitants of this insignificant little village—it was so then, and I suppose is so now—were fishermen, pilots, and boatbuilders; a simple, industrious, kind-hearted people. How often have the little shoeless urchins slyly thrust me a slice of their dark-brown bread through the trellis-work of the flower-garden, in front of the house; and many a weather-beaten handful of forbidden fruit has been dropped into the ready pin-a'-fore of "Master Joe," and devoured with ecstasy in the most private place on the premises.

The county of Devon is called, and justly so, the garden of England. Climate gives character to all animals, and in that calm, yet genial spot, where, in the open air, the simple jessamine twines its perfumed tendrils amid the dazzling beauties of the passion-flower, the blood so smoothly flows to work its task of life, that man's nature partakes of the serenity of the atmosphere, and all is health, and peace, and calm content.

At the period to which I allude (I shall purposely avoid all useless dates) *Tor-Bay* was the chosen rendezvous of the Channel fleet. The satirical couplet of

" Lord Howe he went out,
And, lord! how he came in,"

would have been equally applicable to the fleet then under the command of Earl St. Vincent, but that the Saint precluded the pun. Adverse winds, in that most adverse channel, and the nothing-to-do-duty this then terror of the ocean had to perform, made even mooring and unmooring a precautionary employment, for thousands of men to be kept in subordination literally by one: all old *man-o'-wars men* know it is safe policy never to let Jack have time to think of anything but his duty. Frequently the fleet would be in harbour two and three weeks at a time, diverting the people with cleaning, painting, polishing, and punishing; then to sea for a like period, and into port again.

The beauty of the climate, the facilities for sea-bathing, and the joy which every sailor feels at being surrounded by "wife, children, and friends," induced many of the superior officers to hire the better sort of houses which could be procured, or build slight compact ones for the accommodation of their families. In a large fleet, carpenters, masons, mechanics of all sorts, and labourers by hundreds, are readily obtained; houses were built, furnished, and occupied as if by magic, and the country, for miles around, being thickly studded with the rural residences of the nobility and gentry, Tor-Quay, at that time, became suddenly the most exclusively fashionable watering-place in the kingdom.

In a small, neat house, fitted up in elegant simplicity, situated on a gentle ascent from the beach, and overlooking the whole harbour, lived my protectress—my more than mother. Here, loving and beloved, I passed three innocently happy years.

The arrival of the fleet was the signal for joy and festivity; sailing-matches, boat-clubs, pony races, banquets, balls, and concerts occupied a portion of each day and evening. In compliment to Earl St. Vincent, on his birthday a more than usually splendid festival was given at Carey Sands, a country seat a few miles distant from our house, and "the *children*," indulged in everything (which health and morals would permit), were allowed to see the commencement of a masked ball, walk through the rooms, and return early home. Here I first saw Lord Nelson, a mean-looking little man, but very kind and agreeable to children; he prophesied a very different fate for me from what it has been, and some trifling anecdotes of himself, which he probably invented to please a boy, made so strong an impression on my mind as greatly to influence my conduct while in the navy.

A spacious hall, fitted up as a theatre, attracted our particlar notice. As I afterward learned, a company of players, from the adjacent town of Totness, were engaged to give two or three exhibitions, the festival lasting a week. The fireworks, ox-roastings, balls, and concerts were all described and explained to us, and all perfectly understood, excepting the play, and that was incomprehensible. To satisfy our tortured curiosity, this angel woman (her name is too sacred to be put on record with the adventures of a poor player) actually engaged a portion of the company to give an entertainment at our house *to please the children.* Shrink not, ye props and ornaments of the profession, when I tell you you have often, perhaps without thinking it, been placed in the same position. How frequently have I heard a fond parent say, "If you are good children, I'll take you to see Kean, or Forrest, or Macready." For my own part, many a time has some fat-headed patron of the drama said, "Cowell, my boy, I'm going to take my little girls to see your Crack to night, so do your best."

The day, big with fate, at length arrived, and "the best actors in the world"—I *think* four in number. One didn't speak, but merely rung a little bell, and snuffed the candles, and when he put one out we all laughed, and he made a very formal bow; he was a comical-looking creature, dressed in large, white Turkish trousers and a footman's jacket. Preparations immediately commenced; the dining parlour was speedily unfurnished, and the adjoining room "thrown into one," that is, as far as wide-opening a common-sized door could make two rooms into one. Chairs, sofas, and ottomans were placed in rows, and elevated, in the back apartment, where the servants and humble neighbours were to be accommodated, to peep through the open door over our heads. All the flat candlesticks in the house were put in a line, in front of the seats intended for the family, and separated from them by a long board nailed on edge. How well do I remember with what wonder and admiration I looked on at the adroit manner in which signal Jacks, ensigns, and blue-peters, window and bed curtains, were furled, puckered, tacked, and tied, by a slim, long-nosed young gentleman, in shirt-sleeves, knee-breeches, and blue worsted stockings, to form the wings and drops of this mimic stage! At length all was completed—the performance was to commence " at early candle-light:" never do I recollect so long an afternoon as that was but once since, and that was, five hours passed in a sponging-house waiting for bail. At length the day drew in, "and night, the lover's friend," advanced; the bell was rung, and the seats in the rear immediately occupied, according to the age and grade of the party. We were placed in front, the governess at our backs, ready to explain any doubtful point, and direct our deportment: our general instructions were, to clap our hands when she did, and not to laugh; this latter command I made up my

mind to disobey; and I did. To her supposed superior judgment in juvenile matters had been left the control of the entertainment, and she had selected "*Hamlet*" (only a portion of the tragedy, I suppose), but whether to suit her own taste, or her pupils, I can only imagine. She was a romantic little body. She hated me with all her heart, but was too prudent to say so; and I hated her with all my soul, and said so to everybody. She had a very pretty, ill-natured looking face, and small neat figure, in despite of one very crooked leg; this fact I discovered in consequence of her tumbling, head foremost, over a stile one slippery day; and for laughing most heartily—who could help it?—I was locked up in a cupboard, at the door of which I kicked so lustily for half an hour, they were obliged to let me out, "*I made such a noise!*"*

I forget if there was any overture, or an apology for one in any way; but music, from my infancy, being as familiar as a household god, it was not likely to live in my memory. I suppose they began the play where Horatio informs Hamlet of his "last night of all" adventure, for I recollect nothing preceding that dialogue, which I was astonished to find I had often read in that excellent book for children, "Enfield's Speaker." I love that book still; it gave me the first relish for more substantial food, and if I can sell this, I'll buy a copy for my grandson. Presently the Ghost glided in from behind a French flag—there was one on each side of the room, with the English ensign over it—enveloped in a white sheet, something white on his head, his face white-washed, and a white truncheon in his hand. All was breathless attention; but, before he had time to reply to Hamlet's earnest inquiries, I shouted out, with all my might, "That's the man who nailed up the flags!" For, in defiance of his white-all-over-ness, I recognised in the Ghost my friend in the knee-breeches, for whom I had held the hammer, and helped so nicely (as he said) in the morning. The governess gave me one of her withering looks, but all the rest of the audience laughed most heartily; so did Hamlet, so did the Ghost, till his white sheet shook again.

Hamlet—" methinks I see him now"—was a slim, round-faced, good-looking young man, and, I imagine, rather effeminate in his manner; for all agreed he was very like our very pretty housemaid Sally. He was dressed in a suit of modern black, a frill about his neck, with a silver cord and tassel, his head powdered (the fashion of the time); a spangled red cloak; the order of the garter around his leg; a broad-brimmed, black velvet hat, turned up in front, and a large *diamond* shoe-buckle, supposed to enclasp one tall, white feather. But Horatio had five (we all counted them); his waistcoat, too, was nearly covered with gold, and his cloak was spangled all over; he wore light blue pantaloons, and red shoes—I forget the colour of his hat. He was decidedly my favourite, and I believe the favourite of all; at any rate, the children and servants thought as I did, *that he was worth all the rest of them put together;* besides, "in the course of the evening," he sung a fine loud song, about ships and the navy, and danced a sailor's hornpipe; but whether they were introduced in the tragedy or after it, I know not. He appeared to have twice as much to say as Hamlet had, and what he did say he said three times as loud; all the

---

* I cannot but regret these delightful visions of my childhood, which, like the fine colours we see when our eyes are shut, are vanished forever.—Alexander Pope.

auditors in the next room could hear every word he uttered; and, as more than half could not see him through the open door, it was quite enough to make him a great favourite in their estimation. The coachman said he heard one speech while he was feeding the horses; and the stable was at least one hundred yards from the house; no doubt the same speech which frightened two of the youngest children. They cried, and, at their own request, were sent to bed.

Hamlet made several long soliloquies, and as he looked me straight in the face, I thought he addressed me in particular; so when he inquired,

> " Whether 'tis nobler in the mind to suffer
> The slings and arrows of outrageous fortune,
> Or to take arms against a *sea* of troubles—"

I replied, "If I were you I'd go to sea." This called forth a most joyous shout from the next room, for even then I was the low-comedian of the household; but my female Mentor said I was a very bad boy (I was used to her saying that), and if I spoke again I should be sent to bed. So when I thought Hamlet was going to make me another long speech, I shut my eyes, and made up my mind to go to sleep till it was over. But my friend Horatio soon roused me. In fact, he was one of the many actors who are determined to be heard, at any rate; and "tired Nature" must be very tired indeed if she could take her "second course" while he was declaiming. I have met with many *Horatios* since, and they, like my *first impression*, are always great favourites with children and the uninformed. There was a *star* Horatio engaged in the last company I played with, and nine tenths of the audience thought and said he was a very fine actor. Well, let them think so; I'll not contradict them; I was sorry myself when I was undeceived.

Hamlet spoke Collins's beautiful " *Ode on the Passions;*" he didn't deliver it as the governess read it; I thought then he was right and she was wrong: I have changed my opinion since. The Ghost sang a comic song, and the whole party

> " Ye mariners of England,"

the candle-snuffer giving his "powerful aid" in the chorus.

Exhausted with wonder and delight, I went to bed. I prayed every night that I might be *made a good boy* and *go to heaven*. I fell asleep, and dreamed that I had got there, and was surrounded by dozens of Hamlets, and Horatios, and Ghosts in red wigs and striped stockings, dancing, and singing "all manner of songs," and the angels applauding them in the most boisterous manner; but when I waked, I didn't "cry to dream again," for, to my astonishment, I heard Horatio singing away with all his might in the housekeeper's room, amid clapping of hands and shouts of laughter.

Before I closed my eyes again that night, I made up my mind that I would rather be that Horatio, and do "all that," than be Horatio Nelson, though he had lost an eye, and banged the French.

> " Where then did the Raven go ?
> He went high and low ;
> Over hill, over dale, did the black Raven go.
> Many autumns, many springs,
> Travell'd he with wandering wings ;
> Many summers, many winters—
> I sha'n't tell half his adventures."
>
> COLERIDGE.

CHAPTER III.

> "Truly, in my youth I suffered much extremity for love."
> —SHAKSPEARE.

I was just "turned sixteen," as the children say, but in manner and appearance much older. Three years in the navy, the usual hardships of a sailor's life, a complexion stained with salt water and the sun of many climes, are materials to make boys into men at very short notice. I had three weeks' leave of absence, prior to a twelve months' cruise on the West India station. My mother lived next door to Grosvenor Chapel; and on Sunday morning, determining to see all that could be seen (as my days were numbered), I "dropped in" to witness the service. In using Paul Pry's flippant expression, I must not now, nor then, be understood to have any but the most profound respect for all religious ceremonies; but, having been educated a rigid Roman Catholic, at that period my entering an Episcopal house of God was induced by pure curiosity. In the adjoining pew sat an elderly, tradesmanlike-looking man, with a pug nose, and a round, unmeaning face, resembling altogether a very good-natured bulldog; with him a plump old lady, and an elegantly-dressed young creature—their daughter, of course; but where could she get such an abominable, plebeian-looking father and mother? I felt angry that nature had made herself so ridiculous. She was most beautiful, refined in her deportment, and a perfectly aristocratic face. Her fine eye, I thought, sometimes wandered towards me; a naval uniform, in those days, was quite as attractive as a soldier's is in these; she sat close to me, nothing but the abominable bulkhead of the pew between us,

> " Where she kneel'd, and, saint-like,
> Cast her fair eyes to heaven, and pray'd devoutly."

An angel's whisper! there is no preaching I ever heard can produce on my mind such a pure devotional feeling as listening to little children and pretty women saying their prayers; I always want to go to heaven along with them directly. I thought I heard her sigh. Our eyes met as she said Amen; my heart palpitated, and "Amen stuck in my throat." I had been in love two or three times before, and have been in love ever since, and perfectly understood all the symptoms; but, as Ollapod says, there were "matrimonial symptoms in this case." In my own mind, I had got the consent of my mother (who could refuse to permit a union with such a divinity?), and had retired, *on a British midshipman's half pay*, to a "cottage near a wood," with a cow, cabbage-garden, chickens, and children. The only impediment that appeared to cross my path to pre-eminent felicity was her puddingfaced, pug-nosed parents; my mother would decidedly object to them, whatever she might think of their daughter. In my confusion of thought, I stood up in the pew, and popped on my hat with the cockade behind ; the old gentleman pointed out my error; I thought I saw a childlike giggle play over the beautiful face of my adored; I would have given two years' pay to be shot on the spot, or tossed overboard in a gale of wind, or mast-headed, out of sight of land or petticoats, for the rest of my life. The service ended, I gained the door as they did, and tendered an awkward acknowledgment of thanks to the old man for correcting my ridiculous position.

"Sir," said he, with a plethoric kind of chuckle, "you gentlemen of the navy, sir, don't often go to church, I suppose, sir; but, sir, I love a sail-or, sir; I'm a loyal subject, sir; God bless the king, sir, and God Almighty bless the queen, sir. She, sir, is, sir, the mother, sir—that is, the queen-mother, sir—and I'm blessed, sir, if she oughtened to be blessed, sir, for blessing the country, sir, with such a blessed lot of royal highnesses, sir. Sir, I'm a true-born English-man, and a loyal subject, sir, and have the hon-our to be leather-breeches-maker, sir, to His Roy-al Highness the Duke of Sussex, sir," pointing, at the same time, to a sign over a bow-window, by the side of which he stopped, and rung a bell at the private entrance. The door was opened by a boy in undress livery; we bowed and part-ed. I looked up. Sure enough, there was "the precious evidence," "*William* (I think) *Creek, Tailor and Breeches-maker in ordinary to His Royal Highness the Duke of Sussex*," in green and gold letters, and the King's Arms in a semicircle over it, exactly four doors from my mother's house. I had followed my charmer (who was on the outside) at an angular distance of about three feet, sometimes on the curbstone, some-times in the gutter, or, as a sailor might say, about two points to leeward. Now this was not *mauvaise honte* on my part, but prudence; for, upon coming alongside in the first instance, I found, to my astonishment, she was at least three inches taller than myself. In everyday language, she was what is called a magnificent creature,

> " With beauty too rich for use, for earth too dear ;"

a very effeminate, Miss Clifton style of woman. Over her sculptured form she had thrown a splendid scarlet mantle, trimmed with white er-mine; a white hat, with a drooping red feather, adorned her classic head. I am still, and for years have been, allowed to possess great taste for ladies' dress, but at the time I speak of, per-haps, it was a little Goldfinch-ish : " Sky-blue habit, scarlet sash, white hat, yellow ribands, gold band and tassel—that's your sort !"

I was in love—most horribly in love—

> " 'Twas through my eyes the shaft had pierced my heart ;
> Chance gave the wound that time could never cure."

But she was (oh horrible thought !) the daughter of a leather-breeches builder, and my mother, like Rob Roy, had " an utter contempt for weav-ers, and spinners, and all such mechanical per-sons." But then he made breeches for His Roy-al Highness the Duke of Sussex ! how might that soften down the bowels of aristocratic au-thority ? There was hope in that thought, and I determined to be measured for a pair the next day : though I had but little time to wear them; for, on the station to which I was ordered, even if the service would permit the costume, the cli-mate would not.

On the following morning I called on Mr. Creek.

"Sir, he's at breakfast, sir," said the knock-kneed boy in the gray livery I had noticed the day before; " but, sir, if 'tis anything partic'lar, sir, I'll call him, sir."

"Do so, sir; I wish, sir, to see him, sir, di-rectly, sir," said I, following the *sir-ish* fashion.

The bow-window apartment I had entered was covered with a handsome carpet; in the centre a billiard-like table, on which were wri-ting materials, and the papers of the day; and the walls decorated with numerous mirrors. My prospect of consent began to brighten. If he was a breeches-maker, he didn't breakfast till ten o'clock, and kept a sort of livery-servant. I had barely time to think so much, and peep through a glass case, the width of the shop, covered with a demi-transparent green curtain, behind which at least thirty men were employed on a platform, stitching away at his royal highness's small-clothes, I suppose—when Mr. Creek appeared. His fat face was buttered from ear to ear, which he proceeded to wipe with his folded handker-chief, while in his peculiar style he paid me the compliments of the day. When he came to a pause, I begged him, in my most urbane man-ner, to measure me for a suit of clothes.

" Sir, with pleasure, sir. A uniform suit, of course, sir ? I pride myself on my uniform fits, sir. This coat is a little too much—"

I interrupted, no doubt, a learned lecture on what a uniform coat should be, by quietly say-ing, " I wish a plain suit, Mr. Creek."

" A plain suit, sir ? Bless me, sir ! have you left your ship for any length of time, sir ?"

" I may shortly leave the navy altogether," said I, with a sigh. I thought of the cottage and the cow; and as my mother cheerfully paid my bills at that time, and might not after I had retired from the service and married the tailor's daughter, prudence prompted me to order a green coat, red waistcoat, and leather breeches—a very fitting dress for rural felicity. The red vest I ordered in compliment to the colour of my wife's cloak—that was to be; and I hinted, that if it could be made off the same piece of cloth that his daughter's mantle was composed of, I should prize it more highly. I imagined it was cabbage on an extensive scale.

" Oh, sir," said the old man, his little blue eyes twinkling on either side of his bit of putty-like nose, " she's not my daughter. I—"

" God be praised !" exclaimed I, not waiting for his " *wish she was*" conclusion of his sentence, I suppose.

" Sir !" said he, his face suddenly assuming an expression of gravity which its fat-encumber-ed muscles seemed impossible for it to achieve, " sir—I beg pardon, sir—but I should like to know, sir, why you should appear so thankful, sir, that Anna is not my daughter, sir ?"

ANNA ! I heard her name for the first time; a pastoral, poetical, and pretty name—a real sail-or's name :

> " I call her Anna, Anne,
> Nan, Nance, or Nancy."

I blundered out, that I had thanked God that, in addition to her natural protector, she had a friend of his age and respectability to guide her moral deportment, of which I judged from the sacred place to which he had conducted her when *we first met*. A shade of doubt passed over his countenance; but he recollected I was his customer, and his natural good-humour and common sense prevailed. In his own way, he went on to explain that Anna had no father; he had died when she was an infant; and had left her mother " well to do in the world," with three children, all girls, two much older than Anna, and one long since married to a cousin of his wife. She was a native of ——, in Berkshire; at her father's death, her mother had taken a milliner's shop, where Anna had learned the ru-diments of the business, but had been sent to London under his care, and was now articled for three years (two and a half of which were yet to stretch their slow length along) to the Misses Twicross, the celebrated dressmakers in Bond-street, with a premium of fifty guineas, to be *finished*, as he called it.

Upon giving my name and address, the old man exclaimed, "Why, bless me, sir! I have, sir, the honour, sir, to be in great favour with your mamma, sir; my neighbour, sir; and, you know, sir, it's very few people as is, sir—" with a kind of confidential chuckle. "You see, sir, her kitchen-chimney was on fire, sir, and the maid-servants set up a terrible screeching, sir; and there was so much smoke, sir, that you could not see where the fire was, sir; and the parish engine, sir, being in the basement story of the chapel, sir, next house to hers, sir, as one may say, sir; I, sir, and my boy, sir, and the poor apple-woman, sir, that she kindly gives leave, sir, to sit at the corner of the court, sir, pulled it out, sir, and I dragged the hose into the passage, sir; but the fire went out, sir, before we could get any water, sir; but your good mamma, sir, coming down stairs, sir, and seeing me with the brass nozzle in my hand, sir, thought I had extinguished it, sir; and so, sir, whenever she speaks of me, sir, she always says, ' *The good man that saved my property by putting out the fire —Mr.—what's his name? something that puts my teeth on edge?*' ' *Mr. Creek, ma'am,*' says Mary. ' *Yes, Mr. Squeak—that's it.*' " The jolly old man chatted himself into a most familiar good-humour. I recounted some of my ship-shape adventures, and, well pleased with each other, we parted, with my promising (oh, how gladly!) to take a cup of tea with himself and wife, and Anna, "just in the family-way," that evening. I am not going to tantalize my readers with a rodomontade of love-making; suffice it to say, Anna had received an education far above her station: affable, nay, even free in her manner, "than those who have more cunning to be strange," but with a mind as simply pure and unpolluted as the stream that wanders through and adorns her native village. I readily obtained permission, to save Mr. Creek the trouble, of conducting her to Bond-street in the morning. The jovial old tailor had made us stand back to back, to decide our height; and he declared, "Anna, sir, is only an inch taller, sir, than you are, sir—*good measure*, sir." When, at an early hour the next day, we met, I had heels to my boots that placed me on a level with her at any rate ; and, before we had crossed Grosvenor Square, I had good reason to believe that our hopes and wishes were more on an equality than our persons. Doubt not I was most punctual in my attendance to and from South Audley-street to Bond-street. Three times that week, and four the next, accompanied by the old people, we attended the theatre. The first legitimate play I ever beheld Anna sat beside me— 'twas Romeo and Juliet. "They must have played it on purpose," said the innocent Anna, in a whisper, and her cheek wet with tears; and I, in my heart, damned the author for not letting them live and be happy.

Charles Kemble was *the* Romeo—the *great* Lewis, Mercutio—Miss Norton, Juliet—la, la (but I never saw a Juliet such as Shakspeare intended)—the glorious Mrs. Davenport, the Nurse—and Murray, the silver-toned, serene, and beautifully-natural Charles Murray, was the lovers' friend, the botanical Friar Lawrence. I passed two whole, dear, delicious Sundays in her society. Oh how sweet

> "To walk together to the kirk,
> And all together pray !"

I spoke not of my difference of creed, for, for her sake, I would have turned Turk.

The old man was our confidant and councillor. "Sir, you must join your ship, sir, at the proper time, sir; and Anna, sir, must finish her time with the Misses Twicross's, sir, and get the worth of her fifty guineas, sir; and you must fight the enemies of Old England! Oh! I'm a loyal subject, sir; and when you're a lieutenant, sir, and the old lady won't consent, sir, if you both, sir, think, sir, as you do now, sir, and there should come a peace, sir, you'll get your half pay, sir; you can teach transportation, navigation I mean, sir, and drawing, and painting, sir" (I had been well instructed, and had taken his and his wife's portraits, and Anna's "picture in little"); "and she will be mistress of her art, sir; I am well to do in the world, sir; have neither chick nor child; Anna's father was a good friend of mine, sir—lent me money when I first went into business, sir; but never fret, sir; take things cool, as I do, sir," wiping the perspiration from his fat forehead; "all will be right, sir; take my advice, sir." *I wish to God I had.*

The fatal second Sunday at length arrived— I thought, in the middle of the week. I had to set forth post, at 7 P.M., to ensure my being on board by gunfire on Monday morning; but it was past nine before I could finish all my oaths of constancy, and exchange those tokens sailors think so sacred.

With hope decking the future in the rainbow colours of love at seventeen, I rushed into the chaise, on a bright autumnal evening, and, faster than the sun, I seemed to travel on the same road to Portsmouth, to overtake him in a few weeks in the West Indies.

The tedium of many a weary middle-watch in that sunburned sea has been relieved of its monotony in (castle-) building, the cottage, and the cow, the chickens and the children ; and then,

> "Look'd on the moon,
> And thought of Nancy."

CHAPTER IV.

> " Hope, thou hast told me lies from day to day
> For *nearly* twenty years."
>
> Young.

With my last shilling in my pocket, and my heart pretty nearly in the same place, I was seated about the middle of the high flight of stone steps leading to one of the entrances of the dockyards, watching the gambols of some boys bathing on the shore beneath. "To myself I said," if I could only take courage, and keep my head under water as long as that lad does, "in a merry sport," I might speedily end all my troubles, and the anxiety of those who still care for and love me.

The red sun was dodging now and again behind some fantastical long gray clouds, and apparently descending with more than usual rapidity, as if in derisive imitation of the friendship of man. "Good-by—I'm sorry for your misfortunes, but—I'm in a hurry—good-by."

I had arrived at Plymouth Dock about three weeks previous to this period, with "time cut from out eternity's wide round" before me, and fifty pounds in my pocket—an inexhaustible sum to my nineteen years' old experience—probably five guineas was the largest amount I had ever had in my possession before, at one time, in my life; all my necessities had been amply supplied, and every member of a cockpit knows that, as to money, "man wants but little *there* below." Young minds are more easily depressed than those which have had long experience of "fortune's buffets and rewards;" my landlady at the White Horse, who was the gray mare of that establishment, had that day given me notice of "no liquor and no credit," and two days more had elapsed than necessary to bring me an answer to my letter, praying for *positively the last assistance I would ever ask for.* I had "wasted myself out of my means" in boarding every outward-bound merchantman, and treating the captains to "five-pound suppers and after-drinkings," to bribe my way as a mate in some craft bound to any land, "so not again to mine." But in those days my finished theoretical knowledge was an impediment to a command under these prejudiced, ignorant, "petty traffickers." The British navy, with two wars at her back, seized upon all who could be serviceable, and many a three and four hundred ton merchant vessel would go to sea with a skipper, two mates, and five or six landsmen or boys, to follow in the wake of a convoy, content with a dead reckoning, if any at all, kept on a black board with a piece of chalk.

In the frame of mind I then was, I might, when the sun and little boys got out of my way, have wet myself at any rate, but that just as they were all preparing to depart, the arrival of a man-o'-war's boat immediately at the foot of the stairs where I was sitting formed a new impediment to my cold-water experiment. "A gross, fat man," in a warrant officer's uniform, landed, followed by a seaman bearing a large-sized chest: as he reached the step on which I sat, I rose to let him pass; he, in a rough, authoritative manner, exclaimed, in a broad Scotch dialect, "Od, but it's queer what can mak shore people sae fond o' sitting on sic a gangway as this—it's fu' small way—and no' intended for ony but his majesty's officers and sic like."

Before the conclusion of his rude address, I had recognised him for an old shipmate; our eyes met—he stood for an instant the picture of penitent astonishment, and in the next I was half crushed to death in his ponderous embrace.

He had been before the mast of a sloop of war I belonged to for a short time, and in boarding a French lugger privateer, was wounded twice, and his bravery was instantly rewarded by making him a quartermaster, the first step for promotion to a warrant. Our corvette was condemned as no longer seaworthy on her arrival at the very port where we now again met, and by accident he was sent on board the same ship I was then ordered to join. He had always been a great favourite with me, for, apart from his being a brave man and a good sailor, his childlike blessing in the hour of peril on his old father and mother and his native home, proved the kindness of his nature; and though he had not seen either since he was a boy, his tongue still retained as strong a love for its language as his heart did for its soil.

Trinculo says, "Misery acquaints a man with strange bedfellows:" it certainly levels all distinctions. Pride and poverty had so struggled away the strength of my boyish mind, that even the rough kindness of this weather-beaten Scotchman so subdued my *care-devil* nature, that "tears, the heart's best balm," flowed in torrents, and I sobbed long and loud in his arms; had he been my father, I am sure I should have felt as I did then, but

> "I never a father's protection knew—
> Never had a father to protect."

"Dinna fret man, dinna fret; there's na use i' fretting—I ha' heard o' your scrape. Deil scoup wi' the feller as caused it—he's an awsome body that, and naebody su'd care till anger him—but ye was a'ways a rattling cheel. But ye ha' a gude friend i' the admiral, and he'll pass it a' ower easy."

"He has passed it over *easy*," said I: "he has obtained my discharge by sick-list, to save me from a court-martial, who, in its mercy, might have condemned me to be shot. Damn the service! and all that belongs to it."

"Nay, nay," said he, soothingly, "ye wold na' damn me?"

I could not speak—my heart felt as if it had overflowed up to my neck—I grasped his honest hand.

"I didna' ken the case was sae bad," said he: "let's say na mair about it; you must awa home wi' me. Oh, you need na stare, I ha' got a home and a wife too—

> "'In every port we find a home,
> In every home a wife, sir.'

"Oh, she's a real wife—I was na' but bleating out an auld snatch of a song just to cheer ye up like. Heave a head wi' the trunk, Steeney—" to the seaman, a long, red-whiskered fellow; a countryman, no doubt. "I ha' gotten a wee dribble o' Port wine in a keg in it, whilk I'm taken right through the yard"—with an amateur smuggler's look—"so they mayna' suspect onything; the puir body at home is fond of a wee sup, hot wi' sugar, afore turning in."

His explanation of the contents of the box was superfluous, for I heard the well-known squish, squash, as the man again lifted it on his shoulder. After passing unmolested through the dockyard, a few short turns brought us to a shoemaker's shop; behind the counter was a little man with wax-ends and upper leather written in his face (what a strange thing it is that shoemakers always look like shoemakers): he was employed in lighting a second candle, for it was then dark.

"Awa' above wi' the prize, Steeney, and tell Missus Mackay," with a strong emphasis on the *Missus*, and a twinkle of his good-natured eye at me, "tell Missus Mackay to put a' to rights, as she ca's it—I ha' gotten a gentleman wi' me. Mr. Hobblin," to the shoemaker ('twas his real name), "this is the gentleman I tell'd ye of, as got me made" (here he gave me another disabling shake of the hand). "I'll tell ye a' about it—and that'll gi' the auld woman time till get a' ready—she's a wee bit fussy; but, gude sir, gude—take a chair—I can sit anywhere," pouncing his ponderous person on a pile of sole leather in the corner, which his weight brought immediately to within a foot of the floor; "ye need na' mind, Master Hobblin; no harm done; it's got till be hammered, ony how. Weel, ye see, I was on liberty, taking a cruise on the Holy Ground, as they ca' it; if ye was ever at Cove o' Cork, ye maun ken, there's na sic a place for fun in a' England, or Scotland till boot—weel, I was having a crack wi' an auld shipmate as belanged till the *Yolus*—he was braggin' o' his ship, but na braggin' o' his captain; ye ken when fellers are afore the mast," here he polished one of the anchor buttons on his sleeve, "they will a' grumble sometimes wi'out cause—but in his case, I dare say, he was na' far out in his reckoning. Weel, ye see, as I could na' brag my ship against his, I bragged on our captain—he comes frae puir auld Scotland—and naebody had muckle chance till say onything against him; he wad but just walk up the 'commodation ladder every day at twal o'clock, and if there was na' ony punishment, he'd mak his bow and gang down again; and if there sud be a needcessity to punish some puir dewil, he'd na' seem to tak ony pleasure in it—just read the articles o' war, and ask the feller if he wad prefer till be tried by a court-martial, and mair than likely get hanged, or take twa or three dozen at aince. In course they a' did, whiles I belanged till the ship, but ane puir, daft toad o' an Irishman, and he wad insist till be tried by the laws o' his country, as he ca'd it; and he dangled at the ear-ring o' the foreto'sail yard—there's na gude in being ower obstinate—weel, ye maun ken, if it was for naething mair than owerstaying liberty, or the like o' that; when they'd gotten a dozen or sae, he'd whisper till the doctor, and the doctor wad whisper till the captain, and he'd say, 'Master-at-arms, take him down;' then they'd pipe the sidesmen, and he wad make his bow and shove off. Weel, ye see, as I had got till windward o' him as till our commander (that is, our captain—the admiral was the commander, o' course, though I ne'er seed him but aince, and then he was a horseback; I bow'd till him as in duty bound, and he bow'd till me becase he liked it), I thought I wad brag o' the ship a wee bit; ye ken frae Mother Oakley's door ye can see her, moored off Haul-bowlin Island; weel, ye see, just as I was pointing out the beauty o' her model—crack! crack! goes the muskets o' the twa centries o' the Tender, and in a minute a'terwards three out o' four marines blazed awa frae the Trent, but they did na' ken at what; the Tender lying in-shore, they could na' see, as I did, that four men had cut the painter o' the yawl frae the guess-warp o' the Tender, and were making for shore. I gave chase till overhaul 'em, as they made up hill, and just came up as young master, here, had brought them to; ye see, the sight o' a uniform till a round jacket, is like till a constable's stave till you landsmen; they were fresh press'd men, and wad a' gaed quietly aboard, but, in a minute or sae, full a hundred women and bairns a' thegether, set up a yelloch that made a' ring again, and came rampanging like so many devils, wi' sticks, and staves, and a' kinds o' kitchen furniture; the women fought like furies, and the bairns a bletherin a' the time in full chorus, we suld ha' been murdered but that his boat was a' ready at the landing, and sae we managed till get the men o' board. I gat this gash on my cheek, and young master wi' a big bump on his head instead o' his hat. We had baith been in a *real fuss* thegither, a short time afore, and was baith on the list for promotion; there's naething like untill a friend at court, Mr. Hobblin; he had gotten the ear o' the admiral, and sae he put baith this and that thegither, and I was made a gunner, and sent on board the Dryad. But let's awa aloft and see the auld woman."

Eve, they tell us, was made out of one of her husband's ribs; Mrs. Mackay (as far as bulk was concerned) could have been made very easily out of one of her husband's legs; he was a remarkably large man, and she a remarkably small woman, but the best brewer of punch I ever met with before or since. We had a jovial evening—in vino veritas—I tolu all; and Mrs. Mackay insisted that she should make me up "a nice bed on the sofa," and remain and take "pot luck" with them till pay-day came, when my old shipmate would settle up arrears, and I should quit the mess at the White Horse. His vessel was undergoing repairs, and he was on shore-duty at the navy yard, having flint-locks shipped on the carronades. "A maist abominable invention," as he said, "just as much as till say that every captain o' a gun at the Nile, St. Vincent, or Trafalgar was o' no gude till the service."

To gratify my friend and amuse myself, I had taken an "inveterate likeness" of my old shipmate, and another of his little wife; these were shown to Mr. Hobbling, their landlord. His brother was the *deputy-mayor* of the little *Rotten Borough* of Saltash in Cornwall, at that time called so with justice, for it could boast of sending two members to Parliament to represent a population six or eight houses were sufficient to contain; while Birmingham, and Manchester, and other large and densely-inhabited places, had no "sweet voices" in the councils of their country. The chief magistrate, as I have observed, was "despatched by deputy," and this dignitary requested I would take two such likenesses of himself and wife, for which he was willing to pay any price. I undertook the task for thirty guineas, and gave such satisfaction that I received twenty more for making copies. During the time occupied in this operation on the mayor and his wife, I called, with my friend Mackay, at an extensive manufactory of glazed leather hats: a regulation had just been introduced in the navy, to have an initial of the ship's name, or some fanciful device, on the hat of each of the crew, as a good mark to know what vessel he belonged to, in the event of desertion or ill conduct on shore. All the mystery of the process I learned by looking on, the design and execution "came by nature;" and I actually decorated with a 𝔅, in genuine gingerbread style, the hats of the crew of a ship on board of which, a short year ago, I was an officer.

An old messmate, a lieutenant of marines, who had borrowed a guinea of me "for an hour" three weeks before, called one day (perhaps to borrow another) and caught me at my degrading employment, as he chose to consider it, and the next morning he crossed a muddy street to avoid speaking to me. But for my own part, conscious pride and confidence in my own resources made me for the first time in my life *feel independent*, and that feeling has never forsaken me midst many turns of

> " Giddy fortune's furious, fickle wheel, —
> That goddess blind."

But for meeting with the character to whom I devote the next chapter, I might have been painting hats or faces " at this present writing."

◆

CHAPTER V.

" Jig off a tune at the tongue's end, canary to it with your feet, humour it with turning up your eyelids ; sigh a note, and sing a note ; with your hat penthouse-like o'er the shop of your eyes ; with your arms crossed on your thin belly-doublet, like a rabbit on a spit ; or your hands in your pockets, like a man after the old painting ; and keep not too long in one tune, but snip and away. These are accomplishments, these are humours ; these betray nice wenches,

13

I was seated in the reading-room of the hotel, thinking away the half hour before dinner, when my attention was attracted by a singularly-looking man. He was dressed in a green coat, brass-buttoned close up to the neck, light gray, approaching to blue, elastic pantaloons, white cotton stockings, dress shoes, with more riband employed to fasten them than was either useful or ornamental; a hat, smaller than those usually worn, placed rather on one side of a head of dark curly hair; fine black eyes, and what altogether would have been pronounced a handsome face, but for an overpowering expression of impudence and vulgarity; a sort of footman-out-of-place-looking creature; his hands were thrust into the pockets of his coat behind, and in consequence exposing a portion of his person, as ridiculously, and perhaps as unconsciously, as a turkey-cock does when he intends to make himself very agreeable. He was walking rather fancifully up and down the room, partly singing, partly whistling " *The Bay of Biscay O*," and at the long-lived, but most nonsensical chorus, he shook the fagends of his divided coat tail, as if in derision of that fatal "short sea," so well known and despised in that salt-water burial-place. I was pretending to read a paper, but, in fact, puzzling my brain in endeavouring to recollect on what side of this many-manned world I had met this human being before, when a carrier entered, and placed a play-bill before me on the table. I had taken it up and began perusing it, when he strutted up, and leaning over my shoulder, said,

"I beg pardon, sir; just a moment."

I put it towards him.

"No matter, sir, no matter; I've seen all I want to see—the same old two-and-sixpence— *Hamlet, Mr. Sandford*, in large letters; *and Laertes, Mr. Vandenhoff*—oh !"

And with an epithet not in any way alluding to the "sweet South," he stepped off to the *Biscay* tune, allegro. I was amused; and perhaps the expression of my face encouraged him to return instantly, and with the familiarity of an old acquaintance—and that he was, I was convinced, in some way or other—said,

"My dear sir, that's the way the profession is going to the devil: here, sir, is the ' *manager* ' "— with a sneer—" one of the damnedest humbugs that ever trod the stage, must have his name in large letters, of *course;* and the *and* Laertes, Mr. Vandenhoff—he's a favourite of the Grand Mogul, as we call old Sandford, and so he gets all the fat; and d'ye know why he's shoved down the people's throats ? Because he's so damned bad the old man shows to advantage alongside of him. Did you ever see him ?"

I shook my head.

"Why, sir, he's a tall, stooping, lantern-jawed, asthmatic-voiced, spindle-shanked fellow." Here he put his foot on the rail of my chair, and slightly scratched the calf of his leg. " Hair the colour of a cock-canary," thrusting his fingers through his own coal-black ringlets; "with light blue eyes, sir, trimmed with pink gymp. He hasn't been long caught; just from some nunnery in Liverpool, or somewhere, where he was brought up as a Catholic priest; and here he comes, with his Latin and Lancashire dialect, to lick the manager's great toe, and be hanged to him, and gets all the business; while men of talent, and nerve, and personal appearance,"

shifting his hands from his coat pockets to those of his tights, " who have drudged in the profession for years, are kept in the back-ground; 'tis enough to make a fellow sweat !"

Very adroitly blowing his nose with his fingers, and cleaning them on a dirty, once-white pocket-handkerchief.

"You, then, sir, are an actor ?" said I, calmly.

"An actor ! yes, sir, I am an *actor*, and have been ever since I was an infant in arms; played the child that cries in the third act of the comedy of ' The Chances,' when it was got up with splendour by Old Gerald, at Sheerness, when I was only nine weeks old; and I recollect, that is, my mother told me, that I cried louder, and more naturally, than any child they'd ever had. *That's me*," said he, pointing to the play-bill—*Horatio, Mr. Howard.*

"A thought, more like a dream than an assurance," flitted past my mind, and I was about to ask a question, but he proceeded.

"I *used to make* a great part of Horatio *once;* and I can now send any Hamlet to h— in that character, when I give it energy and pathos; but this nine-tailed bashaw of a manager insists upon my keeping my ' madness in the background,' as he calls it, and so I just walk through it, speak the words, and make it a poor, spoony, preaching son of a how-came-ye-so, and do no more for it than the author has. But, sir, I'll pledge you my honour that when I belonged to Old Lee's company, at Totness, a lady, who resided at Tor-Quay, had heard so much of me in this very part, that she engaged me, at an *enormous expense*, to represent the character at her own house."

I was right in my suspicions: it was, indeed, an old acquaintance, the beau ideal of my childhood, *the identical Horatio.*

"And after," he continued, " I had enchanted them with my performance, I was had into the *drawing-room*, had a damned good supper, gave them the ' Bay of Biscay,' one of my best songs—

' There she lay, all the day—'

You know the thing, I suppose; the old lady plied me with bottled porter, hot, with nutmeg and sugar" (I thought of good-natured C——, the housekeeper), "plenty of preserves, cold chicken, and pickles ; and in the morning, after a thundering breakfast, she clapped a knuckle of ham and a piece of pound-cake into a *clean* sheet of paper, as she said, to pass away the time in the coach."

"That was a high compliment, Mr. Howard," said I, without knowing what I said: I was again at home, with all my hopes unblasted. "A high compliment, sir! it was the most high compliment that ever was paid to any tragedian of eminence, except the compliment that was paid to John Kemble, when he was engaged, at two-and-sixpence an hour, to read to the Duke of Norfolk, when he was laid up with the gout."

I cannot vouch for the authenticity of this anecdote, as I never heard of the circumstance before, nor since. Dinner was announced; without expecting or intending him to accept my cold invitation, I artificially said,

"Will you join me, sir ?"

"My dear sir," he replied, "nothing could give me greater pleasure than to cut your mutton and tap your tankard, as we say; but I have a very particular engagement at three o'clock, to promenade two charming girls, the Misses Buckingham—splendid creatures, I assure you

—I'll introduce you. I want to *beau* them up
and down George-street once or twice, just to
make a widow of my acquaintance miserable,
who lives in that neighbourhood. You understand me; ha, ha, ha! Have you the time?"

"I have not," said I, with a suppressed sigh.
I thought of my watch, pawned past hope of
redemption. "But as I ordered my dinner at
three, I presume that is the hour." And was
slightly bowing my way between him and the
door, when, suddenly hooking his arm within
mine, he exclaimed,

"But what have we to do with the time of
the day? unless minutes were capons, and hours
were cups of sack, as jolly Jack Falstaff says.
I have taken a great fancy to you, and shall be
happy to befriend you in any way in my power.
I'll get you an order for the play to-night, and if
you'll go, dam'me if I don't let out a little. The
girls will play the devil with me for disappoint-
ing them, but I'll gammon 'em; say I had a part
to study; it does me good to tease 'em sometimes, they like you the better for it; and, as
you're so very pressing, I'll accept your kind
invitation."

I had seen enough of the world to perfectly
understand all this; but I was amused, so led to
the dining-room and ordered another chop.

"Two," said he, "two; and harkye, sweet-
heart," picking up a pickle with his fingers and
popping it into his mouth, "let's have a pot of
porter directly."

I always adored character, and though I didn't
believe him to be a very estimable one, to me,
then, he was an original. He ate fast and
slovenly, frequently using and praising the good
old adage of "*fingers were made before tongs;*" he
called, in a tragic tone, for "*another chop and some
cheese!*" and "a PINT of porter at *my expense!*"

The last part of the order I instantly contradicted.

"Well, well, just as you say," said he. "Then
bring Mr. Cowell another *pot* of porter, and make
haste, d'ye hear!"

Not being aware that I had mentioned my
name during our conversation, if it might so be
called, where he had had nearly all the talk to
himself, I inquired how he had learned it.

"Why, my dear sir, I happened to be in the
bar-room this morning, and the landlord came
in, and says he to his wife, 'What do you think,
my dear—Mr. Cowell has paid his bill.' 'He
has!' says she; 'well, now, I declare, I always
thought he was a very nice young man; and, no
doubt, as he has got the reminiscence as he expected—' Remittance, of course, she meant. I
know well enough what remittances are; I often
have occasion for them myself. For, with the
paltry sum of five pounds a week—my salary in
the theatre—I find it very difficult sometimes"—
retying his shoestring in a large bow—"to make
both ends meet. You happened to pass by at
the time she was speaking. 'There goes Mr.
Cowell,' says she; 'the most perfectest gentleman as ever stopped at a house.' I was pleased
myself with your appearance, and resolved to
form a friendship with you. But I must be off.
I'll call and take a cup of tea, and make it up
with the girls. I've got to break the neck, too,
of a blasted part for to-morrow night. Nay,
keep your seat. 'My love as yours to mine.'
Adieu!"

True to his word, he sent the order. I visited
the theatre—*and was disgusted.* It was one of
the plays I had seen in my halcyon days with

Anna. I only remembered Kemble in the cast;
who but a professor could or would remember
any one else? "A combination and a form, indeed, where every god did seem to set his seal,
to give the world assurance of a man."

I was well acquainted with the text; having,
when quite a boy, been presented with an elegant edition of Shakspeare by a scholar and a
gentleman, the chaplain of a ship I belonged to;
and, next to the Bible, he recommended it to my
particular perusal.

The manager—*the large-lettered humbug*—was
decidedly deserving the distinction "himself had
made," but the rest were villanous, and *Horatio*
the worst of all. I was shocked and angry at
my boyish judgment.

How is it that children—I mean children with
a fair proportion of brains—are so contradictory
in taste? I have heard a little girl bestow such
pretty praise on a primrose or a butterfly, that I
have blushed for my own incompetence so rich-
ly to express my feeling; and, in the next half
hour, have seen the same child in ecstasies of
admiration and delight at the antics of some vulgar clown in the arena of a circus.

My visit to the theatre that evening glanced a
ray of sunshine on my clouded path, and I argued thus: "If such a man as this Howard can
get five pounds a week for what he does, I can
do the same, or more. By ——, I'll turn actor!"

I went to my room and wrote the letter which
will be found in the next chapter.

◆

CHAPTER VI.

" 'Tis easy then for a new name,
And a new life, fashioned on old desires."
SHELLEY.

"TO GEORGE SANDFORD, ESQ.

"Plymouth Dock, January 11, 1812.

"SIR—I wish to become an actor. I will be
content to receive a small amount of pay, until
I get acquainted with the duties I have to perform. I have learned *Iago*, in Shakspeare's play
of Othello, and could easily get perfect in *Belcour*, in Cumberland's comedy of The West Indian. I have seen Elliston in that character in
London, and have vanity enough to believe I
could play either of them. Your early reply
through the postoffice will oblige

"Yours respectfully,
"LEATHLEY IRVING."

Three anxious days passed, and "*nothing for
Leathley Irving!*" was all I could get from the
postoffice. On the fourth, "*one penny!*" was
demanded, and a very gentlemanly-looking note
was pushed through the hole to the following
effect:

"George Sandford presents his compliments
to Mr. Leathley Irving, and will be happy to
have a conversation with him at his house on
Thursday next.

"To Leathley Irving, Esq. Tuesday evening."

His address, I found, was at a handsome fan-
cy-shop in George-street. Of a tall, sedate, elderly lady, seated behind the counter, I inquired
for Mr. Sandford, and handed my card. An answer returned in a minute, "that Mr. Sandford
had an appointment with a gentleman at that
hour, but I might name my business, or please
to call again." I was turning towards the door,
with an indignant "no matter," when the thought
occurred to me that I had sent in my real name;

15

and, in some embarrassment, I stated that I had made a mistake in the card—that it was *Mr. Leathley Irving*, with whom he had an engagement, who desired to see him. I was immediately conducted through the parlour at the back of the shop, then through the kitchen, by a pretty little servant-maid, who, after knocking at a door on one side, and waiting for a pompously-sounding "*Come in!*" on the other, lifted the latch, dropped me a courtesy, and I found myself in the presence of a rather (had been) handsome man, of middle stature, about forty years of age, with a profusion of hair (the remains of last night's powder still discernible), rubbed up in all directions and striking individual attitudes, resembling the angular, dislocated curls shreds of leather would make if suddenly popped into a broiling-hot frying-pan. He was enveloped in a large-patterned calico morning-gown (will anybody tell me why managers of theatres have such a predilection for morning-gowns? I have found but one exception to the fashion in eight-and-twenty years, from George Sandford down to Ludlow and Smith). He was pacing, with "Tarquin's ravishing strides," an apartment as large as "parlour, kitchen, and hall;" a book in one hand, and my card in the other. "Sir," said he, as he turned and met me, "whom have I the honour of addressing—Mr. Cowell or Mr. Leathley Irving?"

"Sir," I replied, in the same authoritative tone in which he had asked the question, "the card bears the name I'm known by; but, if I turn player, I choose to be called Irving." "What for, sir?" said the manager, handing me a chair, and drawing another close to me: "what the devil for, sir? I have been an actor more than twenty years, and have known many serious inconveniences occur to men in after life from the folly of changing their names when boys. It's damned nonsense, sir! There can be but one excuse for a young man's assuming a false name upon entering my profession, and that is, that his previous course in life has made him damnably ashamed of his own." I felt the blood mount to my forehead, and I instinctively rose from my chair. "Oh, sir," said my new friend, with a peculiarly bland and placid smile, "keep your seat; don't imagine I suspect you of having cause to be ashamed of your name; 'tis the reverse case with you: you assume another name because you are ashamed of a pursuit either your taste or your necessities induce you to adopt. Now, sir, with such a feeling you can never be an actor. No man can ever be eminent in a profession he considers it a disgrace to follow. The Drama, I confess, '*bears but an ill name in the forest*,' but the blame lies with the professors, and not with the profession.

"There are myriads of men who are a disgrace to the pulpit, the bar, or the stage; but the frightful responsibility of daring to unfold the cloak pretended piety assumes, and the legal cunning of the advocate, often lets the parson and the lawyer pass unscathed, while the poor player walks, with his hundred errors, stark naked through the world, for every *daw to peck at*."

There was much good sense peeping through his enthusiastic style of thought; and I, in very honesty of heart, told him, in few words, my painful history.

"My good young friend," said he, in a tone of voice well trained to assist his meaning, "keep the name you say you have a claim to, and now are known by—you have good requisites, and, by industry and perseverance, may become an ornament to the stage. But 'tis a briery path to preferment in this profession; it requires time and laborious study to make even a passable performer; your figure, face, and voice must be apprenticed, day and night, to nature. A refined and well-educated mind may be formed by art and industry; but it must naturally possess the wonderful instinctive capacity to seize upon and *feel* the thoughts and language of others, and use them with the same ease and freedom as if they were your own. To be a great actor ' *is to be one man picked out of ten thousand.*' Have you a good study?"

I replied in the negative.

"I'm sorry to hear that; without a good study your labours will be so severe you'll be disgusted with the undertaking before you reach the threshold of success."

"Oh, sir," said I, "that I can easily remedy."

"How, sir? how? Practice will improve it, I'm aware, but how can you so *easily* remedy a bad study?"

"By changing my apartment," I replied; "my chamber is next the dining hall, and unless they give me one more privately situated, I'll move to another house."

"You reprove me well," said he, with a smile: "we actors use the term study for the attributes of memory; the place and time for its exercise are varied by circumstances and the habits of its owner."

He appeared pleased to hear me say I had great facility in acquiring anything I wished to learn.

"Come, to the proof, then," said he, jovially; "let's have a speech straight. You say you are perfect in 'Iago;' let's have one of his soliloquies, with good emphasis and good discretion."

He saw my embarrassment, and, in pure good taste, waived the subject; not like some puppies I have since seen sit, in satirical pomposity, enjoying the tortures of some trembling tyro, though that very sensibility is the best indicative of talent, and the sure attendant upon genius.

"Sir, I propose you shall make your appearance in Belcour this day week; but—" he continued, "be most *dreadfully* perfect, not only in what you have to say yourself, but in whatever any one else has to say to you; get so *awfully* perfect that, if you are suddenly awoke in the night, you will be able to repeat the whole character without hesitation. In the mean time, it will smooth your path to get acquainted (in the way of business) with the company—and I am proud to say I have *some* gentlemen in my employ; Mr. Moore, an excellent low comedian, and a proper man, and Vandenhoff, though with very little talent, possesses a superior mind, and an excellent education. Inquire for me at the stage-door this evening, and take a tête-à-tête dinner with me at three to-morrow, and any advice or assistance you may require, and I can give, you may command."

This was the man "Horatio" had described as an insolent, tyrannical blackguard.

Poor George Sandford. He died a few years since, regretted and respected by all whose good opinion he would have condescended to care for while living. He was a native of the city of New-York; and 'tis somewhat strange that my best theatrical friend and manager first saw the light in the same city where my last born opened her eyes, and in a country I by choice have been a citizen of for more than half my thinking life. I shall like to meet that man in the other world, and tell him all about his native country. He was an excellent general actor. I have reason to believe his education was intuitive (the better, after all). His King Lear and Doctor Pangloss were the most finished representations of the characters I ever saw.

I visited the green-room, where I was favourably received, particularly by the ladies, among whom was a sister of Alec. Drake, for many years the favourite comedian of the "West." She had a pretty voice, pretty face, but waddled like a duck. She was my Louisa Dudley. I tried very hard to be really in love with her, for the sake of increasing the effect, but I believe she succeeded better than I did in the experiment. I had three carefully-conducted rehearsals, each one serving to convince me more strongly that I was incapable of the task my self-esteem had induced me to believe so easy.

The night arrived—*January the twenty-third, 1812.*

" *The part of Belcour by a gentleman, his first appearance on any stage,*" attracted a full and very fashionable house. Admiral Calder, the commander of the port, and a large party, occupied the stage-box. I had many shipmates in harbour at the time, and some relatives: all, of course, attended, induced by pity; how I hate the word—scorn or curiosity.

I had been used to danger in many shapes, and fear is not an attribute of my nature, but I was most damnably frightened on that occasion. I spoke the words mechanically, but I could neither see nor hear; my mouth was parched; what to do with my hands I knew not; I deposited them in all sorts of places; if both arms had been amputated, I felt assured I should have been relieved of an abominable encumbrance. Embarrassed by my embarrassment, *Stockwell* bungled in one of his speeches: I repeated it, and then spoke mine in reply; the audience, confound them, laughed and applauded. I felt I had done wrong: my brain whirled in confusion, and I rushed off the stage before the conclusion of the scene, amid deafening shouts, yells, and huzzas, such as are generally humanely bestowed upon the retreat from a butcher's-stall of some poor devil of a dog with a tin kettle tied to his tail; and at that moment, I have no doubt, I experienced precisely the same sensations.

"For God's sake give me a glass of grog!" I stammered out; "and, my dear sir," grasping the hand of the manager, kindly extended to me at the entrance, "finish the part for me: I feel my incapacity, and only regret my conceit caused me to make such a jackass of myself."

" Pho, pho! *you must conclude* what you have begun," said he, in his positive but gentlemanly manner; "the first plunge is over, you'll feel your power in the next scene; your great fault is, you try to do too much; stand still, *don't act,* and speak louder; think you are talking to some one in the gallery, and then, if you only whisper, you'll be heard all over the house: take another sup of brandy and water—there—that's your cue."

I felt encouraged by grog and good advice, and the next scene is a very effective one: I imitated Elliston as well as I could, and was admirably supported and encouraged *by the manner* of the excellent actress who performed Mrs. Fulmer, and I retired amid *the unbounded applause of a brilliant and overflowing audience.*

"There," said my mentor, triumphantly, "didn't I tell you how it would be! 'tis decidedly the best first appearance I have seen for years."

I gained courage as the comedy proceeded; and at its conclusion, the manager, amid thunders of applause, announced it for repetition on the Saturday following: " *The part of Belcour by the young gentleman who had been so favourably received that evening.*"

The barbarous fashion was not then invented of demanding the presence of the object of supposed admiration or ridicule, to add to his miseries, by expecting him to speak, or bow, or make a fool of himself in some way or other, which, *nowadays,* these victims of vanity on both sides usually do.

CHAPTER VII.

"What, wouldst thou have me go and beg my food?
Or with a base and boisterous sword enforce
A thievish living on the common road?
This I must do, or know not what to do:
Yet this I will not do, do how I can;
I rather would subject me to the malice
Of a diverted blood."

SHAKSPEARE.

EVERYBODY said my performance was most excellent *for a first appearance,* but I felt no self-satisfaction. To the inexperienced, the more pure and true to nature acting is, the easier it appears; but to rant, and shout, and "out-herod Herod," distort the face and form in a way that no human being ever did *off the stage,* in his senses or out of them, seems a most arduous undertaking. This caused the delusion under which I laboured. In the seven plays I saw with Anna (we ne'er shall look upon their like again), all difficulty was so concealed by the refinement of art, that I foolishly, yet firmly, believed I could sustain any of the characters quite as well, without dreaming I should ever be put to the test. I have no *data of any kind, I am sorry to say,* but the impression they made on my memory is as fresh at this distant period as it was the morning after I saw the performance, and I will name part of the "casts" of some of them.

The West Indian.

Belcour - - - - - Elliston.

James H. Caldwell is the only actor on this side the water I have seen approach him in *genteel* comedy.

O'Flaherty - - - - Johnstone.

Worth a hundred Powers, if even Power had been really what he had the tact to make the public believe he was.

Charles Dudley - - De Camp.

Then a most elegant young man, and an excellent actor, in spite of his conceited, *paw! paw!* voice.

Varland - - - - - Dowton.

Then in his prime; a shadow of his former self came to this country about three years ago.

" All that's bright must fade."

Stockwell - - - - Powell.

Charlotte - - - - Miss Duncan.

A delightful actress in such characters.

Louisa - - - - - ——

I forget her name, but she was a most beautiful creature (almost all that is necessary for the part). I remember I praised her so highly, that poor Anna declared she thought "she was a perfect fright."

Hamlet.

I recollect nothing but *Kemble*, and that his brother Charles was Laertes; but "the King, the Queen, and all the Court," are all buzz.

Isabella.

The principal characters by Brunton, Charles Kemble, Kemble, and Mrs. Siddons.

On the Saturday I was more collected; my hearing and sight were restored; though I was often interrupted by some sea-phrase applicable to the sentence I was uttering, or a well-meant expression of encouragement, every now and then, from, probably, some old shipmate, to the great amusement of the rest of the audience; and, at the conclusion of the performance, "Three cheers for the blue jacket!" was announced, and performed in full chorus. This latter compliment I was in the habit of receiving upon the slightest occasion, during the season; for, though I had been dismissed the navy with a "flea in my ear," my offence was "a feather in my cap" in the estimation of my comrades of my own grade, or those beneath me. "By the Eternal! I had the popular vote," as my friend General Jackson would say.

The pit, gallery, and upper-boxes of the Dock Theatre, at that time, were crowded with sailors and marines, with their *wives for a week*, and dock-yard ma-tes, as they were called, between whom and the round-jackets existed a continual "well-fought war." These jolly "gods" had a nick-name for nearly every member of the company. I found they greeted my friend Horatio with, "Hurra for Sky-blue!" This appellation he had gained in consequence of his great attachment for the very "tights" he wore the first morning I met with him. He played Major O'Flaherty; there they were, with a gold band down each side. He rendered them, as actors say, "a very useful property." They could be worn, "for a change," with black Hessian-boots, or russet, or shoes of any colour with stockings; but sandals they set at defiance; for shabby-genteel characters, a red or white patch or two made them "very characteristic;" and as to stripes, they would bear any but blue.

About this period there was a certain "odd kind of a new method of swearing" ran through the fleet, and "*By Cheeks the marine*" was a favourite oath. A very old actor, of the name of Chambers, whose weakness it was to boast continually that he had "had his ancestors too," on that evening was struck by an apple, thrown from the gallery; taking it up, he stepped forward, and very pompously said, "I'll give twenty pounds to know who threw this apple!" "Cheeks the marine!" cried a voice from above. When the shout the response created was over, drawing himself up, and glancing at the commander of the port in the stage-box, he said, with a sigh to bygone greatness, "In my *schoolboy* days I knew an admiral of that name." "Huzza, boys! huzza! three cheers for Admiral Cheeks!" He had christened himself most effectually forever in that company, to his own annoyance, and the destruction of any serious scene in which he was concerned. For the last five-and-twenty years I would have gloried in them as a *low comedy* audience; but at that time they often played the devil with my *juvenile tragedy*.

Mackay and his wife were loud in their encomiums.

"Ye looked sae slick-like," said my honest friend, "wi' ye'r white silk wash-boards till ye'r coat; ye looked mair like a sailor than a' the rest thegither, wi' ye'r bonny leg a leetle bow'd, and baith ye'r taes turned in, as if ye'r war stonding firm on ye'r shanks in a chappin sea; an' the hitch ye gave ye'r small claithes when ye said onything clever was the best o' a'. I ne'er seed but ane actor as guid, and he was na sae much better nether — 'twas a leetle Scots pony, at Portsdown Fair. He was a saucy wee bit toad that, that when his master wad say till him, '*Billy, what's the hour, my chiel?*' he'd paw, and paw—ane, twa, or as mony as it was, as natural as a quartermaster makin' eight bells."

Now this I considered the highest compliment paid to me by any of my friends; and how often since would I have preferred being said to be "*almost as good as a learned pig, or pony,*" than "*to be nearly equal*" to some two-legged baboon, with a red tail, black eyebrows, and a mouth from ear to ear!

The following day (Sunday) I dined with the manager. After the cloth was drawn, his good lady had retired, and he had twice thrust the decanter towards me, he said, "I requested this interview, Mr. Cowell, that we might talk over and consider in what way I could serve you; but a letter I received this morning, most fortunately, points out a path for you at once. I candidly tell you, I have no doubt on my mind as to your ultimate success in the drama. Mr. Fisher, a friend of mine, who has a small company travelling in Cornwall, writes me here to recommend (if in my power) a young man to supply a vacancy in juvenile tragedy and light comedy; there you will gain confidence by constant practice, and next season I will be happy to receive you. I will, therefore, if you say so, write to him to-day, and name you."

I thanked him, but respectfully declined his offer: to engage to play juvenile tragedy and light comedy, without knowing a single character, with a stranger for my manager, and perhaps a *stranger* company, was an undertaking too appalling for me to accept. "But, my dear sir," I continued, "if you will permit me to remain with you, and play at intervals any parts you may think me capable of sustaining, I will paint portraits and teach drawing in my interims of leisure for a living, and not require any pay."

"Sir," said he, with emphasis, "an amateur I have a horror of; we have actors enough already, '*e'en as many as can well live one by another;*' the line of business you are fitted for at present is already filled, and it is the etiquette of the profession never to dispossess an actor of a character he has once played, if he is at all capable of sustaining it."

I felt and looked, I imagine, mortified and disappointed. "Then," said I, "since there is no hope of an engagement this season, I will teach drawing and navigation (if I can get any pupils), and wait till next year."

After a pause of a minute, with his expressive eye looking through me, he said slowly,

"I know what it is to have our youthful ardour blighted. I adore my profession," he continued, with enthusiasm, "and am always proud to enlist a gentleman in its ranks: my only reason for hesitation in the matter is, that though I have the whole control here, I am connected with Mr. Hughes, the proprietor of Saddler's Wells, and he is unwilling to add to our expenses; but," he continued, carelessly, "I'll manage it. Let me see; we must try you in

Shakspeare. Can you get perfect in Ross and Lennox, in Macbeth, by Thursday? We make the two parts into one, for want of numbers. Wednesday we wish to do it, if you can get ready—the lines are difficult."

"Easily, sir," I replied. "I believe I'm perfect in the whole play."

"Well," said he, "that's more than the last gentleman was, even in the parts I speak of, and he has been on the stage these twelve years. As to the *teaching*, get Mrs. Sandford to place one or two of your beautiful drawings in her shop, and I'll engage she'll obtain you more pupils than you can attend to, as you cannot possibly spare more than two or three hours a day from your studies. Now as to the shillings and pence part of the business. The highest salary we give is a guinea and a half per week, and I will put your name on the books for one-pound-one."

I thought of Horatio's boasted *five pounds* a week, and I felt, and appeared, astonished, I suppose. The manager, with disappointment and anger joined in the expression, gave me a severely scrutinizing look; this increased my embarrassment, and, with the blood mantling in my face at the horror of his suspecting (after all his kindness) that the small sum he offered me was the cause of the feeling I displayed, I exclaimed, with energy, "You wrong me, sir, indeed you do. I have not the power to give utterance to the high sense I have of your kindness to me; the sum you name is much more, I am confident, than I can at present earn, and you have wrongly construed my thoughts if you imagine, for a moment, it was that which caused my surprise; it was my astonishment that Mr. Howard should have gratuitously told me that he received five pounds."

"My dear young friend," said he, stretching across the table to shake me heartily by the hand, "you have much to learn of my profession yet. I make it a rule never to name the amount of an actor's salary to anybody, but in this case it is necessary. Mr. Howard receives twenty-five shillings a week, and if his intellect was valued, instead of his utility, he wouldn't obtain five."

I expressed my indignation that he should, unasked, have told me such a falsehood.

"Oh! he meant no harm," said he, laughing; "'tis the fashion or habit of nine actors out of ten to declare their income is at least three times as large as it really is, and their benefits are always said by them to be fashionable and overflowing houses; they boast on these points so continually, that they at last actually believe it themselves, and run in debt, generally, in the same proportion."

Both apparently well pleased with the termination of our negotiation, we parted, with a glass of wine to my success as an actor.

What strange animals we poor human beings are! I had, for two hours or more, felt as if my very existence depended on my obtaining this employment, and I had scarcely let the door close behind me when I felt as if I ought to go back and decline the engagement. A thousand contradictory feelings filled my mind at once. I hurried on, as if to outwalk my own thoughts. I stopped, out of breath, at the corner of a street —looked up at the new moon with the inquiring gaze of an old acquaintance, but before I had time even to ask advice from that quarter, a cloud, "black like an ousel," hid her from my

view. "*My conscience, hanging about the neck of my heart, said very wisely to me,*" "If you take this step you must resign all hope of your ever regaining your past position." Pride—revenge—yes, revenge!—I know no other word nearer to my meaning—and a sort of "dam'me-if-I-care-for-anything-or-anybody" sensation, carried the point. I went home and read Ross and Lennox from the acting copy, and have been an actor ever since.

CHAPTER VIII.

"Then to the well-trod stage anon,
If Jonson's learned sock be on;
Or sweetest Shakspeare, fancy's child,
Warble his native wood-notes wild."

MILTON.

On the Monday morning I was formally introduced as a member of the company, and most kindly welcomed by all; but particularly by the gentleman with whose interests I was most likely to interfere. This display of indifference by those who are suffering in dread and dismay lest you *push them from their stools*, is very common in the profession, and generally overdone: they are usually what may be called too d—d affectionate. In England, they conclude a sort of negative complimentary chat with "Suppose you take your dinner with me?" supposing they have got one to offer; and on "this side of the water" they always say, "Let's go and take a drink?" The arrangement of my dress for the twin Scotchmen the manager had promised to attend to; but the loan of "*properties*, or anything I have, is perfectly at your service," was iterated by all. Howard said, "My boy, by —, I'll lend you my blue tights—oh, you're perfectly welcome, I don't wear them till the farce; Banquo's one of my *flesh parts*—nothing like the naked truth—I'm h—l for nature. By-the-by, you'll often have to wear black smalls and stockings; I'll put you up to something: save your buying silks, darning, stitch-dropping, louse-ladders, and all that: grease your legs and burned-cork 'em—it looks d—d well ' from the front.' "

All my worldly experience had been gathered in a cockpit, the members of which are heterogeneous enough in all conscience, but they have all exactly the same duty to perform, the same pay, same living, same law to abide by, and, generally speaking, are of about the same grade in the scale of society, even before the service has levelled all distinctions. Judge, then, how incapable I was of understanding or appreciating the eccentric and contradictory habits and manners of my new allies. The quantity of materials thought necessary by the three witches in Macbeth to "make the gruel thick and slab," are not more opposite and various in their compound than the origin and character of the "*Ladies and Gentlemen*" attached to the theatrical profession. "There lies the villany:" if there could be instituted a college—a school—an ordeal of any kind to be passed before man or woman were admitted to be an actor or actress, the Drama, blazing in its own brightness, would be honoured and respected. 'Tis true, many have risen from the lowest dregs of society to the topmost pinnacle of theatrical ambition — Mrs. Abington and Kean may be named as extraordinary instances—but how many remain floundering in their original mire, sullying the fair fame of those deserving moral estimation!

19

The world never thinks of drawing a distinction; and, indeed, by what rule could it make one? We don't stop a man in the street with a muddy coat to ascertain if he had soiled it by helping some blackguard out of a gutter, but content ourselves with thinking he's a dirty fellow.

The kindness of the manager, and the prejudiced indulgence of the audience, made me a favourite with both. Sandford's prediction was verified as to the teaching, and I was in the receipt of a handsome income immediately. I charged a high price, and undertook to instruct those only who had already gained some proficiency in the art, with one exception. I did teach one "young idea"—a lovely girl of about fifteen, a step-daughter of Major Watwyns—a Jewess-like divinity. Is there a style of beauty on earth that can compare with the Oriental, poetic loveliness of those *chosen females* when they are young? But then, they will get married, and make it a rule to "increase and multiply," which undoubtedly makes them more interesting as wives and mothers, but it spoils the poetry. There are, to be sure, exceptions, and the lady I allude to is one of them.

> "How long hath *Chronon* wooed in vain
> To spoil that cheek!"

A few years since I had the pleasure of being again introduced to my charming pupil, at Cincinnati. She is the wife of a merchant there, has a large family, and is as handsome as ever.

Incledon, "the inspired idiot," was the first *star* I ever played with. He has helped, most innocently, to make so many books, that in his case "the wine of life is drawn, and the mere lees is left (for me) to brag of;" so let him rest with the "sainted Jane and Mary."

Munden, who had been *underlined* for a week, arrived at last; the company were engaged in the rehearsal of the "Road to Ruin," he having written from Exeter to desire that he might be advertised for Old Dornton and Crack for that night; and his nonappearance at the time he stated had caused some uneasiness; he was followed by a porter with a large trunk. After cordially greeting the manager and the members of the company, with whom he was before acquainted, he said, "Sandford, my dear boy, lend me sixpence." And (in a voice, oh, how rich—rich is a mean phrase to convey an idea of its round, articulate, expressive power) he continued:

"I have had my wardrobe brought to the theatre; it saves trouble, and the expense of little boys bothering you for a penny a piece to carry a bundle. You left the other trunk at my lodgings, my good man?"

"Yes, sir," said the porter, shaking into the crown of his hat a tattered handkerchief, with which he had just removed the sweat of his brow.

"Here's a shilling, Mr. Munden," said Sandford; "I haven't a sixpence."

"Have you the change, my man?" inquired the great comedian.

"Have I change for what, sir?" said the porter.

"For the shilling, my dear boy," replied Munden.

"And is it less than a shilling that a gentleman like you would be offering a poor devil like myself for wheeling two big boxes nearly a mile? Sure the law allows sixpence a parcel, if it's only as big as your fist."

The law might have been argued, according to the statute in that case made and provided, till Munden had made the fellow laugh himself out of his pay altogether, had not Sandford sent the man off with a shilling, and requested the great actor to go on with the rehearsal.

"We have waited two hours for you already; your letter stated you would be here last night," said the manager.

"And so I should; but I couldn't come without wheels," replied the comedian; "the stage broke down just as we got to Ivy Bridge, on purpose, no doubt, that the robbers might pillage me at the hotel there; the bloodsuckers took every shilling I had for bed and board, and bit me to death with fleas into the bargain. I had but threepence left when I made my escape from them this morning; I offered them to the guard, after he had collected my baggage, and he told me *to keep it, sir!* the impudent scoundrel told me to keep it, and so I did," he continued, with a laugh worth the whole stage fare from London to Plymouth, "and treated myself to a pint of porter, and the odd ha' penny I gave to Roache's children to buy lollipops—to buy lollipops, sir, and bull's eyes; I stopped there on my way, to let them know I had arrived, and see if my room was ready."

This said Roache was an old friend of Munden's, and it is highly probable he had the room without charge. He kept a circulating-library, of dirty, worn-out books, quack-medicines, jobprinting, and children's toy kind of shop. The same man had exactly the same sort of establishment, a few years since, at the corner of Frederic and Market-streets, Baltimore, where he died; the members of his large family, who shared Munden's lollipop, are now all engaged in increasing the population of different parts of the Union.

"Sandford, it will only be necessary to go through my scenes—who's the Harry Dornton?" I was introduced. Surveying me from head to foot with a serio-comic look from such an eye! setting at defiance description, and the shade of enormous shaggy eyebrows, one of which would be amply sufficient to make two pair, even for Billy Wood.*

"Are you perfect, sir, in the words?" said Munden.

"Quite, sir," I confidently replied.

"You will find Mr. Cowell," said the manager, "though a young actor, very attentive to any business you may instruct him in, when explained to him in the manner you are so well aware a gentleman expects."

Probably the hint was superfluous, for I ever received from that great actor the most marked attention. The day was so far advanced that

---

* William B. Wood, Esq., formerly manager, and still a member, of the Chestnut-street Theatre, Philadelphia, has remarkably long eyebrows, amounting to a deformity; but of which nature has very kindly made him excessively proud; this amiable weakness, as well as his passion for speaking "an infinite deal of nothing," is notorious among his friends; and 'tis said "once upon a time," finding himself a stranger on a steamboat, and in vain ndeavouring to get into a "*fine weather*" conversation with a gentleman whose acquaintance he was anxious to make, after failing in several efforts to get a "*talk*," at length abruptly accosted him with, "I beg your pardon, sir, but by —, sir, this is a perfect natural curiosity—a genuine N. K. I pledge you my honour, sir, I just pulled this extraordinary hair out of my eyebrow," holding his hands up to the light, about five inches apart. He carried his point, and had a most delicious *hairy* discussion on the merits of that ornament, or inconvenience to the human form divine, from the crown of the head to the first joint of the great toe.

we couldn't repeat our rehearsal, and he invited me to take a chop with him at his lodgings, and after dinner go over the scenes we were together in; which, for the sake of such instruction, I readily agreed to—it was literally *a chop;* we had one a piece, and a single sole between us (a very delicate flat fish about the size of the sole of your boot, both cheap and plentiful at Plymouth), and a pint of porter, of which I declined partaking, apparently to his great satisfaction. The whole dinner, which he praised both as to quantity and quality, he explained to me with great glee, "Had only cost a shilling: sixpence for the chops, three ha'pence for the fish, and the remainder for the bread, potatoes, and porter." The extreme parsimony of this most delicious actor induced every one to believe he was enormously rich, but at his death his fortune was proved much below the general calculation. Even his meanness was smothered in fun. He once told me in the Drury Lane Green-room, very seriously, that he had that morning advertised his grounds for rent, and discharged his gardener, because he had met a girl crying radishes "at three bunches a penny!" On asking a lady for the loan of an umbrella one wet day, she retorted, "Why, Mr. Munden, why don't you buy one? you are rich enough."

"My dear, I've got a bran new one at home, I've had these two years."

"Then why don't you use it, sir?"

"My dear child, if I brought it out it would be sure to rain, and I should get it wet and spoil the beauty of it."

Till the hour of going to the theatre we went over the scenes again and again; my willingness to receive instruction appeared to give him great satisfaction, and he prophesied a glorious reward for my perseverance, and instanced himself as a proof of the consequence: who could doubt he practised what he preached, when, in defiance of the labour before him for the night, and the fatigue of a journey, he, with all the enthusiasm of youth, for hours directed the support he required in his great character, which he had then played probably two hundred times?

He was, in my opinion, the best comedian I ever saw. He identified himself with a character, and never lost sight of it—his pathos went to the heart at once, and his humour was irresistible. In his latter years he was accused of sacrificing too much for the sake of gaining applause, but I believe he endeavoured to alter his pure and natural style to suit the declining taste of his auditors, and compete with the caricaturists by whom he was surrounded. In playing Ralph to his Old Brumagem, at Drury Lane, I objected to some business he pointed out, as being unnatural. "Unnatural!" said he, with a sneer: "that has been my mistake for years. Nature be d—; make the people laugh."

But he's gone! and if there is any fun in the next world, he's in the midst of it.

"Sic transit gloria *Munden.*"

By great industry I rapidly improved, and before the close of the season I had become a very *useful performer* at any rate. My connexion as an artist was of great service to me at my benefits, and I had two really "overflowing houses;" the last, "By desire of the officers of his majesty's ship York," nearly the whole of the crew, with the band at their head and the marines bringing up the rear, marched to the theatre,

crowding the pit and upper portion of the house. The play was the Iron Chest, which I had selected for the sake of acting "Wilford," to perform which character I had been sighing all the season; but Moore, the comedian who was to play Sampson, thought proper to be taken ill at four o'clock in "the posteriors of the day," as Shakspeare hath it, and Sandford urged me to undertake the part, as the best apology to offer to my friends instead of this general favourite. Laughter and applause, no doubt, much more than I deserved, rewarded my first effort in low comedy; and all declared it was the line of business in which I was destined to excel; and I thought so too; but for the next six months I had engaged for the *amiable* and *interesting*, at fifteen shillings per week, at the Theatre Royal, Plymouth, so that my comical propensities had to do penance for that period, at any rate.

During the performance that evening, a request was made by an officer that one of the crew, who had written a comic song, might be permitted to sing it, which was readily granted; and between the acts a fine black-whiskered, six-feet-high fellow made his appearance, amid the cheers of his shipmates, and sung at least fifteen verses, each ending with a *Toll-loll-de-iddy-tiddy-toll-loll-loll.* The composition consisted of a long string of sailor's wit at the expense of Poll, and Sue, and Jack, and Ben, and so on, which appeared to be greatly relished by those who understood the joke. At length he came to a pause— looked embarrassed—hitched up his trousers— turned his quid—scratched his head—and said, "Shipmates, *you know* there's two more verses, but they are not fit to sing before the ladies; they are rather b—. Toll-loll-de-iddy-tiddy-toll-loll-loll," and away he went. Either as a tribute to his modesty, or in the hope of hearing the other two verses, he received a general *Encore!* from all parts of the house; but at the same place he stopped again, made his bow, and said, "You know I told you why I left off here before," and quitted the stage amid shouts of laughter.

——◆——

CHAPTER IX.

"Meantime, I would not always dread the bowl,
Nor every trespass shun. The feverish strife,
Roused by the rare debauch, subdues, expels
The loitering crudities that burden life;
And like a torrent, full and rapid, clears
Th' obstructed tubes. Besides, this restless world
Is full of chances, which by habit's power
To learn to bear is easier than to shun."
ARMSTRONG'S *Art of Preserving Health.*

The borough-town of Plymouth is about two miles from Dock, and literally connected with that (then) densely-populated depository for sailors and soldiers of every grade, from admirals and generals down to the after-guard and awkward squad; marines, ma-tes, Jew pedlers, pickpockets, blackguards, and bum-boat women, and other ladies with a claim to only half the title, by a long lane with no turning, called "Stonehouse," on either side of which, leaving room for a barracks on the right, was then a row of small houses whose inhabitants were notoriously of the feminine gender. For the information of the curious in topographical knowledge, I must state, that Dock can now boast of a mayor and corporation, and the name of Devenport, but in my day its fame emanated from

"The armaments which thunder-strike the walls
Of rock-built cities, bidding nation's quake,

21

> And monarchs tremble in their capitals;
> The oak leviathans, whose huge ribs make
> Their clay creator, the vain title take
> Of lord of thee (*the ocean*) and arbiter of war."

The Plymouth Theatre, at Frankfort Gate, by courtesy called Royal, because the Duke of Clarence had once entered it, probably without paying for his ticket, was then conducted by Mr. Foot, in connexion with Mr. Percy Farren, of the Dublin Theatre, whom I never saw. His son, George Percy Farren, is now in this country, and in the same cast of characters, I think quite equal to his uncle of the London theatres. Foot had been a captain in the army, and looked like a gentleman of the *roué* school. Talking of looks, he had one real eye for service, and another, of glass, for show; if he got *gouged* in love or war I never learned, but a side glance conveyed the most irresistibly comical kind of squint ever invented by art or nature. His manners were agreeable, and what is falsely called gentlemanly, but his mind was most depraved; all moral obligations he set at defiance, and his charming daughter, innocent and young, was even then in training, by her father, for the life of splendid infamy in which she moved for years, with pity's finger pointing at her fallen state. Poor Maria! A few days before I left England I met her with a servant following in Colonel Berkley's livery: "She was beautiful, and if ever I felt the full force of an honest heartache, it was the moment I saw her."

As I before observed, my teaching put me in possession of a handsome income; I therefore readily entered into a bond with Foot to receive only fifteen shillings per week, and play nothing but good parts; thereby curtailing my utility as an actor, and increasing my leisure.

The salary for each performer was put up weekly by the treasurer, sealed and directed, and handed round to the company, during the rehearsal, by Mrs. Foot. After I had been in this employ a short time, I had (in consequence of not being wanted at the theatre during this shower of gold) allowed my pay to accumulate for five or six weeks; but one day, after making my bow to the lady of the house, and putting my little arrears in my pocket, was walking off, when Mrs. Foot stopped me, in evident embarrassment, and said,

"Mr. Cowell, I have made a mistake; be kind enough to let me have that money again."

I immediately restored to her (as I then thought) the whole of the packets; in a few minutes, the call-boy handed me (as I supposed) the amount due, in one parcel; but, on gaining my lodgings, I discovered I had unknowingly retained one of the little billets she at first gave me, directed and dated two or three weeks gone by, and containing, to my astonishment, twenty-five shillings, and the larger one the whole of the balance due me, for the time, at the rate of fifteen shillings per week. In the evening I called on the treasurer and explained the circumstance, and presented him with the five-and-twenty shilling parcel I had unintentionally retained; he to my *disgust* assured me that my salary had been always charged on the books at one pound five; that he had regularly enclosed me that amount, and such was the sum named as paid to me on the balance-sheet, copied by him every week and sent to Percy Farren at Dublin. I kept my own counsel; played, when I did play, *very* good parts, and got the twenty-five sealed up every Saturday.

Once Foot said,

"Cowell, you're a queer fellow; you have never taken any notice of my raising your salary."

"Yes, I am rather queer," I replied, with a laugh. He gave me a look with his real eye over his nose, right through the glass one, and walked away.

"What do you smile for in that satirical manner?" has been often asked of me, after listening to an eulogium on "dear Mrs. Foot being so kind as to save one the trouble of going to the treasury, and handing one one's salary in such a ladylike manner."

The Dock Theatre closed on a Saturday night, and Plymouth opened on the Monday following, with the comedy of the "Heir at Law," as best calculated to display the strength of the company, and I was cast the *good part* of Henry Moreland; but, on the Sunday intervening, Sandford gave a dinner to Foot, my manager that was to be, Vandenhoff, Moore, D'Arcey, and myself, and a few private friends. Though a very retiring, business-like man in his mode of conducting his professional duties, he was a *bon-vivant*, in the fullest sense of the word, in his own house. Wine of the best was passed rapidly round; speeches were attempted till we were all speechless; songs were sung till we couldn't remember the first line; and the manager's, our own, and everybody's health drunk, till we were too "far gone" to swallow. My Scotch friend D'Arcey, well seasoned with usquebaugh in the Highlands, and myself, were the last to retire. I make it a rule, up to the present hour, to be last at a feast, whatever I am at a fray. D'Arcey couldn't remember the beginning of Burns's ballad, but all he could recollect I assisted him in singing:

> "We are na' fu', we're na that fu',
> Only a wee drap in our e'e,"

and that's all I do recollect of the matter, but was told I was found, long after daylight the next morning, seated on a turned-up washtub, drinking gin with a dozen damp women employed in washing sheets and table-linen in General Nelson's coach-house. I went to bed instead of the rehearsal, and sent the plain state of the case to the manager, and Polly Lambert, as he was most appropriately called by the gods, for he was a very ladylike man, played the part. I, of course, concluded I had forfeited my engagement, and I think it more than probable I should, but for the weekly profit I was destined to prove to the "wide-awake" partner, while the other was sleeping at Dublin.

The second morning, while sipping chicken-broth and reading "Taylor on Drunkenness"—by-the-by, a more philosophical and physiological work than any temperance pamphlet produced for five-and-twenty years—I received a pleasant note from Foot, and the next morning I went to the theatre. He appeared to think it an excellent joke.

"I know my friend George of old," said my new manager; "he's a d— high fellow in his own house; a regular Charles Surface, though demure as a Joseph in his business. By ——, I think you got off very well; I knew the consequences, and made my escape about ten o'clock, for the d— rascal laid me up for a week once, and, by ——, I'm called an honest four-bottle man."

The company was more efficient than the first I was associated with, the best portion of which had been selected, and several of considerable talent added to the list, among whom was my friend Barnes, even then called "Old Jack," and "Old Barney," and he admired the title then, for so he used to designate himself in his benefit-bills; but now, when he has an honest claim to that venerable appellation, he don't apply it to himself, nor appear quite so well pleased at being named so by others. His amiable wife, in addition to her well-known talent, was then the most sylphlike, beautiful little creature in existence. Ye gods! how awfully I was in love with her! Platonically, of course, I imagined then; but, in thinking over the events of that period, I confess I recollect catching myself accusing Anna of being a little too tall.

Byron had not then made his Don Juan excuse for inconstancy, but I was very much of the same opinion at that time, in prose, that

> " That which
> Men call inconstancy is nothing more
> Than adoration; due where nature's rich
> Profusion with young beauty covers o'er
> Some favoured object; and, as in the niche,
> A lovely statue we almost adore,
> This sort of adoration of the real
> Is but a heightening of the beau ideal."

But, then, more than once I remember wishing most earnestly that my friend Jack was divorced, or dead, and decently buried—but it's all over now. What an abominable contrivance this getting old is!

Young Betty, the Roscius that had been, was our first star. He was of my age, within a month one way or the other; a great, lubberly, overgrown, fat-voiced, good-tempered fellow, with very little talent, and just tolerated as a man by those who were ashamed to confess they were deceived in thinking him a divinity when a boy.

I have seen many infant phenomena in the course of my theatrical career, and witnessed the "drillings and trainings;" and if the humane Martin had known as much as I do, he would have included these little prodigies in his act "for the suppression of cruelty to animals."

I once had a conversation with a fellow who exhibited a learned dog at the Adelphi Theatre, and he assured me that he had found, from experience, that the description of animal best fitted for his purpose was, as he expressed it, " A cur that's not good for nothing else in the whole world;" and the poor beast I saw playing cards and casting accounts fully came up in appearance to his idea of the necessary requisites: even Burns's " Tanted tyke, tho' e'er sae duddie," had some fun in his composition, but the pitiable wretch I saw " get all the applause" did not deserve even to be called a dog—a long-backed, short-legged, sleek-haired, ungentlemanly-looking thing, went slouching round a circle with his stupid-looking eyes half closed, and his tail between his legs; had he been a calculating boy, he would have done precisely the same, only, for the want of a tail, he would have had his hands in his breeches pockets. Astonishing animals and astonishing children are schooled in exactly the same way—extreme and continual rewards and punishments—raw beef and a whip for the one, and sugar-plums and a rod-in-pickle for the other. It cannot be denied that there are many instances of precocious genius, both in the theatrical world and out of it, and if such favoured creatures were left solely to nature, they would be always pleasing, though never astonishing in after life; talent and time must walk hand in hand to form the clever man. But should a

child unfortunately " sing a little song," or imitate some caricature actor, God help the little creature! especially if the parent be a player; and I have generally found these scions are of some " stick," not fit, as Garrick coarsely said, " to carry guts to a bear:" they are instantly taught to play on the pianoforte, and the drum, and the fiddle, and the flageolet, and jig about at the same time (as Ellen Tree's sister used to do), and fencing, and dancing, and everything but reading and writing, till their poor susceptible little brains are so overwhelmed with the mass of knowledge crammed into their little box, that no wonder they sink under the weight of their own pressure; and if they live long enough, prove to be extremely stupid men and women.

So as some bud which nature in a freak bids to peep forth before its usual time, if forced and nurtured by artificial means, soon sickens, droops, and withers, and in the excess of its own luxuriance, dies, and is forgotten; but if left in the care alone of Him who made it, it would have bloomed its bright and brief career, and its sweetness would be remembered and regretted.

It is necessary to state that about this period *I got married by accident—but not to Anna.*

◆

CHAPTER X.

> " How changed since last her speaking eye
> Glanced gladness round the glittering room
> Where high-born men were proud to wait—
> Where beauty watch'd to imitate
> Her gentle voice—her lovely mien—
> And gather from her air and gait
> The graces of its queen!
> Now—what is she ?"
>
> PARISINA.

CHARLES YOUNG succeeded Betty; a delicious change; equal to a squeeze of lemon after a dose of jalap—a perfect gentleman and most amiable man. I have often heard him called an imitator of Kemble, but I never saw any resemblance; it is true, his good sense made him believe he had not the genius to soar above his great coadjutor, and he prudently contented himself to adopt his conceptions; if you saw Kemble in Hamlet one night, and Young the next, you would discover no beauties stepped over, and nc new ones displayed; but all that Kemble had done for the character would be done by Young, twenty-four hours after him, in every sense of the expression. During his sojourn at Plymouth, he played several characters to prepare himself to sustain them at Covent Garden, among them *Richard* and *Sir Giles Overreach*; of course he was worse than Kemble was in both of them, and I don't know if he ever attempted their murder in London.

For the sake of comparison, 1 presume, soon after Young departed, Foot played the Stranger. I was Francis; and a very bad actor, but a talented, eccentric man, of the name of Reymes, the Tobias. The house was very thinly attended, and on such occasions actors in country theatres are very likely to try more to please one another than the audience.

"Nay, should I lose my son, still I should not wish to die. Here is the hut where I was born. Here is the tree that grew with me; and—I am almost ashamed to confess it—I have a *dog* which I love," he should have said; instead of which, he substituted, "a *duck* I love."

This unexpected alteration, of course, made me laugh.

"Smile if you please," he continued, with per-

23

fect gravity, "but hear me. My benefactress once came to my hut herself. The poor *bird*, unused to see the form of elegance enter the door of penury, *quacked* at her. 'I wonder you keep that waddling, ugly *fowl*, Mr. Tobias,' said she. 'Ah, madam,' I replied, 'if I part with my *duck*, are you sure that anything else will love me?' She was pleased with my answer."

He was excellent company, and being very fond of a ramble in the country, would frequently attend me in my sketching expeditions. I was employed one day in making a drawing of Stoke Church—strange, too, that I should desire a likeness of that matrimonial manufactory, for it was there I was bound in the holy ties of wedlock; but it was very picturesque and pleasing on paper, for all that. Several times I was disturbed in my occupation, to look round to inquire the cause of a crash, every now and then, like the breaking of glass; and at length I caught a glimpse of Reymes, slyly jerking a pebble, under his arm, through one of the windows. I recollected twice, in walking home with him, late at night, from the theatre, his quietly taking a brickbat from out of his coat-pocket and deliberately smashing it through the casement of the Town Hall, and walking on and continuing his conversation as if nothing had happened. Crack! again. I began to suspect an aberration of intellect, and said,

"Reymes, for heaven's sake what are you doing?"

"Showing my gratitude," said he; and crack! went another.

"Showing the devil!" said I; "you're breaking the church windows."

"Why, I know it—certainly; what do you stare at?" said the eccentric. "I broke nearly every pane three weeks ago—I couldn't hit them all. After you have broken a good many, the stones are apt to go through the holes you've already made. They only finished mending them the day before yesterday; I came out and asked the men when they were likely to get done;" and clatter! clatter! went another.

"That's excellent!" said he, in great glee. "I hit the frame just in the right place; I knocked out two large ones that time."

"Reymes," said I, with temper, "if you don't desist, I must leave off my drawing."

"Well," said he, "only this one," and crack! it went; "there! I've done. Since it annoys you, I'll come by myself to-morrow and finish the job; it's the only means in my power of proving my gratitude."

"Proving your folly," said I. "Why, Reymes, you must be out of your senses."

"Why, did I never tell you?" said he. "Oh! then, I don't wonder at your surprise. I thought I had told you. I had an uncle, a glazier, who died, and left me twenty pounds, and this mourning-ring; and I therefore have made it a rule to break the windows of all public places ever since. The loss is not worth speaking of to the parish, and puts a nice bit of money in the pocket of some poor dealer in putty, with probably a large family to support. And now I've explained, I presume you have no objection to my proceeding in paying what I consider a debt of gratitude due to my dead uncle."

"Hold! Reymes," said I, as he was picking up a pebble. "How do you know but the poor fellow with the large family may not undertake to repair the windows by contract, at so much a year or month?"

"Eh! egad, I never thought of that," said the whimsical, good-hearted creature. "I'll suspend operations until I've made the inquiry, and if I've wronged him I'll make amends."

Being acceptable to the audience, and a very youthful appearance, the manager was induced to cast me for George Barnwell, "though, heaven knows, against my own inclining;" for I never had a particle of sentimental tragedy in my composition. On reading the character, I was disgusted with the "fool, as well as villain." My whole life had been passed in the unrestrained society of young men, but I never met anything like a George Barnwell in any mess I ever belonged to; and I felt my incapacity to invent the delineation of a character I did not believe ever existed in nature; and I entreated Foot to take me out of the part. But my objections appeared to him extremely comical; no prayers I had "wit enough to make" could move him, and he persisted, I believe for the sake of the joke, that I should perform the character. As usual, I had waited till the last hour to swallow the bitter morsel, and on the day it was to be performed, I was fuming and fretting up and down the room, endeavouring to get the mawkish language into my head, when an old messmate, an assistant-surgeon, whom I had not seen for two years, paid me a visit. I excused myself from attempting to entertain him, by explaining the torture I was enduring.

"Why don't you send word you're ill?" said the doctor.

"Why, my dear fellow," said I, "I have made so many objections, that Foot would suspect at once that I was hoaxing him, and be here on the instant."

"Give me a pen and ink," said my old companion. "I've saved many a good fellow from disagreeable duty in the same way—there—send that, and a shilling, to an apothecary, and let me know about half an hour before you want to be very sick, and I'll make you so, without doing you any harm; go myself as your physician to Foot, as you call him—bring him here to be convinced of the dangerous state you are in—lay it all to excessive anxiety of mind, and make him believe you won't live the night out. So throw away the book, and let's have a glass of grog together. I met Spencer, and he told me who you were, and where to find you."

The plan succeeded to admiration, and, thank Heaven, I have never played, or read, that worse than an emetic since.

Wilson the rope-dancer, long since forgotten by most thinking beings, was then all the rage; crowding his own pockets and the houses wherever he went; but, in my opinion, he was very inferior to John Cline, now in this country, and christened in German, very appropriately, "*the little gentleman rope-dancer*," by Charles Gilfert, who took out the first patent for theatrical humbuggery in the United States.

At about this period the British government took it into their heads that the Duke of Clarence—having, as it was supposed, in all probability, sowed his wild oats, should take unto himself a lawfully-wedded wife, leave off breaking the ninth commandment, and use his royal highness's best efforts to produce an heir to the throne in the event of its ever coming to his turn to supply such a deficiency. Whether the novelty of the thing tickled the old gentleman's vanity, or if "just for a bit of fun," as the boys say, he consented to the operation, I know not; but he did, and thrust forth from his protection the mother of his children, to earn a living, for her few remaining days, by the reputation of her transcendent talent, the exercise of which, in its zenith, had literally supported him in luxury for years. She might well exclaim, with the creator of her own Rosalind,

> " My way of life
> Is fall'n into the sear, the yellow leaf:
> And that which should accompany old age,
> As honour, love, obedience, troops of friends,
> I must not look to have."

And with probably just such feelings, slaking former fire, the great Mrs. Jordan arrived at Plymouth, to play a round of characters.

She opened in the " Widow Cheerby;" I was the " Charles Woodly."

" Can you laugh, Mr. Cowell?" said Thalia herself. " I used to laugh very naturally once; and to laugh well is of great importance, even to a tragedian."

" Upon my life, madam, I do not know what I can do," I replied; " I have only been on the stage five months."

" Then you are a very promising young man, and your good sense will make you think you don't know what you can do when you have been upon the stage five hundred years." I laughed. " Oh, I see you can be merry," continued this Momus in petticoats—perhaps with an aching heart. " The effect of this scene depends entirely upon you; keep it up, no matter where you are, and, scarcely, what you say; but be most joyous; I want the whole scene to go well while I'm upon the stage; I don't wish the foolish people in front to praise Mrs. Jordan only; I want them to be intoxicated with the general effect; but don't go so far forward—act between the second entrances."

Munden, a short time before, had particularly desired me to get close to the footlights; but it was very easy to account for the contradiction in the instructions of these great artists. The fact is, she was getting old; dimples turn to crinkles after long use; besides, she wore a wig glued on; and, in the heat of acting—for she was always in earnest—I have seen some of the tenacious compound with which it was secured trickle down a wrinkle behind her ear; her person, too, was extremely round and large, though still retaining something of the outline of its former grace;

> " And, after all, 'twould puzzle to say where
> It would not spoil a charm to pare."

There is no calamity in the catalogue of the ills " that flesh is heir to" so horrible as the approach of old age to an actor. I must beg it to be clearly understood, I am not speaking from my own experience in this matter. In the line of business I profess, a few gray hairs sometimes saves a wig; and a wrinkle or so supersedes the trouble of marking the face, which I was obliged to do for many years, till lately; but juvenile tragedy, light comedy, and walking gentlemen with little pot-bellies, and have-been pretty women, are really to be pitied. Fancy a lady, who has had quires of sonnets made to her eyebrow, being obliged, at last, to black it, play at the back of the stage at night, sit with her back to the window in a shady part of the green-room in the morning, and keep on her bonnet unless she can afford a very natural wig. As long ago as Garrick's time, Churchill tells us,

> " All actors, too, upon the back should bear
> Certificate of birth—time when—place where.

> For how can critics rightly fix their worth,
> Unless they know the minute of their birth?
> An audience, too, deceived, may find too late
> That they have clapp'd an actor out of date."

And in the United States, at the present day, the very same feeling exists to a nicety. In every city on the Continent—for I have visited nearly all of them—you will meet some half dozen or more *Paul Pryish* old bachelors to inquire of you, " How old is Fanny Drake?" or, " How old is Fanny Kemble? or Fanny Jarnian? or Fanny Fitzwilliam? or Fanny Hill?" And just now they were all full cry to discover the birthday of Fanny Ellsler. Ellen Tree had scarcely made the usual theatrical tour before dates were collected in circumstantial evidence. I played with her during an engagement in Baltimore, and was cross-examined on the subject by Col. Jack Thomas, and other amateurs in such matters, but *I didn't tell.*

In this country, too, particularly,

> " The eye must be fed."

A *fine-looking young man* and a *beautiful girl* can get an excellent living on the stage by such material alone; but when they begin to get old, *God help them!*

Always an adorer of genius in any shape, I worshipped Mrs. Jordan. Her encouragement fired my ambition, and her advice and example I adopted as my creed. Sandford made up a company to play with her at Exeter, and she insisted that I should be one of the party. I felt flattered by her good opinion, and gave up my teaching for the honour, and received a compensation for the loss of my benefit at Plymouth in an increased salary, of which she paid the half. Sandford, she declared, " was like an old horse; would neither go with begging nor beating." The fact is, he had a style of his own, and was too old to bear dictation or alter his manner. I was young, and would do as she bid me, as well as I could, and therefore was selected to play all the off-parts to her that it was possible for me to undertake; among others, Beverly, in *All in the Wrong*, to her Belinda. All the principal actresses that I know of always choose to play Lady Restless in preference; but when Mrs. Jordan was the Belinda, you would not remember, at the end of the comedy, that Lady Restless was even in the piece. Her Nell, in the *Devil to Pay*, was a huge lump of nature throughout. Her making the bed, smoothing it down, admiring the quality of the linen, and the simple expression, " I've often heard of heaven, and this is it," defies description. I have seen many Jobsons, but I never saw but one Nell.

At the close of the Exeter campaign I returned to Dock, with a better salary, and a share of the low comedy business with Barnes. I was the original Gregory, in the *Turn Out*, in that company; the scene being laid at Plymouth, I thought myself privileged to correct some inaccuracies in localities and other matters. Among them, the author speaks of " pickled salmon," which is an article scarcely known there: I substituted the very popular delicacy, pickled cockles, using the same abbreviation the old women used, to call them about the streets—it was very effective then. Barnes was Restive; his wife, Marian Ramsay; and Vandenhoff, Forage, an excellent actor in such characters. I saw him make his first appearance in London afterward, at Covent Garden, and it was either too bad or too good an imitation of John Kemble for the public to more than tolerate then: I have not seen him perform since.

Barnes was an overwhelming favourite at both Plymouth and Dock; he owned some houses in the neighbourhood, and appeared to be settled for life; and, therefore, it was no place for my advancement in the line of business I was desirous to sustain. Out of a number of applications I received three offers. One from Macready, the father of the great actor, at Newcastle-upon-Tyne; one from Kelly, Collins, and somebody else at Portsmouth; and one from Beverly, at Richmond, in Surry, which, being the nearest to London, I accepted.

◆

CHAPTER XI.

"'But tho' he was o' high degree,
The fient a pride nae pride had he:
But wad hae spent an hour caressin',
Ev'n w' a tinkler gipsy's messin':
At kirk or market, mill or smiddie,
Nae tauted tyke, tho' e'er sae duddie,
But he wad stan't, as glad to see him,
And stroant an stanes, an' hillocks wi' him."
TWA DOGS.

SIR LUCIUS O'TRIGGER boasts of there being "very snug lying in the Abbey" at Bath; now, in my day, I can boast of there being very snug lodging in the churchyard of Richmond-upon-Thames; in a very nice little house, intended, no doubt, as the parsonage, and most conveniently situated for such a purpose, immediately opposite the door,

"Where sinners enter, and like saints come out—"

but be that as it may, there I took up my quarters, and there my first child was born, now nearly nine years older than his father was then. This circumstance makes the yard interesting to me, while the church must be so to everybody, in consequence of a brass plate in one of the aisles: "To the memory of James Thomson, author of the Seasons."

But all this has nothing to do with theatricals. But if my readers will only imagine this a "long stop," and walk with me through a crowd of cricketers, and "playful children just let loose from school," across the "grassy-vested green," I will introduce them to William R. Beverley, Esq., manager of the Theatre Royal, Richmond.

Of a great lubberly boy of eighteen or nineteen, who was leaning against the stage door, in a long begrimed apron and shirt sleeves, with a pound brush in one hand, and half a pound of bread and butter in the other, I made my inquiries. In addition to his face being very much marked with the smallpox, it was well daubed with blue and yellow paint, and its assumed expression of "serious gravity" formed altogether an excellent broad hint for a caricature of Liston looking through a rainbow. After rubbing his nose against his knuckle, and at the same time the brush against his ear, with an air of importance he directed me to the dwelling part of the establishment, where, he told me, I should find his "pa," for it appeared I had been addressing Henry Beverley, the son of the proprietor. His extraordinary likeness to the great comedian I afterward found was notorious, and on which much hope of future fame was predicted, but never was realized.

Mr. Beverley met me at the entrance, and I introduced myself.

"Oh, you are Mr. Cowell—walk in—take a seat. Well, my young 'un, what part have you ever gone on for in Alexander the Great?" said my third manager, in a *slang* kind of voice, after the manner of a coster-monger or a hackney-coachman, without a hoarseness.

"Sir!" said I: "Alexander the Great! There is nothing in the play in the way of low comedy but Clytus, and I'm not able to play that."

"Able or not able, you must play what I want you to play, or I shall not choose to be able to pay you your salary; but as to Clytus, it's one of my pet parts—I do that myself. Young Betty opens on Monday in Alexander, and I want you for Hephestion."

"But, sir, your letter of engagement," which I produced, "expressly says that I am to play all the low comedy, save only such characters as you think proper to perform yourself."

"Well, that's all very fine, my rippin—I know all that—but you see I engaged you *expressly*, as you call it, to supply the place of little Dornton, who was to have gone to the Haymarket, but Coleman, Winston, and Morris have had a b—row, and the little theatre don't open this season, so Dornton keeps his situation. But I'll tell you what I'll do: if you'll agree to make yourself *generally useful*, I'll give up some of my characters, and I play all the best; if not, I can get plenty of young 'uns at the Harp or Finches" (favourite haunts for would-be actors at that time), "and there's no harm done."

But there was a great deal of harm done; I had taken a long journey, which I could not repeat, with Mrs. Cowell "in the way that women wish to be who love their lords," and had refused the other two offers I had received. I therefore very prudently put a good face on the matter, and made my *début* in Hephestion, and Ralph in Lock and Key, which the manager *gave up* for this night only.

He was a tall, gaunt-looking man, vulgar, both in appearance and manner—a dirty shirt, open at the neck; worn-out sandals for slippers; and an old drab greatcoat, his dressing-gown, I suppose. But I was rejoiced to find, upon acquaintance, that he was a very different human being from what might be imagined from a first impression: he proved to be a kind, open-hearted, honest man; I was in his employ for more than a year, greatly to my advantage; and we parted, and continued the best of friends.

His circuit consisted of Richmond, Woolwich, and Croyden; and the villages being all within a few miles of London, the distinguished members of Covent Garden and Drury Lane were able to pay short and continual visits—we had a "star" nearly every night; in consequence, all that was required of the stock company was utility; and I was the most useful of the party. When I entered the profession, I had determined to succeed, and, therefore, no labour could appal me; I played anything and everything, from high tragedy to low comedy; and to the excess and variety of practice I had in that company, I feel myself indebted for all the experience I have put up in one parcel since. I have played Mr. Oakley to Miss Smith's (the successful imitator of Mrs. Siddons, now Mrs. Bartley, if she's alive) Jealous Wife, one night, and Squire Beadle, with Charles Young as Oakley, another; Caleb Quotem to *Paddy* Webb's Looney; Captain Beaugard to Matthews as Caleb, and so on. Beverley used to boast that "The young 'un"—that was his affectionate title for me—"in case of necessity, could go on for Hamlet, from night to night, without missing a line."

Among the celebrated actors I played with in this company, I remember the following: *Mesdames* Glover, Davidson, Edwin, Smith, Kelly, Matthews, Cubit, and Booth: *Messieurs* Young, Matthews, Munden, Webb, Elliston, Emery, Sinclair, Incledon, Taylor, Blanchard, Samuel Russell, Dowton, Oxberry, Rae, Betty, Richard Jones, with fifty others, and the ridiculous "Amateur of Fashion," Romeo Coates. He played six or seven times during the season, gratuitously, to crowded houses; and, as Beverley expressed it, "The nasty beast paid the rent." He was like a very ugly monkey in the face, with long, frizzly, black hair, turned up behind, usually with a woman's comb; but in Romeo it was allowed to take the natural position of a horse's tail, which it resembled, and was decorated with a large bunch of white ribands. His wardrobe was of the most costly materials and ridiculous fashion; his jewelry was said to be of great value, and for its protection he was always accompanied by Bishop, the Bow-street officer. I had the misery of playing Mercutio, Ensign Dudley, and Horatio to his Romeo, Belcour, and Lothario. His dying scenes were always encored, and so were many of his speeches, amid shouts of laughter, and he seemed to relish the ridicule heaped upon him quite as much as the audience.

After one of his exhibitions, I performed Artaxomines in Bombastes, in imitation of him throughout, and the identity was so great that many wagers were laid that I was really the man. A piece at this time called *At Home* was in rehearsal at Covent Garden, in which Matthews had a part intended to represent Coates, and the great mimic used to drive to Richmond during its preparation to get me to read the part in the way Coates would be likely to play it.

It is notorious that an imitation can be much easier caught from an imitation than from the original; the very best must partake of caricature, and the outline, in consequence, is bolder, as a copy is much easier made from a drawing than a drawing is made from nature. The stock company are not worth talking about on the stage, and off of it I knew nothing of them, with the exception of Klanert, Hughes, and *little Bob Keely*. The first was our principal man; he had been for some years at Covent Garden, and his name will be found, in the original cast of "Speed the Plough," as young Handy's servant, and in that line of business, I have no doubt, he was excellent. Hughes went to Drury Lane that season, and has been there, with scarcely anybody's knowing it, ever since. Keely was a sort of second prompter, a very talented young man in every way but as an actor then, nor did he give any promise that he could ever become the excellent comedian I am told he now is. He was very successful as a star in this country, a few years since, but I never saw him act.

The immortal Kean had this year burst from his obscurity, to dazzle all the world with his transcendent talent. I was most anxious to see this wonder, and the first night I was out of a performance, Keely, who was my sworn friend and companion, walked with me from Woolwich to London, and at about four o'clock in the afternoon we joined a crowd already assembled at the pit entrance of Drury Lane Theatre, which continued to increase by thousands before the doors were opened.

Half crushed to death, we found ourselves, after a desperate effort, at the back of the passage which surrounds the pit, from whence I could, by straining to my utmost height, catch a glimpse of the corner of the green curtain nearest to the top, but little Bob hadn't even that satisfaction. There, at any rate, we could not see Kean, nor live to see anything else at the end of a few hours' squeeze such as we were then enduring, and we agreed to pay the extra three and sixpence and go into the boxes; but as to obtaining a pass check, it was impossible. We had nearly as much trouble to get out as we had to get in, and were content to lose our three and sixpence apiece, and pay fourteen shillings more for the privilege of standing on a back seat of the upper tier of boxes, at the corner next the stage, an excellent point of sight for a perspective view of the crown of a man's hat, or a bald spot on a lady's head in the pit, who had been obliged to take off her bonnet whether she liked it or not.

"Bruised in body," and "sorely afflicted in spirit" and pocket, we were just in the mood not to be easily pleased with anything or anybody.

When Kean came on I was astonished. I was prepared to see a small man; but diminished by the unusual distance, and his black dress, and a mental comparison with Kemble's princely person, he appeared a perfect pigmy—his voice, unlike any I had ever heard before, perhaps from its very strangeness, was most objectionable—and I turned to Keely, and at once pronounced him a *most decided humbug;* and, if I could have got out then, I should have said so to everybody, because I honestly thought so; and if, afterward, I had been convinced of his enormous genius, I might, like Taylor, the oculist, and editor of the Sun newspaper, have persisted in my denunciation, rather than confess my incapacity, at the first glance, to comprehend the sublimity of Shakspeare and Nature being upon such familiar terms. But I was obliged to remain, and compelled to be silent; so invoking patience, and placing my hand on a young lady's shoulder for support, I quietly gazed on through three tedious scenes—for all the actors seemed worse than usual—till it came to the dialogue with the Ghost, and at the line

"I'll call thee Hamlet—king—*father*—"

I was converted. I resigned the support of the lady, and employed both hands in paying the usual tribute to godlike talent. *Father* is not a pretty word to look at, but it is beautiful to hear when lisped by little children, or spoken by Edmund Kean in Hamlet.

In private life Kean was the most contradictory character I ever met with: affable and overbearing by turns—in either case without sufficient cause. Lavishly, nay, foolishly liberal, or niggardly mean and suspicious. With a refined taste for music, he would listen attentively, and laugh heartily, at a blackguard's song in a beerhouse. Devotedly fond of children and animals, he was sometimes brutal in his domestic behaviour. An enthusiastic admirer of flowers, birds, shrubs, and Nature in her simplest garb, he would spend days and weeks in a den of vice and depravity. His chosen associates were selected from the lowest dregs of society—prizefighters, thief-catchers, and knaves and fools of low degree, "as gross as ignorance made drunk"—though sought after and courted by all the rich and noble in mind or station. When

27

sober, he was elegantly courteous and gentle-manlike in his deportment, *if he thought proper;* but when intoxicated, he was disgustingly coarse, and vulgar in the extreme.

Kean had his degrees of drunkenness, according to a calculation made by a faithful servant of his, I think named Miller. This man was devotedly attached to his master—all menials adored him—and if Kean happened to be dining with a party of gentlemen, which he was obliged to do sometimes, Miller—who was as anxious about his conducting himself with propriety as a father could possibly be—when it was getting late, and the servants were ordered to leave the room, would take his station near the door, and, from time to time, make the following inquiries of any of the party who might pass him.

"How is master getting on, sir?"

"Oh, very well, Miller," would be the probable reply.

"Is he getting—eh?" says Miller, significantly.

"Getting what?" says the stranger.

"Getting tipsy, sir! if you must have it."

"Oh, just a little."

"Ah! I thought how it would be," Miller would say, with a sigh. "And he promised me he'd behave himself!"

In half an hour he would make another inquiry to the same effect, and receive for answer,

"Oh, he's just a little high—glorious company! He's going to sing us a song."

"Going to sing?" says Miller, with anxiety. "What is he going to sing, sir? What's the name of the song?"

"'The Storm.'"

"'The Storm!' Ah! I see how it is; if he's going to sing 'The Storm,' he must be getting very drunk."

Another half hour would pass, and he would listen at the keyhole, or, perhaps, open the door quietly, and thrust his head into the room, withdraw it in an instant, and, shutting the door, turn round with a look of horror, and exclaim, "It's all over! he's past hope! he's out of his senses! *he's talking Latin!* And now he's sure to make a damned beast of himself!"

◆

CHAPTER XII.

"The same persons who would overturn a state to establish an opinion often very absurd, anathematize the innocent amusements necessary to a great city, and the arts which contribute to the splendour of a nation."—VOLTAIRE.

AFTER an unprofitable campaign at Richmond, the company moved to Craydon, a very small, anti-theatrical town at any time, but then made more so by a long and severe controversy between two popular preachers, who, having exhausted their identical rhetoric, and the patience of their congregations, agreed, as a last resource of notoriety, to unite their whole remaining stock of damnation, and hurl it wholesale at the drama and its humble professors. The effect of this fire and brimstone eloquence, if it may be so called, was to half ruin poor Beverley, and half starve some ten or twelve poor players.

> "The first and wisest of them all professed
> To know this only—that he nothing knew.
>
> *　　*　　*　　*　　*　　*
>
> Alas! what can they teach, and not mislead,
> Ignorant of themselves, of God much more;
> And how the world began, and how man fell,
> Degraded by himself, on grace depending?
> Much of the soul they talk but all awry,
> And in themselves seek virtue, and to themselves
> All glory arrogate, to God give none."

Thus sung the pious Milton, but our persecutors used language better suited to convince their feeble-minded flock that *Paradise* could only be *Regained* by prostrating the playhouse. After six weeks of patient endurance, we made our retreat to Woolwich. Beverley had no scene-painter employed, and to aid my worthy manager, I engaged gratuitously to "*get up*," as the phrase is, some showy pieces. At that period of my life I was an enthusiast in anything I undertook. Through the kindness of Mr. Murray, of Covent Garden, I obtained an introduction to Phillips, the then celebrated scenic artist, and gained from him some general instructions as to the colours, &c., and the privilege of visiting the painting-room. He was of the old school, and though his productions were beautiful specimens of art, the elaborate *finish* he bestowed on them rather decreased than added to their effect; and while in the same room, the elder Grieve (who first pointed out the path Stanfield has since trod to fame) was every day *splashing* into existence a cottage or a cavern, with a pound brush in each hand; Phillips would sit for hours with a rest-stick and a camel's hair pencil shading the head of a nail. My success in this department of the arts, in the opinion of the kind-hearted Beverley, was superlative. He said, and I am sure innocently believed, I was "the best scene painter in the kingdom!" and as he was too poor to pay me the price at which he valued my talent, he, like an honest, liberal-minded man, recommended me to Trotter, who had become the lessee of the Brighton Theatre, and with him I engaged as actor and painter, at the highest salary I ever got in England, out of London. Harley was the principal comedian, and as I would not play a secondary part, I appeared less frequently than he did, but shared equally with him the favour of the audience. He was only a few years older than myself, but the most parsimonious *young* man I ever knew. The next season he appeared with great success at the English Opera House, and has continued a favourite in the metropolis ever since. A weak-minded, *wanted-to-be-thought-great* actor (he was foolish enough to drown himself a few years since), of the name of Faulkner, was a member of the company. He, with a Mr. Anderson, who had got rich in the employ of Stephen Kemble, as his treasurer, had leased the northern circuit from that good, easy man, and Faulkner, the *acting* partner, was recruiting for the establishment. To me he made an offer to lead the low comedy business, but with a salary of less than one half of what I was then receiving, which his persuasion, my own vanity, I called it ambition then, and the flattering prophecy of Mrs. Jordan, induced me to accept; and after due notice, Trotter and I parted, with sincere regret, I believe, on both sides.

Faulkner and Anderson's circuit consisted of North and South Shields, in Northumberland; Sunderland, and the city of Durham, in the county of that name; Stockton-upon-Tees, and Scarborough, in Yorkshire. Upon my arrival at the first-named place, I found, to my astonishment, four low comedians besides myself, engaged on precisely the same terms as to business. Four to one were great odds, but I distanced them all. First, "Lewis;" he got too drunk to play the first night, and was discharged, and for spite, kept the "same old drunk," as the sailor said, for the six weeks we remained in the town, and may not be sober yet, for any-

28

thing I know to the contrary, for I have never seen him since. Next, Brown, a brother to John Mills Brown, for many years in this country, but unlike him in talent; he did more good than harm. Then Smith, nicknamed Obi, from his excellent pantomime acting in Three-fingered Jack; but he was a most melancholy low comedian, and *couldn't sing*. And last, Porteus; he was an elderly, baldheaded gentleman of forty-five, who had made his *first appearance on any stage* a few months before, as a last resource, having failed in a saddler's shop at Liverpool. I had everything my own way, and was, of course, a great favourite, but the *treasurer-manager* had so cunningly contrived the terms of the benefits, that if an actor didn't lose by taking one, which, by his engagement, he was compelled to do, he thought himself well off. The journies were long and expensive; I was the father of two splendid children, and only a guinea and a half a week, and my good spirits to feed and clothe them; I never suffered the inconvenience of poverty, while on the stage in *England*, but during the year I was in this company.

At Durham I had the happiness to gain the firm and lasting friendship of the *great and good Stephen Kemble;* he there resided in a beautiful little cottage, a short distance from the city, on the bank of the river. In early life he had married a Miss Satchell, the daughter of a then celebrated pianoforte maker. She had retired from the profession before my time, but had left a high reputation behind her, and in parts requiring simple pathos, was said never to have been excelled; her sister was still on the stage, and married for some years to a distant relation of Mrs. Jordan's, by the name of James Bland; as actors, they were without talent, but had two fine children, from ten to twelve years old.

When Stephen Kemble leased his theatre to Faulkner and Anderson, he made a proviso that they should receive each five-and-twenty shillings per week for the services (such as they were) of themselves and children. The boy made the calls, the pretty little girl "went on" for one of the Stranger's offspring, or a *Child* in the *Wood;* the mother played *short old ladies;* and the father delivered the messages. Thus the claims of Plutus bound them to a daily intercourse, though those of Hymen had been broken for years; the man's dissipation, I imagine, was the cause of their separation—*I believe that women are never in the wrong*—but they met and spoke to each other as indifferent persons would, and 'twas droll to hear the old gentleman say, "I must put on my other shirt today, for I'm invited to take a friendly cup of tea with the old lady," meaning his wife. His carelessness of character was naturally increased by the certainty he had of receiving his salary. The theatres, as is usual in all countries, were surrounded by some half dozen taverns, and at one or other Jemmy would wait to be called; for 'twas his boast that he had never been known to be in a theatre a minute before or after he was wanting. He was a great shot, and always dressed in a hunting-coat, with large leather gaiters, and small-clothes; and no matter what the costume of the play was, he never changed any part of his apparel but his coat. He was well informed, a ready wit, and of great amiability and simplicity of manners; his company was, therefore, unfortunately, much sought for as a brother sportsman, or a pot companion. When his services were required on the stage, his son, from long practice, would have him at the wing just in time to slip on a tunic or a jacket, pop a little red on his face, and push him on. He knew every message in every old play that ever was delivered, but the new ones he either would not or could not learn. In the opera of the Devil's Bridge he had to say a couple of lines to the effect that "The Count Belino's escaped from his confinement," instead of which he rushed on and said,

" My lord, the Count Belino's taken prisoner."

"No, no!" said his son, who was always his prompter.

"No, no," echoed Jemmy, "and so they've cut off his head."

" Escaped! escaped!" said the boy.

" And so he has made his escape," said Jemmy, amid a roar of laughter. The part of Catesby, in "Richard III.," he boasted he was "letter perfect in ;" and so he was; but Richard had so impressed on his mind the high importance of his being very quick in saying, " The Duke of Buckingham is taken," that he announced the joyful tidings two minutes too soon. Again, at the first pause, he popped on his head and stammered out, "My lord, the Duke of Buckingham is taken," and again was pulled back by the tail of his tunic; when the right time actually arrived, he was a little too late, and Richard, foaming with rage, shouted out,

"Now, sir?"

"The Duke of Buckingham," said Jemmy, very calmly, "is taken now, by God."

He was intrusted with the part of the Priest in Hamlet, who really has one very difficult speech, beginning with

" Her obsequies have been as far enlarged
As we have warranty ;"

instead of which, Jemmy substituted,

" Her obsequies are as large as we can make 'em ;"

and the audience heard no more of the excuse for the omission of the usual forms at the funeral of the "fair Ophelia."

As he "opened an account" at every grog-shop in the town, his benefits were always fully, though not very fashionably, attended; he used to call them "a meeting of creditors." His son was a good-tempered, intelligent boy, but showed little respect or deference for the opinion of his father. Children soon learn to neglect that duty when they see a parent neglecting to respect himself. On a Saturday they usually held a consultation as to how the five-and-twenty shillings should be disposed of to the best advantange.

"Now, John, my boy," the old man would say, "let me see: I owe eight shillings at the sign of the Saddle; well, that's that," putting the amount on one side; "well, then I promised to pay part of my score at the Blue Pig—well, say five shillings; there, I'll stop Mother Pepper's mouth with that. How much does that make, John?"

"Why, nine, ten, eleven, twelve, thirteen shillings," says the boy, touching his five fingers.

"But I mean, you goose, how much have I got left ?"

"How should I know?" says John; "why don't you count it? you've got the money."

"But you ought to know, you young rascal," says the father, with true parental authority; "you ought to know: take thirteen from twenty-five, how many remain? why, twelve, to be sure," counting the balance slyly in his hand; "that's the way you're neglecting your education, is it? I shall have to talk to your schoolmaster."

"Yes, you had better talk to him," replies John, "for he told me, yesterday, that unless you let him have a little money, I needn't come to school no more."

"Ay, true, my dear, that's true; you mustn't lose your education, at any rate," says the kind old man; "take him round five shillings after dinner, my dear. I had a pot with him last night, and he agreed if I would let him have that much now, he'd take the rest out in tickets at the *Ben*, and treat the boys."

"I want a pair of shoes, father," says John, taking advantage of the old man's softened mood.

"How much will they cost, my boy?"

"Why, father," says John, "I can get a capital pair for three and sixpence."

"You must get them for three shillings, John; we owe the butcher four, and he must be paid, or we get no beef; there, that ends it," says the poor old fellow, with a self-satisfied air; but his vision of independence was in an instant destroyed by John's simply saying,

"You've forgot the landlady, father."

"Yes, that's true, so I have; yes, d— her, she must have her rent, or out we go. John, my dear, I'll tell you how I'll contrive it. I'll put the Saddle off with four shillings, and *open a branch account* with the Yew-tree."

"Yes, that's all very well," says John, very quietly, "but we owed her sixpence on last week, and she paid for the washing."

"Well, how much does the washing come to, John?"

"Two and tup'ence," says the boy.

"Well, then," argues the old man, "Mother Pepper must be content to take three shillings instead of five."

"But then, father, that won't do; and we want tea."

"Who wants tea? I don't care a d—for tea."

"But I do," replies the boy, with provoking calmness.

"You want tea! you'll want bread, you young scoundrel!" shouts Bland, in a rage.

"Bread! that's true," exclaims John; "you forgot the baker."

The old man's schemes to pacify his creditors with the distribution of five-and-twenty shillings were all knocked on the head by the recollection of the baker, and sweeping the money off the table into his breeches pocket in a passion, he roared out,

"They may all go to hell together; I'm damned if I pay any of them."

The frequenters of the theatre, both at Shields and Sunderland, were of the sort Shakspeare so excellently describes: "Youths that thunder at a playhouse, and fight for bitten apples; that no audience but the tribulation of Tower Hill, or the limbs of Limehouse, their dear brothers, are able to endure."

At Durham they were fastidiously refined, and at Scarborough exclusively fashionable; but I was fortunate enough to suit their varied tastes, and was a great favourite everywhere. We had a month to remain at the latter town, when, through the influence of my good friends, Major Topham, of sporting and dramatic celebrity, and Stephen Kemble, I received an offer from Fitzgerald, of the York circuit, to lead the comedy, with the highest salary in the company. I, of course, was delighted; instantly accepted the proposal, and informed my managers of my anxiety to leave at the end of that season; but no prayers could move them; they insisted on their bond of six weeks' notice, which obliged me to go to Shields for two weeks, and take a very long journey out of my way to get to Hull, where I was to join the York company. I was very poor, too, and "more proud than poor."

"And the worst of it was, the little ones were sickly,
And if they'd live or die, the doctor didn't know."

Both my children were ill with the measles, which parental anxiety magnified into the small-pox:

"The dragon now,
Which Jenner combats on a cow."

The last night arrived. With scarcely enough to pay my stage-fare alone to Shields, broken in spirit, I was bustling through Blaisot, in one of the "Maid and Magpie" translations, for the first and only time—Heaven be praised—when I was informed a gentleman at the stage-door wished to see me. I had two or three creditors in town, very gentlemanly men, but they had kindly promised to wait—for their *money*, I mean, though not at the stage-door—but at the end of the act a very elegant man handed me a card, on which was engraved Mr. Alston, which he explained, understanding I was engaged, he was about leaving with the porter. On the back of it was written, in pencil, "Lord Normanby, and a few friends, will be happy to see Mr. Cowell at supper this evening." I was not in the humour to make myself agreeable to Lord anybody, but politely declined the honour, and stated, as a reason, the indisposition of my children, and the necessity of leaving town in a couple of hours, in the mail-stage, for Shields. Before conclusion of the performance I received a packet, which I found contained fifty one-guinea notes, with the following epistle:

"Messrs. W. T. Denison, Mr. Alston, and Lord Normanby, great admirers of Mr. Cowell's comic powers, beg he will accept the enclosed as their contribution to his benefit, which they were unable to attend; any influence they may possess he may freely command. They wish him every success in a profession of which he is already so great an ornament."

I paid off my four or five pounds' worth of debts in the morning; wrapped my dear children in blankets; hired a postchaise; played out my two weeks at Shields; and, in high spirits, started for York, as the theatrical phrase then was, *the stepping-stone to London.*

◆

CHAPTER XIII.

"I do remember him at Clement's Inn, like a man made after supper of a cheese-paring; when he was naked he was, for all the world, like a forked radish, with a head fantastically carved upon it with a knife: he was so forlorn, that his dimensions, to any thick sight, were invisible: he was the very genius of famine; and now is this vice's dagger become a squire."—*Henry IV.*, part ii.

THE York circuit, under the long and able management of the eccentric Tate Wilkinson, had for years held the first rank, next to London, in theatrical estimation. In this school the talent of a Siddons, Jordan, Kemble, Emery, Knight, Matthews, and a host of other celebrated actors, had been matured; but, at the time I speak of, it had fallen from its high estate, though it still maintained a feeble superiority among its compeers from the recollection of what it had been. Learning, at the theatre, that Fitzgerald (the manager) was confined to his room with the asthma, I called at his lodging over a seed-shop, on a short, wide, flat street, called Corn-hill. I had taken up my abode at a watch-maker's opposite. I found my new ruler seated on four chairs (all there were in the apartment), before a large fire, wrapped in a white flannel gown, a pair of green slippers peeping from underneath, and a crimson velvet cap, confining a head of hair which might with justice have been called *red-hot red*, but that the contrast with the cap cooled it down to a yellowish tinge. His "reception was the north side of friendly, that I must say," to use Nicol Jarvies' expression, but that might be attributed to bodily suffering—people are not often sick and civil at the same time—but a poodle dog made ample amends for the lack of hospitality of his master (he had been trained by some other gentleman), for he insisted on taking my hat, licked my hand, and, no doubt, would have wagged his tail if he had had one; but as the negro said of a similar animal, "dat tail must ha' been cut berry short off, or else him drave in." Poor Dragon deserves this much notice as connected with the drama; he was the *real original dog* in the Forest of Bondy, and shared the applause with the great Liston.

The old saw says, "Judge of a man by the company he keeps;" but the companionship and apparent kindness of Fitzgerald to this animal must not be placed to his credit as the outward sign of goodness of heart. He liked the dog because he drew him money; on the same principle that Elliot was civil to his amiable wife Celeste, until Fanny Elssler interfered with her attraction.

After standing a reasonable time, I took a seat on the table; he took the hint, and kicked towards me the chair on which his feet were partially resting; and, in the unnecessary energetic action he used, he displayed a leg, in point of size, very much resembling half a pair of large kitchen tongs. He was a tall, good-looking man when *made up*, but had a bad countenance; "his brow, like a pent-house, hung over" his small, gray eyes, a fine Roman nose, and a mouth struggling to be handsome in defiance of a continual sensual expression. He professed to be a very gallant man; and his poor little wife—who could not bring herself to rejoice with him at his triumphs in that department of the arts—through excessive love, or folly, attempted to poison herself a short time before I made his acquaintance. Her life was saved by miracle, to drag out a wretched existence, with prostrated nerve and a broken spirit. Some plausible, but peremptory objection, was raised to every character I named for an opening; and, after some heat on both sides, he *wheezed* out his consent that I should play *Crack* the next night, without previous announcement, or any of the usual formalities thought favourable to all parties in making a first appearance. But I made a great hit notwithstanding. The fact I found to be, that his offer of an engagement to me he had been obliged to make at the suggestion of my powerful friends; but that Mr. Bailey, an objectionable actor to the audience in general comedy (poor fellow! he died long since in a poor-house), had a wife, "all of her that *was* out of door most rich," and on her the lion had put his paw; and the advancement of the husband on the road to theatrical preferment was the M'Adamizing means most in his power to smooth the path to the wife's dishonour. They had, of course, an excellent situation, and a large family; and the good woman, I believe honestly, for the sake of her husband, did "beguile the thing she *was*, by seeming otherwise." But the audience claimed the exclusive privilege of protecting and rewarding a favourite actor, "all in the olden time," and, with the exception of some petty annoyances, I passed a pleasant and, profitable year in the York circuit. The manager feared and hated me; I have explained how innocently I had caused the latter feeling, but the first must also be accounted for. His extreme rudeness induced me, after my first visit, to make my necessary communications in writing, and, in reply to one, he, in plain English, called me *a liar*. I have the will yet, but I had most powerfully the way then, to fulfil, "on good occasion," old Scotia's motto. I entered his apartment, and firmly, yet civilly, desired him to *unwrite* the expression; he refused, and I cured his asthma for that bout. I had not then heard the anecdote of the rough-mannered and celebrated Dr. Moseley, setting-to with a patient suffering under the same disease, and, after pommelling him all round the room, and ultimately flooring him with a "hit in the wind," standing over him, and saying, very calmly, "If you ever draw your breath again, you'll be entirely cured." And I have no doubt in the efficacy of the remedy myself; but people are so averse to take "what will do them good," if it's at all unpleasant, that many sufferers from this long-lived disease, I have little hesitation in supposing, would rather wheeze, and cough, and smoke stramonium, sitting upright for a month in bed, than take the thrashing I gave Fitzgerald. The dog Dragon, not having the cause of quarrel explained, was too prudent to show a preference; but his canine feelings becoming excited, he had a little fight of his own, taking the odds, and a small bite out of the calf of my leg, and half a mouthful of skin off the bone of his master's. Fitzgerald promised to be more civil for the future, and I promised never to name the matter to the company—"the lion preys not upon carcasses"—but he and the dog had called murder so loudly, when the voice of the one was cleared and the other exasperated, that the landlady "came in at the death," and, notwithstanding her assertion "that she never meddled with anybody's business but her own," it *leaked out*, and I encountered several anonymous shakes of the hand, behind the scenes, a day or two afterward.

He was actually the *unnatural* son of old Gerald, the manager of a little strolling company through some small towns on the coast of Kent; the same man with whom Howard made his first appearance in his successful crying capacity. Ashamed of his father and his name, when he joined the Norwich circuit, some years before, he clapped the Fitz to it—wished it to be understood he was an Irishman—and gained some sympathy as a supposed descendant of the patriot of that name. He was a tyrant, in the fullest sense of the word, to his inferiors; but, as is always the case with such animals, he was fawning and sycophantic in the extreme to those above him.

Johnny Winter (by the excellent imitation of whom, and the anecdotes related so exquisitely by my lamented friend Charles Matthews, he could alone have supported a large family) had

been for years the tailor and wardrobe-keeper of
the theatre, but, when Wilkinson died, he had
gone into business as a breeches-maker; for the
cut of which article, "according to the fashion
of the time," he was inexpressibly talented. And
to use his own words, in reply to "How are you
getting on, Winter?" "Eh, beautiful, beautiful!
I ha' gottin a large shop and no custom—Ize
doin' fine!"

I was introduced to this curiosity by Cummings, the contemporary of John Kemble, who
had been in the York company for more than
forty years! and died upon the stage, while performing Dumont, in the tragedy of Jane Shore,
the season after I left the company. Winter
must then have been at least seventy years of
age, but retained, in figure and manner of address, all the flippancy of youth in an extraordinary degree. He was a great admirer of the
turf (all classes of Yorkshiremen usually are),
and always dressed like a jockey, or trainer, in
a frock-coat, small-clothes, topped boots, striped
waistcoat, fancy neckerchief, with a horse or
dog brooch, and a whip or ash-sapling in his
hand. His opinion in theatrical affairs—which
he always (often without being asked) gave
without respect to the feelings of the party—was,
from its whimsicality and blunt honesty, both
sought for and dreaded. Matthews he couldn't
"abide;" his great and admired particularity in
his dress was very objectionable to Johnny, and
he used to say,

"Dang the feller, he's niver sooted; there's
John Em'ry 'ull put on ony ko'it as cums to
hand, an' gang on, an' mak the peepl' laagh
twice as much as what he can."

It was part of his duty to provide clean tow-
els for the gentlemen; and the nervous, anxious
Matthews would soil a napkin from one end to
the other in cleaning, and painting, and marking
his face, again and again, to obtain some particular expression; this was a great offence to
Winter; and when he had left the room he'd
hold it up and exclaim,

"Did ye iver see sic a nasty beast as that
Mathoos? all'ays a washin' himsen; noo Mistre Cummins is the cleanest man amang ye, an'
he ne'er washes himsen at all."

Poor Cummings, being afflicted with a disease of the heart, generally dressed at home, or
nearly so.

The sensitive, fidgety Matthews was actually
annoyed that he couldn't obtain any approbation
from Winter; and when the farce of the Review was first produced, he prevailed upon Johnny to go in the front, and give him his opinion
of his personation of Caleb Quotem, in which
he intended to make (and did) a great hit. At
the conclusion of the performance, while un-
dressing, Matthews inquired,

"Well, Johnny, how did you like it?"

"Beautiful, sir! beautiful! I ne'er seed nau't
like it."

"Ay, indeed!" said Matthews, delighted;
"I'm glad you were pleased, Johnny."

"Wha could help but be pleased?" said Winter: "i'twar the varri best actin' I iver seed i' my
life."

"Yes, I think it was a decided hit," said
Matthews, gratified at having at length made a
convert of Winter. "And how did you like my
song? it went capitally, didn't it?"

"Ye'r song?" said Johnny, with a vacant
stare. "Oh, e'es, I remembers; i'twar a poor
jibber-jabber thing; I thou't nau't on't—but I
ha' seed mony sic creturs as thim, an' i'twar
na'thral as life; i'twar beautiful, sir! beautiful!"

Rejoiced at obtaining such unequivocal approbation from Winter, who had never praised
him before, Matthews continued,

"Yes, Winter, I never was in a better humour for acting; I think it's decidedly my very
best part; don't you, Johnny?"

"Me, sir?" said the implacable Winter: "I
niver thou't nau't aboot ye—not I!"

"Why?" said Matthews, astonished, "haven't
you just been paying my acting all sorts of compliments?"

"You?" said Johnny: "I niver once thou't o'
ye; I wur praisin' Mistre Hope i' Dubbs; he
wur th' varri best i' th' hul piece."

Fitzgerald, though a vile actor, to give the devil his due, had a very superior, and even clas-
sical knowledge of costume; and he had employed Winter to make him a suite of dresses for
Macbeth. When he was a lad, and bearing his
real name, he had been engaged by Wilkinson,
but discharged after a week or two, in consequence of his impertinence and incapacity. This
Winter recollected, and, while fitting on a robe,
some departure he had made from his instructions caused Fitzgerald to fly into a violent passion, and use some coarse and insolent language
to the old man, who very calmly said, when the
gust was over,

"Now, ye see, ye mun get some ane else to
finish t' job, or do't yersen; ye see, I recollect
ye when ye wur a poor ragged lad, an' wur
kick'd out o' theatre, Mistre *Gerald*; ye hadn't
Fitz then!" and very coolly walked away.

Charles Wood was another heir-loom in this
establishment; no manager dared discharge him;
he had been a member of the company even
longer than Cummings, and was a much older
man; he was stone deaf, but the most cheerful,
good-tempered creature in existence; he had
been a singer in his youth, and was the original
Eugene in the Agreeable Surprise, at the Haymarket; he was always humming or whistling
a tune about the theatre, as "gay as a lark;"
his wife was in her dotage, and he had a large
family of children, most of whom had turned out
badly; *id est*, the boys were all very wicked, and
some of the girls very good-natured; but he
drew comfort even from them, and would say,
"Ay, ay, plenty of — and rogues in my family,
but no cowards," in reference to the care-for-
nothing behaviour of one of his boys on receiving sentence for some petty crime.

In endeavouring to pull on a tight boot one
night in a hurry, I boasted that I had "the patience of Job"—which people are very apt to do
when they have lost all their own—in the hearing of Winter, who, from long habit, was a frequent visiter of the dressing-room.

"Talk o' 'the patience o' Job!'" said Johnny. "Look at Charley Wood, wi' twenty-ane
scamps o' childer, a queer wife, an' a guinea a
week! 'Patience o' Job,' indeed! Job be d—!
look at Charley Wood a whislin'!"

During my sojourn in this company I formed
some friendships both lasting and valuable.
Among them I made one in rather a singular
manner. Paul Bedford, an actor and singer,
had introduced me to his brother, a professed
gambler, and a partner in a fashionable hell in
Pall Mall. During the York races he attended
an E. O. table in the gentleman's stand, to which
I had the entrée. There were three horses to run

for the cup—Catton, Fulford, and, I think, Everlasting. Catton was the favourite, at great odds, but the knowing ones had some notion of Fulford; and Bedford instructed me that if, at a certain point of the race, Fulford was ahead, to "*bet all I had.*" He was ahead at the right time and place, and *I did bet a guinea* with an elegant little old man, with powdered hair and a cue; and when the sport was over, he inquired loudly for the gentleman to whom he had lost a guinea. I presented myself.

"Why, my dear sir," said he, with great glee, "how is it possible you came to bet on my horse? Why, I had not the most remote idea he could beat Catton; my dear sir, it was my own horse I was betting against; I merely entered him for the sake of the sport, and to please some friends who were anxious to see what he could do. Why, you must be a most excellent judge; haven't I the pleasure of knowing you?"

"Cowell, sir, is my name," said I.

"What, of the theatre? why, certainly, certainly! I thought I knew your face; I saw you in Goldfinch last night; an excellent performance — excellent. Allow me to give you my card—Neville King; you must dine with us to-day; I'll introduce you to my friends."

And the bustling, agreeable little old man, named me to some dozen noblemen and gentlemen as his friend, "Mr. Cowell, of the theatre, a great judge of horses, and *a winner on the race.*" His invitation to dine with the club was earnestly repeated by several, and as I only had to perform Tiptoe, in the farce of "Ways and Means," I consented. We had a jovial time; I sung them some songs suitable to the occasion, was induced to remain longer than was prudent, and when I got to the theatre I was *conscious* that I was very *drunk.* I had, fortunately, little change to make in my dress, merely a footman's jacket instead of my coat, and a silver band round my hat, for, of course, I always wore topped boots and breeches in the race week. Johnny Winter dosed me with tea and pickles, for, to his taste, I had suffered in a good cause, and my brother actors managed the first scene among themselves; the last chiefly consists in a very long speech, in which Tiptoe is supposed to have been taking a drop too much, and in depicting which I had gained some reputation; but it had "pleased the devil drunkenness to give place" to qualmish stupidity. I cunningly avoided any effort at acting, and as a large portion of the audience were suffering, probably with exactly my sensations, the whole affair passed off insipidly enough. I had just gained my dressing-room, and began to sip some brandy-toddy, which Winter had declared "the sovereign'st thing on earth," when Fitzgerald strutted into the room. "Why, Cowell!" said he, "I never was so disappointed in my life! Some of your admirers," with a sneer, "told me you were very fine in a drunken character, and I was induced to see the last act. Why, my good sir, you have mistaken the style of Tiptoe's intoxication altogether; he has but a very short time to get drunk in, and, of course, is highly excited from the immediate effects of wine, swallowed in large quantities; but you lost sight entirely of the exhilarating character of drunkenness, which the author intends, and looked like a man who had *been very tipsy,* and wanted to go to bed and sleep off its narcotic remains. It was very bad, I assure you—you were entirely mistaken."

When he had closed the door, Winter said,

"That poor ignorant thing knows more aboot na'thral actin' than I iver thou't he did."

During Colonel Neville King's stay at York, he showed great attention to myself and family. I painted a portrait of Fulford, with which he was highly delighted, and had it splendidly framed and sent to Lincoln, where he resided.

Probably in the history of the turf, no two human beings were ever so perfectly pleased at

Losing a guinea and winning a guinea.

CHAPTER XIV.

"'Tis thou, thrice sweet and gracious goddess! (addressing myself to Liberty), whom all in public and private worship; whose taste is grateful, and ever will be so, till Nature herself shall change. No tint of words can spot thy snowy mantle, or chymic power turn thy sceptre into iron: with thee to smile upon him as he eats his crust, the swain is happier than his monarch, from whose court thou art exiled."—STERNE.

OF all the members of the York company at that time, none ever arrived at any eminence in the profession excepting Mrs. Humby. She had been educated a singer, was excessively pretty, and in simple, innocent characters, a charming actress. She was the best Cowslip I ever played with; her husband was a very estimable, and in money matters, an extremely prudent young man, and went by the name of "Young Calculation." Playing Solomon, in the Quaker, one night, I made use of the usual distich,

"Who sees a pin and lets it lay, may want a pin another day. I'll pick it up and stick it here; a pin a day's a groat a year."

When Humby met me in the morning, he said, "Cowell, you must alter that rhyme of yours: it isn't correct; I've made a *calculation,* and a pin a day is tenpence ha'penny a year, if you purchase by retail."

The circuit consisted of York, Hull, Leeds, Doncaster, and Wakefield, and at the latter town I left the company—I am glad to say, to the great annoyance and inconvenience of Fitzgerald, for I was an enormous favourite, and at that time there were few professors of my line of business out of London. Kilner succeeded me, an excellent actor in hearty old men, which then I didn't play; he came soon after to this country, and was long a great favourite at Boston, but of late, like the genius of old, he has kept himself *corked up in a bottle.* I was tempted to join the Lincoln circuit, by the offer of one half more salary than I received at York, to play only four times a week; to have the book sent to me to choose the character I preferred performing in every piece; to visit seven towns in a year, nearly close together, and have half the clear receipts of one night in each for a benefit. This company had been for many years under the direction of Thomas Robertson, but through the ridiculous speculations he had entered into at the instigation of a *particular friend,* he had been thrown into prison for debt, and I was engaged by a committee of gentlemen who had undertaken to regulate his affairs, and had secured to me the strict fulfilment of their contract. It was sundown on Sunday when I arrived at Lincoln. I had, with my wife and two children, *posted* all day from Wakefield, where I had finished my engagement the night before, and performed Domine Samson and Baron Willinghurst; and after putting my person in repair, I accompanied my friend Armstrong, the leading actor (whom I had known in the York company), to the lodging of the lady manager. I am not considered a faithful historian where women are concerned. In consequence of my adoration of the sex, I have been accused of being too partial in my descriptions; but if any of my readers are acquainted with John Mills Brown, the comedian, and will imagine him dressed in a very low-necked, short-sleeved, black velvet gown, large black necklace and ear-rings, dark sorrel hair turned up behind, with ringlets in front, and a very beautiful hand, and arm bare to the shoulder, they'll have a very correct likeness of Mrs. Fanny Robertson, whose half-sister she was on the mother's side. Her maiden name was Ross, and her father the manager of the Edinburgh Theatre, "long time ago," and celebrated in Irish characters; and her mother was said to be equal to Mrs. Jordan.

I was never introduced to a queen, but the etiquette observed and exacted by Mrs. Robertson, I imagine, is all that will be required, if I ever do go to court. Her boudoir was small, but elegant; an easel with drawing materials on a stand in one corner, a superb harp in another, a pianoforte and a profusion of books, music, drawings, and other "knick-knacks." Her reception of me was most favourable, and had she really been a queen, I should have felt certain of a seat in the cabinet.

The next night the theatre opened with the comedy of Speed the Plough, and a Chip of the Old Block; I playing Sir Abel Handy and Chip. The house was crowded, and I made a prodigious hit.

The following morning I paid my respects to the manager at the Castle, and was introduced to the deputy-governor, alias the jailer, a very pleasant, intelligent man, as everybody described him, by the name of Merriweather. Though his appellative didn't agree with his gloomy occupation, he had the reputation of being highly qualified for his office; he was formerly a tailor, but having "a soul above buttons," he preferred the name of his trade should begin with a J instead of a T, had chosen to turn keys instead of coats, and to lock up rather than to cut out. He was a great amateur in horticulture, mineralogy, conchology, zoology, and perhaps all the "ologies" excepting, probably, ontology; his power of expression in matters of science was a perfect oglio, and in attempting to convey his "useful knowledge" to the uninformed, he more unintelligibly mixed it up for his own exclusive gratification. The walls of his dining-room (he gave excellent dinners) were decorated with stuffed ducks, distorted cockle-shells, and "other skins of ill-shaped fishes." His admiration of the arts and sciences had caused him to enclose nearly the whole of the Castle yard for a private garden; though it was originally intended for the use of prisoners for debt (then often for life) and traitors, and other delinquents to stretch their legs in, before the law decided upon stretching their necks; but as the dessert-tables of the bishop, the sheriff, and the judges were seasonably supplied with the delicacies it produced, his taste, and that of his pineapples, were greatly admired. It was cultivated with both care and skill, under his direction, by some petty rascals who were indulged in digging to the clanking music made by their own fetters encountering the blade of a spade; all wicked gardeners were sentenced to six months' prison discipline at least, if he had any influence in their case.

"Mr. Robertson is a particular friend of mine, Mr. Cowell," said this St. Peter: "I am devotedly fond of the drama, and have given him liberty to walk in my heaven on earth, as I call my rural sanctum."

Unlocking a huge iron bar, which secured a small, though high gate, overarched with two prodigious jaw-bones of a whale, the merits of which, after explaining, I have do doubt, in very scientific, ossified language, we thridded the "narrow pathway" till we overtook my new manager, the privileged Jonas.

He was a small, handsome-featured man, with amiability and humility quietly claiming possession of the only expressions his countenance was capable of. He was dressed in a dark-coloured morning-gown, soiled with powder on the collar, though he had none in his hair; his beard was long, shoes untied, and his whole appearance forlorn and slovenly. Every debtor I ever saw in prison in my life always looked as if he owed money and could not pay it—though I'm told sometimes their looks belie them.

His welcome was painfully polite, and our short conversation ended with his expressing a hope that he might shortly meet me in some other than "*this wretched place.*" Looking round upon the most beautiful garden I ever beheld, I thought of Sterne's Starling, and imagined I saw "*I can't get out*" glistening in his moistened eye.

On my return to my lodging, if Falstaff had met my landlady in the passage as I did, he would very probably have said, "Heigh, heigh! the devil rides upon a fiddlestick," for as she described her sensations, she was all in a "flusterlication." Following me up stairs, she flounced herself into a chair, and with scarcely breath to utter, exclaimed,

"Oh, sir, what do you think? the high-sheriff has been here and inquired for you, asked me when he could be sure to find you at home, and has left his card. Heaven help me, that I should have ever let my lodgings to a player; but as what's done can't be undone, get out the back way as fast as you can, and make your escape."

As a visit from this important functionary in England is never paid, in his official capacity, but to gentlemen who are either suspected, or guilty of high treason; and as my poor landlady couldn't imagine he would call upon me in any other way, she had pictured to herself my incarceration in the keep of the Castle, thence drawn on a hurdle to the place of execution, my head popped upon a pole like a robin redbreast, and the balance of my body dangled from a gibbet.

The direction of her astonishment was changed, though rather increased than diminished, when, on reading the card, I calmly said, " Colonel Neville King—oh, my dear madam, he's a particular friend of mine."

"A friend o' yourn, sir!" said the woman, almost in a scream. "My goodness gracious! a friend o' yourn? Why, he's one of the greatest gentlemen in the county; he's the high-sheriff, sir: only to think of his being a *particular* friend o' yourn. Why, sir, I assure you he never darkened my doors afore, though I've always had the most genteelest of lodgers. Sally! put some more fire on in Mr. Coward's parlour! That's your name, I believe, sir?"

"No, madam—Cowell," I replied.

"Yes, Mr. Cowen. I'll recollect," said she; " only being so put out makes a body forget. That gal has never dusted these chairs, I declare. My last lodger was a lawyer's clerk and his lady, and Colonel King never once thought o' calling upon him. I can't help thinking of the colonel's being your *particular* friend. I must get another gal; she's too lazy for anything, I do declare; there's not a drop of water. Sally! bring a nice fresh pitcher of water for Mr. Cowitch! There, I believe I have called you wrong again."

"*Cow-ell*, madam," said I, with emphasis.

"Yes, sir, *Cow-hell*; yes, *hell, hell!* I shall be sure to recollect it now. As I said before, Mr. Cow-*hell*, I always let to none but genteel people; never took in a player before, and wouldn't you, only you was so highly recommended. I must make that gal put this room nice to rights every day; perhaps Colonel King may call again. What sweet children you've got, Mr. Cow—"

"Ell," said I.

"Yes, Mr. Cowhell. Send 'em down to get a cake when they're hungry. I'll have your windows cleaned to-morrow, and put you another little strip of carpet in the bedroom, and try to make you nice and comfortable. If Colonel King calls, I'll tell him to walk up?"

I nodded, and away she bustled to tell the wonderful event to her husband and her customers, for she kept a pastry shop. It was still long before a decent dinner-hour, and, minutely directed by my landlady, I set off to return the colonel's call. On the almost inaccessible hill, called the Strait, which divides the lower from the upper town, I met the "fine old English gentleman" on his way down to request me to dine with him and his brother, a clergyman, with whom he was desirous I should be acquainted, which I readily accepted, and we continued our walk through the city; he introducing me, as we went, to those who were *worth knowing*, and stopping several times to relate the *guinea anecdote* and extol my judgment in horseflesh. His brother I found more of the man of the world than the colonel, but extremely kind and agreeable; my picture of the horse was criticised with judgment, softened by politeness and partiality; he was very conversant with Shakspeare, and regretted that the theatre, being under the "shade of the Cathedral," he couldn't with propriety witness my performance; but, out of the Fulford cup, drank to his speedily having that pleasure in London. I believe the prayers of priests are attended to sometimes. A conversation between the player and the parson, on the inutility of the drama in a moral point of view, he armed with kind feeling and George Barnwell, I with experience and the Beggar's Opera, was suddenly interrupted by the colonel's saying abruptly,

"Brother, I have an excellent idea. Mr. Robertson has for years been urging me to lend my name to patronise a house—you know what I mean—to put at the top of the play-bill, 'By desire of Colonel King,' and all that sort of thing; but, though I wish him well, yet I have always refused, for I should feel mortified by having anything to do with the matter unless I had a good house, that is, an overflowing house; but I was thinking Mr. Cowell and myself could make a great thing of it between us at his benefit, eh? High-sheriff of the county, and all that—Lady Monson's in town, and she'll get the Earl of Warwick to go; and then there's Heron—I never asked any favours of these people before, and I'll ask everybody; and, eh—what do you think, brother?"

The parson thought it excellent; I thought it capital, and the next day, Wednesday, he was to go electioneering for "our benefit," as he called it, and I was to open a box-sheet in the morning. I did, of course, as he desired, and on the following day every seat was taken; the receipts were larger than any ever before in Lincoln. Singular to relate, the manager, who was respected by everybody, was released from prison on that very evening, and I led the good old man on the stage amid the deafening cheers of the audience.

After a pleasant and profitable season, the company moved ·to Newark-upon-Trent, the distance performed in about two hours. I had introductions to everybody from everybody. The pride of the theatrical population caused an effort to be made to exceed the Lincoln receipts, on my benefit night, without the aid of individual patronage; and, though the house was smaller, some well-applied guinea tickets gave them a powerful pound-and-shilling victory over their more aristocratic neighbours. The same success attended me at Grantham, Spalding, Boston, Peterborough, and Huntingdon; and my return through the circuit made "assurance doubly sure." The only unalloyed period of perfect content and comfort I ever experienced (in a theatrical poiht of view) were the nearly two years I passed in this company. We never played more than four nights in a week, with the exception of the race week at Huntingdon, and then we received one third more salary. To the off-play days the manager laid no claim, for rehearsals or any other purpose; the actor's time was his own; it was considered not paid for, and, therefore, not taxed; excepting probably twice in a year, the production of some showy piece would make a night rehearsal necessary; and then, the voluntary assistance of the company was *requested* in a respectful and affectionately-worded note addressed to each individual, from the highest to the lowest, and the business of the evening closed with an economical repast. Stars were never engaged to "strut their hour upon the stage," for twenty pounds, to the disadvantage, by comparison, of the poor stock-actor, *working hard for twenty shillings à week*. The performers were selected with a rigid regard to moral worth and deportment, and with as much talent as is (I am sorry to say so seldom) met with, hand in hand. The consequence was, the actors and actresses were treated like human beings by the citizens, and, according to their grade and acquirements, had social intercourse with their fellow-men: they remained, generally, in the company for years. Among themselves they were like brothers and sisters, but paying the respect due to age and superior talents always observed in well-regulated families.

Show me a manager on this wide continent of America who has ever had (or has) the instinctive moral propriety of feeling to pursue such a course. No: they say, "Any way to make money or get a living." But, as Colman observes in one of his plays, "the ways be so foul and the bread be so dirty, that it would turn a *nice stomach* to eat on't."

On each play day we rehearsed the performance of the night, with scenery, properties, and the most scrupulous exactness; this over-and-over-again drilling was a nuisance to those who understood their business, and I was one who thought so, but it secured the pieces being letter perfect, and you were sure to have a subordinate stand where you wished, say what he should, and when he ought. No Richard in that company would say, "Hark! the shrill trumpet," and then hear a Too-ti-to-too! two minutes afterward; but there the sound was "echo to the sense." The same plays and farces which were performed in one town were repeated in the next, in the same rotation; and each performer retained the same entertainment he had at first selected for the whole year; as, for instance, I took Charles Dibdin's very agreeable operatic play of the Farmer's Wife, and Midas, for my first benefit, and they were only played on that occasion everywhere through the circuit, and the next year considered stock property. In every town one or two plays or farces were "got up," of which the performers were provided with books or parts at least a month before; and these collectively formed a fresh list to start with at Lincoln. The manager, with very good taste, proved his superior confidence in the probity of the softer sex, by employing a female money-taker or *treasuress*, a fine, fat, handsome woman, by the name of Stanard, and mother of the amiable "Sister Rachael," now in this country.

Mrs. Robertson was a highly-accomplished, strong-minded woman, and, notwithstanding her uninteresting appearance, a very superior actress; but often loose and careless, from the absence of that wholesome stimulus to ambition—competition. Her husband was humility personified; he employed a stage-manager, and when he visited the theatre of a morning, you might, from his manner, imagine it belonged to any person but himself; as he passed round the scenery on tiptoe, to take a seat at the corner of the prompter's table, he'd bow to each actor he met in the most respectful manner. The inner lapel of his coat would be literally lined with scraps of paper about two inches big pinned to it, on which were written his memoranda for the day; watching a leisure moment, he'd beckon you towards him, and unpinning one of his little manuscripts, read as follows: "Mr. Cowell will be good enough to name what song he will sing on Thursday evening, the 17th day of June next"—it would then be probably the latter end of May—"the performance being by desire of the Lincoln Sharp Shooters."

"Oh, any you please, sir," I would reply.

"I would rather you would be kind enough to name one," he'd say, timidly.

"Well, sir, the Nightingale Club."

"Wait an instant, if you please;" then turning the paper, he'd write on the back, "Mr. Cowell is good enough to say he will sing the song of the Nightingale Club on Thursday evening, the 17th day of June next, the performance being by desire of the Lincoln Sharp Shooters," and repin it in the vacant place. Now this was all very ridiculous, but it was very inoffensive, and infinitely preferable to the arrogant, insolent manners of some living managers, whom I shall as faithfully describe in the next volume.

◆

CHAPTER XV.

"Why, everything adheres together; that no dram of a scruple, no scruple of a scruple, no obstacle, no incredulous or unsafe circumstance—What can be said? Nothing that can be can come between me and the full prospect of my hopes. Well, Jove, not I, is the doer of this, and he is to be thanked."—*Twelfth Night.*

At about this period, Stephen Kemble had been appointed manager of Drury Lane by the committee for the trustees, and immediately proved his friendship, and the high opinion he entertained of my talent, by offering me an engagement of six pounds per week, to be increased to seven and eight, in the event of my success, for the following seasons; explaining, that the salaries were greatly reduced, but that this sum gave me all the privileges of the theatre usually granted to the principal performers; that neither Harley nor Munden were expected to return, and the opening, therefore, was an excellent one; and assuring me he had the greatest confidence in my being received most favourably by a London audience.

Highly elated, I instantly submitted the affair to Mrs. Robertson, for her advice and opinion.

"It cannot be disguised nor denied, Mr. Cowell," said this clever woman, "that the loss of your services will be severely felt by Mr. Robertson; it may be long (if ever) before he may be able to obtain a gentleman so highly esteemed by the friends of the theatre to supply your place; but I most solemnly pledge myself that no selfish consideration influences my advice one atom, but, in the spirit of sincere and disinterested friendship, I urge you to *refuse this offer*. Your income here, you are aware, with your benefits for the last year, was eight pounds per week, within a few shillings, and this year it will exceed that sum; this, you must recollect, is for every week in the year; there you have a vacation; and without a name long and conspicuously known in London, you can employ your talent to little profit during that period in the country. Lent, Passion-week, and other holy-days, with the respect demanded to be paid at the death of every member of an aged and extensive royal family, will reduce your yearly income nearly one half, and your expenses in London will more than double what is required to live as you do here. There is not the most remote probability of a diminution in your popularity, and the fact that you have refused a London engagement for the sake of remaining in this company, would so flatter the vanity of these kind-hearted people, that they would feel bound by gratitude to support you, with their utmost means, forever. Mr. Robertson is getting old"—here she gave a little shake of her head, and curled down her mouth as people usually do after taking a glass of sea-water, or a seidlitz powder without sugar—"and he has more than once spoken of your succeeding him in the management; nature never intended you to be in a subordinate situation in life; here you have everything your own way; but in London, no matter what success you may meet with, envy, jealousy, and various petty annoyances (the most tormenting of any), will inevitably surround you; the management encumbered by a committee of noblemen and gentlemen totally ignorant or unmindful of the feelings and rights of actors, and quarrelling among themselves who shall most embarrass the interests of the theatre to advance—in defiance of public taste—some favourite mistress, and, through her influence, probably those who may impede or interfere with your advancement; and—*you may fail*—and then, to return here, with diminished lustre, would be vexatious to yourself; and these good people, relying on a London judgment, might suspect they had been mistaken in your talent, and adopt their opinion. There, I have made you a long speech, and given you my most honest opinion; and now do as you please; I shall never say a word farther on the subject."

Half convinced of the truth and policy of her advice, I might probably have adopted it, but that she unfortunately said, "*You may fail;*" this wounded my pride, and, to remove all doubt of such a possibility, I "screwed my courage to the sticking place" and accepted the engagement. Every day, prior to my departure, I became more fully satisfied with the decision I had made. From the first hour I became an actor, every energy of mind and body had been stretched to its utmost to achieve this grand desideratum, and now the hoped-for stake for which I played came to my hand without my seeking it, with advantages unprecedented—Stephen Kemble, my proved friend, the manager, and a vacancy in my line of business in the theatre that might not occur again for years. My success with the public my vanity and experience would not permit me to doubt for a moment, for, after passing, with the highest approbation, "the rough brake" of a York audience—the most difficult to please in England—I had little to fear from the acknowledged liberality of a London one. On my last night the company and the manager gave me a handsome supper, and, with the good wishes of a host of friends, I set off for London, and the first play-bill I saw, on entering the metropolis, announced *Mr. Munden's re-engagement at Drury Lane.*

I found the theatre in a deplorable condition; an indifferent company, and badly selected, playing to literally empty benches, excepting when Kean performed, and his attraction had, from the constant repetition of his plays, been worn to a shadow of what it had been. To appear on any night when he didn't act, was assuredly to have an empty house; therefore, by the advice of Stephen Kemble, I opened in Samson Rawbold, in "*The Iron Chest,*" and Nicholas, in the "*Midnight Hour.*" My success was equal to my warmest wishes. Several members of the committee, particularly Colonel Douglass, paid me some high compliments, and Kean, Kemble, and the enthusiastic "little" Knight were warm in their congratulations. The song, which is not an effective one, was loudly encored, which Mr. Smart, the leader, assured me, in the green-room, he did not remember to have been so honoured since the part was originally played by Suett. The newspapers were all very approving; numbers of my Lincolnshire friends had visited London for the simple-hearted purpose of giving me their support, and, by using their influence with their friends in town, the house was better than usual, though it was the same night that Farren made his *bolstered-up* hit at Covent Garden.

Everything in the power of Stephen Kemble to aid my advancement was attended to with great care; I was never called upon to play anything but a principal character, and his personal kindness gave me an enviable position in the company; my chiefest annoyance was my not having enough to do. The Lyceum closed, after a few weeks, to make room for Matthews with a new entertainment, called "A Trip to Paris," and Harley rejoined Drury Lane; he was an established favourite with the audience, and a very general actor. He had founded his style originally on Fawcett and Bannister, but he didn't hesitate to draw largely on Munden, Liston, Knight, Matthews, De Camp, and others, according to the nature of the character he had to represent, or all of them at once, if the part required their varied powers; but out of the patchwork he made a very agreeable performance, and only a nice observer would discover the stitching together. He was most indefatigable in his profession, and in private life an inoffensive man, though worldly-minded, and extremely penurious. We had been old friends at Brighton, and when I first went to London he took me to his lodgings to see his collection of prints. He had a handsome apartment over a book-shop in Bedford-street, Covent Garden, the wall of which was decorated with a large number of portraits of actors, all guaranteed to have been *given to him* in the handwriting of each on the margin. Being so early in the day that a refusal was certain, he ventured to point to the sideboard and invite me to take a little brandy, and made me promise, very faithfully, that *some day* I would take a chop with him, which promise, while in England, he more than a dozen times made me repeat; but *the day* never arrived, nor did I ever hear of any human being ever taking a meal at his table. He was a good son and brother. His mother and two sisters resided with him. They kept no servant, and when he played they would be seen seated above, at the corner next the stage, in the second tier of boxes, for the double purpose of starting the applause and saving fire and candle at home; and frequently, when it happened to be a dull, poor house, they would have all the applause to themselves, and, being very persevering in their approbation, they were often noticed by the audience, to the great amusement of the actors and the constant visiters of the theatre. But they continued most faithfully to discharge this duty for years, and to their timely hints Harley was indebted for many an encore and round of applause.

Mr. Barnard, who was the walking gentleman of the establishment, had solicited the services of Russell, Gattie, Oxberry, myself, and Harley, to play for his wife's benefit, who belonged to the Greenwich company. We hired a glass-coach, alias a better sort of hack, for the day, and at about ten o'clock in the morning we called and took up Harley, the last of the party. After the rehearsal of Wild Oats, with "*the following powerful cast,*" Rover—Russell (who would cheerfully travel a hundred miles, get up in the middle of the night, and give five pounds into the bargain to play that character at any time); Ephraim—Oxberry; Sir George—Gattie; Sim—Cowell; and John Dory—Harley, it was agreed that each should write down an order for a cutlet, or chop, or anything they pleased for dinner, without the knowledge of the others, and then make it a general repast; when it came to Harley's turn he declined, stating, as an excuse, that he had *dined before he set out.* "What, before ten o'clock?" says Russell: "why, Jack, you dine as early as poor Tokely used to do, but I hope it's not from the same cause." Tokely was a very intemperate, but extremely clever man. Fawcett was stage-manager of the Haymarket Theatre, where Tokely was an immense favourite; he frequently came quite inebriated to rehearsal, and Fawcett undertook to advise him to refrain from drinking liquor in the morning.

"I am fond of my glass of wine after dinner," said Fawcett, "and a glass of grog after supper, but to taste liquor before dinner is a vile, ungentlemanly habit; and for Heaven's sake, Tokely, oblige me and yourself by refraining for the future; promise me you'll never drink anything till after dinner."

Tokely pledged himself that he would not; but a few days afterward he was absent after the time called for the last rehearsal of a new piece; when he arrived Fawcett was about to rebuke him for his neglect, but caught a whiff of his breath.

"Faugh!" said Fawcett, "Mr. Tokely, I'm ashamed of you; you've been drinking again; remember what you promised!"

"But, sir, I've dined," said Tokely, very demurely.

"Dined?" said Fawcett: "what, before eleven o'clock in the morning?"

"Yes," said the comedian, "I dined early, and that caused my being rather late at rehearsal."

Poor Tokely continued to dine early, and died very soon afterward.

When the varied dinner was served, Harley seated himself at the window with a newspaper, but the savoury odour of the viands was too much for his hungry resolution.

"That smells deliciously," said Harley: "allow me to take a little bit on a morsel of bread."

And though we all invited him to have a plate and chair, and partake, he still continued to refuse, and "pick a little bit" of everything, and cheerfully took a glass or two of wine with us all. Russell, who was a great wag, borrowed a pound note of him; and when we made the settlement, before starting home at night, he charged Harley for his equal share of the dinner, supper, and wine, and handed him two and sixpence as the change of his note. He looked daggers, but he never uttered a word the whole way to London.

The eldest Miss Tree, a most amiable woman, was the principal dancer of the theatre. She had been married to, and separated from an advertising dancing-master by the name of Quin. Harley paid her great attention, and everybody imagined it would be a match. Some one was praising her very highly for her performance of Columbine, in the Christmas pantomime:

"Yes," said Tom Cooke, "she's very clever as Columbine, and I'm told shortly she's going to be *Harley Quin*."

But she never was, for she was in this country with her sister Ellen, and *still Miss Tree*.

In society Harley was agreeable and gentlemanly, could sing a comic song extremely well, and tell a *studied, droll story* with effect, but I don't believe he was ever known to say a witty thing naturally, or perpetrate a joke of his own in his life.

During this season I played as an apology for Munden, Knight, Harley, and Oxberry, in consequence of the indisposition of one or the other, at very short notice, and frequently with their names in the bill, and was always most favourably received by the audience; as I made it a rule all my life to be at the theatre every morning at ten o'clock, whether wanted or not, and generally in the green-room at night, if any one was sick whose place I could supply, I was the first to be called upon; as it placed me frequently in a favourable point of view before the audience, in characters in which I was prepared—and even if I had never seen the piece, having an extraordinary quick study, great presence of mind, and *tact* to get through anything—these sudden calls upon my services (particularly as they obliged my good friend the manager) were rather pleasing to me than otherwise; and they occurred so frequently, that it became a joke for the actors, and when I entered the theatre, at morning or night, they'd salute me with,

"Here he is! Munden's sick!" or, "Cowell, my dear fellow, you can go home; everybody's quite well," as the case might be. Even Kemble would join in the joke, and say, in his fine, fat, good-humoured manner,

"Doctor Cowell, I'm very sorry to inform you that all your patients are in fine health this morning."

I had just finished playing Cosey, in "Town and Country," one night, when a message came to me in my room that Harley, while preparing for the afterpiece, had been seized with an epileptic fit, and inquiring if I would undertake the part of Goodman, in the Barmicide; a splendid spectacle, which had been long in preparation, and produced for the first time the night preceding. It was a very long character —some melo-dramatic business, interspersed with two concerted pieces of music and a song. I undertook to *get through it*, with the part in my hand; the only advantage I had was, that I had seen it the night before, for there was no time to read it—nothing puts an audience so out of humour as delay. An apology, stating the dilemma the management was placed in, was made, and I was received with the hearty encouragement a London public know so well how to bestow. During the intervals of the scenes, I got so far possession of the part that I referred to it but seldom, and in the last act did without it entirely. To show the aptness with which an audience there seizes upon and applies any portion of the dialogue which serves to express their feeling, I'll state the following as a proof. The lovely Mrs. Orger had to say, in reference to some aid I had afforded to the virtuous part of the plot, "I'm sure we are all greatly indebted to Goodman; I don't know what we should have done without his assistance." The house applauded to the echo that applauds again; and at nearly the end of the piece, my last speech was to the effect, "Giaffar has done his duty, *somebody else* has done his, and I trust, with submission, I have done mine." And the curtain fell amid deafening peals of applause. The management and the critics gave me infinitely more credit for the undertaking than it deserved, and I, of course, retained the character during the run of the piece. Harley's illness was continuous, and I pledge myself *I never once prayed for my friend's recovery*. Actors are the most selfish people in the world, and feel for one another on the same principle as the midshipman's favourite toast, "A long and bloody war!" explains their sentiments. His death, or absence from the theatre, would have greatly aided my advancement; but, unfortunately for me, and fortunately for the theatre, about this time Howard Payne's tragedy of Brutus made a prodigious hit, and was played nearly the whole of the season.

The theatre was so entirely prostrate at this epoch, that the salaries failed in being paid, and as a last resource, Payne's play, which had long lain neglected, was, by Stephen Kemble's good taste, put in rehearsal, and Kean was prevailed upon to study the part. After a number of vexatious delays, which Payne bore with exemplary patience, walking with the permission of a "day rule" to the theatre (for he was a prisoner for debt at the time in the Fleet or Bench) to meet Kean by appointment, and then find him *not to be found*, or not *fit to be seen*, it was at length produced to an indifferent house. It was shockingly cast; Harry Kemble, whom the audience would hardly tolerate, was the Tarquin; D. Fisher, who had good sense enough since to turn dancing-master, was the Titus; and the balance of the characters *un*supported by a parcel of people that it would be annoying even to mention their names; the fat, vulgar, housekeeper-looking Mrs. Glover, who now plays a line of business she was only ever fit to sustain, was the Tullia; Water-gruel Mrs. W. West was the other woman, and the pretty little dawdle, Mrs. Robinson, the Lucretia. On the first night, a scene between her and Harry Kemble nearly ended the fate of the play; but the next, Tarquin smothered her, or did something or another to her immediately, without saying a word about it, much to the satisfaction of the audience. The public were greatly prejudiced against the establishment, and assisted, no doubt, by the emissaries of the rival theatre, the play, on its first representation, made three or four narrow escapes; greatly to my annoyance, for, independent of my interested motives, I had a warm feeling in favour of the author, both for his talent and amiable deportment. But Kean was the Atlas of the night, and took the whole play on his shoulders; his assumed folly elicited the first general approbation from the house, and his speech to Titus ending with

> " Tuck up thy tunic, train those curled locks
> To the short warrior-cut, vault on thy steed:
> Then scouring through the city, call to arms !
> And shout for liberty !"

caused John Bull to shout too with all his might: in fact, he always does shout when liberty's mentioned, whether because he thinks he's the possessor of the blessing, or " *wants to*," as the Yankees say, I know not. The oration over the body of Lucretia was the most heart-thrilling, pathetic appeal to the passions I ever heard: equal in solemn beauty to his manner of bidding *farewell* to the attributes of war in Othello, which never was spoken by any actor but himself as Shakspeare conceived it. At this time Le Thiere's large painting of the Judgment of Brutus was exhibiting at the Egyptian Hall, Piccadilly, and being the work of a Frenchman, everybody, of course, went to see it. The last scene was grouped exactly after its manner; *Le vivant tableau* had a most happy effect, and the play, to my great delight, after all its struggles, was announced for repetition amid universal approbation.

In defiance of its almost unprecedented success with the public, nearly the whole newspaper press seized their dissecting-knives to cut up it and its author; columns were filled with extracts from obsolete dramas, which Payne had used for his purpose with all the freedom of an old acquaintance; though scarcely one actor or playgoer in fifty had ever heard of, or read them, with the exception of himself, and those crossexamining critics; one long and able article, I remember, was wittily headed : " The labour we delight in *physics Payne*."

At all events, he deserved higher praise than the compiler of *Shakspeare's play of Richard the Third*, as it is called, for out of far inferior materials, he placed in the front rank of public opinion an excellent tragedy, on a subject four or five authors of celebrity had failed to make dramatic;

revived the drooping laurel on the brow of Kean, and with his overwhelming assistance saved Drury Lane Theatre at that time from *total ruin*.

<hr>

CHAPTER XVI.

" Love's very pain is sweet ;
But its reward is in the world divine,
Which, if not here, it builds beyond the grave."
SHELLEY.

IF you were to listen to and believe half the gruntings and grumblings of the peevish atoms who inhabit this " wretched world," as they call it, you might be led to imagine they were most anxious to " shuffle off this mortal coil." This goodly frame, the earth, is described by them as a " steril promontory," " a foul and pestilent congregation of vapours ;" that man delights not them—" no, nor woman neither !" as Hamlet says ; and they try to persuade you and themselves that any change must be for the better. And yet I never saw one of these " discontented papers" who didn't use " the little left of strength remaining," in struggling with the grim tyrant when it came to the awful pause. Now I believe that there are quite sufficient delicious little inventions for our gratification to amply keep pace with all " the natural shocks that flesh is heir to," and among them, can any one be more delightful than the unexpected renewal in manhood of a sincere boyish friendship ? This I experienced in an unushered visit from George Maryon.

He had been a midshipman in the navy, and at the close of the war, had been left with a bullet in his body to remind him of his youthful folly, and a very superior education for his future support; his brother was an artist with considerable talent, and together they had established an academy for young gentlemen at East Lane, Walworth. My dear boy Joe, who always loved everything and everybody his father admired, took a great fancy to my sworn friend, and he was intrusted to his care as a pet and "parlour boarder." Each succeeding Sunday they paid us a visit; but my uncertain engagements at the theatre deprived me, for some weeks, of the power of absenting myself so far from its purlieu. But the death of Queen Charlotte, causing the establishment to be closed till she was enclosed in the vault at Windsor, among her poor relations, gave me an unenviable holyday—"no play, no pay"—and on a fine day after dinner, I set off to walk to Walworth, which I understood to be only two or three miles distant. All my life I have suffered great inconvenience from the absence of the faculty of remembering names. Once, in playing Lazarillo, in " Two Strings to your Bow," I insisted that my name was Pedrillo, to the great amusement of the actors. Calling at the stage door to look for letters, I inquired of West, the messenger of the house, my shortest route to Wandsworth instead of *Walworth*.

" Why, sir," said this experienced directory, "it's a pretty good walk to Wandsworth—but it's a straight line. Your best way will be to go over Westminster Bridge ; and you'll find dozens of coaches will set you down there for a shilling or eighteen-pence."

I did as he advised, and, soon after passing the Marsh Gate, I was overtaken by a long fourhorsed stage, with " Wandsworth" named on its end, as its place of destination. I hailed the driver, and took a seat by his side. As he was not able to give me the desired information, when we reached the village I alighted at the first tavern, and requested to be directed to East Lane, and Mr. Maryon's academy.

"I knows of no Heast *Lane*," said the landlady—I suppose, for she was very fat—"but some calls this *Heast Hend*, I'm sure I don't know for what; and there's Mr. M——, he's a harchitect, and keeps a sort of a 'cademy. He teaches some young men to draw churches, and build 'ouses, and such like, I believe."

"That's the very man, madam," said I. I thought of his brother, the artist, and the name (which I purposely suppress, for fear, even at this distant date, of creating a difficulty between an elderly lady and gentleman, if they are still alive) was as much like Mar-yon, as Mar-von is, as she pronounced it. According to her direction, I entered a small garden, and rang the bell at the door of a handsome house, standing back from the road. After waiting a reasonable period, I repeated the summons more energetically, and in a few seconds I heard a female voice say, pettishly, "That boy is never in the way;" and the door was instantly opened by—Anna! I caught her in my arms—I was afraid of her falling, and, if she had, she would have hit her head against the foot of the stairs, for the passage was not more than eight feet long, and she was standing on the inner edge of the mat—a little, fat man, and a maid-servant, made their appearance — but how they got there, Heaven only knows!—and, with their assistance, I placed her, senseless, on the sofa in the parlour. After the lapse of a few minutes—passed by me in a delirium, and by the man and his maids in applying, in hurry and confusion, the usual remedies, all which I remembered as a dream afterward, but then I had not the power to assist—she opened her heavenly eyes, gazed, with a vacant stare, around the apartment, concealed her face with her hands, and burst into an agony of grief.

"Anne, my dear, Anne!"—if he had called her *Anna* I believe I should have knocked him down—"why, Anne, my dear," said the little fat man, looking up at her as she was leaning back on the sofa, with "the heart's blood turned to tears" oozing through her taper fingers over her wedding-ring, and chasing each other, like dewdrops tinted with rose-leaves, down her snowy arm, "what is all this, and who is this gentleman?"

"Wait a minute—don't speak to me!" sobbed poor Anna; "you shall know all—indeed you shall—I—I'll tell you what a wretch I am—in—in a minute."

The little fat man looked at me for information, but I was so stultified with horror and regret at this promised confession, which would, in all probability, involve the happiness of her I had so purely and innocently loved, that my bewildered thoughts deprived me of the power of words to arrest the "evil communication;" and I stood firmly, with the same apathetic, indifferent expression of face and manner, so often seen in some poor wretch, listening to be told quietly, that he is to be hanged by the neck until he is dead, and his body given to the surgeons for dissection—and which natural display of intense suffering is always placed to the account of undoubted courage and magnanimity of soul, in Newgate Calendar criticism. After a lengthened pause, she suddenly rose up, and, with hysterical playfulness, said hurriedly,

"The surprise—the—no, not the joy—the astonishment, overcame me — it's — my cousin you've heard me speak of," and again sunk upon the sofa.

"Thank Heaven! I'm her cousin, for the sake of all parties," thought I.

"Oh yes; why, bless me, no wonder!" said the little fat man. "Oh dear, yes, I remember. I'm glad to see you, sir. I caught Anne one day crying over your picture; she told me that it was her cousin—why, really, no wonder you were surprised, my dear—she said, I think, you were shot, or drowned, or something. I'm glad to see you. She's got your picture yet. There, that's it, tied to the black riband. Show it your cousin, Anne—well, never mind, by-and-by—I declare it's an excellent likeness! a little too fresh-coloured, perhaps—but, then, the uniform makes a difference. But you must take a glass of wine—Anne will get over it presently—and I'll send for the children."

And away the nasty little fellow went. The only balm I could lay to my tortured feelings at that moment was, that he was *very fat*—and I knew Anna could not bear fat—and that he was a head and shoulders shorter than myself. But "the children" made me sick at my stomach; I felt faint; and, without my saying a word, Anna answered my look,

"Don't despise me. What could I do? You never answered my letters. Everybody said you were dead, or had married some one else. God help me! he was rich, and all my friends persuaded—"

Me she would have said, and perhaps a great deal more I'm glad I did not hear, but that the door opened, and in came the father, without doubt, of a little pot-bellied brat, the image of himself, whom he was leading by the hand, and followed by another "like the first," crying, and sliding into the room, with a dirty nose.

"Take the baby up, Betsey," said the father.

"He won't let me, sir," said the maid.

"Ah, he's a spoiled child; but here's a fine fellow," said the foolish-fond parent; "only three years and a half old; shake hands with the gentleman, Joseph; come, that's a good boy—it's ma's cousin, my dear, that you were named after."

But, thank Heaven! my namesake wouldn't do anything of the sort.

"We only breeched him yesterday," said the father, his eyes half out of his head with delight.

And a pretty business they had made of breeching the little beast. A nankin jacket and trousers all in one piece, bedizened with mother of pearl buttons all over the top, and daubed with gingerbread over the bottom; and a slit in the back, wide open, to let the little ball of fat in or out, I suppose.

"Well, I'm heartily glad to see you—take a glass of wine," said the good-natured man, though I hated the sight of him. "Sir, here's to ye. Oh do, my dear, take a little; it will do you good—now indeed it will; well, if you won't, you won't, I suppose. Anne has fretted a good deal about you, I assure you."

I took my hat.

"Oh, you mustn't think of leaving us so soon. Anne will be quite lively presently, now you've got back. I've often heard her declare she couldn't die happy unless she either saw or heard something certain about you."

I moved towards the door.

"You mustn't think of going to town to-night;

we have plenty of spare beds, and you must tell us how you escaped getting drowned, or shot, or whatever it was."

I felt that victory could only be gained by an immediate retreat; pleaded that business of the last consequence demanded my presence in London that night, but promised to return early on the morrow, and pass the day with them; took the privilege of an affectionate cousin to embrace his wife—*whispered an eternal good-by*—stumbled over the mat, down two steps at the street door, and departed.

> " She gazed as I slowly withdrew :
> My path I could scarcely discern.
> So sweetly she bade me adieu,
> I thought that she bade me return."

But I didn't, and have
Never seen Anna since.

* * *

CHAPTER XVII.

> " Say what abridgment have you for this evening ?
> What mask ? What music ? How shall we beguile
> The lazy time, if not with some delight ?"
>
> SHAKSPEARE.

STEPHEN KEMBLE, and his sister, Mrs. Siddons, to my poor thinking, shared between them all the *genius* of that wonderful family. Extraordinary natural advantages, highly-cultivated minds, and long and intense study of the mechanical attributes so important to an actor, rendered both John and Charles Kemble (but particularly John) for years " the observed of all observers ;" though I, in defiance of general opinion, always considered Charles the superior artist. " An two men ride on a horse, one must ride behind ;" and when John Kemble was at the very zenith of his glory, with no shadow within reach of his shade, his brother, with a better voice, and finer face, was playing walking gentlemen in the same theatre—Alonzo to his Rolla, Lewson to his Beverly, Laertes to his Hamlet, Cassio to his Othello, Prince of Wales to his Hotspur, and so on. How would it have been had their positions been changed? And even in those comparatively subordinate characters, Charles gained a most exalted reputation, and the recollection of his excellence in that description of business painfully derogates from the merit of any performer in that walk of the drama since. After the retirement of the " great Kemble," his most prejudiced worshippers were obliged to admit that Charles was his equal in most characters, and even honest enough to allow his superiority in some, and in a certain grade of high comedy he stood alone—Mercutio and Don Felix, for instance ; and it was wittingly said of his brother John, when he attempted the latter part, " that he possessed too much of the *Don*, and not enough of the *Felix*."

Stephen Kemble's extraordinary bulk deprived him of the power of entering the arena with his gladiatorial brother ; but his Macbeth and Hamlet, by the adorers of mind, not body, will never be forgotten ; and his readings of Milton and the Bible were superhuman. In his latter days, from necessity, not choice, he only performed Falstaff ; but even in that resource, for his transcendent talent, he stood without a rival.

Fawcett delivered the wholesale wit of Falstaff in small parcels, with the pungent quaintness of Touchstone. Bartley would make you believe the knight had got fat behind the coun-

ter, while keeping a retail shop in the city. Dowton made him a very large-sized Sir Anthony Absolute. Matthews played it as he did Grunthrum, in " The Fortunes of War," or the very whimsical character in one of his entertainments, who inquires of everybody, " Am I thinner, think ye ?" Warren had a great reputation in the part in this country, and a sign for a porter-house was painted in compliment to his performance, in Philadelphia ; but he, though a very sensible actor, portrayed Sir John as if his favourite beverage was beer, not sack. Hackett and John Quincy Adams have paid one another some high compliments lately through the newspapers on their true conception of the character, which I think is highly probable to be the case ; but when I saw Hackett in the part, some years ago, I thought it was a very excellent imitation of Matthews.

Stephen Kemble's face and figure were a guarantee for the character he gave himself: " Sweet Jack Falstaff, kind Jack Falstaff, true Jack Falstaff, valiant Jack Falstaff, and, therefore, more valiant, being, as he is, old Jack Falstaff;" and alive to all the minute beauties of the author, he pointed them naturally, without force or effort ; and if the cavillers to excellence deny that the performance was perfection, they must admit that it put all competition in the background. In private life he was a good man, a ripe scholar, a warm friend, and a delightful companion.

During this season the principal green-room was conducted with all the etiquette observed in an apartment designed for the same purpose in private life, and very properly too. A well-appointed room, especially when ladies are part of its occupants, has great influence on the conduct of its visiters in all classes of society, from the magnificent drawing-room down to the splendid " gin palace." There was an obsolete forfeit of one guinea for any one entering it in undress, unless, of course, in character. This being perfectly understood, was never likely to be incurred. But Alderman Cox, *one of the committee*, in defiance of this well-known rule, dropped in one evening in a riding-dress, with very muddy boots and spurs. Tullia's train getting entangled in one of them, Oxberry good-humouredly reminded the alderman of the forfeit, which he appeared to take (and I think did) in high dudgeon ; but the next day a note was addressed to the gentlemen of the green-room, begging them to accept a dozen of very fine Madeira in lieu of the guinea forfeit ; pleasantly stating that, " as he was a very bad actor, he must be a member of the second green-room, if of any, and, therefore, did not consider himself amenable to the laws of the first." To meet the matter in the same spirit, with this wine, and other, we agreed to give the alderman a dinner at the Freemasons' Tavern, and a non-playing day in Lent was selected. Sir Richard Birnie (the Bow-street magistrate), Mr. Vaughen, M.P. (an esteemed friend of Kemble's), and Fauntleroy (the unfortunate), were invited to meet him ; and the party completed by Stephen Kemble, his son Harry, Carr, Hughes, Rae, Gattie, Oxberry, Harley, Kean, Munden, Henry Johnston, *Irish* Johnstone, Russell, and myself. Who would not like to be one of such a party once a week ? But they are nearly all gone now to— " not where *they* eat, but where *they are* eaten · a certain convocation of politic worms are e'en at *them*." " Oh, the mad days that I have spent!

and to see how many of my old acquaintance are dead." Kean was observed to refrain from wine, and when urged by his jovial companions to "drink and fill," Alderman Cox said,

"In my official capacity" (he sat opposite to Stephen Kemble), "I have excused Mr. Kean. The fact is, I have made a promise for him that he shall spend the evening with my wife, and if he takes too much wine, I don't know what may be the consequences."

The alderman laughed like an accommodating—alderman, and we smiled at his very considerate philosophy. Kean withdrew early in the evening, and the good-natured husband remained with Kemble and four or five others, myself among the number, till three in the morning. This is the same Alderman Cox who was awarded heavy damages in a court of *justice* against Kean, for destroying his domestic felicity; and this is the very Mrs. Cox whose injured innocence "bellowed forth revenge" across the wide Atlantic, and induced the good people of Boston and New-York, in very purity of purpose, to use her name as a watchword to drive from the stage, as a punishment for some offence given to the audience, "Shakspeare's proud representative."

Though not a member of the institution, I received the compliment of being appointed one of the stewards at the annual Theatrical Fund Dinner, at which the Duke of York presided, with Kean facing him as master and treasurer; and the talent of that great actor was even displayed in the simple matter of reading over the list of subscribers. The amount given, or the name of a popular donor, elicited, generally, some demonstration of approval, according to the sum or character of the party, and his peculiar mode of announcing, "*the veteran Michael Kelly, ten pounds*," obtained three rounds of applause. In the anteroom, appropriated to receive our distinguished guests, I met, for the first time in London, my friend W. J. Dennison, Esq., M.P., who had so unexpectedly assisted to help me out of my scrape at Scarborough. Shaking me heartily by the hand, and pointing to the bit of blue riband at my buttonhole, he, laughing, said,

"You see, Cowell, I told you how it would be."

Grimaldi, the celebrated clown, whom I had never before seen without a red half-moon on each cheek, was one of the stewards, and I don't know why, but I felt astonished at finding him a very agreeable, gentlemanly-looking man: we formed an acquaintance which lasted while I remained in England.

Tom Dibdin, the author and celebrated punster, also one of the stewards, arrived very late, on a very miserable-looking nag, and his appearance altogether called forth some remarks and merriment from those at the windows.

"Gentlemen," said he, on entering the room, "you mustn't judge of anything by its looks; that's the pony that plays the marble horse in Giovanni in London, and can get as much applause as any of you; it's the celebrated Graphy."

"Graphy! that's a strange name for a horse, Dibdin," said some one.

"Most appropriate, though," said the punster. "When I made up my mind to buy a horse, I said, I'll bi-o-*graphy*; when I mounted him I was a *top-o-graphy*; when I want him to canter, I say, *ge-o-graphy*; and when I wish him to stand still, and he won't, I say, but you *au-to-*graphy; and, therefore, I think Graphy is a very proper name."

On the last night of the season, for the benefit of *Old* Rodwell, the box-book and housekeeper, a gentleman was to make his first appearance as Sylvester Daggerwood, and give imitations of celebrated performers. I had played *Frisk*, in *My Spouse and I*, on the same evening, and could, therefore, only go in the orchestra to see an excellent performance. He possessed all the ease and familiarity of an old favourite, and his mimicry was admirable. This was no other than the irresistibly comic actor, and emperor of topers, John Reeve, who a few years since paid a visit to this country.

The theatre closed in a state of bankruptcy, and was advertised for rent soon afterward; but I had been prudent enough to provide an expedient for the vacation, at any rate. Matthews had been most successful in his entertainment called "A Trip to Paris," and had rendered that description of performance popular; and by secretly robbing him of all his jokes and songs, and localizing them to suit my hemisphere, I compiled an excellent three hours' olio, called "*Cowell Alone*," or a "*Trip to London*." The use of all the theatres in the Lincoln circuit I obtained gratuitously, and my success was enormous. I played two, but never exceeded three times, in each town to crowded houses; wisely leaving off to the regret of my friends, with the intention of returning. I merely visited the theatres belonging to my old circuit, with the exception of Louth, in Lincolnshire, thirty miles from Boston; and at the urgent solicitation of my friend Jackson, the printer (whose name was nearly always found at the foot of the last page of schoolbooks for boys of my age), I consented to become his guest for a week, and "show my show" in the town-hall, the use of which was tendered me, through his influence, by the authorities. It is the only picturesque spot in the country, and the inhabitants the most hospitable, jovial set of fellows (if they have not degenerated) that can be found anywhere; here I gave three entertainments, and had some difficulty in getting away at the end of a fortnight. There was a sort of moving festival among Jackson's friends while I was there. Smoking was greatly used as an abracadabra, in that fever and ague country; and a *certain set* had a room, or "snuggery," as they called it, detached from their houses, for the purpose of freely enjoying that fumigating propensity. At about three o'clock one morning *I was assisting* Jackson home, in broad daylight, from one of these noctes ambrosiæ, but being full of wine, he couldn't find his way there; and I, *being a stranger*, couldn't conduct him in a town so laid out that every house is, in fact, in the country; and, after a number of efforts to gain the right path, he stopped and inquired of a country boy,

"My lad, can you tell me where John Jackson lives?"

"Eh," says the boy, "why you be John Jackson."

"Hold your tongue, you fool!" said my unsteady friend: "I know I'm John Jackson, but where do I live?"

Elliston, that "diverting vagabond" and scourge to actors, had become the lessee of Drury Lane, and made me an offer of *four pounds* a week (it was said he made Munden an offer of *eight*) to return, with great inducements as to business—which, of course, I declined.

I had got as far as the beautiful little city of Peterborough, and had still two towns untouched, when I received a letter from Mr. Lee, stating that the two young Rodwells, in conjunction with Willis Jones, had purchased the Sans Pariel from old Scott, and intended opening it with as strong a company as they could get, and a superior style of performance; and offering me an engagement for the light and low comedy, and that if I accepted, to come immediately to town; which I did. I performed that night, and the next I was in London.

Scott's fame for manufacturing ink, pink saucers, and liquid-blue dye, was coeval, and equally notorious, with Day and Martin's blacking. At the time when all the little boys and girls in London wanted to be Master Bettys and Miss Mudies, Miss Scott developed strong symptoms of this dramatic disease; and though her extraordinary talent was undoubted by her father and her friends, it was delicately hinted that the greedy public not only expected intrinsic merit (which she possessed) for their money, but also that it must be hallowed o'er with beauty to secure *the first impression*. No paragraph, however laudatory in its imbodying, would ever excite curiosity, the grand point to be obtained, unless it commenced or ended with, " This transcendent little loveliness, this sylphlike masterpiece of Nature in her most bounteous mood, whose cerulean beauty conjures the wandering stars, and makes the little cherubim close their wings with envy, to think they are not so fair, last night astonished and delighted an overflowing house; among the distinguished persons present, we observed Lord Castlereagh in the stage-box, and Mrs. Siddons (as she thought, out of sight) in the corner of the orchestra, with tears in torrents bedewing their experienced faces."

Or, to bring the position more home to the feelings of old Scott, argued his worldly adviser, " How could you expect to sell your true blue, if *not to be equalled*, and to *imitate this is forgery*, were not flourished all over the label in pink and green ?"

Now Miss Scott, in addition to some natural defects, had had the smallpox and rickets unfavourably; but as genius comes in all disguises, she really had talent both as an actress and a writer; and as a resource for the world's prejudices, old Scott gutted the back of his warehouse and fitted up a theatre, where his daughter might safely indulge her predilection for the stage. Here for two or three years, assisted by some young people, her pupils, she dramatized and acted away to a subscription party of her own friends. In all cities there are certain sides of the way in certain streets which the population, from some cause or other, prefer to crowd, and leave the opposite comparatively empty : just so it is with the location I speak of; the best in London for a theatre, hundreds of people enter there attracted by the red baize doors and a galaxy of gas, who, when they set out on their ramble, never dreamed of visiting an establishment of the kind at all. And old Scott very wisely obtained a license for a minor performance, chiefly provided by his clever daughter; and thinking of her alone, called it the " Sans Pariel," opened the doors to the chance customers, and made a fortune; and this was the very place Rodwells and Jones had purchased.

I had never seen the interior in Scott's time, but its origin was still strongly developed. A wide passage under the first floor of a house, leaving room for a small shop, on the right, in the same building, led you to the entrances of the boxes and pit, the latter being placed in the back cellar. Though comparatively small, it was most excellently planned, both for seeing and hearing. The name was changed to the Adelphi; a good direction, being nearly opposite to the street leading to that well-known terrace on the Thames, where the immortal Garrick once resided, and appropriate in reference to the brotherly managers.

The whole of Scott's engagements had been purchased, with the property; but of the merits of the performers there was no means of judging, for they were put far in the back-ground by the new company, with the exceptions of Jones, the singer—the " Braham of America," as he was foolishly called till Braham himself came, in his old age, to dispute the title—and Gomersal, who had been Miss Scott's " amiable footpad" for years, and he grumbled through the heavy business. *Our party* consisted of Mr. and Mrs. Chatterly, who had both been great favourites at the English Opera-house—he in old men, and she in high comedy ladies; Mrs. Alsop, a daughter of Mrs. Jordan's, but no relation, by blood, to William the Fourth. She had been at Drury Lane, and was highly admired in romps and chambermaids; Mrs. Waylet, who has been a great favourite in London ever since, played boys, and lively singing characters; Mrs. Tenant, long favourably known at the nobility's concerts, the principal singer; Mr. Watkins, who was in this country some years, with Burroughs added to it, the principal serious young man; Wilkinson, the celebrated Geoffrey Muffincap—and if he had never played anything else but that and Dogberry, he would have been considered a great actor—was the low comedian; John Reeve—a changeable part, and two other characters, suited to his style then—and myself, eccentric light comedy. Beautiful walking ladies, well-dressed young gentlemen, and dancers by dozens.

The pieces were all original, and written expressly to fit the peculiar talent of the principal performers; and Wilkinson and myself, both overpowering favourites, had the privilege of producing any piece that we thought we could make successful. The elegant little Planché was my chosen author; but a piece was acted at the Olympic, called " Where shall I Dine ?" in which Wrench had a part called Sponge, to which I took a great fancy, and, by introducing an appropriate song, which I was always required to repeat twice, I had the advantage of him—supported, also, by our superior company—and I played it every night, with the exception of three weeks, during the remainder of the season, and for six in succession, *twice on each evening*. Wrench was taken sick, and, to save the run of the piece being stopped at the Olympic, and show the magnanimity of the rival establishment, after performing the part first at the Adelphi, while our ballet was proceeding I drove to the other house, played it there, and returned in time to dress, and act my character in the farce.

As this book professes to be exclusively a history of *my theatrical life*, my domestic joys and sorrows should remain " untouched, or slightly handled;" but, in common justice, and to show the difference in the hearts of men I am bound to describe, I must in this instance deviate from my allotted path. Mothers and fathers who read this page will readily believe I considered my attendance on the deathbed of my youngest child—a daughter, nearly five years old—paramount to any other duty upon earth, and I absented myself from the theatre. But every pay-day the sum supposed to be due to me was enclosed, with the earnest good wishes and anxious inquiries of Jones and Rodwells—though my salary was a large one, the run of two favourite pieces suspended, and my absence from the theatre highly injurious to its interests, and painfully inconvenient. At the end of three weeks, *Maria died;* and setting at defiance "all forms, modes, shows of grief," I instantly sent my desire to be announced, and *played the same evening.* Even at this distant period this recital is painful to me, and, for some years after its occurrence, I dared not trust myself to refer to it; but Time, who smooths the wrinkled brow of care, has long since taught me to thank God, in the same spirit that inspired the pretty lines of Coleridge, that

> " Ere sin could blight or sorrow fade,
> Death came with friendly care,
> The opening bud to heaven convey'd,
> And bade it blossom there."

CHAPTER XVIII.

> " If thou wert honourable,
> Thou wouldst have told this tale for virtue, not
> For such an end thou seek'st ; as base, as strange.
> Thou wrong'st a gentleman, who is as far
> From thy report as thou from honour."
>
> *Cymbeline.*

WHILE I was in treaty with Jones and Rodwells for an increase of salary for the next season, I very unexpectedly received a note from Elliston, requesting to see me. I found him seated in his room, enveloped in a morning-gown ; his hair thrust up from his forehead, and standing in all directions, after the manner of a mad poet; a pen behind his ear, and another in his mouth, and before him, on the table, a quire or two of scribbled paper, and a folio edition of Shakspeare, open at King Lear, which he informed me he was revising, and intended to place upon the stage " in a garb 'twas never dressed before." In his bland and most insinuating manner, " he regretted, *with all his heart and soul,* that such *enormous talent* should be wasted at a *petty minor theatre—the Sans Pariel.*"

" It's called the Adelphi now," said I, interrupting him. " I know it, my dear sir," he continued: " these young men have called it the Adelphi; but old True-blue's connexions, and the apprentice boys, who constitute the audience, will see them d—d before they call it anything but the *Sands Parill,* and look upon an actor, no matter what talent he may possess, as a *Sands Parill* player." After pointing out the degradation attending belonging to a minor theatre, though he had conducted one for years, that " best of cut-throats," who had " a tongue could wheedle with the devil," induced me to sign an engagement for three years, at the same salary I was receiving at the Adelphi, to commence the Monday after Passion-week. The description of business I was only to be called upon to sustain was named in the following form : " All such parts as are usually played by Messrs. Munden, Dowton, Knight, Oxberry, and Harley, or other performers holding the same grade in the profession." This unexpected arrangement greatly annoyed my friends Jones and Rodwell, who produced the articles drawn as I wished, and only wanting signatures, and all parties regretted the hasty proceeding. But they prophesied, from Elliston's dishonourable reputation, that he would be sure to break the engagement, and if he did, I promised to return to them. Among many verbal inducements held out to me by Elliston (whose powers of persuasion amounted to fascination), he suggested that I might always command a few days, or a week, to take a trip with my entertainment, and so increase my salary, and relieve the treasury. " As," to use his own words, " I shall not bring you out till Harley goes to the Lyceum, which doesn't open till June, and then I'll place you so carefully before the public, that that prince of impostors will never want to come back again." It so happened that Crisp, the manager of the Worcester circuit, made me an offer to go to Chester for three nights, in the race week, commencing on Easter Monday, for which he offered me twenty pounds, and to pay *all* my expenses there and back. Fully relying on my services not being required at Drury Lane, I accepted the proposal, and, as a mere matter of form, mentioned the arrangement I had entered into to Elliston.

" You can't go, sir," said the barefaced cajoler.

" Why, sir," I replied, " you yourself pointed out the advantage to the treasury my occupying as much of my time elsewhere as possible would be between this and June."

" Why, so I did," said he : " that's all true enough; but if you refer to your articles, you will find that permission for your absence must be first had and obtained in *writing,* and I don't think proper to write; for," continued he, in a very important tone, " I find the interests of the theatre demand that I should immediately bring you before the public, and I intend to produce ' *Blue Devils*' on Thursday next, with a *powerful cast,* and you must make your first essay this season in the part of James !"

The man's style was so bombastically comic, that to be angry, or even refrain from laughing, was impossible; but I never asked for leave of absence afterward. Though I generally played excellent business—for, for the sake of annoying Munden, Harley, and others, he'd frequently cast me into parts they had a better claim to—I still had my share of disagreeables, though always carefully kept within the letter of the law ; for, secure in my engagement at the Adelphi, which was purposely kept open, I was rather desirous than otherwise that he should "tear the bond." At length he cast me for Aruns, in Payne's play of *Brutus,* and I remonstrated.

" Sir, this part of Aruns must surely have been sent to me by mistake," said I ; " it was originally played by Mr. Yarnold, or some secondary young man, without any pretensions to comedy."

" That, my dear sir," said he, in his soft, soothing manner, " was a great oversight in the management; its being given to the serious young man you speak of was a great injury to the play, which is a very dull, tedious affair, at any rate, and this little bit of delicious comedy will be a great relief to its monotony."

" Comedy, sir !" said I : " my dear sir, read the part; there is not a comic line in it."

" I know it," said he, calmly, " I know it; the author has left the character entirely to the actor, as he has every part of the play; who could tell what Brutus was meant to be, if Kean didn't act it? This part is intended as a comic relief, such as Shakspeare desired Oswald to be in King Lear; only this is infinitely more capable of effect, and in your hands 'twill be irresistible."

Thus assured as to its *comic capabilities*, for the sake of the mischief, I learned the few lines. On the night, I dressed myself, with the assistance of the wardrobe-keeper, who entered into the joke in the most outre manner possible, and kept out of sight till the very moment I was wanted. Kean not being at rehearsal, was unprepared to meet a comedian in the character, and when I ran down the stage, after the manner of Crack or Darby, in the burlesque dress, he burst into an uncontrollable laugh, in which the audience heartily joined, and after gabbling over the few lines, to which Kean couldn't reply, I made a comic exit at the opposite prompt side, amid yells, shouts, hisses, and applause, and the first person I met was Elliston.

"You can take off your warrior's dress, sir," said he, with a half laugh, for he was as fond of mischief as I was; "we'll not trouble you any farther; Mr. Russell will finish the part."

"You know you told me to make it as funny as I could," said I.

"Yes, that's very true," he replied, "but I didn't expect you to make it so *d— funny*."

And Russell retained the part for the remainder of the season.

A burletta, called Giovanni in London, founded on the pantomime of Don Juan, had been dramatized in rhyme by Moncrief, and produced by Elliston some time before, when he had the Olympic, with great success; and to the great astonishment of the *old school*, this illegitimate manager had it rendered into prose, and some additions made to it, for Drury Lane; engaging the fascinating, and much-wronged Madame Vestris, to represent the gay seducer. And the number of hard male hearts she caused to ache, during her charming performance of the character, I am satisfied, would far exceed all the female tender ones Byron boasts that Juan caused to break during the whole of his career. Harley was cast Leporello, and I was desired to understudy it, and left out of the piece; but at the first rehearsal, Oxberry and Knight both refused the parts allotted them, and Oxberry's was given to me — "Mr. Porus, a coachmaker," without one redeeming line, and on the stage, with little to do all through the piece. I remonstrated, but was answered that it was according to the spirit of my engagement; that it was Mr. Oxberry's part, or such as he ought to play, and that, for his refusal, he had been forfeited; and that, if I declined the character, my night's salary should be stopped during the run of the piece, though the fulfilment of my articles would still be claimed. For an ambitious actor to have to play an objectionable part for one night is bad enough, but he can grumble through it, and forget the annoyance in the morning; but every night in the week, for months, to be so afflicted, is putting patience to a severe penance. Every scheme I could invent to distress the performers, so that I might be taken out of the piece, failed; in fact, rather rooted me more firmly in my disagreeable position. Madame Vestris had to sing a very long song, to the tune of "Scots wha' ha' wi' Wallace bled!" which was always encored, and to which I had to stand quietly by right, and listen; but I made up my mind I would get clear from that nuisance, by "cutting mugs" at the musicians, and making the people in the front of the pit giggle all through the song; but, to my horror and disappointment, when we came off, the dear kind soul, instead of being angry, as I wished and expected, said she thought "it was extremely comical, and begged I'd do it every night." Harley was the only one I succeeded in annoying; I could give an excellent imitation of him, and by speaking outside, and going down the stage after his manner, I got the reception intended for Leporello, and when he came on, the audience, for fear of being again taken in, took no notice of him at all. The first night I even deceived his mother and sister, and got the first and last approbation I ever received from them, I'm quite certain. After about five weeks of this never-likely-to-end vexation, I consulted my friend Rodwell, and we agreed to have two guineas worth of Chitty's opinion, the celebrated Chamber counsel, and he gave it decidedly as his conviction that the article was rendered void; and relying on this authority, Rodwell bound himself to keep me harmless, and I signed and sealed for the Adelphi, on my proposed terms, for three years. Rodwell retained Adolphus as counsel in the event of an action, and Elliston was apprized of my leaving the theatre according to law; and after some preliminary forms, meaning nothing, I suppose, the affair was dropped.

Elliston was a magnificent actor and delightful companion, but a most unprincipled man: his "Liar" could only be equalled by his "poetical prose" off the stage. When manager of the Olympic, an actor by the name of Carles, who was an overpowering favourite with the audience, had been discharged, in consequence of intemperance, and, of course, he stated to his friends that he had been shamefully ill used. The frequenters of the Olympic, in Elliston's time, were a very different class of persons to the elegant audience Madame Vestris, in after years, attracted there; and they, with fellow feeling, sympathized with his supposed injuries; for though he told the truth, all his offence was "only taking a drop too much;" and a most powerful party was arrayed, one evening, to demand his reinstatement, and Carles took a seat in the pit to await the joyful result. When Elliston appeared, he was greeted with one universal shout of "Carles! Carles! engage Carles! let's have Carles! Carles! Carles! Carles, or no play! Carles! Carles!" When, with his hand on the spot the uninformed in anatomy imagine the dwelling-place of the heart, and a face expressing veneration and submission, which he possessed such unequalled power to portray, he, in action, entreated silence, and with all the unhesitating bluntness of truth, he burst forth with pathetic energy,

"My best, my warm friends! this ebullition of feeling in behalf of one you suppose to have been wronged shows the nobleness of your nature, and I adore you for it:" intense silence. "The man who would hesitate to stretch forth his utmost might to rescue from the bitter fangs of oppression the object of tyranny and persecution, is unworthy to enjoy the blessings of that liberty for which our forefathers fought and bled!" loud applause, and one little "huzza" from an apprentice-boy, nearly out of his time, in the pit. "I loved that man," pointing to Carles: "oh! how I loved him; I idolized his transcendent talent, and took him to my heart like a brother:" here he produced a white handkerchief, and several gentlemen were heard to blow their noses in the gallery. "To my poor thinking, he appeared the moving picture of all that could adorn humanity; he would, to be sure, get a little tipsy sometimes:" here there was a slight murmur among the audience; "but I always looked upon it as an amiable weakness—we all get tipsy sometimes—*I do:*" here there was an acknowledgment of the fact in the shape of a *little laugh.* "But for the last week"—here he looked directly at Carles—"he has been in a continual state of intoxication, and has never been, near the theatre." Carles rose from his seat. "*Down in front! hat's off! down in front!*" was declared in a voice as *double as the duke's,* and Carles sat down, and Elliston continued, with a thick voice and hurried manner: "And on going to his lodging this morning, to coax him to return, which I have often done before, judge of my horror and astonishment when I found his wife and children starving for the want of the common necessaries of life:" here some one in the gallery was imprudent enough to shout out, "*Carles hasn't got no wife!*" but a universal cry of "*Pitch him over!*" prevented any farther remarks from that gentleman, and Elliston proceeded: "His lawfully wedded wife, the most lovely, thin young creature I ever beheld, whom this villain"—pointing at Carles in the pit—"had torn from her fond, gray-haired father's arms, to bring to misery, and leave her to perish for want: the infant at her breast screaming for the nourishment the starving mother couldn't give; the little ones, four lovely boys, clasping my knees and shrieking for bread; and in the corner of the room lay his infant daughter, the most lovely, angel form I ever beheld, a frightful, distorted corpse, too horrible to look upon, who, the day before, had died for want of food." Here there was a general murmur round the house, but Elliston interrupted its explosion by continuing, "I instantly sent for food for the little ones, and with the sum this villain," looking at Carles, and blubbering, "could easily have earned, I provided a coffin for the little cherub, and only half an hour ago I returned from the funeral. Now, I appeal to you as men, as husbands, and as fathers, should I engage this inhuman monster?" pointing at Carles. "If you say so, he shall instantly be reinstated."

"No, no!" Carles got up to speak. "Knock him over! out with him! pitch him out!" and a hundred such expressions, issued forth in one enormous torrent, and poor Carles, *who never had a wife in his life,* nor *a child, to the best of his knowledge,* escaped, by miracle, from the infuriated multitude, into the street, and Elliston got peal on peal of applause, and the performance proceeded.

◆

CHAPTER XIX.

"Oh, gracious God! how far have we
Profaned thy heavenly gift of poesy?
Made prostitute and profligate the muse,
Debased to each obscene and impious use:
Whose harmony was first ordained above,
For tongues of angels, and for hymns of love?
Oh, wretched me! why were we hurried down
This lubrique and adult'rate age
(Nay, added fat pollution of our own),
T' increase the streaming ordures of the stage!"
DRYDEN.

WHEN Stephen Kemble took the government of Drury Lane Theatre, his ambition led him to believe that he could replace the drama on that proud and purely classic pedestal from which the rude hand of ignorance had hurled it headlong; and his refined taste gave him the intellectual power for the Augean labour, but the kindness of his nature deprived him of the strength of heart necessary to begin the task: dozens of actors and actresses he had remembered when a boy, grown gray in the theatre, and passed the day of pleasing, he humanely retained to choke the outlet of a limited treasury, and thereby fettering the means which should have been applied to furnish material for a market always requiring a quick return. His very name, too, contradictory as it may appear at the first glance, was an impediment to popularity. The exalted station his brother John and Mrs. Siddons had achieved, rendered them unapproachable to the multitude; this was a heinous fault. The mob must ever have their idol, whether in religion, politics, or the drama, upon familiar terms; the privilege of calling them, behind their backs, "Old Sall Siddons," and "Black Jack," was not sufficient; they must meet them at the Harp, or Finche's, or the Coal-hole, as they could "Charley Incledon," or "Neddy Kean," or they were not content; they therefore looked up to their splendid talent with *awe* for its sublimity, with *wonder* at its attainment, and with *envy* at the *feeling distance* at which, by comparison, it placed themselves; and, in consequence, the *vulgar public* worshipped and hated them. Though past the reach of prostration from their "high estate," every trifle was seized upon with avidity for the purpose of annoyance. Kemble, in Prospero, alive to Shakspeare's meaning, that the smooth current of the language should flow with no grammatic bar to ruffle its enchanted calmness, changed the harsh plural of the "ear-piercing" *ache,* and filled the measure of the line with pure poetic propriety. The scribblers by rule seized upon this piece of pedantry, as they called it, to cavil at, and, ridiculous to relate, every night a portion of the audience, too ignorant to know the *patois* of St. Giles's was not their mother tongue, whooped, yelled, and shouted at the justly "lengthened line." With such a prejudice existing against these two ornaments of the profession, no wonder the scions of the race were doomed without mercy to "expire before the flower in their caps;" and, instigated by this feeling, poor Henry Siddons, with every advantage of mind and education, was *written off the London stage* for no offence but his name; and, sad to tell, his disappointed ambition helped to dig his early grave. His amiable wife, too, an overwhelming favourite as Miss Murray, suffered from the same cause, and the metropolis of England lost the adornment of talent infinitely superior to the overrated Miss O'Neil's.

Stephen Kemble, playing only one part, always appeared as a stranger to the audience, who valued him merely as the "gross fat man" who could play nothing but Falstaff, and his son Harry was, unfortunately, too nearly fair game to easily escape. The committee, too, had five opinions in every proposed amendment, and, of course, made bad worse, though I must do them the credit to say that, thanks to them, there were more pretty women in the first and second greenrooms than any one manager was ever able to collect together again in my time; among them, the beautiful Mrs. Mardyn, who a short time before, in the Plymouth theatre, was considered incapable of delivering a message; but at Drury

46

Lane she played four or five principal characters during the season, *to empty benches*, and 'twas said (and I believe, for I know the cost of such material) received thirty pounds per week! No wonder the theatre went to ruin, and my esteemed friend, Stephen Kemble, retired in disgust to his pretty cottage at Durham.

Elliston took the reins under very different auspices. He was the lessee, and literally uncontrolled, and a long and distinguished favourite with the public; his nature, too, admirably fitting him not to allow old friendships, humanity, or kindness of heart to interfere with his interests. His theatre, to use his own expression, was not "intended as an hospital for invalids;" all the old servants of the public were, therefore, discharged, or those only retained on salaries graded to the extreme of what their abject necessities obliged them to accept. For years the manager of the Surrey and Olympic, he brought with him the experience purchased in that school to add to his admitted knowledge of the legitimate drama, and followed by crowds of the *utile*, who, for the honour of belonging to Drury Lane, would act for little salary, or none at all; always ready, and possessed, in an unequalled degree, of the fascinating power of persuading the public to anything he wished, he took the direction of the theatre with the best possible chance of success—for a time, at any rate. His right-hand man was Winston, long associated as the drudging partner with Coleman and Morris, at the Haymarket. He had been disappointed in his hopes of becoming an actor himself, and, with the same acrimony of feeling an elderly virgin hates a blooming bride, he detested the professors of an art he hadn't warmth of soul enough to advance in. It was his province to measure out the canvass and colours for the painters, count the nails for the carpenters, pick up the tin-tacks and bits of candle, calculate on the least possible quantity of soap required for each dressing-room, and invent and report delinquencies that could in any way be construed into the liability of a forfeit; of course, his prey was "such small deer" that the gentlemen of the theatre wouldn't even condescend to spit upon him; but Smart, the leader, who, in the legitimate sense of the word, deserved that title, literally did void his rheum upon his face, one night, before the company, which the dastard wiped off, and, "with 'bated breath and whispering humbleness," sued for pardon for some dirty act. In the course of my experience I have noted many such "valuable creatures," as they are always called till they are found out, pinned to the fortunes of a manager; and generally they get rich, and their employer gets poor, and, in his tattered authority, exclaims, "How strange it is that I should have been so deceived in that man!"

King Lear, as threatened, was produced after loud proclaim of preparation, and the tragedy published as revised by the manager, and the poor " *nice-fruit-and-a-book-of-the-play*" women were obliged, on pain of dismissal, to add to their *ancient melody*, " *as adapted to the stage by R. W. Elliston, Esquire !*"

Full measure was taken of the taste of the Surrey and Olympic audience, in rendering the beautiful play as much like a melodrame as the nature of its action would permit. I wish I had a bill to refer to; but I remember great credit *was advertised* as due to the management in correcting the hitherto inaccurate costume, and Kean was clad in a *crimson velvet gown*, bedizened with gold buttons and loops down to his feet! and Russell, as Oswald, in white *silk stockings* and the same dress he wore for Roderigo! But the chief dependance of success was placed on a bran-new hurricane on shore, "designed and invented" by somebody, "after the celebrated picture, by Loutherburg, of a *Storm on Land;*" but, to give this additional effect, the sea was introduced in the back-ground, the billows, painted after nature, "curling their monstrous heads and hanging them with deafening clamours"—trees were made to see-saw back and forth, accompanied with the natural creak! creak! attending the operation; Winston had hunted up, *without any expense to the management,* every infernal machine that was ever able to spit fire, spout rain, or make thunder, and together were brought into full play behind the entrances. Over head were revolving prismatic coloured transparencies, to emit a continual-changing supernatural tint, and add to the unearthly character of the scene. King Lear would one instant appear a beautiful pea-green, and the next sky-blue, and, in the event of a momentary cessation of the rotary motion of the magic lantern, his head would be purple and his legs Dutch-pink. The common fault of all mankind is vaulting ambition, and, in the true spirit of that feeling, every carpenter who was intrusted to shake a sheet of thunder, or turn a rainbox, was determined that his element should be the most conspicuous of the party, and, together, they raised a hurly-burly sufficient to "strike flat the thick rotundity o' the world," and not a word was heard through the whole of the scene. Kean requested that it might "be let off easy" the next night. "I don't care how many flashes of lightning you give me," said he, "but, for Heaven's sake, Winston, expel your wind and cut out your thunder."

To keep his own name and that of his theatre constantly before the public, he knew, from every quack's experience, was most important, and every means to achieve this object was resorted to by Elliston. A portico to the front entrance was *built on one night* by torchlight, and the police reports were continually decorated with a long account of an aggravated case of assault and battery, committed by R. W. Elliston, Esq., on the person of a check-taker or an apple-woman. The poor, persecuted Queen Caroline, about this time had arrived in England to demand redress for the unmanly accusations brought against her by her husband, and Elliston, taking good measure of the weak point in the character of his " *friend, George the Fourth,*" as he always called him, showed his one-sided loyalty and ignorance at the same time, by omitting "et regina" at the bottom of the playbills, and leaving " *vivant* rex." And so the *singular plural* remained for weeks till noticed by the newspapers, which, perhaps, was what he desired. But this paltry attempt to wound the feelings of a suffering female, for the dirty desire of pandering to the malignity of her depraved husband, was held in contempt and derision by every thinking mind, and, I hope, by even his King among the number.

By a succession of degradations, heaped unsparingly on the drama and its professors, he laid the groundwork of that ruin to which his followers brought

Poor Drury Lane.

CHAPTER XX

> " Sir, I desire you do me right and justice :
> I am a most poor woman, and a stranger,
> Born out of your dominions ; having here
> No judge indifferent, nor no more assurance
> Of equal friendship and proceeding."
>
> *King Henry VIII.*

AFTER leaving Drury Lane there were six weeks to elapse prior to the opening of the Adelphi, but, fortunately for me, when it was first rumoured that I was about retiring from that establishment, Moncrieff applied to me to undertake the character of Leperello, which he offered to prepare expressly for me, in a new piece called "Giovanni in the Country," which he was then dramatizing for the Cobourg. I consented, on condition that my salary should commence immediately, and that I should have the privilege of resigning before the Adelphi opened, which was readily acceded to; and on a Saturday night I bade farewell to "Old Drury," and on Monday commenced an engagement "over the water," in my favourite character of Sponge.

Glossop was the manager; a very vulgar, ignorant man. I had little to do with him but in the way of business, and he was always extremely civil and correct in his dealings where I was concerned. His father was a soap-boiler and candle-maker, and through some speculations he had made, which appeared most ridiculous to everybody, had unexpectedly, perhaps even to himself, realized an immense fortune. His son married Miss Fearon, whom I knew at Plymouth as the "*English Catalani!*" She was the pupil of a violin-player called Cobham, had a delicious voice, and, from having been taught from that instrument, her execution ever retained the brilliant, articulate character peculiar to the "soul-awakening viol." She was, soon after her marriage, separated from Glossop, and, as *Madame Feron*, visited this country as a *prima donna* some years since. His connexion with that lady probably induced him to dabble farther with theatricals, for which he was totally unfitted, "*and the way he made the old man's soap and candles melt was curious*," as poor Moreland would say. The decorations of the theatre were the most gorgeous and costly of any in London; good taste was thrust out of the way to make room for gold, and silver, and brass, and glass, and gas, in all directions, till "the sense ached" at the dazzling profusion. No expenditure was spared in the production of the pieces; and the house was crowded every night. I was a great favourite, and I passed a pleasant and profitable time till the day arrived to walk over Waterloo Bridge, and be once more welcomed at my pet theatre, the Adelphi.

The trial of Queen Caroline, at about this time, created the most intense and universal excitement among all classes of persons ever witnessed in London during my recollection. There were two parties, equally violent in their opinions—the king's, cruel and vindictive in their accusations; and the queen's, boisterous and vehement in their declarations of her innocence. It absorbed every other topic of conversation; and the rancour with which either position was maintained severed the bonds of old friendships, and ruffled the social compact round the domestic hearth. Politics, of course, made "confusion more confounded;" the Radicals took side with the queen, and had a most overwhelming majority. The particulars of the case "*non mi recordo*," and if I did, they have no claim to a place in these pages; suffice it to say, I was one of her most enthusiastic supporters; for, admitting all they brought against her were true, *she was a woman*, and I always make it a rule, in taste, to be on their side, whether they are right or wrong. In our theatre, both the Rodwells and all the actors were of my opinion, excepting good-natured, foolish old Lee, the stage-manager, Willis Jones, his father, who was the treasurer, and *Mrs. Waylett;* she declared she thought the queen had acted very imprudently!! On the night of her acquittal the excitement was terrific; the military were ordered out, to intimidate the multitude by their presence, and instantly suppress any treasonable outbreak by the joy-intoxicated myriads who were parading the streets, and rending the air with shouts of triumph. Our theatre was crowded, and it so happened that in the first piece some fifty supernumeraries were employed. Highly elated by the success of my party, I met these fellows, ready dressed for the stage, awaiting the commencement of the performance ; and, without thought, in the fulness of my feeling, I proposed "*Three cheers for the queen !*" which was instantly given, with due dramatic precision, and responded to *nine times* by the audience, in a voice of thunder! All the actors rushed upon the stage, dressed and undressed, and old Lee, the stage-manager, in his morning-gown; but no remark was made, and, delighted at so excellent an opportunity of expressing my joy, I proceeded to dress for the performance. At the conclusion of the first act, there was a universal cry for "God save the Queen !" The number and temper of the audience were tools too dangerous to trifle with, and old Lee, who was foolish enough to adore the king, and, in consequence, hate the queen, had to address them in his "official capacity;" after, in his usual style, stating that he was instructed "by Messrs. Jones and Rodwell to inquire their pleasure ?" and being answered by a thousand voices, " trumpet-tongued," that they wanted "God save the Queen !" he went on to say that "we agnize no anthem called 'God save the Queen,' but if it be the wish of the audience, at the end of the first piece, the company will sing 'God save the King.'" As he had stated, the whole of the ladies and gentlemen (as is usual on such occasions) appeared at the appointed time, and Mrs. Tennant commenced the first verse, amid some interruption by the audience,

> " God save great George, our king ;
> Long live our noble king ; God save the—"

"Queen !" I shouted with all my might. The effect on the actors and audience was electrical, and peal on peal of applause drowned the hearing of the termination of the verse; the second was intrusted to Jones, now of the Park, who, in a very gentlemanly manner, paused for my "Queen !" some followers of my own and the audience joined in the chorus according to my reading, and after an encore, either I or the "anthem," as Lee called it, got nine rounds of applause. Not a word was said by the management; Rodwells appeared delighted; and Lee's opinion no one considered worth looking at; but, before the pay-day came, I heard it rumoured that I was to be forfeited a week's salary, and my participators in the treason, whom I had seduced from their allegiance, were to be punished in proportion; I was, therefore, prepared for a defence, and proposed we should all go in a body to the treasury, and that I should enter alone, and endeavour to obtain a mitigation of the sentence. When I presented myself, Mr. Jones, an amiable and most gentlemanly man, addressed me in the following manner:

"Mr. Cowell, I assure you it is with feelings of the deepest regret that the management consider it a duty they owe themselves to mark, by the highest penalty in their power, the most unparalleled breach of decorum ever committed within the walls of a well-regulated theatre. Of the correctness of this charge against you you must admit the justice; and of the offence itself, I have no doubt your calm good sense has long since made you both sorry and ashamed."

Here was a loophole for me to sneak out of, but, heartily despising such means of escape, I replied, "You are greatly mistaken, sir, if you imagine that my conduct was influenced by anything but a cool, deliberate feeling of a right I had, as an honest man, to unite my poor voice with thousands to rejoice at the escape of a wretched lady from her malignant oppressor."

"Sir!" said he, with some warmth, "you and I hold very opposite opinions on that subject, and, however romantic yours may be, the theatre was no place to express it in."

"Sir!" said I, with equal temper, "my *romantic* feeling in the cause of an injured woman will ever cause me to set at defiance any *arbitrary* law oppression can ever invent; and there is no admitted one, in any theatre, under which my supposed offence can be comprehended."

"Why, I admit," said he, hesitatingly, "that there is no specified rule, but you are aware the management has the power—"

"Yes," interrupting him, "they have the power over those—"

"But, my dear Mr. Cowell," said the kind old man, not allowing me to end my angry sentence, "if your feelings were so violent in the cause, why didn't you control them till after the performance, and then give vent to them in the street?"

"So I did!" I replied: "I assisted some hackney-coachmen to break old Lee's windows, and made him light up, in spite of the love he bears to George the Fourth. But, sir, instead of condemning this ebullition of mine, it ought to be applauded as an act of policy; for, if the singing of 'God save the *king*' had been persisted in, the exasperated public would have possibly destroyed the theatre."

"Well, sir," said he, firmly, "I would rather the property had been razed to the ground than that an expression of partisanship so different from my opinion should be bruited abroad. I think very differently, though quite as enthusiastically on the subject as you do; the friendship of many I hold dear would be jeopardized by my allowing such a wanton abuse of decorum to pass unnoticed; I therefore must, in self-defence, retain your week's salary; but no doubt your general anxiety to forward the interests of the establishment will soon give the management an opportunity of justly restoring the sum."

"Sir, I shall decline receiving it in any shape but as a right!" I replied. "Understanding that this stretch of power was to be assumed, I prepared for the Times newspaper this little paragraph, which, to prove how anxious I am to exonerate you from any participation or approval of my conduct, I'll read to you." And I produced the following:

"UNPRECEDENTED CRUELTY AND OPPRESSION.

—On the night our beloved queen was acquitted of the vile and infamous charges that were fabricated to achieve her ruin, a poor actor, in the fulness of his heart, substituted 'queen' for 'king' in a fulsome song the overstrained loyalty of the managers of the Adelphi Theatre endeavoured to thrust upon the patience of the audience, and for this heinous offence, in their opinion, these lawmakers have taken from him his week's wages, and his only means of support for a wife and large family of children."

"Why, surely, Mr. Cowell," said the old gentleman, placing his spectacles on his forehead, and leaning back in his chair, "you never intended to publish such a mischievous article?"

"Most decidedly I do, sir," I replied. "In yesterday's New Times, that *queen's scourge*, as it's properly called, there's a very mischievous article at my expense, which *I know* emanated from the theatre, for the expression, that *I am as illegitimate in my politics as I am in my acting*, is the very words Lee appeared so tickled to have hit upon, when I confessed to breaking his windows."

"Well, Mr. Cowell," said the good old man, "I see 'tis vain to convince you of your error—there's your salary—destroy that foolish paper, and let us forget the circumstance."

"But there are others implicated," said I.

"Oh, never fear," said he, "I shall not mention the subject."

We conspirators met on the stage after rehearsal, and gave three loud cheers, but "named no parties."

My engagement at the Adelphi being for three years, with a probability of a lease, renewable forever if I pleased, I was desirous of establishing myself in some other theatre for the summer months. Glossop offered me an increase of salary, provided I would remain the whole season; this, of course, I couldn't consent to. Morris made me an offer for the Haymarket, which he intended to open that season by himself, which I accepted; but in arranging the points of business, he stated the opening play was to be the "Belle's Stratagem:" Dorecourt, Charles Kemble; Flutter, Richard Jones; and I refused, very foolishly, to open in Courtall, and ended that affair. I had made up my mind to another trip to Lincoln with my entertainment, when, at the seventh hour, I received an offer from William Barrymore, the author and stage-manager for Astley, to undertake the principal character in a magnificent equestrian drama, called "Gil Blas," he was preparing. To obtain admitted talent in those days, a high price had to be given at a *minor establishment;* and Astley, following the example of the Adelphi, and the fashion of the time, had already engaged Henry Johnston, and Mrs. Garrick, a delightful singer, from the Haymarket. Astley's always opened on the Easter Monday, and we closed in Passion-week, and their season ended about the time the Adelphi commenced. The time suited me exactly; the salary was unexceptionable; I should probably have to play but the one part all the season, and, in consequence, no rehearsals. I therefore made the engagement, and with the assistance of a jackass, caparisoned like a mule, with false ears and a tail, for he had been "curtailed of his fair proportion" of either to make him sometimes look like a pony, I was carried up hill and down dale as the renowned Gil Blas, with great success.

——◆——

> "*Poins.* Come, your reason, Jack—your reason.
> "*Falstaff.* What, upon compulsion? No: were I at the strappado, or all the racks in the world, I would not tell you on compulsion. Give you a reason on compulsion! if reasons were as plenty as blackberries, I would give no man a reason upon compulsion, I."—*First part of King Henry IV.*

STERNE says, in one of his sermons, "There are secret workings in human affairs, which overrule all human contrivance, and counter-plot the wisest of our councils, in so strange and unexpected a manner, as to cast a damp upon our best schemes and warmest endeavours." Some such a "secret working" induced me about this period to be most anxious to bid "my native land good-night."

Oxberry was publishing an edition of plays, with portraits of the principal performers; his engraver lived immediately opposite to my lodging, and when he had business with him he generally paid me a visit. He was in some trouble one day in consequence of his not being able to procure a likeness of Charles Kemble, in Romeo, for which the publication of the tragedy was detained, and though I had never spoken to Charles Kemble in my life, his face was so "screwed to my memory," I undertook to make a drawing. He stayed to dinner with me, and during our conversation while employed upon the sketch (which was published with my name as the artist), he happened to mention that Stephen Price, the American manager, was a constant visiter of the Drury Lane Green-room, introduced by Wallack, who had been to the United States, and went on to say that he had made him an offer to cross the Atlantic. "Upon this hint I spake."

"By Heaven, Oxberry, that would be the very thing for me."

"Why, that never entered my head," said he— *he knew my reason*; "but how will you be able to manage with your engagement at the Adelphi? Price will jump at you, for to get a comedian is the principal object of his visit to England."

"Why, Rodwell and I are old friends," said I, "and the management collectively have a warm feeling towards me, and under the *circumstances*, I have no doubt of their consent; at all events, if this American and I agree, I'll go at any risk."

"Oh, of that there is no danger," said Oxberry, "and I'll see him to-night, and name you to him; he's a devilish pleasant fellow, when you get used to him, but his manners are coarse in the extreme; if he is a fair specimen of the Yankees, they must be a d— rough set. But they say he's very rich, a counsellor, and a colonel in the army, and the devil knows what. He's the *Mr. Harris* of America, and owns *all the theatres in the United States!*"

On the following day I got a note from Stephen Price, requesting that I would breakfast with him at ten o'clock the next morning. He lodged in Norfolk-street, in the Strand. The door was opened by a servant-girl; in answer to my inquiry, she said, "*I'll see,*" and in a minute a negro man appeared, and showed his own teeth and me into the parlour, where a cloth was laid for breakfast. In a short time he returned to say, "Mr. Price would be glad to see me up stairs." I was conducted to a chamber; and on the bed, with his feet wrapped in flannel, and his body in a wadded silk morning-gown, lay Stephen Price. In a peculiarly distinct, drawling manner, which, till you got accustomed to it, had a very singular effect, he said the usual civil things on a first meeting. The hesitency in his style of delivery, didn't convey an idea that he was waiting for words, for he appeared a very well-informed man; but rather, that he was weighing the value of each, and its probable consequences, before he gave it utterance. As some one remarked of him, "Stephen Price is not a man to eat his words, but he always chews them well up before he spits them out." Of his person no opinion could be formed, in consequence of its attitude and costume; his countenance was anything but what would be called *good*, though capable of an extremely agreeable expression; small, bright, mischievous eyes, an abominable nose—looking like a large thumb very much swollen, and nearly "coming to a head," but decision and firmness strongly marked around his mouth; his appearance and manner were greatly at variance, for he looked like fifty, and talked like twenty.

"I must apologize to you, Mr. Cowell," said he, "for asking you to take your breakfast in my bedroom; but after calling in at Astley's to see you, *Jeemes* Wallack and myself finished the evening at Vauxhall, and I didn't get home till four this morning; and the cons'quence is I caught cold, and have got a fit of the b— gout —I'm very subject to the d— thing. But Wallack's the d— b— I ever met with—nothing ever hurts him."

I, of course, was exactly of his way of thinking.

"Mr. Oxberry informs me, sir," said he, "that you have a desire to visit New-Yo-ork."

"I have, sir," I replied.

"Well, sir," said he, "I'll tell you, cand'dly, that I'm d— if you'll do for New-Yo-ork, if you are not a better actor than you a'peared last night. I'll tell you what 'tis, there's a little b— in the Park Theatre of the name of Nexon, who can play that character quite as well as you can, and he merely d'livers messages *there.*"

"You have, I conclude, then, an excellent company," said I, a little nettled, "on your side the water?"

"A d— deal better company than they have in any theatre in London," said he, faster than anything he had said yet. "I have a young man, a countryman of yours, of the name of *Simp-son;* he's a much better actor than your cel'brated Jones, *somewheres* about his size, and the most industrious b— in the world. I have given him one quarter of the Park Theatre, and made him my stage-manager," looking at me as if to give me a hope I might get a quarter if I minded my hits; but I said, as if ending the treaty,

"Well, sir, surrounded as you are by such a galaxy of talent, it will be advisable for me to remain in London?"

"Why, sir," he replied, quickly, "I'll tell you what 'tis: Jeemes Wallack and sev'ral of my friends say that you're a b— good actor, but that you won't act at Astley's. What will you take to go to New-Yo-ork?"

"Fifteen pounds a week," I replied.

"I'll give you ten pounds a week for the first season," said he, "and twelve for the second."

"Agreed," said I.

"When can you go?" said he.

"To-morrow," said I.

"Well, sir," said he, smiling, "I'm d— but you are certainly the easiest man to make a bargain I ever dealt with."

If he had known, however, as much as I did, he would have offered me a guinea a week, and

I would have taken it; but, Heaven be praised! he didn't, and he continued,

"There's an eternal fine ship, called the *T'ames,* sails from London on the first of September, and another, called the Albion, on the same day from Liverpool, in which I shall sail. The only dif- 'rence in the thing is, you get to sea a d— deal quicker by going to Liverpool."

I gave the London ship the preference, as more convenient on account of baggage, and that I might once more visit my old cruising-ground the British Channel, and perhaps forever bid farewell to the scenes of my boyhood.

The terms of benefits, and other important items of the engagement, were pointed out and specified in a plain, honest, business-like man-ner. He was to see Captain Charles H. Mar-shall, and secure the passages, and have the arti-cles prepared for signature, during the little week that was to elapse before my departure. We had a long and extremely pleasant conversation, chiefly descriptive of the country I was about to adopt. His style was peculiarly suited to mi-nute detail, and information in that shape, then so interesting to me, was highly entertaining; and, to his honour be it said, I did not detect by experience the most remote exaggeration in any of the matters he named, always excepting the talent of his dramatic corps, and even there "his failing leaned to virtue's side." And upon acquaintance, I found he made it a rule to speak of all, while in his employ, in the most exalted terms of praise, but, the moment they left him, they were "d— impostors and b— scoundrels." The coarse and highly objectionable epithets with which he unsparingly larded his conversa-tion were delivered, apparently, so unconscious-ly, and, from long habit, were mixed up so mi-nutely with his discourse, that by those familiar with him the peculiarity would pass unnoticed.

My lamented friend Rodwell met my case with the feeling of a brother, but Jones was out of town, and, without his concurrence, the neces-sary form of release from my obligation could not be effected; but, as "the affair cried haste," he undertook to write to him. As Price very justly said, "Anybody could play Gil Blas as well as I did;" the part itself was little better than a *walking* gentleman, and the jackass sus-tained that part of the character; and though the author intended we should divide the ap-plause, I quietly resigned my share in his favour. I felt, therefore, confident that Astley would be delighted to save my useless and large salary for the next four weeks, but, to my great astonish-ment—for I put the cause of my wishing to re-sign on that footing—he declared himself more than satisfied with my engagement, and refused, in the most positive manner, to give up my arti-cles. To him, of course, I said nothing of my intention of sailing to America. On Friday evening Willis Jones sent for me to the stage door, presented me with a letter, full of kind wishes, from Rodwell, and the documents of our agreement, and we parted—as warm friends al-ways part. I complained of indisposition, and Astley, who, unlike his father, was a most gen-tlemanly creature—in manner and appearance more like an eminent physician or a clergyman than the manager of a circus—insisted that I shouldn't play; and some young man, who had been instructed, in case of an accident, to under-study the character, took the jackass ride for me, and I packed up my baggage. The next morn-ing I signed and sealed with Price, was introdu-ced to the captain, who was our witness on the occasion, and on Sunday evening I joined the ship at Gravesend.

It was a dark, drizzly, melancholy night—a fair specimen of Gravesend weather and the parts adjacent—no "star that's westward from the pole" to point my destined path, and furnish food for speculative thought; and, after sliding five or six times up and down some twenty feet of wet deck, I groped my way to the cabin. The captain was not on board, and I found myself a stranger among men, for there were four besides myself, or, rather, three, for one was asleep, I suppose, for he was snoring very loud, in a berth next to my state-room. Such stopped-headed gentlemen are an abominable nuisance, near, or in your dormitory on shore, in harbour, or "caught in a calm;" but under way on the At-lantic, he may breathe as loud and in any way he thinks proper, without inconvenience to any-body but himself. Of all gregarious animals, man is the most tardy in getting acquainted: meet them for the first time in a jury-box, a stage-coach, or the cabin of a ship, and they al-ways remind me of a little lot of specimen sheep from different flocks, put together for the first time in the same pen; they walk about, and round and round, with all their heads and tails in different directions, and not a baa! escapes them; but in half an hour some crooked-pated bell-wether, perhaps, gives a South-down a little dig in the ribs, and this example is followed by a Merino, and, before the ending of the fair, their heads are all one way, and you'll find them bleat-ing together in full chorus.

Now, in the case of man, a snuff-box, or a mull, instead of the sheep's horn, is an admira-ble introduction; for, if he refuses to take a pinch, he'll generally give you a sufficient reason why he does not, and that's an excellent chance to form, perhaps, a lasting friendship—but to "scrape an acquaintance" to a certainty; and if he takes it, perhaps he'll sneeze, and you can come in with your "God bless you!" and so on, to a conversation about the plague in '66, or the yellow fever on some other occasion, and can "bury your friends by dozens," and "escape yourself by miracle," very pleasantly for half an hour. But in this instance it was a total failure: one said, "I don't use it;" another shook his head, and the third emptied his mouth of half a pint of spittle, and said "he thought it bad enough to chaw." Well, as I couldn't with propriety ask why he "didn't use snuff," and the mandarin-man might be dumb for anything I knew to the contrary, and expect me to talk with my fingers; and if I had contradicted the last I might, from his appearance and manner, have got into a fight instead of a chat, I quietly took a seat at the table, snuffed two tallow-can-dles, and took a synopsis of the floating apart-ment. There were two horse-hair sofas on either side a table, twelve berths with red cur-tains and sea-sick-yellow fringe, and, properly, four state-rooms forward of the mizen-mast, one of which Price had engaged for myself and Mrs. Cowell, and the one next to it was used as a pan-try. I was speculating as to what kind of hu-man beings were shut up in the other two, when my curiosity was half removed by a female leading out a beautiful little boy from one of them. No matter what I may be with men and women, I am always a great favourite with dogs, and cats, and infants of a certain age, and we generally get acquainted in an instant. He had just gained that delightful period when children think more than they have power to utter; and I love to translate their innocent thoughts. I had been obliged to leave my two dear boys to follow me; and this little fellow, by reminding me of them, seemed to have a claim to my affection; his mother was a simple, amiable creature in her deportment, and myself and wife were rejoiced at meeting companions for our voyage so suited to our feeling. She, with artless eloquence, told us that her husband, an English farmer in good circumstances, had sailed for America more than three years before, and that she had been prevented accompanying him in consequence of the sudden illness of her mother, "who is in heaven now," and, with her beautiful baby, whom his father *had never seen,* was journeying to her new home in the United States.

In the morning the captain arrived, and introduced me to the gentleman who didn't *use snuff,* as Mr. Scovell, a part-owner of the vessel; he was a resident of New-York, and in partnership with his brother, a merchant in South-street, but a native of Connecticut; and after the river in that state, which wanders "his silver winding way," the ship was named, and pronounced by him as spelled, the *Thames;* contrary to the usage of

> "Full many a sprightly race,
> Disporting on the margent green"

of "father Thames;" whether "bound 'prentice to a waterman," or "on earnest business bent," all there agree to call it "*Tems.*" The gentleman who *shook his head* was a Presbyterian clergyman, of the name of Arbuckle, of Pennsylvania, a most amiable young man. The *chaw individual* had a sick wife on board, a sufficient excuse for his being very disagreeable; and I make it a rule never to remember the names of persons I don't think it worth while to like or dislike. My friend with the impediment in his nose was Mr. John Kent, who claimed to be a brother actor; he was engaged by Mr. Price, but I had never been introduced to him before. The captain was Charles H. Marshall, a very good-looking, and very fine fellow, with "no drowning marks upon him." The mate was a weather-beaten, humorous "sea-monster;" upon asking his name, he replied,

"If you're an Englishman, and I once tell you my name, you'll never forget it."

"I don't know that," I replied; "I'm very unfortunate in remembering names."

"Oh, never mind!" said he, with a peculiarly sly, comical look: "if you're an Englishman you'll never forget mine."

"Then I certainly am," I replied.

"Well, then," said he, dryly, "my name's Bunker! and I'm d— if any Englishman will ever forget that name!"

"All in the Downs the fleet lay moored," as usual; perhaps twenty sail, bound to all sorts of places, and waiting for all sorts of winds, and we were obliged to follow the fashion of that abominable stopping-place; but the few days' detention gave our small party time to get acquainted e'er that

> "The vessel spread her ample sail
> From Albion's coast, obsequious to the gale."

My pet and playfellow and myself were sworn friends; and 'twas delicious, each night, to listen to him while, with his little hands towards heaven held, kneeling at his mother's feet, and gazing with childish earnestness on her face, made beautiful by the expression of pure piety, repeat in lisping tones, soft and sweet as music at a distance, prayers and blessings on *a father he had never seen.* On a Saturday night he went to bed apparently well, and the next morning he was a corpse! he had died of the croup.

A fair breeze had sprung up, and orders were necessarily given to unmoor. He was hurried to the burial-ground at Deal. The mother's agony was frightful; and when she saw him placed in "his narrow cell," "Oh! the cry did knock against my very heart!" and the last tear I shed upon my native land moistened

AN INFANT'S GRAVE.

> "As one who, in his journey, bates at noon,
> Though bent on speed,"

I'll here end the first volume.

THIRTY YEARS

PASSED AMONG THE PLAYERS

IN

ENGLAND AND AMERICA:

INTERSPERSED WITH

ANECDOTES AND REMINISCENCES

OF A VARIETY OF PERSONS,
DIRECTLY OR INDIRECTLY CONNECTED WITH THE DRAMA DURING THE

THEATRICAL LIFE OF

JOE COWELL, COMEDIAN.

WRITTEN BY HIMSELF.

IN TWO PARTS.

PART II.—AMERICA.

" So many particulars may perhaps disgust a philosophical reader; but curiosity, that weakness so common to mankind, deserves a higher name when it is employed upon times and persons of which posterity has no other means of forming an opinion."—CHAMBAUD.

NEW-YORK:

HARPER & BROTHERS, 82 CLIFF-STREET.

1844.

THIRTY YEARS

PASSED AMONG THE PLAYERS.

CHAPTER I.

> "Home of the free !   Land of the great and good,
>   Whose heritage is glory !   Hail to thee !
> Thou oft, undaunted, nobly hath withstood
> Europa's best and proudest chivalry ;
> And, conquering, won a mighty destiny
>   First mid the nations ; and thy flag of light
> Gleams on all climes, a brilliant galaxy,
>   To guide to Freedom from foul Slavery's might ;
> Typing thy hero-sons' apotheosis bright."
>   LEWIS FOULKE THOMAS.

WE left the Downs on the 8th of September, 1821, and, after a tedious and most boisterous passage, on the 23d of October, as the sun "went down into the sea," the welcome cry of "Land, ho !" from the foretop, cheered the spirits of the mind-tired passengers and worn-out crew.   We had a light, fair breeze and fine weather, and we stood boldly on all night.   For though "the A. No. 1, copper-bottomed, good ship Thames," as she was rated on the books at Lloyd's, had well-nigh sent "Old Kent and I," parson and all, to the bottom, the captain was "of very expert and approved allowance," and at daylight—for be sure I was in his watch—for the first time in my life, I beheld the Highlands of Neversink. Marshall and myself had become great friends, and, being most anxious to get to the city, he kind-ly allowed me to take the yawl with four hands, and as Scovill was equally desirous, he accom-panied me.   After four hours' good rowing we met the tide, and were obliged to make a landing on Staten Island, about two miles from the Quar-antine ground.   Leaving the boat in the care of the people, the owner and myself walked to the ferry.   The steamer Nautilus, which was still puffing and blowing in the same line of business when I was last in New-York, six years ago, landed us at the Battery.   Scovill took me to his counting-room and introduced me to his brother, who very sedately, yet kindly, welcom-ed me to his country, and their porter conducted me to the Park Theatre.   Price was standing on the steps, and as the ship was not yet even reported "below," he had no expectation of see-ing me, and, in fact, had begun to suspect the ship was *below* in the genuine sense of the word. It was after the time of rehearsal, and Simpson had left the theatre.   Price gave me the address of a boarding-house he had kindly provided for me, and, of course, asked me to dinner, which I declined, on the score of having placed myself, as it were, under the conduct of Scovill for the day, and he would, of course, expect me, but promised to be at the theatre in the evening.

I returned to the counting-room.   Both the merchants inquired if I had seen Mr. Price—how I liked the city.   "*Wasn't it very superior to London?*" and so on; handed me a news-paper, turned the top of a candle-box inside out, and begged I would be seated.   For an hour or more they continued in conversation, and I to read the *National Advocate*, every advertisement decorated with a woodcut of little boys pulling on boots, ladies having their hair dressed, and other useful and necessary arts *illustrated*, on a sheet of paper about the same size as two pages of the Penny Magazine.   I had read it all through once, and got so far the second time as the price for advertising, and "*published by —— Phillips and edited by M. M. Noah,*" when one Scovill looked at his watch and the other asked the time—they were partners even to a watch—and they both agreed it was the dinner-hour; took their hats; begged I wouldn't disturb myself; "*would be happy to see me at any time; I should always find the morning news,*" and walked off. During the passage Scovill had been very un-well, and very frightened, and, under the cir-cumstances, I had been able to render him some very valuable services ; any attention while suf-fering from terror or sea-sickness is very apt to produce strong symptoms of gratitude at the time, and I don't know what Scovill had not promised to do for me when he got to New-York. But I had *a right to expect a dinner ;* for soon after leaving the ship in the morning, in conse-quence of shipping a spray now and then, and the boat, having been so long out of the water, leaked a little, we were obliged to bail ; at the sight of this operation his heart failed him, and he entreated us to go back ; but upon assuring him that there was not the least cause of alarm, to change the subject of his thoughts, I presume,

> "Trembling and talking loud,"

he said, "Of course you'll dine and spend the day with me and my dear brother?" and I said, "Yes."   But I conclude his dear brother didn't *calculate* there was any advantage to be gained, in a mercantile point of view, by an acquaint-ance with a play-actor, and as I was not likely to be of any farther use to my sea friend, the little expense was very prudently saved.

Tumbling by accident over such specimens of humanity, on first landing in a strange country, frequently lays the foundation of a lasting prej-udice against a whole people.   I stood for a few seconds on the threshold of that inhospitable door,

> "And sighed my English breath in foreign clouds."

My acquaintance with Price was too slight to return to him and explain my disappointment, and accept his proffered dinner; and, indeed, how could I tell but that he had also repented of his impulsive civility, and that I might receive a second, and, from him, a more severe mortification? I had refused to be introduced to the boarding-house Price had selected, preferring that my dear wife should form an unbiased opinion of the necessary comforts required for our new home. There was no human being to my knowledge I was acquainted with in New-York, with the exception of Barnes, who, I found, was a member of the company; he had ever been very kind to me while at Plymouth—he used to call me his son—and if I had been, he could not have shown more anxiety to give me every instruction in his power, in my early attempts at low comedy. But some years had elapsed since we parted, and the Atlantic rolled between the land where our friendship had been formed, and inviting myself to dinner was rather an odd way of renewing it. I could not tell, too, if change of air, as well as circumstances, might not have an effect on that "charm that lulls to sleep," and give likely cause "to steep his senses in forgetfulness."

When we left the ship, Scovill had provided himself with a "hunk" of gingerbread—that is, if a cake of molasses and flour, without spice, could be so called—and myself and the men with some bread and pork, and a keg of water; nearly all the luxuries the ship could boast of, with the exception of some sea-sick ducks, a pig with the measles, and a sheep in a consumption; for, as the *never-to-be-forgotten* Bunker said,

"It coughs like a Christian, don't it, parson?"

It will readily be imagined that I had a most devouring appetite, for, with the exception of a "bite" in the boat, I had not tasted food since the night before. I had put in my pockets, more for show than service, some thirteen or fourteen English shillings: New-York was then a very different place of accommodation for travellers from what it is at the present day; no oyster-cellars that you could tumble into at every corner; "restaurat" staring you in the face in every street; and coffee-houses, and all sorts of houses, capable and ready to accommodate a stranger. The only two places of the kind in existence then, even when you were directed where to find them, was "Morse's," a very humbly-fitted-up cellar, where a table-cloth was never seen, and a clean knife only by waiting till the operation was performed, under a store in Park Row, where now, I suppose, there are thirty; and there you could get a fried beef-steak, raw oysters, or soup made of the same material, which at that time I considered sauce for codfish by another name; and one of a little better class, kept by a Frenchman, under Washington Hall, then the second best hotel in the city. After wandering about I knew not whither, "oppressed with two weak evils," fatigue and hunger, I entered what in London would be called a chandler's shop, put some money on the counter, and inquired if they would sell me for that coin some bread and butter and a tempting red herring or two I saw in a barrel at the door.

"Why, what coin is it?" said a fellow in a red-flannel shirt and a straw hat.

"English shillings," I replied.

"No," said the fellow, "I know nothing about *English* shillings, nor English anything, nor I don't want to."

I thought, under all the circumstances, and from the appearance of the brute, it might· be imprudent to extol or explain their value, and therefore I "cast one longing, lingering look behind" at the red herrings in the barrel, and turned the corner of the street, where I encountered two young men picking their teeth, for which I have never forgiven them.

The feelings created by the war with England, then long since over, was still rankling in the minds of the lower order of Americans, as if it were yet raging, and their hatred of an Englishman they took a pride in showing whenever in their power. In every quarrel, domestic or national, it will always be found that the conqueror is the last to forget, and generally the last to forgive. The language necessarily used in boasting of success rekindles the fury of a fire the dews of peace should always quench. In England it had ceased to be spoken of, or even alluded to. But, it must be acceded, a war there, or in any monarchical government, creates very different feelings (if any at all) from the "one spirit" which actuates a free and sovereign people, whose lives, whose fortunes, and whose sacred honour were pledged by their fathers to defend their homes and liberty, and who with one accord exclaim, "United we stand, divided we fall." But in my country, such an event being declared against any power, with a large portion of its inhabitants only occasions regret, or delight, according to *how much* it may interfere with or advance individual interest; and the combatants themselves, hired to fight, never care for what, nor even inquire the cause of quarrel, but, with bulldog courage, seek the "bubble reputation, even at the cannon's mouth."

The turning I had made from *the grocery* was into a badly-paved, dirty street, leading up a slight ascent from the river to Broadway, and at about half the distance, to my joy, I beheld, over a dingy-looking cellar, "*Exchange Office. Foreign gold and silver bought here.*" I descended three or four wooden steps, and handed my handful of silver to one of "God's chosen people," and, after its undergoing a most severe ringing and rubbing, the (I have no doubt) honest Israelite handed me three dirty, ragged one-dollar bills, which, he said, "s'help me God is petter as gould." As all I wanted then was that they should be better than silver, my politics at that time didn't cavil at the currency, and I hastily retraced my steps to the red-shirted herring dealer, and, placing one of the dirty scraps of paper on the counter, I exclaimed, with an air of confidence, "There, sir, will that answer your purpose?" He was nearly of the Jew's opinion, for he declared that it was "as *good* as gold," and I gave him a large order, *and made my first meal in the United States seated on a barrel, in a grocery at the foot of Wall-street.*

The best sauce to meat is appetite, and my herrings and bread and butter put me in a much better humour with myself and everybody else. From information gleaned from my anti-English friend and his customers, I was assured that the ship would be up by the evening tide, and anchor for the night in the stream, by nine or ten o'clock, and I engaged an owld counthryman to take me on board. Thus relieved in mind and body, I sallied forth again, up Wall-street and through Broadway. The pavement was horrible, and the sidewalks, partly brick and partly flagstones, of all shapes, put together as nearly as their untrimmed forms would permit. *The Park*, which Scovill had spoken of with enthusiasm, I found to be about the size of Portman Square, but of a shape defying any geometrical term to convey the form of it. It had been surrounded by a wooden, unpainted, rough fence, but a storm on the first of September, the power of which we had felt the full force of, twenty days after, on the Atlantic, had prostrated the larger portion, together with some fine old buttonwood-trees, which either nature or the good taste of the first settlers had planted there, and the little grass the cows and pigs allowed to remain was checkered o'er by the *short cuts* to the different streets in its neighbourhood. The exterior of the theatre was the most prison-like-looking place I had ever seen appropriated to such a purpose. It is not much better now; but then it was merely rough stone, but now it's rough cast, and can boast of a cornice. Observing the front doors open, I ventured in, and, opening one of the boxes, endeavoured to take a peep at the interior of the shrine at which I was either to be accepted or sacrificed; but, coming immediately out of the daylight, all was dark as Erebus. A large door at the back of the stage gave me a glimmer of that department, and groping my way through the lobby, I felt, at the extremity, a small opening, and proceeding, as I intended, very cautiously, tumbled down three or four steps, and was picked up at the bottom by some one in the dark, who led me on the stage.

"Have you hurt yourself?" said this immensely tall, raw-boned fellow, with his shirt sleeves rolled up over an arm the same size from the wrist to the shoulder.

"No," I replied, "but I wonder I didn't."

"Have you any business here?" said he.

"No, nothing particular," said I.

"Then you can go out," said he, and he pointed to the opening at the back.

I took the hint and direction, and found myself in an alley knee deep with filth the whole width of the theatre. I continued my walk up Broadway, and as I went the houses diminished both in size and number, and in less than a mile I was in the country. On my return, the theatre doors were open, and the audience already assembling. Phillips, the singer, was the "star," and the performance, "Lionel and Clarrissa." The opera had not commenced, but I took a seat, with about twenty others, in the second tier. The house was excessively dark; oil, of course, then was used, in common brass Liverpool lamps, ten or twelve of which were placed in a large sheet-iron hoop, painted green, hanging from the ceiling in the centre, and one, half the size, on each side of the stage. The fronts of the boxes were decorated, if it could be so called, with one continuous American ensign, a splendid subject, and very difficult to handle properly, but this was designed in the taste of an upholsterer, and executed without any taste at all; the seats were covered with green baize, and the back of the boxes with whitewash, and the iron columns which supported them covered with burnished gold! and looking as if they had no business there, but had made their escape from the Coburg. The audience came evidently to see the play, and be pleased, if they possibly could, with everything; the men, generally, wore their hats; at all events, they consulted only their own opinion and comfort in the matter; and the ladies, I observed, very sensibly all came in bonnets, but usually dispossessed themselves of them, and tied them, in large bunches, high up to the gold columns; and as there is nothing a woman can touch that she does not instinctively adorn, the varied colours of the ribands and materials of which they were made, were in my opinion a vast improvement to the unfurnished appearance of the house.

Phillips as Lionel, and Mrs. Holman as Clarissa, shared equally the approbation of the audience: the current of whose simple, unsophisticated taste had not then been turned awry by fashion, obliging them to profess an admiration of the enormities of the German and Italian school, which, in these days of humbug and refinement, they alone pretend to listen to. Simpson was the Jessamy. As it happened, 'twas one of Jones's very good parts. The audience appeared to back Price's opinion, judging from the applause, but, for my own part, *I was of a very different way of thinking.* Barnes was Colonel Oldboy: in vulgar old men, such as Delph or Lord Duberly, he was excellent; but, though Oldboy is extremely coarse in his language, he is still a gentleman of that school, and, therefore, a character out of Barnes's direct line. It was either the *very* first or second appearance of my friend Peter Richings, one of the best general actors now on the continent; he was the Mr. Harman, and I honestly believe he was even more stupid than I was at the same point of experience. But for the friendly interference of the amiable Miss Johnston, through his embarrassment he would inevitably have been shut outside the drop at the *finale* to the first act, and his narrow escape seemed greatly to add to the amusement of the good-tempered audience.

Fully satisfied that I had nothing to fear, judging by the way the portion of the performance I had witnessed that evening had been approved of, I set off in good spirits to my appointment at the foot of Wall-street. The night was very dark, not a lamp was to be seen, save a twinkle from a little light through the closed glass door of a solitary chemist's shop, in the whole distance; 'twas about eight o'clock, and every store was shut; nor did I meet more than thirty persons during my walk. Look at Broadway and Wall-street now! I found my Irish Charon true to his appointment, but the ship was not expected for two hours at least. I inquired of mine host if I should be an intruder by remaining in his shop, and being answered in the negative, I ordered some more bread and butter, and a herring "to close the orifice of the stomach," and took my old seat on a barrel of pickled shad, as it proved to be; for, after a while, the head slipped in, and so did the tail of my new black coat, which I had had made out of respect to the memory of poor Queen Caroline. To make myself as amiable as possible in the estimation of four or five gentlemen, short of shirt and long in beard, who may frequently be found in such places, I treated, "like a man," to two or three rounds of grog and cigars. I was then no connoisseur in the latter article, having never smoked tobacco in any shape in my life; but to act up to the pure agrarian principles I professed, I undertook a "long nine" and a couple of glasses of "excellent brandy," as old red shirt said. On the passage I had never even tasted wine or spirits, though those luxuries were included in the thirty-five guineas apiece cabin fare. So illy prepared, the "*long nine*" soon knocked me over as flat as a *nine-pounder* : I was sick;

"The dews of death

Hung clammy on my forehead, like the damps
Of midnight sepulchres."

I was perfectly in my senses, but was incapable of sound or motion, or, I should more properly say, voice or action. In these days the march of improvement in such matters, would have doomed me to the certainty of having my throat cut, then stripped, and thrown into the dock; and the next day a coroner's inquest would have quietly brought in a verdict of "*found drowned*," and no more would be said about the matter. But at the untutored period I speak of, they were content to take *only my movables, id est*, my hat, cravat, watch, snuffbox, handkerchief, and the balance of the dirty dollars. My incapacity to make resistance saved my coat, for I was so limber they couldn't get it off whole, and after, in their endeavours, splitting it down the back, and the tail being in a precious pickle, they concluded it would be more honourable to let me keep it—carried me down to a boat, rowed me off to the ship, and delivered me to Old Bunker, as "a gentleman very unwell."

This is "*a full, true, and particular account*" of my manner of passing one day out of upward of EIGHT THOUSAND *I've seen in the* UNITED STATES.

◆

CHAPTER II.

"My name is Pestilence: hither and thither
I flit about, that I may slay and smother;
All lips which I have kissed must surely wither,
But Death's—if thou art he, we'll work together."
Revolt of Islam.

THE next day the ship got into her berth long before I got out of mine, and it was nearly sundown when we drove to our new abode at the corner of Greenwich and Dey streets. Price had selected a boarding-house kept by an English widow, considerately thinking our tastes would be better understood by a countrywoman of our own. It is too late in the day to give advice on this subject; but I soon learned that in any dealings in which an English man or woman should properly be the subordinate party, to avoid them as I would a pestilence. Intoxicated with the supposed sudden possession of what is called *liberty* and *equality*, they mistake "impudence for independence." To use a homely phrase, "*They don't know which way their 'ed 'angs*," and their unbridled ignorance, as well as being inconvenient, has often made me blush for my country.

This lady had been a lady's maid according to her own account, and, to use her idiom, "*Had moved in the first society, till left by her dear husband, who was gone to Abraham's bosom, to keep a boarding-house!*" She had two *very genteel* young women for daughters, who, in London, might have got a living by clear-starching and stitching; here, the foolish mother prided herself upon "*their not being able to do anything at all.*"

It was a large house, the lower story occupied as an extensive grocery. The private entrance was carpeted all over, and crowded with household furniture; some of it appeared as if it had no business there, but I soon found out it was all the fashion; for example, there were *two dining tables*, one with mahogany leaves down to its ankles, very much in the way, against the wall, and another more so, making believe to get out of it, by being turned up on its tripod leg behind the street door.

There were two well-appointed parlours, one for dining and the other for sitting, with sofas, mirrors, and a pianoforte, upon which, I was delighted to hear, the *ladies couldn't play*. The apartment allotted for the use of myself and Mrs.

Cowell was *all over* the store and the two parlours into the bargain; a sort of sized room that any strolling company in England would be delighted to meet with, in the event of not being able to procure the Town Hall. There were eight *large windows*—three on one side and five on the other; a *little fireplace* in one corner, with four bricks, instead of andirons, supporting two or three sticks of green wood, hissing and boiling to death, and making water instead of fire all over the hearth; a bedstead, without posts or curtains; four chairs, about twelve feet apart, by way of making the most of them, and a piece of ragged carpet, about the same portable size of those used for little spangled children to dislocate their bodies on, to a tune on the tambarine, about the streets of London. After starving with cold and hunger, and taking lessons in the Cockney dialect, whether I liked it or not, for two weeks, I moved to a plain, honest Yankee woman's — Mrs. Gantley — where I remained till I could procure a house.

There is still a remnant of the custom, but then it was universal, for all classes of citizens, tradesmen or otherwise, no matter how advantageously they were situated for either business or comfort, to change their abode on the first of May. From that date all houses and stores were rented for one year; and the hurry, bustle, turmoil, and confusion into which that day threw the whole population of New-York, from the highest to the lowest, cannot be conceived; it could be compared with nothing but itself. A town besieged, or a general conflagration, would fail to convey an idea of the ridiculous effect of an immense mass of men, women, and children, loaded with articles of household utility or ornament, taking shelter, with much seeming anxiety, in some abode, from which another party, loaded in the same manner, were making their escape. The streets crowded with carts, wagons, and carriages of every denomination—engaged, perhaps, three months before—teeming over with chairs and tables, in the hurry, apparently, packed on purpose to tumble off, to the great delight of the cabinet-makers and others, who took no interest in the matter beyond the mischief. No better proof of the national forbearance, and government of temper natural to the Americans, than such a trial of patience as this could possibly be invented; and yet even the demolition of a favourite basket of china, or a dray carrying a load of furniture nobody could find out where; or the porter's placing a ponderous piece of furniture in the fourth story of No. 80, when it was expected in the front parlour of No. 1, were causes for merriment, especially to those who had the right to be annoyed; and, with the exception of some disputed points of etiquette among the Irish carmen, the whole day's "toil and trouble"—for

"My business in this state
Made me a looker-on here in Vienna"—

appeared to be considered an excellent frolic.

Simpson I found to be a blunt, plain man, who welcomed me without either warmth or ceremony; he *hadn't a morning-gown*, but the most amiable expression of countenance I think I ever beheld. For the convenience of the theatre, I was to appear in L'Clair, in the "Foundling of the Forest;" and Crack, in the "Turnpike Gate," was suggested, or, rather, insisted upon by Price as the farce; for, having formed a "*Gil Blas*" opinion of my talent, he was determined to be satisfied at once if I was equal to what my friends in London had represented. Barnes was a great favourite in that character, and him, I found, I was expressly engaged to supplant in the favour of the audience.

I was merely underlined "from Drury Lane," my "first appearance in America," on one of Phillips's off-nights, and, in consequence, the house was very little better than it probably would have been without my playing at all. My reception was kind in the extreme; and at the end of the first piece, Price came round and paid me some very high compliments. Simpson said some civil things; but I could plainly see peeping through them that he thought me "very dear for the money." I was then *only* twenty-nine years of age, and the contrast between the young soldier and Crack was very great; and my appearance, when disguised for the latter part, I suppose, gave hope to the junior partner, from his altered manner, that I might be worth my salary. Old Kent and Simpson had been together in the Dublin theatre. I had never seen Kent play, but I found great expectations were formed of his making a hit. He had selected Sir Anthony Absolute and Looney M'Twolter, "to astonish the natives in," and, without any consultation of my taste on the subject, I, of course, was cast Acres and Caleb Quotem. His next night was to be the "Road to Ruin," for the sake of his Old Dornton—I to play Goldfinch—and to show his versatility, he was to *sing* Belville, in "Rosina," and I to play the pretty part of William. To all this I had no right or cause to make the least objection; but the first act of the "Turnpike Gate" changed the state of affairs. Captain Marshall, whenever it didn't blow, would blow the flute, exclusively to please himself—

"How sour sweet music is when time is broke and no proportion kept!"

and two tunes, which I couldn't discover to be *at all* like any air I had ever heard before, I found were great favourites with my friend, and these, I was informed, were "Yankee Doodle" and "Hail Columbia;" and unexpectedly introducing these then unhackneyed tunes in a song I manufactured for the occasion, produced a great effect, and my success altogether was immense.

"Simp-son," said Price, hobbling down the same steps I had tumbled, "look here; as to playing the 'Review' on Thursday night is all d—nonsense; the farce will be this Crack-thing. Cowell," giving me a hearty shake of the hand, "you've made the greatest hit, sir, that ever was made in Ameri-ca. Look here, Neddy, what's the play o' Thursday?"

"The 'Rivals,'" said Simpson.

"Well, here, Cowell," said Price, "if you don't like that part of Acres, say so, and you can play whatever you choose."

"I have already said so to Mr. Cowell," said Simpson; "but he assures me 'tis a favourite character."

And so he had, and, like a sensible man, he paid me all the attention the good opinion I had earned deserved. I became at once a decided favourite with the audience; and that enviable position, I am proud to say, I have maintained, in all the principal cities of the Union, up to the present hour. At the termination of the performance I was introduced to some half dozen critics and admirers of the drama, among them M. M. Noah, then the high-sheriff, who has ever since, when in his power, shown me great kindness and attention. *That night I felt a triumphant, self-satisfied sensation, I never experienced before nor since.*

Simpson had only been married a short time, and, like myself and others, was waiting till the first of May to go into housekeeping; but he gave a very handsome dinner, on Sunday, at his boarding-house, kept by the widow of George Frederic Cooke, where I met Price's two brothers, William and Edward, Noah, Jarvis, the celebrated painter, and most eccentric character, and a large party of gentlemen. Simpson, true to Price's description, was the most industrious man I ever knew; he generally played in every piece that there was any necessity for his appearing in, whether in his line or not, greatly to his own disadvantage, for in a certain range of characters he was excellent. For six days in the week he was scarcely out of the theatre; but on Sunday, it must be a very urgent point of business that would induce him even to write a letter. He seldom visited, but generally gave a dinner to a choice circle of friends; and it was some engagement, more for policy than taste, which prevented my being his guest on those occasions while I remained in New-York. At the end of some twelve nights I had a benefit, the profits arising from which I had sold to Price for our passages, which it considerably exceeded, and he generously offered me the overplus; but I, like John Astley, stuck to my bargain, whether good or bad.

I was now strongly urged by Simpson and Price to go to Boston for two weeks, and receive half the proceeds of an engagement there; but to this no persuasion could induce me to consent. My argument was, that as I had never achieved the position of a "star" in my own country, I would not subject myself to ridicule in attempting to shine out of my sphere in this. My foolish *modesty* on this point, if it might so be called, has been amply compensated for by the host of impostors who have yearly scoured the country since, till they have drained it dry as hay; with nothing under heaven to recommend them but an announcement from one of the London theatres, and T. R. C. G. or T. R. D. L., in gilt or conspicuous letters, on every book or manuscript they have an opportunity to place upon a prompt-table. The managers, secure in a profit, aid the imposition; they demand their charges, and, should the he or she humbug prove too gross, even for the indulgence of the most indulgent audience in the world, no blame can attach to them for introducing novelty so highly self-recommended. The theatres being numerous and "far between," if some well-paid-for puffs succeed in exciting curiosity for a night or two, they travel round the Continent, and escape to Europe before they are fairly found out; often with a well-lined purse, as proof of the easy gullibility of the hospitable Americans, and send "his fellow of the self-same flight the self-same way."

Some years since, in travelling down the Mississippi, a Swiss or German steerage-passenger made himself conspicuous by singing all manner of outlandish songs an octave above common sense—a squeaking falsetto, resembling the excruciating appeals to humanity a pig makes while having his nose bored, or undergoing other necessary or ornamental surgical operations—and collecting, by this unnatural exertion of the lungs, divers *bits* and *picayunes* from the deck-hands and other admirers of "music out of tune, and harsh;" and, a few days after my arrival at New-Orleans, Caldwell underlined "*Signor Carl Maria Von Bliss, from the Royal Academy of Music at Vienna!*" or somewhere; and, to my astonishment, it proved to be this yelling German, who had put my ear out of joint, and helped to wood the boat on the passage down. Of course, this was too much of a joke; but the warm-hearted Southerners, finding the fellow was in poverty, made him an excellent benefit, though they couldn't endure his music.

Cooper succeeded Phillips, then the theatrical god of America; and he behaved like a most disagreeable one to all the mortals beneath him. He was to open in Macbeth; the rehearsal was called at ten o'clock; Mrs. Wheatley, Barnes, and myself were the Witches; we went through our first scene, and so far in the second as Macbeth's entrance; he had been on the stage an instant before he was wanted, but then he was missing.

"Call Mr. Cooper!" says Simpson.

"He's gone in the front!" says the boy.

"Go for him, sir!" said Simpson.

Mrs. Wheatley, Old Jack, and myself told, or listened in turn, to two or three excellent jokes before Cooper arrived. Then he gave long and particular directions to Anderson, the prompter, as to the exact time of the commencing of the march, and the exact time of its leaving off, and had just got as far in the dialogue as to inquire,

"What *ar-re* these,"

when the thought occurred that we should look better, or he could act better, if he had a witch at each entrance. He appealed to Simpson, who grumbled out something, and the *Fuselli groupe* was desired to take open order, and Mrs. Wheatley went half up the stage. This wouldn't do, unless the meeting was supposed to be with three old women, in different streets; and the word was given, "As you were!" and 'twas finally agreed that Barnes and I should stand at the first entrance, and Mrs. Wheatley close to the wing at the second. The manner of directing these alterations and improvements, and the time occupied in making them, put my patience to a severe test; and at this critical juncture a boy entered, and delivered him a note, and he coolly sat down to the table to answer it. This was the climax; and, leading Mrs. Wheatley off the stage, I said, with much temper,

"Mr. Simpson, I can put up with this rudeness no longer; I'm going home!"

Simpson, whose endurance was the wonder of everybody, followed me off the stage:

"Oh! nonsense, Joe! nonsense! come back! it's only his way."

"D— his way!" said I; and home I went.

At night Barnes explained to me the alterations which had been made in the usual business, but I had made up my mind to play the part exactly as I had done it with Kean, at Drury Lane, with Munden and Knight as my allies, right or wrong; and when Barnes and Mrs. Wheatley were stirring the boiling gruel at the back of the stage, I was very coolly standing in the corner. I couldn't but admire the man's splendid talent; and he had administered to my vanity by waiting every night to see my farce, and making it part of his bargain, as he received a per centage, that I should appear on his

nights; but I looked upon him as a brute, notwithstanding; and he never spoke to me, nor I to him. One night, while he was performing Virginius, I was seated on a sofa, placed under a large glass, in the green-room, when he came in to adjust his toga. I moved my head out of his way, and not my person; he came close up to the glass, and then stooped his head within six inches of mine, and stared me straight in the face, and I said, "Booh!" He looked perfectly astonished, and walked out amid a hearty laugh from the ladies, for I was an excellent clown in their estimation. A day or two after he addressed me behind the scenes with,

"Mr. Cowell, no one has been civil enough to introduce me to you, therefore I'm compelled to do it myself!" and, after paying me some very handsome compliments, ended with inviting me to dine with him; and we have been very intimate ever since; nor do I know, in my large list of acquaintances, a more agreeable companion than Thomas Cooper. During my residence in the Northern States, I was a frequent guest, for a day or two at a time, at his delightful cottage, at Bristol, Pennsylvania; where the luxuries attendant upon affluence were so regulated by good taste, that Cooper never appeared to such advantage as when at home. His family was numerous, and very interesting. He used to boast of never allowing his children to cry.

"Sir, when my children were young, and began to cry, I always dashed a glass of water in their face, and that so astonished them that they would leave off; and if they began again, I'd dash another, and keep on increasing the dose till they were entirely cured."

His second daughter, Priscilla, who is married to the son of John Tyler, the present President of the United States, is perhaps indebted to some of her father's lessons for that affable, yet dignified deportment which commands the admiration of all parties.

The Park company was not extensive, but very useful, consisting of

Messrs. Simpson, Barnes, Pritchard, Ritchings, Phillips, Nixon, Anderson, Reed, Banker, Maywood, and myself. Mesdames Wheatley, Barnes, Holman, Barrett; Miss Johnson, Jones, Brundage, and Bland.

If there were more, I have forgotten them. Of course, we all had to play nearly every night, and I never escaped. Gillingham was the leader; a good-tempered, eccentric fellow, with an odd kind of nervous affection, which made him appear as if he was continually endeavouring to bite his own ear; this singularity was most conspicuous when he was under the influence of liquor, which was very frequently the case; and one night, while accompanying one of my songs, he made a more than usual energetic snap over his shoulder, lost his balance, and fell into the orchestra, carrying with him the second violin, his own stool, and a music-stand, to the great amusement of the audience. He was, strange to say, as fond of eating as he was of drinking, and, when searching for a lodging, his first inquiry would be, "Madam, have you a gridiron?" and if the answer was "Yes," the kind of rooms, or the price of them, was a secondary consideration; but if "No," he turned on his heel and vanished without another word. This efficient conductor, with six or eight other *professors*, formed a very wretched orchestra, but then even so many, and of such a quality, could only be obtained at a very high price; they never came to rehearsal but on very particular occasions, and even then they were paid extra, and all the music in the performance was gone through, one piece after another, and an hour selected the least likely to interfere with their teaching, or other out-door avocations. Times are sadly changed. I wonder how many *good* musicians there are at this day out of employment? I know fifty at least. Robbins was the principal artist, and also played the double bass; *he* always came to rehearsal, for he'd do anything rather than paint. H. Reinagle, Evers, and H. Isherwood, an apprentice to Robbins, completed this department, and among them they would perpetrate two scenes in a month. By a law, of their own making, I suppose, they only made believe to work from ten o'clock in the morning till four in the afternoon. In short, at the period I speak of, performers, and others employed in a theatre, couldn't be obtained; nor were there a sufficient number of *American* actors on the whole continent to form a company: fortunately for the young population of that day, they had something better to do. Out of the members I have named at the Park, all were English with the exception of Reed, Woodhull, Phillips, Banker, and Nixon. Woodhull had considerable talent, though he contented himself with being an imitator of Pritchard, and naturally so like him that a stranger could scarcely tell the difference. He died soon after he had formed a style of his own and began to be esteemed a good actor. Phillips was an uncle to Noah—I don't mean "the ancient mariner," but the editor—and through his influence, perhaps to aid his own talent, he was engaged to play walking gentlemen, but was anything but interesting in his appearance; if a profile of his person had been *taken in black*, you couldn't have told the difference between it and the shadow of a boy's top with two pegs. He very prudently took to playing old men, and, in a secondary line, became very respectable. Poor Banker didn't live long enough to "come to judgment;" and Nixon delivered messages then, and was still explaining that "the carriage waits" when I last saw him. All the females worth speaking of were English, with the exception of Mrs. Wheatley, and she, I believe, is a native of New-York, and a much better actress, in my opinion, than all of them put together, without in the least degree intending to speak slightingly of the acknowledged talent of the other ladies. When I joined the company, Mrs. Barrett, the mother of George, played the old women. She was a very ladylike creature, excessively tall, and in her day, no doubt, had been very good-looking, and greatly esteemed in the higher walks of the drama, but brought with her for the task she then undertook nothing but her appropriate age and knowledge of the profession.

Light comedy men and interesting ladies, when they get into years, as a last resource undertake to play old men and women: this is a great affliction to the audience, and to those who have to perform with them; memory, hearing, and seeing, all impaired; the recollection of *what they have been* distressing themselves, and *what they are* everybody else. Acting is — acting; and a young woman of eighteen or twenty is just as capable, or more so, of playing Mrs. Malaprop, or the Duenna, than an old lady of forty-five is to play Juliet, or Sophia in the Road to Ruin; and yet those latter characters are often so represented. Few pretty women will sacrifice their love of admiration, and consent to be

> "An angel of love in the morning,
> And then an old woman at night."

But Mrs. Wheatley was an exception to the general prejudice, and whenever there was an appropriate part in a new piece in which I was interested that Mrs. Wheatley could with propriety be cast, I used to urge all my power with Mr. Simpson to have her in the character; and I boldly assert, that had she had the good luck to have commenced her career in London at that same period, she would have established a distinct path in the intricate maze of the drama, where alone nature, leading truth, and exquisite humour would have ever dared to follow.

The season terminated on the fourth of July, to commence again on the first of September.

Rather as an acknowledgment than a return for the many acts of kindness I had received from both Price and Simpson, I undertook to decorate the theatre gratuitously. Henry Isherwood I selected for my assistant, a lad of great promise as an artist; but the little that Robbins was able to teach him he had neglected to impart, and his after success in his profession I have been much flattered by his attributing to my encouragement and instruction. Glass chandeliers were purchased to supply the place of the iron hoops; the procenium was arched and raised; no expense was spared for material; and, dressed in gray and gold, the next season the "Park" assumed the responsible appearance it has maintained ever since. Price went to England for recruits, and Simpson and the larger portion of the company into the country,

> "To keep the flame from wasting by repose."

The season was unusually warm, and about the middle of August great alarm was created by some cases of yellow fever occurring in the northern part of the city. In a day or two the contagion crossed Broadway, and a death being reported at the Custom-House, in Wall-street, the panic became universal and frightfully ridiculous. The whole population in that section of the city who were well or able, beat a retreat with bag and baggage—the sick and poor at the expense of the authorities—the movement on the first of May would bear no comparison. Well-dressed women with "a blanket, in the alarm of fear caught up," were seen dragging along a squalling child, without a hat, through the blazing sun, and the fond father following with a bed on his head, and perhaps a gridiron or a pair of tongs in his hand. All the ferry-boats to Hoboken, Powles Hook, Staten Island, and Brooklyn were constantly plying, loaded down with passengers, who seemed to think drowning a secondary consideration; and in *one hour* the thickly-inhabited and largest portion of New-York was deserted by every human being. The district supposed to be infected was boarded up, the streets covered ankle deep with lime, and all intercourse prohibited. My family were fortunately in New-Jersey, and my house, though far enough from the point of danger to ensure my own safety, was still too near, in the estimation of my friends, for them to make it a sanctuary, so John Kent and I kept bachelor's hall, for not a soul would venture to pay us a visit. He was a faithful old negro, who for years had been employed in the theatre as a sort of deputy property-maker; he professed a great regard for me in consequence of my being "a countryman!" for, happening to be born on the Island of Jamaica, he prided himself upon being "English." Twice a week we made it a rule late at night to trespass on the uninhabited region, John loaded with a huge basket of coarse provisions for the starving cats, who instinctively believe "there is no place like home," and, after a donation or two of the sort, the numbers that would surround us, the moment they heard us approach, would be past belief: I found it a most whimsical mode of cheating a long, dull night of part of its death-like solitude; not another thing that breathes and stirs would we meet in our walk, excepting a single horse, perhaps, trotting along with an unattended hearse, and the driver smoking a cigar or whistling "Yankee Doodle."

I had once witnessed the full horrors of this scourge to mankind in the West Indies, and though a great number fell victims in New-York, yet, by comparison with what I had seen, to my mind it was disarmed of its terrors; but not so with the generality of the inhabitants, and I firmly believe half the deaths were caused by fright alone.

A fine, jovial fellow, a jeweller, by the name of Irish, had "a dog he loved," who a day or two after his master's flight, it was supposed, had strayed back to the old dwelling, in the very heart of the infected district; and though he valued the animal as dearly as he could a child, and danger in "any shape but that" he would have despised, yet, though suffering actual agony at the thought of the poor little wretch being starved to death, he could not summon strength of mind enough to go in search of him, nor hire any one who would. Though "to do good is sometimes dangerous folly," I undertook the task, and after a fight on the steps with the half-famished wasp, I succeeded in tying him up in my handkerchief, and bundled him back to his master.

Many of the retail dealers from Broadway and Pearl-street, after the first alarm had subsided, had erected temporary sheds for the sale of their various merchandise at Greenwich Village, which could then only boast of a state-prison and some dozen scattered houses, and, in consequence, the place suddenly assumed the appearance of a fair. The young clerks and apprentices, having little else to do, had displayed their wit in various jokes in rhyme on their makeshift signs; Irish applied to me for one "according to the fashion of the time," and I perpetrated the following:

> Charles Irish, that brave-looking fellow,
>   Watchmaker, late of Wall-street,
> Took fright at the fever called yellow,
>   And to this place has made his retreat;
> Now in this don't you think he was right?
>   For had he stayed there and got sick,
> He'd no more wind his clock up at night,
>   Or sell you a watch upon tick.

CHAPTER III.

> "E'en ere an artful spider spins a line
> Of metaphysic texture, man's thin thread
> Of life is broken: how analogous
> Their parallel of lines! slight, subtle, vain."
> *Sickness, a Poem, by* WILLIAM THOMPSON.

THE first of September came, the then regular period of commencing the season at the Park, and no abatement of the epidemic. But the panic which this unexpected visitation had cre-ated having in part subsided, a number of the inhabitants had returned to the city, though but few to their houses; and, in consequence, the town and village were crowded with idlers, including the actors, with long faces and empty pockets. As a resource, it was proposed to fit up the Circus in Broadway, belonging to West, as a temporary theatre; the same building that is now called Tattersal's, and then literally out of town. My friend, Sam Dunn, the long Yankee carpenter, who picked me up and trundled me out the first day I tumbled on an American stage, had all prepared in a few days, and we went into *successful operation;* playing to business which enabled us to pay all the expenditure, and two thirds salary the first three weeks, and then the whole amount, till the Park opened. When the affair was past a doubt, Simpson packed up his fishing-tackle and took the reins of government. Like most large cities, places of public amusement in New-York depend for their chief support on strangers and visiters; but *the inhabitants* then attended the theatre from the fact of there being nowhere else to go; even most of the churches were shut up—I have frequently found the parsons, whether at sea or on land, the very first to run from danger—and the houses were well filled nightly. I took one of my benefits there, and had upward of eight hundred dollars at circus prices.

That excellent actor, John Clark, whom Price engaged upon my recommendation, and Watkinson, to play the old men in the place of Barnes, who had left for England at the end of the season, arrived at the very height of the sickness; and poor Charles Matthews and Price popped in in the thick of it, but, fortunately, none of them suffered from anything but fright.

Matthews made his appearance in Goldfinch, and was very coldly received; he introduced his two excellent songs, "*The picture of a play-house,*" and "*A description of a ring-fight;*" neither being then understood, they were not encored, and the whole performance might be considered a failure; but, fortunately for him and the management, he had studied on the passage M. Morbleau, and Price, who was a great diplomatist in theatrical politics, knowing the advantage of an original part, urged him to play that character in the farce, and in that he made a tremendous hit.

Little dependance was placed on his *entertainments;* but, contrary to all expectation, his main success was hinged upon them. He was more highly relished at Philadelphia and Boston than at New-York, though he drew crowded houses everywhere he went. Price followed him like a shadow, and nursed him like a child. He was really an amiable, good-hearted man; but his nervous irritability—commenced, no doubt, in affectation, and terminated in disease—rendered him extremely objectionable to those who were not inclined either to submit to, or laugh at his prejudices; and his uncontrolled expressions of disgust at everything American would have speedily ended his career, but that Price managed to have him continually surrounded by a certain set, who had good sense enough to admit his talent as ample amends for his rudeness. He actually came to rehearsal with his nose stopped with cotton, to prevent his smelling "the d— American mutton chops!" who could even laugh at such folly? It was positively necessary to his health and happiness to have some fresh annoyance every day. He hadn't been in

New-York a week, when he got a letter from some poor woman, who craved his assistance, on the score of having known him before at *Old York*: this was most deliciously disagreeable; he showed the letter to everybody—explained the persecutions he had experienced in the same way in England: "And now," said he, "dam'me, they are full cry after me in America!" Upon this hint, Price and myself, in disguised hands, sent him two or three epistles every morning, dated from the *Five Points*, or *Chapel-street*, from some "*disconsolate English widow*," or "*a poor forsaken young woman*." And by introducing the names of persons he might happen to mention in his convivial anecdotes, or those whom I had heard speak of him while at York and other places, he had no doubt of their authenticity, and one purporting to be from Johnny Winter's niece, stating that "*she remembered his playing Lingo when she was a child, was now in great distress, and for the love he bore her uncle, claimed his aid*," kept him fully employed in imaginary misery for a week.

At his last engagement that season, his attraction decreasing, Price cajoled him into playing Othello, which drew a full house; and he was actually childish enough to believe *he could play it*—not in imitation, but in *the manner of John Kemble!* But no matter whose manner it was intended to convey, he made the Moor the most melancholy, limping negro I ever beheld. The audience were exactly of my way of thinking; and but for the high favour he had gained, they would have smothered him, long before he smothered Desdemona.

Before I left England *Tom and Jerry* was in preparation for the Adelphi. Burroughs, alias Watkins, was to be the Corinthian; Wilkinson, Logic; and Jerry, Moncrief had written for me, but when I came to America, by omitting the songs and otherwise altering the character, from what was exclusively meant to suit my style, Burroughs played the part, and Wrench was engaged for Tom. Simpson had had the manuscript for some time, but was under the apprehension that an American audience would never tolerate the vulgar slang nonsense. At my earnest solicitation, at length the experiment was made, but so positive was he that the piece could not succeed, that little or nothing was done to assist it; it was even carelessly rehearsed at the back of the stage while business of more supposed importance occupied the front; but, notwithstanding, *Tom and Jerry*, in its day, drew more money than any other piece ever played in the United States!

M. M. Noah, who had already produced several dramatic pieces with success, manufactured a play called The Grecian Captive, which was performed for his uncle's benefit, A. Phillips. I was cast for what was said to be the best part in the piece; at all events, it was the longest; all I ever did know about it was the name, and that was Goodman. The drama was supposed to be written in blank verse, that is, good, wholesome, commonplace language, the wrong end foremost, after the manner of Sheridan Knowles;

> "And to cram these words into mine ears
>   Against the stomach of my sense,"

for one night only, was out of the question, and I made up my mind to speak the meaning of the part after what flourish my nature prompted, and so, indeed, I believe, had all the performers. Simpson and some other captives were discovered, in the first scene, digging away in a Turkish garden; I was a sort of overseer, and entered to them, after the manner of Sadi, in the Mountaineers, and recognised, somehow or another, in the captive I was chiding for idleness, "a beloved master," and Simpson and I were proceeding with an interesting dialogue after this fashion:

> "*Captive.* My faithful Goodman, do I behold once more
> That honest form?
> "*Goodman.* Master, most dearly loved,
> Let an embrace assure me that I do not dream."

And as we were suiting the action to the word, he whispered in my ear,

> "Dam'me, Joe, look at the books."

And, upon turning to the audience, every one in the front had a copy in his hand. To increase the attraction, the play had been published, and every purchaser of a box-ticket had been presented with a book, which arrangement I had never heard of till then. I am not easily embarrassed, but this annoyed me exceedingly. If I had not been the principal victim in the business—for I was on the stage nearly the whole of the piece—I could have enjoyed the anxiety of the audience endeavouring to find out where we were. You might see one thumbing over the leaves one after another, then turn them all back, listen an instant, and then begin again. Another appeal to his neighbour, and he shake his head in despair. I was assured very seriously by a young critic, the next day, that I had *actually sometimes cut out a whole page at a time.* But I could not laugh at it; I was angry, and considered the arrangement a rudeness on the part of Mr. Phillips. At nearly the close of a long and laborious season, a whole company had cheerfully, for the sake of serving him, undertaken to *get through* with a composition that the author himself could never wish should see daylight; and though Phillips knew that not a soul could learn more than the action, he, for the sake of a few dollars, lets an audience into a secret which, for their own sake as well as ours, they had better not have known.

Towards the end of the first act I had to be seized and taken off to prison. Supernumeraries were not easily obtained in those days; generally they consisted of young men *with souls above buttons;* Booths and Forrests in the shell, full of starts and attitudes, and terribly in earnest in all they had to do. If they had to seize you, they really seized you, and left the print of their fingers on either arm for a week; and if they had to knock you down, the odds were large against your ever *coming to time.* I was well aware of their *reality propensities,* and had particularly requested them in the morning to "use all gently." But Woodhull—"a pestilence on him for a mad wag," he's in his grave long ago—delighted at my annoyance, and determining, if possible, to increase it—having taken a leaf out of my own book—told these gentlemen, who were engaged to do as they were bid by everybody, that I had changed my mind, and that at the word they were to rush upon me with all their force and trip me behind, which, I being off my guard, they did most effectively. When I could scramble on my feet again, with all my might I floored the first man I met with, and then rushed off the stage. Poor Nixen was my victim, and he "only gave the order," was not to blame, and therefore promised to thrash me *after the play;* but as I had bunged his eye up by mistake, he looked over the matter with the other. I was most ridiculously angry, and vowed I would not go on the stage again. But Simpson smoothed me down, and my friend Noah acknowledged the bad taste of the books being distributed, and confessed the language "*was very hard to learn.*"

"And so is Peter Piper picked a peck of pickled pepper," I stuttered out; "but it's horrid trash for all that."

In the last scene, Phillips, half frightened to death, came on *wriggling*, on the back of a real elephant; and an unexpected hydraulic experiment he introduced—I mean the elephant—to the great astonishment and discomfiture of the musicians, closed the performance amid the shouts of the audience.

Now, though I and my numerous assistants had effectually damned the piece, the kind-hearted Noah, the next day, in his own paper, wrote an excuse for the performers, and placed the whole blame to his imprudence in permitting the books to be given away.

West, with a fine company of performers, and a magnificent stud of horses, paid a yearly visit to New-York, to the serious injury of the theatre; and, in self-defence, Price and Simpson were desirous to buy him out. To effect this, resort was had to stratagem, in which I played a very useful part. My particular intimacy with the management being notorious, with binding oaths of secrecy, I named to those well fitted to instantly convey the news to West, that the Park proprietors intended erecting a most splendid amphitheatre in Broadway, on the vacant lot where the Masonic Hall now stands; a model, somewhat after the plan of Astley's, was placed in the green-room, and imagination, aided by the whisper abroad, soon gave it a local habitation and a name. A delinquent from the circus (Tatnal) was engaged, and employed to break *two horses* in a temporary ring, boarded round, in a lot on the alley at the back of the theatre. These broad hints at opposition soon brought matters to an issue; and at a fair price, and easy mode of payment—for a large portion of the amount was raised by the receipts after they were in possession—Simpson and Price, and some others, who then objected to be known to be interested, and, through my means, shall not now, purchased the buildings, lease, engagements, horses, wardrobe, scenery, and a prohibition against West again establishing a circus in the United States. And, well pleased with such a winding-up to his experiment, West, with a handsome fortune, went to England; for, when he arrived in America, he had not the means to pay for the passages of his company until Price and Simpson advanced the money, and engaged the horse and foot to "Timour the Tartar" and "Siege of Belgrade" for the Park Theatre.

A Frenchman, by the name of Barriere, had fitted up a small garden at the back of a confectioner's shop in Chatham-street, with two or three dozen transparent lamps, and

" Seats beneath the shade,
For talking age and whispering lovers made ;"

and, by selling "sweets to the sweet" at a shilling a head, had made a great deal of money; which, to rapidly increase, he raised a platform, called it an orchestra, covered it with canvass, engaged a French horn, clarionet, fiddle, and a chorus-singer from the Park, with the gentle name of Lamb, who bleated a song or two, and with this combination of talent attract-ed crowds every night, to the great injury, "in the springtime of year," of the theatre. Price put in force some *fire-proof* law, prohibiting all canvass or skin-deep establishments within a certain limit, and the old Frenchman was obliged to strike his tent; but, with the ice-cream profits, he purchased bricks and mortar, and built the *Chatham Theatre.*

While this was in embryo, Mrs. Baldwin, a sister to Mrs. Barnes, turned the brains of some half dozen would-be-acting young men and women, and a private house in Warren-street into a theatre, and opened a show there. Tom Hilson had been seduced away from the Park, where he had been a great favourite in my line of business, by Charles Gilfert, a German musician, who had married Miss Holman, and was, in consequence, manager of the Charleston, South Carolina, Theatre. On Hilson's necessary return to the North in the summer, being shut out by me from the Park, he accepted a *star* engagement at this old lady's concern, and drew crowded houses. Gilfert, who was a very enterprising, talented man, with some powerful friends, already began to talk of a theatre in the Bowery; and Hilson, in such an event, being a dangerous ally, I sacrificed my taste to aid my friends, and on the *fourth of July,* 1823, took the control of the circus, vacating my position at the theatre, to be filled by Hilson, and Harry Placide as his assistant, in my very extensive round of characters.

Hilson was the son of a picture-dealer by the name of Hill, a man of some wealth; for in that day, copying and repairing pictures, and giving them an ancient name and appearance, was as profitable as passing counterfeit money, and relieved of the disgrace and danger; and, indeed, I have seen copies of pictures so excellent, that they were cheap at the price the originals could command. Who ever grumbled at paying a dollar to see Booth play Richard the Third, provided they had never beheld Kean in the same character?

His family being averse to his imitating Nature instead of art, Tom bade adieu to his country, denied his father by putting the *son* to his name, and came to America, where he might freely indulge his predilection for the drama. But, having entered the profession more after the manner of an amateur, than an actor who had regularly and patiently climbed the rounds of the Thespian ladder, the drudgery of the trade he never could surmount. He required time for study, and a choice of characters, in which for years he was indulged; while Harry Placide quietly filled up the interstices with such care and skill, that ultimately the trifling space Hilson occupied was not worth paying largely for by the management, nor the vacancy likely to be noticed by the audience. Poor Hilson took refuge in the West, and left Placide the undisputed master of the field.

He died suddenly, about two years afterward, at Louisville, Kentucky. In characters requiring homely pathos, if they can be so described, such as the old father in "Clari," he could not be equalled; in humorous parts, in endeavouring to be broad, he was coarse. *As a man he was most estimable.* He married Miss Johnson, one of the very few who make you feel truly proud that you belong to the same profession. They lived but for each other; and when he died, a beautiful little girl was all that tied her to the earth, who, shortly after, being seized with a ma-so happened that my company was always in some city where he was not; but on his return to New-York, I fortunately encountered him, and through the influence of the committee of arrangements, he honoured the circus with a visit, which, of course, produced an overflowing house. The box appropriated for the use of himself and suite I had decorated with as many flags as I could borrow from volunteer and fire companies, mechanic and masonic societies, with the French and American ensigns enfolding each other in divers affectionate attitudes, interspersed with a profusion of every description of vegetable matter, with the exception of boughs of oak and laurel, which Billy Rider had been desired exclusively to obtain.

"There, sir, that's what you sent me for," said Billy, throwing down a huge bundle of shrubs.

"No, sir, it is not; I said oak and laurel."

"Divil a sprig of laurel is there, I believe, in the whole State of Jarsey. By my word, sir, it was down to Weehawk I was, and back again twiced. As to oak, by the powers, there's plinty o' that at the tops o' trees where no mortal man could touch a leaf of it, av he had the legs of Goliath. By my troth, now, they are mighty green and pretty — see the red birries on that darling there—depend on it, sir, d— the difference will the ould gineral know; he's had something better to do than to be bothering his brains about bothany; and all those flags and finery, that's the thing itself, sir, to tickle a Frenchman."

And I believe Rider was partially right, for upon conducting the marquis to his box, for the sake of saying something, I apologized for the lack of preparation in consequence of the shortness of the notice I had received of the honour he intended; and with earnest sincerity of manner, he exclaimed,

"Sir, it is most superb!"

It was notorious that he never remained more than half an hour, at farthest, at any theatre he attended; but (in my opinion) he showed his taste by witnessing the whole of our performance, and expressing his admiration at the practical jokes of the clown. I had, of course, sent refreshments to the party, which the committee, like all committees, appeared to enjoy most heartily; but observing the general didn't partake, I inquired personally if there was anything he "particularly wished," and he requested "a glass of sugar and water." Old Hays, the celebrated police-officer, whom I had stationed at the door to prevent his being killed with kindness, I despatched for the desired beverage; and wishing "*to take a drink*" with the good old man, I ordered two glasses, slyly whispering Hays to put some gin in mine: when he returned, he gave me a cunning sort of thief-catching wink to direct me to my "sling;" but the general having the first choice, got the gin, and I the sugar and water. We drank without a remark; I don't know if the marquis ever repeated his dose, but I pledge my honour I never have mine.

CHAPTER V.

"The south and west winds joined, and, as they blew,
Waves, like a rowling trench, before them threw.
* * * * * * * * * *
Thousands our noyses were, yet we, 'mongst all,
Could none by his right name, but thunder call.
Lightning was all our light; and it rain'd more
Than if the sunne had drunke the sea before.

Some coffin'd in their cabbins lye, equally
Grieved that they are not dead, and yet must dye;
And, as sin-burden'd soules from grave will creepe
At the last day, some forth their cabbins peep,
And tremblingly aske, What news?"—JOHN DONNE.

THE following towns constituted our circuit: New-York, Boston, Philadelphia, Baltimore, Washington City, and Charleston, South Carolina. At the last-named place a large building had been erected, but without a stage; and Blythe had been usually sent there with an exclusively equestrian company, to perform during the winter months; but, on Kean's revisiting the United States, as he had never been to the South, it was thought good policy to engage him, hire the theatre there, which was to rent, make some additions to my dramatic corps, and open both establishments on alternate nights. Eighteen of the most valuable horses were selected; the remainder, with Blythe, and a few of the grooms who couldn't "cackle," were left to occasionally perform equestrian pieces at the Park; and, with fifty-five souls, including musicians, artists, and carpenters, I set off for the sunny South.

The journey by land, in the depth of winter, was out of the question; it was therefore determined that we should sail from Baltimore; and the ship Orbit, Captain Fish, was engaged for the purpose. She was a fine, roomy vessel, and built expressly for one of the line of packets between New-York and Liverpool, but not proving fast enough to compete with her magnificent allies, had been taken out of the trade. We paid one thousand dollars for the use of her, furnishing our own bedding and provisions, and fitting up, at our own expense, the stables upon deck, and the temporary berths and state-rooms between.

On a fine, sunshiny Sabbath morning, though unseasonably warm for the month of January, we hauled off from the wharf, and were towed into the tide, to float down the beautiful river-harbour of the "Monumental City,"

"With glist'ning spires and pinnacles adorn'd."

There was not a breath of air stirring, nor a ripple on the water to disturb the equilibrity of man or horse—a calm so profound as to realize the immortal Donne's beautiful illustration,

"In one place lay
Feathers and dust, to-day and yesterday;"

and, in the language of naval postscripts, "officers and crew all well, and in fine spirits." The ladies had the exclusive use of the regular cabin, and forward of it some divisions were made to form state-rooms for myself and family, and the married folks; and berths, or bunks, were erected on either side of the remaining space for the rest of the company. They formed themselves into different messes; the subordinates, especially those who had had experience in maritime matters, acting as stewards. Billy Rider was in great request; he had crossed the Atlantic three times, and once been cast away in a British bark bound to Belfast. The horses, well trained to go through fire or water, appeared to care little about the novelty of their situation. The grooms and carpenters were divided into three parties, one of which was appointed to constantly watch and attend them, and everything appeared to promise a pleasant trip.

About noon a light breeze sprung up from the northward, and we made sail; towards sundown it freshened considerably, and, as only a solitary lantern was allowed to swing below, all the

65

landsmen unemployed had a good excuse for sneaking quietly to their berths. The next day the wind still continued favourable; and the following morning I was rejoiced to find we had got rid of our pilot, and cleared the Capes. The wind kept in our favour the whole of the day and night, though blowing unequally, in sudden gusts and flurries, with cold and drizzly rain, demanding an additional allowance of blankets for the horses, and an extra glass to the men. About midnight it suddenly chopped round to the southeast, and soon increased to a violent gale, which lasted five or six hours, knocked up a tremendous sea, and then lulled away to an awful calm. The swell was dreadful; and the rolling of the ship, being accelerated by the treading of the horses on either side up and down, according to the action of the vessel, caused everything that was movable below to roll and jump, according to its specific gravity, from one side to the other, at regular intervals; and among trunks, boots, books, demijohns, broken pitchers, and plates, in a sitting posture, looking the picture of patience, was poor Harry Moreland, arm and arm with William Isherwood, sliding to and fro, and exclaiming at every pause, "Curious!" Rider had fast hold of the hanging part of the chain-cable, a portion of which was upon deck, and the rest in the hold; he had mistaken it, I supposed, for a stanchion, and was dangling backward and forward like the pendulum of a clock, expressing, with a woful countenance, his contrition at having "aten a meat dinner with a frind the Saturday before." I gave him absolution and an order on deck in the same breath. His boasted experience was now required. During the blow the spar on the starboard side, that was lashed fore and aft to partly support the divisions of the stalls, and keep the horses in them, had parted, and caused some confusion; and now the ship rolled so heavily, and the horses backing, or actually hanging by their halters at every lurch, it required all the exertion of all the hands I could muster to replace it: from the crew I could get no assistance; they were too busily engaged in sending down the royal-mast and top-gallant-yards, close-reefing topsail, bending storm-stay-sails, and making "*all snug*," to receive the coming tempest, full warning of which was given in the most unequivocal and terrific forms. The air felt hot and thick—you could actually touch it—the swell increased; and when the helpless ship rolled over the sullen liquid hills, the little sail she carried flapped against the masts, which shook to their foundations, as she tumbled, as it were, into the abyss, which seemed yawning to receive her. It was about ten o'clock in the day, but pitch-black clouds, so slowly moving that you couldn't see them move, appeared to crawl all over us from every point—"above, about, or underneath"—and in a minute we were in "darkness more dread than night."

You could not see your hand, nor the ropes to which you clung with instinctive horror; weather-beaten "old sea dogs" trembled and stood aghast, mumbled out God, and mixed up prayers and oaths in whispers. Suddenly the zigzag lightning seemed to tear asunder the curtains of eternity, plash on the deck, and struggle at your feet! And, on the instant, thunder, "so loud and dread" it shook your very heart, made you hold your breath, and feel both deaf and blind.

We heard it rushing on us! "*Look out there, men; take care of yourselves!*" was a broad hint from our jolly fat-headed captain for all my valiant party, with the exception of worthy John Hallam and *little Stoker*, to tumble head over heels below—and well they did. It struck us forward, and with such overwhelming violence we could feel her tremble to the core, as she instantly keeled over on her side. The sea was fairly lifted up and hurled over us in torrents, with a noise so great and uniform it knocked all sound out of the world; we could not hear, and we could not see, but when the instantaneous flash showed a glimpse of horror which made us shut our eyes. By the gasping sensation in my throat, I believed she was quietly settling down, and all was over. I could not pray for cursing my foolhardiness in not skulking below with the rest, and being drowned with my wife and children. I had lashed myself to the belaying-pins, near the weather mizzen rigging, and was literally hanging over the "black profound," and to stir from thence with life was impossible. How long we were in this predicament I cannot even guess at, but, of course, not long—*real hurricanes do not last long*. The ship seemed to labour to get her keel once more under water, and by the more frequent but less effulgent flashes of lightning we could see the fore-topmast, yard and all, hanging overboard, but not a vestige, on the leeward side, of the poor horses nor their stables; but on the other I fancied I still saw a head or two. The mountain-like waves had been blown into something like smooth water by the extraordinary violence of the wind, which had greatly abated, though it still blew tremendously. The clouds began to separate, producing a supernatural kind of light, which would be considered awful even in the last scene of a melodrame. Close by me I found the captain made fast, without his hat, and the mate and several of the crew huddled together around the mizzenmast. I could *see* them screeching to each other, and the mate, a capital sailor—I wish I could remember his name—partly tumbled and partly rolled from his moorings, and with a desperate effort, with life or death at the ends of his fingers, caught hold of the ropes belayed to the main bitts, jerked himself forward, seized the lashings of the long-boat, which still maintained her station, though emptied of her contents—two learned ponies—crawled along under the lee of her gunwale, and, with something like the agility of a drunken monkey, gained the weather fore rigging, and with the assistance of two of the crew, who

"Claimed the danger, proud of skilful hands,"

the wreck was cleared from the ship, and she righted! A good imitation of a storm-staysail was with some difficulty rigged and set, and a mizzen topsail, and she was once more under some control, and very nearly the right side upward.

All the horses on the side that had been under water, of course, were gone

"*No man knows whither,*"

with the exception of a pretty little mare called Fanny. Poor Fanny! she was named after an angel in heaven now. She was nearest the bow, and had, through fright, accident, or instinct, got her fore feet over the spar, intended to secure the stalls in front, and when the ship lay over, some booms and masts belonging to the vessel had shifted, and jambing against her legs, had there held her fast; though skinned and torn, no bones were broken, and in this cruel manner her life was saved. On shore a similar accident would have sealed her death-warrant—*but who could give an order for her execution then?* Charley Lee was her doctor, and she recovered sufficiently to be made a pet of. To windward, three of the horses, wonderful to relate, were still on their legs, Platoff, Wellington, and Jackson. *They were rightly named.* They stood next each other, and the farthest forward, near where the hurricane first struck us, and where even now the " ruffian billows" were

> " Curling their monstrous heads, and hanging them,
> With deaf'ning clamours, in the slippery shrouds."

Of the remaining six two were still alive—Julia and poor old Jack—though dreadfully mangled, and lying panting and groaning in a heap with their dead companions : as soon as possible, with the assistance of the crew, Hallam and Stoker got them overboard.

Soaked to the backbone and stupified, I scrambled below; and there a beautiful scene presented itself. There had not been time to batten down the hatchway after my lubbers had made their retreat, and, in consequence, tons of water at a time had been thrown down, to the amazement and dismay of those between decks; and men, boxes, beds, and barrels of oats were floating about in " most admired disorder."

Alarm for my absence had diverted from the mind of my wife all terror for the real danger, and my children were too young to understand it; therefore, my reappearance made all right in an instant " at home," and a " thundering stiff" glass of grog and a dry shirt soon restored me to myself. The companion gangway having been secured, the cabin was all tight and dry, and so were the ladies, I suppose; for on my arrival at Charleston, I found a barrel of bottled Scotch ale, which my friend John Boyde had put up for me, and placed in the cabin for safe keeping, full of empty bottles. Old Jones and his wife were hugging one another in a corner of my state-room; misery loves company, and they had crawled from their own to make up a pleasant party for the other world. Sam Wisdom, my master carpenter, a fellow six feet and a half high, and stout in proportion, was sitting in his shirt on the deck a foot deep in water, like a wringing wet mandarin, blubbering over his children, and persuading the poor little innocent creatures that they were going to be drowned along with "*poor pa*" in a few minutes!

The gale having sensibly abated, all made snug, and the ship hove to, part of the hands were set to bail and swab. Henry Isherwood was discovered coiled away in his berth, forward, half smothered in wet oats, and immediately reported to me as " killed." When the ship was thrown on her beam-ends, some barrels of " feed" for the horses, piled up in midships, had been tumbled over, and one of the heads coming in contact with his, had started, and its contents emptied all over him; and the sea rushing down the gangway at the same time, he, stunned with the blow, believed he was drowned, and, in his own mind, had quietly given up the ghost. " Don't touch me," said he : " oh, don't touch me ; it's all over with me ; my brains are knocked out ;" placing his hand to his head, and looking up most piteously. Sure enough, he appeared in a woful plight : large black streaks, resembling congealed blood, were trickling down his pale face, and I had no doubt but that his scull was split open ; but on examining more closely, we found the clotted blood to be nothing more than diluted molasses-candy, a large cake of which was still fast in his hair. His father had been a confectioner, and inheriting his partiality for sweets, he had provided himself with a large stock for the trip; which had fallen from a ledge where it was " safely stowed," by the side of his berth, and, in his fright, he had slapped his head into it.

The gale continued with more or less violence for five days, the ship hove to all the time. Our captain had had no experience on that coast, and the weather not permitting an observation to be taken, he didn't know which way to run, so patiently awaited the termination of the tempest.

The company became accustomed to " the great contention of the sea and skies;" and Hallam's favourite slut " Molly" having produced a fine litter of pups in the hour of peril, amply repaid that worthy fellow for all his toil and danger. Platoff and Wellington both died before the termination of the blow; but old Jackson stuck it out till we got into smooth water, and then, as Billy Rider said, " Poor creature, he kicked the bucket in comfort, any how."

After mistaking Georgetown light for Charleston, and bumping us half to pieces on Fryingpan Shoals, we succeeded in reaching our destined port, in the " ship Orbit, Captain Fish, fifteen days from Baltimore, with loss of a deckload of horses."

◆

CHAPTER VI.

" But ye ! ye are changed since I saw you last ;
The shadow of ages has round you been cast ;
Ye are changed—ye are changed—and I see not here
What I once saw in the long-vanish'd year."
MRS. HEMANS

" Alas ! poor gentleman,
He look'd not like the ruins of his youth,
But like the ruin of those ruins."—JOHN FORD.

LEAVING the ship, as a climax, thumping on the bar with which Nature has defended a harbour in appearance only excelled by the Bay of Naples, the Cove of Cork, and perhaps equalled by New-York, the custom-house officer politely landed myself and family at the Battery in his boat. As recommended, I took up my abode at the Broad-street House, an excellent hotel, considered the first in the city, and, to my surprise, kept by a gray-headed negro called Jones. I found letters from Simpson, as yet, of course, ignorant of the loss, stating that, depending on the high reputation of the vessel, he had saved the expense of ensurance, which he had undertaken to effect in New-York at a much lower rate than I could get it done in Baltimore. It seemed as if we had struck a vein of bad luck. Another " discontented paper" gave me an account of Kean's having been driven from the stage in that city, and inquiring if, under the circumstances, his engagement had not better be cancelled. The painful responsibility of my position at this juncture is even now irksome to refer to : a large amount of property, owned by various individuals, exclusively at my disposal, and deprived, by distance, of their advice or assistance. To the performers, whose travelling expenses we paid, and a salary every Saturday in the year, I was indebted, in consequence of the length of the journey, nearly three thousand dollars. A very doubtful point if Kean would be

received, and without him, my company, selected exclusively for his support, most unfit to play
even a saving game; the very sinews of attraction torn from the circus, and the *man-end* of my
numerous Centaurs walking about with nothing
but their hands in their pockets, and heavy wages hourly accumulating.

I was seated at the dinner-table, making believe to eat, when a servant handed me a note.
The address " To —— Howell, Esq.," would
have prevented my examining the contents, but
that the man assured me I was the person intended. It ran as follows:

"Colonel M'Clane presents his compliments
to Mr. Howell: through the newspapers has
heard of his loss, and begs he will send some of
his riders to select from his stable as many horses
as he may consider likely to aid him in opening
his circus. He has a number of horses, and
among them some well adapted for the purpose;
and all, or any, are at Mr. Howell's service, for
as long as he may have occasion for them.
" Charleston, Wednesday."

This from a stranger, who did not even know
my name, spoke the current language of the
warm-hearted natives of South Carolina. I, of
course, accepted the offer, and in an hour the
grooms, with much glee, paraded under my window some dozen animals, as beautiful as were

" E'er created, to be awed by man."

Cheered by this unsought-for proof of kindness,
I addressed a commonplace note—for I despise
the usual " *your-petitioner-will-ever-pray*" appli-
cation—to the intendant and wardens, to request,
under the circumstances, a diminution of the
usual sum charged for a license for each establishment; and the next morning I received the
following:

" City Council, February 7, 1826.
" Read a letter from Joe Cowell, requesting
Council to remit a portion of the license impo-
sed on the Theatre and Circus for the ensuing
season.
" Resolved, that the whole of the license be
remitted. Extract from the minutes.
" WILLIAM ROACH,
" Joe Cowell, Esq."   " Clerk of Council.

This was five hundred dollars saved, and,
what was almost as valuable, a farther proof of
a strong public feeling in my favour. I instantly wrote to Simpson to send me Kean,

" With all his imperfections on his head,"

having hope that the interest created by the
drowned horses would gain him leave to swim.
I have an objection to publish a letter intended
by the writer only for the perusal of the party to
whom it is directed. But the following laconic
epistle so much better conveys an insight of the
character of my friend Simpson than any description that I might undertake to write, that I
cannot forbear making it public:

" New-York, February 13, 1826.
" DEAR JOE,
" The Othello reported the ship Orbit on
Charleston bar, with the loss of a deck-load of
horses, before I got your melancholy letter.
God be praised, we can stand it! I didn't ensure, depending, as I said in my former letter,
on the high reputation of the vessel. Keep up
your spirits. I'm sure you will get out of the
scrape somehow. Yours truly, E. SIMPSON.
" What shall we do about Kean?"

This from the largest sufferer, and the most
responsible of the firm, in case of a failure,
speaks volumes in proof of the calm, Atlas-like
support with which, for so many years, he sus-
tained the fortunes of the Park Theatre.

The amateur horses, whose " very failings
set them off," were an attraction. Dr. Porcher,
Mr. Kennedy, and several gentlemen, followed
the example of the colonel, and parties were
made up, by persons who had never before visited a circus, to see how a favourite horse would
behave in the ring. The inefficiency of my theatrical corps was hoodwinked by sympathy for
my misfortunes, and we performed, in consequence, to much better business than we probably should have done had we offered a superior entertainment, without the difficulties attending its preparation.

Every means in my power I artfully used to
smooth the path for Kean's reception; having it
generally understood by the public that on his
success was hinged the hope of redeeming my
fallen fortunes. But still the Eastern papers
were torturing his offence into a *national insult*,
and calling on the chivalry of the South to
avenge the wrongs this immoral play-actor had
heaped upon the country! I had determined
that there should be no time allowed to organize
a plan of hostility, at any rate, by having the
bills already printed, announcing " *Kean's first
appearance this evening*," and intending, no matter when he arrived, that he should perform the
same night; but in this point of policy I was
in part defeated, by the ship Othello, in which
Simpson had advised me he was a passenger,
being reported " below" early on a *Sunday
morning.* I boarded the vessel before she crossed the bar, and found this wreck of better days
feeble in body, and that brilliant, poetic face, a
Raphael might have envied for a study, " sick-
lied o'er with the pale cast of thought." His
first inquiry was, if the public were hostile to
his appearing; and like a child he appealed to
me: " Cowell, for God's sake — by the ties of
old fellowship and countrymen—I entreat you
not to let me play, if you think the audience
will not receive me. I have not strength of
mind or body — look how I'm changed since
you saw me last—to endure a continuance of the
persecutions I have already endured, and I believe a repetition of them would kill me on the
spot."

I, of course, encouraged him to hope all would
go well; but on landing from the boat, some
twenty idlers collected, and as we turned from
the wharf, hissed and groaned; the well-known,
hateful sound seemed to enter his very soul, and
looking up in my face, with " God help me !"
quivering on his parted lips, he clung to my arm,
as if for succour, not support. I assured him
the disapprobation was meant for an officer of
the customs, in whose boat we had landed, who
was objectionable to the people; and doubting,
yet hoping it was true, I conducted him to my
house next to the theatre, which had been left
handsomely furnished by the improvident Gilfert, and which I had hired for the season.

He passed the day with me and some new-
found friends, and made himself, as he always
could when he thought proper, most agreeable.
" *The sweetest morsel of the night we left unpick-
ed*," and early in the evening I conducted him to
his quarters which I had prepared for him at
Jones's. He was delighted with his black landlord, and astonished to find that a negro could

amass a fortune, and possess all the rational advantages of a well-behaved white man, in the same situation of life, in a slave state. His notions of slavery had more than likely been altogether formed by acting in the opera of Paul and Virginia.

Though most comfortably lodged, he assured me the next day he had never closed his eyes; his anxiety had brought alone such rest

> " As wretches have o'er night
> Who wait for execution in the morn."

What would be the night's event, **who** could tell? The public is a hard riddle to find out, but when you do happen to hit upon it, how simple it is. Fifty friends gave fifty different opinions, each with an "*if*," so that each might after say, " There, I told you so." For my own part, I, of course, most earnestly desired his success, and therefore honestly believed his genius would triumph.

Not a place was taken, but the house was filled soon after the doors were opened. Before it was uncomfortably crowded, I stopped the sale of tickets, for nothing puts an auditor so soon out of humour as a disagreeable seat.

Kean had set his "soul and body on the action both," and I never saw him play better. At his entrance, all was " hushed as midnight"—a quiet so profound "that the blind mole might not hear a footfall;" and this *awful attention* continued during the whole performance, whenever he was on the stage; and when the curtain fell, some few "amazed spectators hummed applause." *There was but one lady in the whole house!* the wife of the district attorney, and a warm friend to the drama. *Woman, in thy purity, how powerful thou art!* The presence of this *one* acted like a charm. She sat alone, the beauteous representative of the moral courage of her sex, and awed to respectful silence the predetermined turbulence of twelve hundred men!

Poor Kean was in ecstasies at his escape. The next morning nearly all the places were secured for Wednesday, and a splendid houseful of ladies, as well as gentlemen, assembled to witness his master-piece, Othello. At his entrance, some ill-advised applause was instantly drowned in a shower of hisses; and in the early portion of the play, several sudden expressions of disapprobation occurred; and in the third act, at nearly the end of his fine scene with Iago, the storm so long pent up burst forth; some oranges, thrown on the stage, appeared to be the signal for a general tumult

> " Of roaring, shrieking, howling,
> With strange and several noises,"

in the midst of which I had the curtain lowered, opened the stage door, and presented myself to the audience. It was my intention to have made an appeal to their indulgence on my own account; but remembering

> " The silence, often, of pure innocence
> Persuades when speaking fails,"

I assumed as innocent an appearance as I knew how, proceeded quietly and slowly to pick up the atoms of oranges and apples, looked unutterable things, and once

> " *I* lifted up *my* head, and did address
> *Myself* to motion, like as *I* would speak ;
> But even then—"

I bowed myself across the stage and departed, amid thunders of applause! and, before it had subsided, thrust Kean on with Desdemona, who,

" As a child, would go by my direction ;"

and the same people who, a minute before, were pelting him with rubbish, rose on their seats, and with "caps, hands, and tongues, applauded to the clouds," and the play proceeded with undisputed approbation!! At the end, Kean was loudly called for; but, from experience, knowing that for him to open his mouth, filled with language of his own, would probably ruin all, I pleaded his exhaustion as an excuse for his making me the means to express the grateful sense he had of their kindness, and tendered his respectful acknowledgments.

The next day some of the first men in the city left him their cards; dinner-parties were made expressly for him; carriages were proffered for his use; the rarities of the season or climate poured in upon him; and the numerous attentions shown him by the kind, yet aristocratic inhabitants of Charleston, equalled, and were more gratifying to his feelings, than the hollow-hearted homage paid to him by a crowd of flatterers in the sunshine of his career. He received fifty pounds sterling per night: that is, two hundred and twenty-two dollars and twenty-two cents; but our profits, notwithstanding, went far towards redeeming the pecuniary part of our losses.

I had some really talented people in my employ; but, from the want of numbers, many of my grooms and riders had to be trusted with subordinate characters, and their Shaksperian blunders were actually serviceable in keeping the audience in good humour. Charley Lee— the father of the now juvenile rival to Ellsler— a most valuable creature in a stable, and excellent in a monkey, performed one of the officers in King Lear, and in reply to Kean's saying,

> " I killed the slave : did I not, fellow ?"

answered, in his *natty* manner,

> " 'Tis true, my lord ! see where the good king
> Has slew'd two on 'em !"

My *king* was an ignorant, dissipated brute, whom I had, unfortunately, engaged on his own recommendation. His incapacity was most vexatious, but sometimes very droll. As Duncan, where Lady Macbeth enters to receive him at the Castle, instead of a speech of some four or five lines, he merely said, "Ah! here's the hostess! we thank you for your trouble." And after her speech, in lieu of continuing the dialogue, in a pompous but familiar manner he said, "Where's Cawder? Is he not home yet? Well, no matter; we'll sleep with you to-night. Give me your hand; walk in, madam; we intend to be very particular with you;" and off he went, with a good laugh at his heels. His King, in Hamlet, could not be described. In the last scene, after mixing up "the kettles and the trumpets, the cannons, the thunder, and the heavens," in a most ludicrous manner, he ended with, "Stop a minute! give me the cup; here's your good health! Come, Hamlet, take a drink."

The easy, tavern-style in which this was said was too much for Kean's gravity; the audience caught the laugh from him, and the curtain went down, as it ought to do, at the termination of a very broad farce; but it ended his career with me. The next day I gave him two weeks' salary, paid his passage to New-York, and have never seen the poor devil since.

Kean was so delighted with the place and the people that he determined to remain until the season was concluded. A friend gave him the use of a country house on Sullivan's Island—a most romantic sandbank in the centre of the harbour. With two Newfoundland dogs of mine, a pet deer, and the *Fanny mare*, he was "alone in his glory;" for it was literally uninhabited in the winter, with the exception of a few soldiers in the fort. He played Bertram for my benefit, on the last night, to the largest amount then ever received at the Charleston Theatre. He took his passage with me in the ship Saluda, and with

"Calm seas, auspicious gales, and sail so expeditious,"

that in three days, recruited in mind and body, he arrived at New-York, "in the merry month of May," 1826.

Poor Kean! I never more saw him act; and though, for years after, his brightness flickered at intervals on the gloomy path of the declining drama, it never blazed again with its uniform, unequalled brilliancy. His neglected early life had grafted habits on his nature totally at variance with his pure poetic taste, and giant-like strength of admiration of all that was great and noble in art, and made him the contradictory, and, at times, objectionable creature which, in general, he is so exclusively described. The truth of the adage in his case was painfully proved : *he knew not who was his father.* When all the thinking world were awe-struck in contemplating his genius, several were named as having a title to that honour, and among them the late Duke of Norfolk; and Kean was weak enough to appear proud of this parental appropriation. A Mrs. Carey, who was an inferior actress at one of the minor theatres, claimed him as her son; and whether he believed her to be his mother or not, he supported her and her daughter for years.

The startling effect of his style of acting, boldly and suddenly setting at defiance the law and decorum of the long-accustomed school of which a Siddons and a Kemble were the models, cannot be conceived at this day, where every aspirant to dramatic fame totters in the path his genius boldly trod, and "drags at each remove a lengthening chain;" for, though he left behind no parallel to his excellence, he created a host of imitators, down to the third and fourth generation. The novelty of his manner may be understood by the following anecdote, which he told me himself. At his first rehearsal at Drury Lane, "steeped in poverty to the very lips," wrapped in an old, rough greatcoat—though it was warm weather—and his appearance altogether bespeaking his estate, several of the well-clothed and well-fed minions of the drama did not condescend to rehearse with him at all; and those who did, refused to deviate from the accustomed business of the stage, which, right or wrong, they had followed for years, and turned into unconcealed ridicule his temerity in presuming to suggest any alteration of the acknowledged laws. Among others, he particularly named De Camp—he, poor fellow, long since died of a dysentery, mixed up with old age and abject poverty, in Texas! He eloquently, yet playfully, described the laceration of his feelings at hearing his peculiarities of voice imitated behind the scenes, accompanied by

"The loud laugh, that speaks the vacant mind."

Amid these "outward and visible signs" of contempt for his talent, old Miss Tidswell, who had played small characters in the theatre since Garrick's time, I believe, and who afterward called herself his aunt, poked him in the back with her umbrella "to entreat listening," beckoned him to the wing, and petitioned him not to persevere in playing : explaining, that all the *actors* and good judges were laughing at him; and pointing out to him the horrible disgrace of his inevitably being pelted from the stage *would be to her,* as she had acknowledged him as a distant relation, and introduced him as such to some performers of her own class in the second green-room!!

Wounded in spirit, he left the theatre, half inclined to follow her advice; not in consequence of any doubt in his own mind of his capacity—for true talent is always self-informed—but to shrink from the dirty annoyances attending its assertion. But, fortunately, he met at the door an old comrade, from some country theatre, to whom he unburdened his "o'er-fraught heart," and the poor disciple of Thespis being in possession of the extraordinary sum of five shillings, Kean accompanied him to a tavern. After a good dinner, a pot of porter, and the warm encouragement of his ragged but sincere friend, he went to the theatre, desperate in his determination to succeed; played Shylock to a very indifferent house, but sealed his fame forever.

CHAPTER VII.

"The first tragedians found that serious style
Too grave for their uncultivated age,
And so brought wild and naked satyrs in
(Whose motions, words, and shape were all a farce)
As oft as decency would give them leave ;
Because the mad, ungovernable rout,
Full of confusion and the fumes of wine,
Loved such variety and antic tricks."

Roscommon's Horace:

Booth, though not a servile imitator of Kean, founded his manner exclusively on his style. He played precisely the same round of characters, dressed them exactly in the same costume, and, being naturally like him in appearance, the similitude was extraordinary. Kean's transcendent genius had so dazzled the public taste, that his defects of voice and figure, "by the aid of use," were actually considered necessary attributes, and Booth possessed the same advantages. Old Dowton morosely said, when Kean first appeared, "God renounce me! 'tis only necessary nowadays to be under four feet high, have bandy legs, and a hoarseness, and, mince my liver! but you'll be thought a great tragedian."

Soon after Booth's arrival in this country, he declared his intention of becoming a citizen, and purchased a small farm, if it might so be called, near the village of Belle-air, in Maryland—the only steril section of land I know of in the whole state; deposited his wife and family in a log cabin, and shone himself, periodically, as a star of the first magnitude through the theatrical hemisphere. Scrupulously avoiding all ostentatious display, he adopted the reverse extreme: attired in a conspicuously plebeian garb, he would take up his quarters at some humble tavern or obscure boarding-house; and when he visited Baltimore (being near his home), he usually attended the market with some vegetables, a load of hay, or sat with a calf, tied by the leg, till time to rehearse "Richard the Third." His simple Republican deportment, well spiced, when occasion served, with "the jolly dog" and "the good fellow," who was "not too proud" to sing

"Billy Taylor" in a beerhouse, or give you a taste of his quality in an oyster-cellar, rendered him most popular with the multitude; a scholar and a linguist, he was an intelligent listener to the pothouse pedant, and could "drink with any tinker in his own language;" carefully concealing any advantages he possessed above the capacity of his companions, his acquirements were lauded and admitted: for it is the characteristic of the nation, as I have read it, sometimes to allow a foreigner to be equal, but never superior in anything. This probably *accidental* mode of conduct, naturally enough, compared with his prototype Kean's arbitrary offences, aided by Booth's undisputed talent, for years caused him to be greatly followed and admired.

His father, who was a devotee to the doctrines, civil and religious, which clogged with blood the wings of liberty during the French Revolution, named him Junius Brutus, as a type of the stern Republican character he hoped his son would achieve; and with an excellent education mixed the seeds of those dogmas which, no matter how gilded o'er by the poetic imaginings of a Voltaire, a Byron, or a Shelley, are to a mind early tutored to adopt them, and undefended by Christianity, dangerous to the happiness of the social compact, and fatal to the ties with which conscience should bind the intercourse with our fellow-man.

It is a dreadful mischance to be early cast upon the world without a guide or protector; but worse, far worse, to have our way of life pointed out by those in whose direction nature tells us to believe, and pursue, at their instigation, a path through this world's pilgrimage at which our young, pure feeling hesitates at the outset, and experience proves leads to a death-bed divested of hope beyond the grave.

Kean's irregularities were coarse and brutal, but their ill effects recoiled exclusively upon himself; Booth's involved the destiny of those nearest and dearest; for years he sheltered himself from their consequences by assuming madness; and the long practice of this periodical "antic disposition," like Hamlet's, ended in its being, I believe, partially the fact. In one of his trips to New-Orleans, two itinerant preachers were on the same boat, whose zeal in distributing tracts, and obtrusive interference with the usual amusements on a steamer, made them objectionable to all, but particularly to Booth, and he invented the following severe scheme of retaliation. He had a large sum of money about him, and, when all were asleep in bed, he placed his pocket-book, with a portion of the notes, under the mattress of one of the parsons, and the balance, with some papers easily described, in the pocket of the other. Early in the morning, before the clergymen were up, he loudly proclaimed his loss, and a general search was ordered by the captain, to which all cheerfully submitted; when the property was found, the astonishment of all could only be equalled by the supposed culprits themselves. In vain their protestations of innocence; the boat was landed, and they, according to "Lynch law," were to receive a severe flagellation, and then oe left in the wilderness. This, of course, Booth could not permit, and he explained the joke he had intended, without dreaming of the consequences.

The indignation of the passengers, influenced by their excited feelings, might fearfully have turned the direction of their revenge, but that

"everybody knew Mr. Booth was an oddity," and "at times supposed to be insane." A sketch of his numerous eccentricities would alone fill a volume; but, being generally divested of wit or humour, and, for the most part, mischievous in their character, an account of them would be painful to either write or read. I don't mean to assert that his having been called after the pattern of severe justice, who assumed the mask of folly in the cause of virtue, had any influence on the conduct of Booth; but baptizing children as if to designate their character is a nonsensical custom, and ought to be condemned. There are enough good, homely Christian names, in all conscience, to satisfy the varied tastes of the most fastidious, and this deviation from the beaten track to please the doting folly of a mother, or the political prejudices of a father, is often, in after life, a positive affliction to the bearer; for if they equal, in mind or station, their illustrious namesakes, the glory they achieve is liable to be passed to the credit of their predecessors; and should their talent, appearance, or opinion be at variance with their title, it will often place them in a painful or ridiculous position. Imagine a politician writing a long tirade against "removing the deposites," and then being obliged to sign himself "Andrew Jackson ——;" or "Apollo," a knife-grinder, with a hump at his back; or "Diogenes" apprenticed to a washing-tub maker. I feel positively obliged to my godfathers and godmothers for having unostentatiously named me after the amiable, ragged-coated, modest Joseph; and the etymology of the designation I have been fortunate enough to prove the appropriateness of, by being *already* the father and grandfather, *to a certainty*, of children in two quarters of the world, at any rate. When Bonaparte was First Consul, an honest old Church and King parson, at Manchester, in England, who was wearied with the frequency of the name of the future emperor being claimed for a child born to be a weaver or spinner, at length determined to christen no more so ridiculously; and upon inquiring the name intended for the next infant presented, was answered, as usual,

"Napoleon."

"In the name," &c., says the clergyman, "I baptize thee John."

"John!" says the astonished father; "I tell'd thee to call the lad Napoleon."

"Pooh, pooh, nonsense!" says the parson; "I have christened him John. Take him away, and call him what you like." I wish all parsons would do the same.

The yellow fever gave so broad a hint as to the necessity of buildings being prepared in the upper sections of the city, that New-York increased in that direction with a rapidity that was truly astonishing. A very superior theatre was erected on the site of the old Bull's Head Tavern in the Bowery, a short time before considered out of town, and used as the cattle mart. The control was placed in the hands of Charles Gilfert, a highly-accomplished German, whose chief ambition was to manage a theatre on an extensive scale, and be considered "*more knave than fool*," in both of which desires he was fully gratified; for the establishment given to him to conduct infinitely exceeded in its extent and appointments any then on the continent, and everybody agreed he was a consummate rogue. Thoughtless, extravagant, and unprincipled as to the means used to obtain on the instant his real or imaginary wants in his private station, he carried with him the same reckless spirit to control the fortunes of others. Large inducements were held out to the various members of the profession to join the concern, and an excellent, but very costly, company was engaged; and though the overflowing houses attracted by the newness, and, perhaps, superiority of the entertainments, were ruinous to the Park, the expenditure quite equalled the receipts. Barrett was the stage-manager; and though at that time not distinguished by the title of " Gentleman George," he was as deserving of the appellation then as now. But if one had been selected which would have more clearly conveyed the idea of an inconsiderately liberal, kind-hearted man, it would better have described his intrinsic character. As an actor in smart, impudent servants, eccentric parts, bordering on caricature, and light comedy, where the claims to the gentleman do not exceed those required for Corinthian Tom, he is excellent. He has attempted to perform some old men lately, in consequence, I suppose, of his whiskers getting gray; but, if he'll take my advice, he'd better dye them, and stick to his old line of business: six feet four is too tall to fit the common run of elderly gentlemen nowadays. He went to England a few years since, and very imprudently made his appearance at Drury Lane as Puff, in the " Critic," a character requiring a long acquaintance with both the *actors* and *audience* to be made effective; the innocent jokes, at the expense of either, always introduced, and the principal means of rendering the character amusing, if called in aid by a perfect stranger, would either be not noticed at all, or considered a liberty. According to Bunn's *sore-minded* book, the performance was a failure, which he merely mentions in proof of the general inability of the Americans to become actors; but for his particular information I beg to state that George Barrett was born in England, of English parents, though he arrived in this country when a boy; and, therefore, his incapacity, according to Bunn's judgment, must be " all owing to the climate," as poor Watkinson said when he was dying, in consequence of drinking too much brandy-and-water.

For years the drama had been generally under the control of foreigners, and the better class of actors were, as I have before observed, exclusively English; but the increase of theatres extending the inducements to make the stage a profession, a number of young Americans became candidates for fame and fortune in that hitherto European monopoly. Of course, they commenced as Keans and Booths; for it is the marked character of the nation to begin at the top of everything, and the energies of the people increase in proportion to the difficulty or danger. In arts or arms, they might with propriety adopt as a motto, individually, " What man dare, I dare." Foremost amid a host of tyros stood Edwin Forrest. He had had the advantage of some useful practice, and had already achieved a trifling reputation in the South and West, to which almost "undiscovered country" in that day but few foreigners had dared to venture. He possessed a fine, untaught face, and good, manly figure, and, though unpolished in his deportment, his manners were frank and honest, and his uncultivated taste, speaking the language of truth and Nature, could be readily understood; and yet so intrinsically superior to the minds of the class of persons among whom his fortunes had thrown him, that he could call to his aid requisites well calculated to make both friends and admirers. Early left to the care of a widowed mother, her fond indulgence or painful necessities had deprived him of an education even equal to his peers. This stumbling-block to his success he most keenly felt. With praiseworthy ambition, and the means his advancing fortunes furnished, with unwearied industry he laboured to remove this obstacle in his path to fame, and may now compare in acquirements with those whose early life was cradled in ease, and learning made a toy. Having had an opportunity of witnessing his unschooled efforts, I strongly urged his engagement at the Park; but, while the dollars and cents were under consideration, Gilfert secured the prize, and, cunningly enlisting the natural national prejudices of the Americans in the cause, Forrest filled the coffers of the Bowery treasury, and received the unthinking, overwrought, enthusiastic admiration of his countrymen, which, after years of unceasing study and practice, he now so justly merits from all admirers of genuine talent.

The destruction of the Bowery Theatre by fire, to such a mind as Gilfert's, seemed only to increase his energies; and in an unprecedented short space of time—sixty days—it was rebuilt and opened, even with increased magnificence. Agents had been despatched to Europe for talent of every description, and the first good theatrical orchestra ever brought to America Gilfert could boast of having congregated. William Chapman, an excellent comedian, was engaged, and George Holland, inimitable in the small list of characters he undertook, proved a deserved attraction, while Forrest, if possible, increased in public estimation. A very capable man, by the name of Harby, was employed, at a handsome salary, to " write up" the merits of the theatre, and such members of the company as the interest of the management desired to be advanced. This, being the first introduction of the system of forestalling, or, rather, directing public opinion, had a powerful effect; and the avidity with which a large class of persons, in all countries, swallow, and implicitly believe what they read in a newspaper, is truly and quaintly enough described by Mopsa, in the " Winter's Tale:" " I love a ballad in print a' life, for then we are sure they are true." All these circumstances combined, and the theatrical population of New-York not being then equal to the support of more than one establishment of the kind, the tide of opinion sat full in favour of the Bowery, while the Park was trembling on the brink of ruin.

In defiance of the somewhat prudish character of the Americans at

" That blushing time,
When modesty was scarcely held a crime,"

Gilfert, whose moral feelings never interfered with his interests, introduced a troupe of French dancers. The experiment was considered a dangerous one; and though all, at the onset, were loud in their denunciation of the immodest exhibition, all crowded to witness it. By comparison with what I had seen in Europe, they were of the fourth or fifth class in the way of talent; and the exposure of the persons of the females, unexcused by elegance and grace, and the ribald remarks indulged in aloud, at the close of every *pirouette*, by the gross-minded portion of the audience, rendered the performance most disgusting to the feelings of the virtuous and refined; while the poor half-undressed supernumerary women, made, for the first time in their lives, to stand upon one leg, bashfully tottering, and looking as foolish, and about as graceful, as a plucked goose in the same position, were pitiably laughable.

This was the first relish given to that false taste which has taken the place of the wholesome mental food furnished by the legitimate drama; and,

> "As if excess of appetite had grown
> By what it fed on,"

"dancers, mimics, mummers" have usurped the claims of poetry and morality, and brought the stage to its present degraded position.

Among the corps was Celeste, then very young and beautiful, and though not in the first rank, there was a native grace and modesty in her manner, by comparison with those by whom she was surrounded, which gained her many admirers. A young man by the name of Elliot, who had nearly squandered a handsome fortune left him by his father, who had been a livery-stable keeper in Baltimore, became enamoured, and after a short courtship, if it might so be called—for, as she could not understand English, and he could not speak French, recourse was had to an interpreter, to say the usual soft things, which, Heaven be praised, I never had occasion to trust any one to say for me—they became man and wife; and for years she maintained the very first reputation in her line, and supported her husband in affluence. Perhaps prejudiced by placing her estimable private deportment in the scale with her acknowledged talent, and my ignorance of the art, may cause me to think she has never been excelled, for, to my untutored taste,

> "An antelope,
> In the suspended impulse of its lightness,
> Were less ethereally light. The brightness
> Of her divinest presence trembles through
> Her limbs, as, underneath a cloud of dew,
> Imbodied in the windless heaven of June,
> Amid the splendour-winged stars, the moon
> Burns inextinguishably beautiful."—SHELLEY.

CHAPTER VIII.

> "When, in this vale of years, I backward look,
> And miss such numbers—numbers, too, of such,
> Firmer in health, and greener in their age,
> And stricter on their guard, and better far
> To play life's subtle game—I scarce believe
> I still survive."—*Night Thoughts*.

I HAVE already said that my company was extensive; and for talent, in many instances it could compete with the best on the Continent. William B. Jones and his lady, omitting their just claims to excellence on the stage, by their private worth alone were ornaments to any establishment. I have just heard of the death of my old friend and companion. I am not one of the crying sort, but the paper got blotted while placing Young's thought upon it, which very appropriately came to my mind on hearing the sad news. Roberts, too, gone long ago, will be remembered by many a lover of fun, as a most chaste and capital comedian. And my ladies! for beauty, utility, in fact, for every decoration but docility, would not suffer by comparison even with our magnificent stud of horses.

Mrs. Tatnall, Mrs. Williams, Mrs. and Miss Pelby, Mrs. and Miss Virginia Monier, Mrs. Parker, and the lovely Mrs. Robertson—now Mrs. Watkins Burroughs—can never be forgotten by the admirers of the

> "Last and best
> Of all God's works!'"

But eighteen or twenty years make an awful alteration in all such matters. Poor Mrs. Tatnall! she died at Texas a short time since—that *last resource* for

> "Talent struggling with despair and death!"

Many years gone by, I strongly recommended her to Simpson, to play the Lady Macbeths, and other would-be queens, with Cooper; he turned up his nose at my circus heroine then, but not long after she was a most successful *star* in such characters at all the principal theatres, and in many of them she was eminent. A comparison with her personation of Masseroni, in the melodrame called the Brigand, would make even James Wallack and

> "All the *stars*
> Hide their diminished heads."

She was really an excellent general actress, a warm-hearted friend, affectionate mother, and, I have no doubt, a most desirable wife. She had but one failing that I know of, if it could so be called, for even that "leaned to virtue's side," and that was an extraordinary propensity to get married every now and then; allowing for the difference of sex and position in society, Henry the Eighth was "*no wheres,*" as Stephen Price would say, in comparison with her conjugal propensities. She was the lawfully-wedded wife of five husbands to my certain knowledge, three of them all alive at the same time, and two, I believe, not dead yet. But for the burying part of the business, she might have sung with feeling Colman's Irish song:

> "To the priest says I, 'Father O'Casey, dear! don't my
>   weddings and funerals plase ye, dear?'
> Says he, 'Ye bla'guard, betwixt church and churchyard
>   you never will let me be aisy, dear!'"

Her maiden name was Pritchard, and, as far as I know, her first spouse was the Mr. Pemberton who some years since played Virginius with some success in London; he was acknowledged to be a gentleman of education and talent, though somewhat eccentric in his mode of displaying his acquirements; from him she was separated, and married Tatnall, one of the earliest American equestrians; from him she was separated, and, undismayed by his notoriously cruel conduct—for Tatnall treated his wife very nearly in the same way he did his horse—she married Hartwig, a very inferior actor, and a widower, in consequence of his first wife having poisoned herself three months before; her separating from him very speedily caused little surprise, and she married Hosack, a nephew of the celebrated physician of that name in New-York, and, by the desire of his family, resumed her own of Pritchard *in the playbills*. Hosack had a small annuity, and was a very worthy young man; they had two or three children, and appeared to live most happily together, but death interfered with that arrangement, and shortly afterward she became the wife of Riley; he claimed the author of the "Itinerant" as his father, and, I am told, *had been* a good actor, and a respectable man. This connubial career soon came to an end, and she left him to close his wanderings and his eyes in the hospital at St. Louis. I doubt much if she ever had an offer of marriage since, for I don't believe she had the heart to refuse one; and in the brief notice of her demise in a Texas paper, "no afflicted husband" was named "to bewail her loss," which, in the familiar idiom of that country, might, under all the circumstances, be called "*d— hard luck.*"

It couldn't be expected that during the increase of successful theatrical establishments, the circus should remain quietly and alone in possession of the field. A large building was erected in Grand-street, New-York, and, like everything new, for a time had its supporters; and though, through bad management, and its then out-of-the-way situation, it was ultimately a failure, it interfered for a time sensibly with our receipts. The loss, too, of the horses was severely felt; for though their place was supplied as regarded numbers, those that were gone had each been worth the price of admission merely to look at, and while they were alive, we could defy any competition "that stood upon four legs."

Mr. Sandford, now General Sandford, who had married Mrs. Holman the singer, and the widow of the well-known old actor of that name, erected a very extensive amphitheatre within pistol-shot of our encampment, and called it, as everything was called at that time that wanted a name, from an oyster-cellar to an omnibus, Lafayette. With every horse that could be purchased with a long tail and a spot in its neighbourhood, a few runaway rascals of ours, with Tatnall at their head, and some nothing-better-to-do boys, who had tumbled into the notice of the amateur manager, outside of our stable on a pile of straw, but whose "vaulting ambition" has long since rendered them superior in gymnastic talent to any that can be produced in Europe, he commenced his campaign with Watkins Burroughs, from the Surry and Adelphi Theatre, to conduct the dramatic department; and by forcing us to an expensive competition, and, at the same time, drawing off a portion of our audience, this powerful opposition took largely from our former profits, though it ultimately brought the proprietor to a state of bankruptcy— was closed in a year or two, burned down, and never rebuilt.

Price, who visited London every year, sent me periodically all the come-at-able talent, humbug, or nonsense to which the English show-shop had given a name, or that he knew from experience would suit the wonder-loving public here. Hunter proved an immense attraction; he was the first rider in this country who dexterously and fearlessly went through all the usual antics on the bare back of the horse, instead of on the oldfashioned flat saddle, the size of a sideboard.

Stoker, a rope-vaulter, was another wonder; he, among a variety of liberties he took with himself, used to hang by the neck, not till he was dead, but just long enough to give his audience reason to believe that he might be; and this faithful imitation of the last agonies of a malefactor, in a spangled jacket, drew together, nightly, quite as large a crowd as a public execution always does. Fortunately for the management, several ladies fainted the first night he appeared; and this fact being named in some of the papers, and the exhibition described as most shocking to witness, and certain on some night, when least expected, to cause the death of the performer, the boxes were always filled with the fair sex whenever the feat was advertised. In short, every novelty that money could procure, *tact* invent, or unwearied industry produce, to excite the creative appetite of curiosity, was served up in unceasing variety. Every spectacle "*got up*" had no rival but its predecessor, and even at this day it is admitted that the Cataract of the Ganges, and other gorgeous affairs of the sort, have never been excelled in splendour and effect.

Mine was a genuine Democratic government: the man who swept the stable received quite as much courtesy from me as he who could vault over all the horses in it, and balance the broom on his nose into the bargain. I, in consequence, had a very high reputation for even-handed justice, and, " against my own inclining," was chosen arbiter in all the private and domestic quarrels and troubles, and the causes of either were sometimes very amusing.

Most of my performers, both horse and foot, had a claim to some share, large or small, of the receipts of a house as a benefit in each season; but to avoid trouble to others, and save them from the very common folly of selecting some piece likely to keep money out of the treasury, for the sake of playing a part they are particularly unfitted for, I always controlled the nature of the performance.

The benefits, on one occasion, came on during the very successful run of El Hyder, and, of course, I would not have its career interrupted. Mrs. Tatnall played Harry Clifton — ay, and played it better than anybody ever did or could play it. Mrs. Williams, who was exclusively an equestrian, when her night came, thought it would be an attraction for her to undertake the part, and I gave my consent that she should show her versatility, to the great annoyance of Mrs. Tatnall. Mrs. Pelby, in turn, claimed the like indulgence on her benefit, and, in common justice, she had as good a right as Mrs. Williams to amuse herself, at any rate, and I advertised her for the character. Mrs. Tatnall was outrageous at this accumulated infringement of her rights, and vowed to be signally revenged. The part is really an excellent one, and any *circus lady* might be justified in even using more than " wild and windy words" to maintain the possession of it. A dashing young midshipman, after the true Saddler's-Wells model, in white tights, fighting broad-sword combats to no particular tune, *audante,* with three or four giant-like assassins at a time; shouting for "*liberty!*" at the end of every speech, and a " dam'me" at the end of every line, and surrounded by blue-fire and piebald horses in the last scene, is not to be sneezed at. I was the old sailor, and quite as unlike a sailor as my master, and, of course, quite as effective.

While the performance was proceeding, I observed Mrs. Pelby to be particularly restless and odd in her deportment, standing sometimes upon one leg, then balancing herself on the other, rubbing the upper ends of them together, thumping herself with her cocked-hat in all sorts of places, twitching her beautiful face about as children sometimes do in the green-gooseberry season, and at the end of every highly-relished Republican sentiment whispering such disjointed sentences as, "I can't bear it!" "What shall I do?" "Good Heaven! it's dreadful!" "I shall certainly go mad!" "I must pull them off!" and bang would go the cocked-hat against the skirts of her coat, both before and behind, with her fingers extended as if itching for the luxury of an uncontrolled scratch. During a pause, in a confidential manner and imploring accent, she said to me, "Oh! I am in torture; for Heaven's sake, make an act at the end of this scene. You don't know what I suffer; I must change them or I shall die. That beast, Mrs. Tatnall, must have put *cow-itch* in my pantaloons!"

And so, no doubt, she had—"to what extremes may not a woman's vengeance lead!" but the supposed culprit strongly denied all knowledge of the ticklish transgression, and very truly said "that no lady could be capable of anything half so villanous." I, and everybody else, believed her to be the *irritator*, but as there was no law, even of my own making, applicable to the offence, I was glad she did not confess. The usual remedies, whatever they are, were applied, and in a pair of blue trousers, a little too large in one place and not big enough in another, Mrs. Pelby finished the part without any farther apparent titillation.

Though my income was large, my outlay was on the same scale; wherever I went, Mrs. Cowell and my younger children went; and in that day, travelling, with all the comfort that could be bought, was a very costly amusement, and living at the principal hotels, with private parlours and other privileges, beyond a joke to pay for.

It is not of the least consequence in this country what a man's profession may be; he obtains a station, and is respected in society, not according to *how* he makes money, but according to how *much* he makes; wealth is the aristocracy of the land, and a *poor gentleman* an incomprehensible character to the million. In my doubtful position —a circus manager—there was no proof so convincing of my being the possessor of wealth, and, therefore, having a claim to consideration, as by lavishly squandering it away. My liberality got quite as much applause as my comic songs; and though the interests of the sleeping partners in the concern were advanced at my expense, at the end of three years of intense toil and annoyance, I awoke to the consciousness that if I had remained in New-York and followed my profession, of which I was then proud, I should have been quite as well, if not better off. All I had gained by my management was a high reputation, which continued success in any pursuit is sure to obtain. I once heard a man who had just lost his last stake at *roulette*, a game which sets all calculation at defiance, say to another, who was staring with astonishment at winning, thrice in succession, thirty-six times the amount of his bet,

"Ah! I wish I understood the thing as well as you do—I'd make a fortune at it."

Warren and Wood, who for years had been associated as managers of the Philadelphia, Baltimore, and Washington Theatres, at about this period dissolved partnership, and Warren, who by purchase had become the sole director, made me an offer of a very handsome salary to undertake the acting management, which hitherto had been Mr. Wood's department. I had long since selected Philadelphia as my *home*, though I could only enjoy the pleasures of one three months in the year; this arrangement, therefore, held out domestic inducements that jumped well with my humour, and at the latter end of 1826 I took the reins of government at the Chestnut-street Theatre.

My seceding from the circus, I was pleased to find, met with less opposition from the proprietors than I had anticipated. My income was a large item saved in the general expenditure, and Dinneford, who had been some time in my employ, and Blythe, the riding-master, with Simpson to advise and control, they had a right to believe would economically, yet amply, supply my place.

My new company, if not eminent for talent in every department, was highly respectable; and having been trained by my predecessor Wood, a gentleman and a man of taste, to submit with cheerfulness to the wholesome subordination on which a well-conducted theatre so much depends, the direction was divested of its proverbial annoyances, and the season proving *profitable beyond all precedent*, I have reason to recur to this period of my life with both pride and pleasure.

Wood and his lady still continued members of the company. He was a most mechanically correct actor, and when his great peculiarities happened to exactly *fit a character*, which in the extensive range he allotted to himself was often the case, he might be considered excellent by those who had long been acquainted with his style; but the singularity of his voice, to a strange auditor, took largely from the pleasure his sensible delivery demanded. There was a kind of *comic pathos* in its two distinct tones, which, though it did not assist a laugh where it should occur, was very apt to cause one in the wrong place. Mrs. Wood was a sterling actress, indebted to nature for a very superior mind, and then—the account was closed. They were both enthusiasts in their art, and most ardent admirers of each other's talent; and in parts they frequently played together, such as Mrs. Haller and the Stranger, they infused so much reality into the scene, that they literally appropriated all the sorrow to themselves; positive sobs and tears by turns, at each other's plaints and penitence, would so interfere with and divert the sympathies of the audience, as to drown all recollection of the imaginary characters in pity for the sufferings of Billy Wood and his wife.

Warren was highly esteemed as a man, and admired as an actor. He had obtained a great reputation as Falstaff, which character his bulk admirably adapted him to represent; and, as far as "unbuttoning after supper, and sleeping on benches after noon," there was an extraordinary similarity in his habits, and the "cause that wit is in other men." Poor Warren was a man of wealth at the time I am now speaking of, but he unfortunately outlived his fortunes.

Jefferson was the low-comedian, and had been for more than five-and-twenty years! Of course, he was a most overwhelming favourite, though at this time drops of pity for fast-coming signs of age and infirmity began to be freely sprinkled with the approbation long habit, more than enthusiasm, now elicited.

I am told "Mr. Jefferson was a native of London, and arrived at Boston, at the age of nineteen, as a member of Powell's theatrical company, in the year 1795."

Literally born on the stage, he brought with him to this country the experience of age with all the energy of youth, and, in the then infant state of the drama, his superior talent, adorned by his most exemplary private deportment, gave him lasting claims to the respect and gratitude both of the members of the profession and its admirers. And perhaps on some such imaginary reed he placed too much dependance; for the whole range of the drama cannot probably furnish a more painful yet perfect example of the mutability of theatrical popularity than Joseph Jefferson.

When Warren left the management, "younger, not better," actors were brought in competition with the veteran; and the same audience that had actually grown up laughing at him alone—as if they had been mistaken in his talent all this time—suddenly turned their smiles on foreign faces; and, to place their changed opinion past a doubt, his benefits, which had never produced less than twelve or fourteen hundred dollars, and often sixteen, fell down to less than three. Wounded in pride, and ill prepared in pocket for this sudden reverse of favour and fortune, he bade adieu forever to Philadelphia. With the aid of his wife and children he formed a travelling company, and wandered through the smaller towns of Pennsylvania, Maryland, and Virginia, making Washington City his headquarters. Kindly received and respected everywhere, his old age might still have passed in calm contentment, but that

> "One wo *did* tread upon another's heel,
> So fast they *followed*."

His eldest daughter, Mrs. Anderson, and his youngest (I believe), Jane, both died in quick succession, after torturing hope, with long and lingering disease. His son-in-law, Sam Chapman, was thrown from a horse, and the week following was in his grave. His son John, an excellent actor, performed for his father's benefit at Lancaster, Pennsylvania; was well and happy; went home; fell in a fit, and was dead on the morning of September the 4th, 1831. And "last, not least," to be named in this sad list, the wife of his youth, the mother of his thirteen children, the sharer of his joys and sorrows for six-and-thirty years, was "torn from out his heart."

> "*The spirit of a man will sustain his infirmity, but a wounded spirit who can bear?*"

Joseph Jefferson died at Harrisburg, Pennsylvania, the 6th day of August, 1832.

CHAPTER IX.

> "The book of man he read with nicest art,
> And ransack'd all the secrets of the heart;
> Exerted penetration's utmost force,
> And traced each passion to its proper source."
> CHURCHILL.

I HAD secured a galaxy of *stars* of the first magnitude: among them, Macready, Cooper, Forrest, Mrs. Knight, and others of distinction; but for attraction, none could compete with the brilliant Lydia Kelly; her extraordinary success must have astonished herself. When she was first underlined at the Park, one of those well-known theatrical insects who flutter round a box-office, and because they are free of the house, conceive themselves privileged to be impertinent, said to Price,

"Why, Price, they say this Miss Kelly is not the celebrated Miss Kelly, but a sister of hers. Is that the fact?"

"Why, doctor," says Stephen, "I'll tell you what it is; there are three celebrated Miss Kellys in London, and as I had my choice, I should have been a b— fool if I hadn't picked out the best."

If Price had his "*choice*," he certainly showed his wit in the selection. Fanny, *the celebrated*, was a delicacy, a nice little bit—five or six green peas on a plate to prove such things can be in the world at Christmas. Now a London audience can afford to pay for such luxuries, but the drama in this country, Price was well aware, required more substantial food. Fanny's perfection of art, too, always savoured of the kitchen, or, at any rate, it never got higher than the back parlour, or the bar-room of an inn; and then, indeed, if she happened to be "*Mary the maid*," you would see the most consummate skill so skilfully concealed, that *acting* ceased to be; all she did was reality, but it was the reality of humble life, and, therefore, she couldn't even *make believe* to be Beatrice or Lady Teazle; and those were the sort of characters that were the most attractive here. Now Lydia could introduce us to the drawing-room: it was one of her own, to be sure, but she was very free, and easy, and agreeable there, and she showed us the fashions; they, perhaps, were her own too; but she was a splendid-looking woman, and they were very dashing and effective, and, therefore, much admired; and so were her songs, and her legs, which she showed her good sense by showing she was not ashamed of showing, when the part she had to perform required such a display. To be sure, some ladies who are engaged to be "generally useful" are often thrust into "breeches parts" whether they like it or not; and then, poor dears, they have a right to seem ashamed of themselves if they like it, and it is highly probable that sometimes they really are.

During the run of the pantomime called "Jack and the Bean Stalk" at Drury Lane, Miss Povey, who played Jack—by-the-by, it was singing a *solo* in the opening of this very pantomime that first brought Miss Povey into notice: I think I hear it now; how exquisitely it vibrates on the memory, as deliciously as the never-to-be-forgotten warble of the tame redbreast, the pet of my childhood! What a pity it was she married little Knight!

Well, Mrs. Knight—Miss Povey, I mean—played Jack, climbed up a pole, and sung like a cock-robin. But the pretty flaxen-headed little creature felt embarrassed in breeches, and, therefore, had permission to use the principal green-room, which, though not more private than the general one, was safe from vulgar eyes. And there, in the right-hand corner next the window, the siren would take her station—looking more like a boy than a girl—at least two hours before she'd be wanted in the last piece. Her little feet, " and the demesnes that there adjacent lie," "folded like two cross boughs;" the skirts of the little brown coat tucked over her knees, and her hat on her lap with the crown upward; and without scarcely moving or looking, there she'd sit, the perfect picture of purity, in pantaloons. But this was all

> "The fault and glympse of newness;"

when she did as she pleased, boys of all sorts were her favourite characters.

What a pity it was little Knight died without hearing Father Matthew lecture on temperance!

John Greene and his wife were both members of the company, but in very subordinate situations. He happened to be cast the Irishman in "Rosina," and I was amazed, both at the fine rich brogue he possessed, and his quaint, natural manner of personating the Paddy. I was the more surprised, because Wood, to whom I had applied for information as to the talent of all the strangers to me in the company, had described this couple particularly *as only fit to be trusted with a line or two*. I inquired of Greene if he could study O'Dedimus, a very long part in the lignant fever, the widowed parent vowed one grave should hold them, and wildly inhaled her infant's poisoned breath till saturated with disease. But God spared the child, and the poor mother perished.

I loved them both as I would a brother and a sister, which is much to say " in this all-hating world."

◆

CHAPTER IV.

" Have they not sword-players, and every sort
Of gymnic artists, wrestlers, riders, runners,
Jugglers and dancers, antics, mummers, mimics,
To make them sport ?"—*Sampson Agonistes.*

I NOW look back and laugh at the contradictory feelings I experienced the first day I walked through the aisle-like stable, to be introduced to the members of the circus as their future manager; each stall occupied by a magnificent animal, knee-deep in unsoiled straw, platted into a kind of door-mat fringe on its outer edge, to secure the particles from littering the snow-white pavement. The childish pride I felt as " to myself I said,"

" I'm monarch of all I survey,
My right there is none to dispute,"

was checked by the recollection of the sacrifice I was about to make of my profession; and for the life of me I could not suppress the thought that there might be some of my *legitimate* associates who, in speaking of my appointment, would apply to me that coarse but common combination of words and wit, " horse — and sawdust" manager; which, though, in point of fact, it amounts to the same thing as " sole director of the celebrated equestrian company," yet, by taking away the dignified name of the office, all that remained was mental slavery of the worst kind, because totally at variance with my taste or former pursuits. But Tom Ash, the chairmaker and celebrated financier, said I should make a fortune " *by the operation*," and, with this imaginary gilding, I swallowed the pill.

My few weeks' experience at Astley's I found of infinite service in my new undertaking; at all events, it gave me the power of backing my directions with " *that's the way we always did it at Astley's*," and such authority was indisputable. To successfully command an army, a banditti, or a circus, it is all-important that the corps should have implicit confidence in the capability of their leader; and who could doubt mine, when *I had graduated at Astley's ?* Large additions to horse and foot had been made, and the company was both extensive and excellent: a stud of thirty-three horses, four ponies, and a jackass, all so admirably selected and educated, that for beauty and utility they could not be equalled anywhere. The concern was already popular, and the powerful influence of the proprietors *incog.* made it (oh, enviable democratic distinction!) a very *fashionable resort*, and our success was enormous. Of course, like others when first placed in power, I made a total change in my cabinet. John Blake I appointed secretary of the treasury and principal ticket-seller; and to prove how excellent a judge I was of integrity and capacity, he was engaged at the Park at the end of the season, and has held that important situation there ever since. A delicious specimen of the Emerald Isle, with the appropriate equestrian appellation of Billy Rider, received an office of nearly equal trust, though smaller chance of perquisites — stage and stable doorkeeper at night, and through the day a variety of duties, to designate half of which would occupy a chapter. He was strict to a fault in the discharge of his duty, as every urchin of that day who attempted to sneak into the Circus can testify. Conway the tragedian called to see me one evening, and in attempting to pass was stopped by Billy, armed, as usual, with a pitchfork.

" What's this you want? Who are ye? and where are you going?" says Billy.

" I wish to see Mr. Cowell," says Conway.

" Oh, then, it's till to-morrow at 10 o'clock, in his office, that you'll have to wait to perform that operation."

" But, my dear fellow, my name is Conway, of the theatre; Mr. Cowell is my particular friend, and I have his permission to enter."

" By my word, sir, I thank ye kindly for the explination—and it's a mighty tall, good-looking gentleman you are too," says Billy, presenting his pitchfork; " but if ye were the blessed Redeemer, with the cross under your arm, you couldn't pass me without an orther from Mr. Cowell."

Bob Maywood, on his benefit night, during my first season at the Park, mistaking the noise made by the call-boy and some of his playmates frolicking behind the scenes, before the curtain was up, for the commencement of the performance, poked his nose through the door in the flat to take a peep at the house before he went on, when one of the lads, supposing Bob's nose was that of his comrade, sneaked softly by the side of the scene and tweaked it most abominably; discovering his mistake, the boy was off and under the stage before Maywood could get to the front. I was greatly amused at poor Bob's astonishment and anger at this mysterious insult. A reward was offered for the discovery of the offender, but as I alone was witness to the deed, he wasn't likely to be found out. In the course of the evening a fine-countenanced, bold-looking, red-headed rascal, with an extraordinary large mole on his chin, exhibiting half a dozen hairs of the same complexion, came sidling up to me, and, with a roguish smile, said,

" Don't you go to tell on me, sir."

" Oh, oh," said I, " then you are the villain who pulled Bob Maywood's nose, are you ?"

" Yes, sir," said the boy; " but indeed I thought it was George Went's."

This was my first acquaintance with Tom Blakeley. I faithfully kept his secret; and he, in gratitude, was always on the alert to run of an errand, or do any little job I required; but if he should see me and Maywood in conversation, he'd come up, with a mischievous twinkle in his eye, and say,

" Will you have a stick of candy, sir ?" or " an apple," and give me an imploring *don't-tell* look.

I liked the young rogue, but the run of the piece in which boys were required being over, I lost sight of him; but a few days after my taking the circus, a well-grown lad presented himself as an applicant for a situation, and by the extraordinary mole on the chin I instantly recognised my young friend of nose-pulling celebrity. For old acquaintance' sake I gave him a small salary to do " *anything*," but his great industry and propriety of conduct soon made him a most valuable member of the company. He afterward became an excellent actor, and for some years was a great favourite at the Park

77

and Bowery. He was the first to introduce *negro singing* on the American stage, and his "Coal Black Rose" set the fashion for African melodies which Rice for years has so successfully followed. While at Philadelphia, Tom was called upon by the city authorities to give security for the maintenance of a "little responsibility;" this he appeared to consider a most vile plot against his moral character, and, indignantly declining any parental honour of the sort, retained Colonel James Page as his counsel, and the cause went to trial. An alibi—that most important point in any case, but particularly so in one of this kind—was, with much plausibility, very nearly established, when the prosecuting attorney begged permission to introduce what he called *a very material* witness. A young woman, dressed in virgin white, with a black veil, advanced, and, removing a cap from the head of an infant, disclosed to the eyes of the court and jury a fine head of bright red hair, and the *fac-simile* of Tom's mole on the chin. The cause was instantly decided to the satisfaction of all parties—perhaps excepting the unexpected father; though I thought I saw a smile of responsible parental pride play over his countenance as he named me as his security to the parish, and declared that, "As I have to pay for a child, I'll have the worth of my money, and keep it myself." And to his credit be it told, that he did, and educated it respectably, and is now proud of an amiable and interesting daughter.

Among the horses was a cream-coloured Hanoverian charger, of extraordinary beauty and immense size, and went so proud in action, "as if he disdained the ground." Though nothing in his life was applicable to his name but the leaving of it (he was killed at sea), he was called Nelson.

Immediately after taking the direction of the establishment, I made myself acquainted with the titles and general character and qualifications of all the horses, but was not so well informed as to how the grooms, minor people, and musicians were called; and among the latter was a clarionet player, with less talent but with the same name as the horse—Nelson. But, as Juliet says,

> "What's in a name? that which we call a rose,
> By any other name would smell as sweet."

On a Sunday, in the forenoon, Rodgers, an equestrian performer, and father to one of the first riders of the present day, called at my house, and requested to see me on very particular business. Upon inquiring his errand, he said, with much solemnity of manner,

"I'm very sorry to inform you, sir, that poor Nelson is dead."

"Dead!" said I, with astonishment: "why, Mr. Rodgers, it's impossible! he was well enough last night;" for, in passing through the stable, I had stopped to caress the beautiful animal, and he was as full of mischief and spirit as usual.

"Oh no, sir," said Rodgers, "he was very unwell for two days, and scarcely able to perform."

"Why, I knew nothing of it," I replied; "why didn't some of them let me know? There was no necessity for his being employed in anything but the entrée; and, indeed, if he was sick, he shouldn't have been used even for that, if I had known it."

"You're very kind, sir, I'm sure," replied the friend of the dead musician. "He'll be a great loss to the concern; and he was such a kind, good creature."

"Why, as to his kindness, I can't agree with you there; he was most difficult to manage; but his loss, as you observe, will be irreparable. When did he die?"

"Early this morning. I was up with him all night. He kicked and rolled about in great agony, and you might have heard his groans for half a square."

"Poor creature! And what did they say was the matter with him, Mr. Rodgers?" I inquired.

"The colic, or something of that sort; and we think it was brought on by his eating cucumbers."

"Cucumbers!" said I: "why, where did he get cucumbers?"

"Mr. Blyth," he replied, "received some as a present, and he gave poor Nelson two or three."

"Well, my dear sir, they never could have hurt him; and if they were likely to do so, Mr. Blyth, of all others"—he was our riding-master—"would never have given them to him; you may depend upon it, Rodgers, it was the bots."

"Oh dear, no, sir," said he, with a confident veterinary manner: "that's a disease as *horses* often dies on; but his was quite different; his body was all drawn up in a heap, and the sweat poured off hin. in pailfuls; we dosed him with brandy and laudanum, and kept rubbing of him, but before the doctor arrived he was a gone horse;" and then, with a sigh, he continued, "There's George Yeaman, and Williams, and a few more as came out with Old West along with him, wishes to pay him the compliment of giving him a funeral, and wants to know if you would be good enough to attend?"

"Oh, pooh! that's perfectly ridiculous, Rodgers. I respect your innocent-minded, good-hearted feeling; I have quite as good a right to be sorry for his death as any of you, but a funeral is all nonsense; we'll have him hauled away early in the morning, and thrown in the river."

"Sir!" said he, looking aghast.

"Are you going back to the circus, Mr. Rodgers?" I inquired.

"No, sir," said he, "but I live within a door or two."

"Well, then, you will greatly oblige me if you will call and tell Peter, or any of the grooms you may find there, to employ a butcher, or any one who understands the business, and have him skinned."

"Sir! what! skinned?" said Rodgers, in astonishment.

"And if you please, tell them to have it done carefully, and be sure not to cut off his ears and tail; I intend to have him stuffed."

"Stuffed!" said Rodgers.

"Yes," said I; "and on the fourth of July, or other great occasions, we'll have him hoisted out for a sign, or use him for a dead horse, at any rate."

This brought our equivocal conversation to a climax; and, highly delighted at finding it was Nelson the musician instead of Nelson the horse who had been killed with cucumbers and kindness, the next morning I joined the mourners, and saw the poor fellow "quietly inurned."

During the time Lafayette was travelling through the Union, receiving the enthusiastic homage of all classes of persons, and, by the only mode in his power, showing his gratitude by kissing all the young women, shaking hands with the old, and blessing the little children, it comedy called "Man and Wife," which I wished to do for Miss Kelly, and, from necessity, had cast the part to myself. Of course, he undertook it, and played it gloriously, astonished everybody, and Billy Wood into the bargain. *I got up* John Bull, principally for the sake of his Dennis, and though, altogether, the play was very well performed, Greene made the great hit; it was acted on the *stars'* off-nights for many times more than the usual number of running a stock piece, to crowded houses, and for four or five of the benefits, his own among the number, filled to overflowing. I have no doubt I have seen a hundred Brulgruderies in my time, including Jack Johnstone and Power, but none of them are fit to hold a candle to John Greene, and I feel certain old George Colman "the younger" would have been exactly of my way of thinking.

Johnstone was the beau ideal of Major O'Flaherty and characters of that class—the *Irish gentleman*, of the *Jonah Barrington school*, he looked, and was—and Power—the thing itself for the valets: the insolence and coxcombry of such parts he hit off delightfully on the stage, though the same style of manner made him exceedingly objectionable in a green-room.

But for the Teagues, the Murtochs, and the Looneys, "*the boys*," the genuine, unsophisticated Paddy, with a natural genius for cutting canals and drinking whiskey, give me the *Native American Irishman*, John Greene.

His good lady, of course, did not remain long in the background. Her high respectability is now too generally known to need any commendation from me. She can play the Queen in Hamlet better than any one I ever saw in America; and for the simple reason, that she can play Lady Macbeth much better than many who would consider the Queen in Hamlet as derogating to their talent.

About this time actors began to be manufactured by wholesale. The great and deserved success of Forrest induced, of course, a host of athletic young men to follow at a distance his career. But something more than a mere imitation of his powers being needed to command attention to their early efforts, *native talent* was the medium through which their claims to excellence were expected to be viewed with increased brilliancy, and their failings entirely obscured. Some few have attained high consideration; but, unfortunately for themselves, keeping you constantly in mind of their great master, they oblige you to take largely from their own intrinsic merits. Pelby was one of the first "native American tragedians;" that is, the first who made a living exclusively on amor patriæ capital. He had a clumsy figure, rather a good face, and a very peculiar voice; he could boast of originality of style, at any rate, for he was totally unlike anybody I ever saw in my life. John Jay Adams was taught to read Hamlet by Pritchard on condition that he would appear for his benefit at the Park, which he did during my first season; and I thought it the very best first attempt I ever saw. He was a wholesale tobacconist, and retail dealer in literature; he wrote very pretty poetry for some of the Sunday papers, and only played now and then; but got worse by degrees; and when I last saw him he was "*shocking bad.*"

Cooper's faults had been so long copied, and, of course, increased in the appropriation, that there was not an objectionable, and, at the same time, original bit left for a new beginner to found

a style on; but Booth, keeping, with truth and purity, a living likeness of Kean's beauties full in view, had, of course, all the smaller-sized mad actors as his satellites; but I know of none worth naming among them except C. H. Eaton. He achieved a sort of popularity, and the distinguished title, *in the playbills*, of the "Young American Tragedian." In addition to his giving a most excellent imitation of Booth's acting, he assumed a lamentable caricature of his eccentricities off the stage. Now there was method in Booth's madness: however ridiculous his antics were, they only excited pity, but never laughter. There was a melancholy responsibility, if it may so be called, about all he said and did while in "phrensy's imagined mood," that if you believed he was insane, it would grieve you to the heart to see a noble mind thus overthrown; and if you thought it was assumed, it would cause quite as painful a feeling to think that one so gifted should condescend to ape degraded nature. But Eaton's secondhand vagaries were disgusting; his distorted fancies, too, like other monstrosities, had to call in the aid of alcohol to perpetuate their first-conceived deformity. Poor fellow! he carried the joke too far at last, and fell from a balcony at his hotel, after performing one night at Pittsburgh, last May, and died in a day or two afterward.

During this season, 1826-7, I had the gratification of introducing two of the "fairest of creation" as candidates for histrionic fame—a daughter of Old Warren and a daughter of Old Jefferson. They were cousins, and about the same age. Hetty Warren had decidedly the best of the race for favour at the start; but Elizabeth Jefferson soon shot ahead, and maintained a decided superiority. Poor girls! they were both born and educated in affluence, and both lived to see their parents sink to the grave in comparative poverty. Hetty married a great big man called Willis, a very talented musician, much against the will of her doting father; and, like most arrangements of the kind, it proved a sorry one. Elizabeth became the wife of Sam Chapman in 1828; he was a very worthy fellow, with both tact and talent in his favour, and her lot promised unbounded happiness. Who could have imagined that this young creature's heart should have been lacerated, and the entanglement of a first and fervent love unravelled and let loose for life, because the Reading mail was robbed? but so it was. Now is this fate? *What should it be called if it is not?*

The Reading mail stage, with four fine, fast horses—*for Jemmy Reeside had the contract*—with nine male passengers and the driver, was stopped by three footpads—Porter, Potete, and Wilson—a few miles from Philadelphia, in the middle of the night. The horses were unhitched, and fastened to the fence, the driver's and the passengers' hands tied behind them with their own handkerchiefs, and quietly and civilly rifled of their property, without their making the slightest resistance! A watch, I think, said to be the gift of a mother or wife, and some other matters of private value, Porter, an Irishman, and the principal robber, politely returned; helped himself to a "chaw" of tobacco, and replaced the "plug" in the passenger's pocket; gave another some loose change; and, in fact, conducted the whole affair with most admired decorum, and then took a respectful leave of his ten victims, sent his *aides*, with the mail-bags, into the woods, and departed. The entire operation was considered the most gentlemanly piece of *highwayism* that had occurred for some time, and caused much excitement. Potete turned state's evidence; Wilson's life was spared by President Jackson, and Porter, whose courage and urbanity were the admiration of everybody, was hanged.

Chapman, who was extremely clever at dramatizing local matters, took a ride out to the scene of the robbery, the better to regulate the action of a piece he was preparing on the subject, was thrown from his horse, and slightly grazed his shoulder. He had to wear that night a suit of brass armour, and the weather being excessively hot, he wore it next his skin, which increased the excoriation; and it was supposed the verdegris had poisoned the wound. At any rate, he died in a week after the accident, and left his young wife, near her confinement, and a widow in less than a year after her happy marriage.

> " Oh! grief beyond all other griefs, when fate
> First leaves the young heart lone and desolate
> In the wide world."

It is the custom in Philadelphia for a vast number of persons to attend all funerals. Chapman being popular, his death sudden and singular, and his poor little wife a native of the city, and adored by everybody, an immense concourse assembled. I walked and talked, as is the fashion, at the heels of some two hundred peripatetics, arm in arm with Edwin, the well known and excellent stipple-engraver, and the son of the great comedian, the original Lingo, and Darby. We were deep in disputation, and over our shoes in mud in crossing a street, when another large funeral procession passed through ours, in another direction, and caused some confusion. Absorbed in listening to anecdotes of his father, and Lord Barrymore's private theatricals, we reached the cemetery, and I proposed that we should make our way towards the grave, that the poor father and brother might be aware of our attendance; we did so, and listened to a portion of the beautiful service, then looked round, with that timid glance always assumed on such occasions; but no sorrowful look of recognition was exchanged; every face was strange; I nudged my companion; we peeped under the handkerchief of each weeping mourner; there was no Old Chapman with spectacles bedewed; turned round at a stifled sob; it was not Williams; no, nor anybody that we knew; all were strangers. The truth stared us in the face—we had got mixed up in the other procession, and had been making believe to cry over the wrong corpse!

A mind such as Forrest's, running riot, like the vines of his native woods, in uncultivated luxuriance, was predisposed to be impressed with an enthusiasm amounting to adoration by the electrical outbreakings of such a genius as Kean's,

> "Who, passing nature's bounds, was something more."

But a model, whose excellence was inspiration, gave an impetus, rather than a check, to its own naturally wild, spontaneous growth; and, untrained by art, Forrest's splendid talent, choked by its own voluptuousness, might even now be rotting in obscurity. Macready's arrival in this country may, therefore, be said to have formed an epoch in the history of the American drama.

> " In ancient learning train'd,
> His rigid judgment fancy's flights restrained,
> Correctly pruned each wild, luxuriant thought,
> Mark'd out her course, nor spared a glorious fault."

This great practical example of the power of art over impulse was not lost upon Forrest. Without condescending to imitate the manner, he imitated the means whereby such eminence had been attained, and has achieved a glorious reward for his industry and self-government.

I had only seen Macready three times before I met him in Philadelphia, and that was in London—once in Rob Roy, and twice in Pescara, a most extraordinary and original conception. The impression that comprehensible performance made on me, time still permits me to enjoy in full recollection, though at the same period I only remember that Charles Young, Charles Kemble, and Miss O'Niel sustained the other principal characters.

Macready could neither boast of face nor figure, but both were under such command, that they were everything which was required, in every character he undertook. By-the-by, it has been often remarked that we are very much alike—of course, I mean off the stage—but I beg most particularly to request those who are not acquainted with my personal appearance to understand *that I am much the better-looking fellow of the two.*

<hr>

CHAPTER X.

" The best actors in the world, either for tragedy, comedy, history, pastoral, pastoral-comical, historical-pastoral, tragical-historical, tragical-comical, historical-pastoral, scene individable, or poem unlimited: Seneca cannot be too heavy, nor Plautus too light. For the law of writ, and the liberty, these are the only men."—*Hamlet.*

MEANWHILE the circus had become so unprofitable that the amateur stockholders were well inclined to sell out. I parted company with Warren, and Simpson and myself became the sole proprietors.

The best of my dramatic company having "got half lost and scattered," I had to form a new one. Fortunately for me, John Hallam was most anxious to go to England for a wife he had chosen there. People often fall in love when they cannot afford to pay for it, but now he thought he might prudently indulge in this expensive luxury; and I gave him an agency, at the same time, to engage any talented people he might meet with likely to suit me. He discharged this trust as he did everything, most faithfully; but, of course, he secured the services of Mrs. Hallam and her sister, Miss Rachel Stannard, and her sister Mrs. Mitchell, and her husband Mr. Mitchell; the rest of the family wouldn't come, I suppose. The only females he introduced to an American audience, with the exception of his new relations, were Mrs. Lane and her talented little daughter, now the beautiful and accomplished Mrs. Hunt, of the Park Theatre.

Warren engaged Francis Courtney Wemyss to supply my place; a very worthy fellow, proud, and justly so, of being the descendant of several earls in Scotland, and some lords in England; he has been buffeting with the spotted fortunes of management ever since, till very lately, and now I see he advertises to sell, in a cellar in Philadelphia, perfumery, tetter ointment, and cheap publications. I hope he will recommend this book to his customers.

As soon as Hallam's mission was known, Warren despatched Wemyss on a similar errand; but Hallam was limited to give only three guineas per week, as the highest salary. Wemyss had to pay much more, of course, as he selected persons who, by talent or circumstances, had achieved some kind of reputation in England. Now my lot had never been heard of out of their own little circle, with the exception of my principal man, Grierson, and Hallam prided himself on having secured the original Duke of Wellington in the "Battle of Waterloo," *at Astley's*. I was in successful operation at Philadelphia when Simpson sent me an account of their arrival in the ship Britannia, my old friend, C. H. Marshall, commander. They could not complain of their mode of conveyance; they had the same skilful captain who landed me here safe and sound, and a magnificent vessel. Charles Irish, of yellow-fever memory, then kept a secondary kind of hotel, where Hallam was instructed to put up and remain a day or two, that the party might recover the fatigues of the voyage and see the lions of New-York. The bill of expenses rendered to me on this occasion reminded me of Falstaff's:

"Item. Sack, two gallons . . . . . 5s. 8d.
Item. Anchovies and sack after supper, 2s. 6d.
Item. Bread, a halfpenny."

This was *supposed* to happen during the reign of Henry IV. The following *did* happen during the reign of Simpson and Cowell:

"Mr. John Hallam

To Charles Irish.
One day's board and lodging for self
   and party $18 50
Refreshments at bar . . . . . . 56 00!!
                       $74 50."

Hallam was a jolly dog himself, and, of course, he took care that the representatives of the British drama, at that day, should do the thing handsomely by their new associates. They were very foreign, both in appearance and manner—English country actors are very odd-looking people—but, on the whole, I was well pleased with honest John Hallam's selection. Of course I made the most of them, and they all had opening parts. Grierson chose Rolla for his *début*, and the same play served to introduce Mrs. Mitchell as Cora. She had a very pretty face and a broad Lincolnshire dialect; and her person strongly reminding me of the great Mrs. Davenport, I doubled her salary, on condition that she would undertake the old women, in which she was highly successful. Pretty women always contrive to get well paid, even to make themselves ugly. Grierson was very tall and very uncouth in his deportment, and so near-sighted that it amounted to blindness; and in the scene where he has to seize the child, not having the little creature thrust into his arms, the necessity for which he had pointed out in the morning, he fumbled about for an instant, and then caught Charley Lee instead by the nape of his neck, and would have whirled him off if not rescued by the soldiers. The public were well inclined to believe all I did was right at that time, but I had put their temper to a serious trial that night. But, fortunately, a most vehement appeal in good plain English, by the beautiful little boy who played Cora's child, to have some domestic matters attended to immediately, and being disregarded, the evidence that it should have been, trickling down the stage, put the audience in such high good-humour, that the play escaped disapprobation. The house was crowded to the

ceiling. I stood for a few minutes behind poor old Warren.

"If this is Cowell's great gun," said he, "why he's a pop-gun."

But it was not: W. H. Smith became an immense favourite. He was one of those pink-looking men, with yellow hair, that the ladies always admire, and in his day was considered the best fop and light comedian on the continent. I doubled his salary directly.

John Sefton was a sort of a failure; though very queer and excellent in *little bits*, he did not hit the audience till he got to Baltimore; and there, his skilful personation of the Marquis, in the "Cabinet," made his two pounds ten into twenty dollars. Some years since he played Jemmy Twitcher, in the "Golden Farmer," at New-York, in a little theatre called the Franklin. The audience were peculiarly capable of appreciating his talent, and his fame is hinged entirely on that one part; his appearance is the thing itself—equal to Sir Joshua Reynolds's picture of "Mercury as a Pickpocket."

The equestrian business ceasing to be *so* attractive, I determined to get rid of that portion of our expenses—sent the company to Wilmington, Delaware, where a temporary building was prepared, and had the *ring* fitted up as a spacious pit, and in September, 1827, opened the Philadelphia Theatre, Walnut-street.

Wemyss returned from England with his party. But too much was expected from them; and in this interim my company had got licked into shape, and had grown into favour with the audience. They underlined *Venice Preserved* and the *Young Widow*, to introduce some of their new people — Belvidera, Miss Emery; Jaffier, Mr. Southwell; and Pierre, Mr. S. Chapman; their first appearance in America—there were not more than two hundred persons in the house. I had the same pieces performed on the same evening, Mr. and Mrs. Hamblin in the principal characters, and had upward of fourteen hundred! The full tide of public opinion was in our favour. We could play three light pieces for a week in succession, to six and seven hundred dollars a night; when the Chestnut-street would prepare an expensive performance, or, rather, display an expensive company to thirty persons.

Among other *stars*, I engaged Cooper, who took his leave of an American audience, with whom he had been so many years the idol, prior to his departure for Europe; and he played his round of characters to crowded houses. He had prepared an excellent farewell speech; but it being his own composition, he had not thought it necessary to fasten it so securely on his memory, as no doubt he would have done had it been the production of another's pen. The veteran, too, evinced much feeling at having to say *goodby*, perhaps *forever*, to a people among whom he had made so long and happy a sojourn; and, in his embarrassment, forgot the words. He is a very incompetent extemporaneous speaker; and thinking it a pity some very pretty thoughts he had put on paper should be wasted, explained the dilemma he was placed in, and begged permission to read what he had written; but, unfortunately, the manuscript was in his own hand; and believing it,

"As our statists do, a baseness to write fair,"

it was almost illegible, and occupying both sides of a sheet of foolscap, which became transparent when held behind the foot-lights, both pages were mixed up together, so that it became impossible to smoothly deliver the sense, and he was obliged at last to give up the task, said a few words warm from the heart, and some honest tears were shed on all sides.

Baltimore had for years been visited by Warren and Wood, with the same jog-trot company and the same old pieces, till they had actually taught the audience to stay away, and it had then the reputation of being the worst theatrical town in the Union. I had always had enormous success there with my circus company; and, encouraged to the undertaking by a host of friends, I leased the theatre from the committee, all of them my personal well-wishers. I had the house thoroughly repaired and decorated, the lobbies carpeted, and stoves erected there and under the stage. The gallery, which had become an unprofitable nuisance, I dispensed with entirely, and made that entrance serve for the third tier, effectually separating the visiters to that section from the decorous part of the house. There was a corporation tax of ten dollars on every night's performance, which Warren and Wood had for years been trying to get removed; but the influence of my powerful friends got it instantly reduced one half! Strict police regulations were adopted, and carried most rigorously into effect; and in November, 1827, we commenced the season.

Hamblin was my first star, to whom I paid one hundred dollars per night, and played to half the amount: a very dingy beginning, but I had " confidence, which is more than hope," of a good season yet.

I was sitting one night at the back of one of the boxes: the play was the *Revenge;* there are but seven characters in the tragedy, and necessarily they are all very long. Smith was Alonzo, and Grierson, Carlos. In the same box with me was a tall, Kentucky-looking man, alone—the house was literally empty—and during a very tedious scene of theirs, he leaned back, and said to me, in a loud tone,

"I say, stranger, has that long-legged fellow got much more to say in this business?"

I answered in the affirmative.

"Then," said he, striding over the seats, "they are welcome to my dollar, for I can't stand listening to his preaching any longer;" and away he went.

My company could boast of little tragic talent, but in comedy we worked together very happily. Wells was my ballet-master, and that department, under his experienced direction, was very effective. The business continued most wretched for two or three weeks; but, fortunately, we were able to make all our payments regularly, and I professed to be perfectly satisfied with the certainty of having a fine season ultimately. Messrs. Dobbin, Murphy, and Bose, the proprietors of the American, had always been our printers; but General Robinson then kept a much-frequented, fashionable circulating library, and I gave him the printing, that it might be to his interest, as well as inclination, to talk in our favour, which he did most successfully and kindly. My worthy host, too, David Barnum — *the emperor of all hotel-keepers* — was most enthusiastic in his efforts to promote my interests. It is delightful to think that, after so many years of checkered fortune passed, that this very night, here in Baltimore, in July, 1843, we should take our glass of "old rye" together, in the same favourite corner; laugh old matters over, and refine upon the refinements of the gout, which we have both so honestly earned.

Simpson sent me all the stars, in increasing attraction; and the season of 1827–8 is spoken of up to this day as the most brilliant *ever known in Baltimore.* Forrest, Hackett, Barnes, Horn, Pearman, Hamblin, Mrs. Austin, Mrs. Knight, Miss Kelly, and the captivating Clara Fisher— worth the whole of them at that day—appeared in rapid succession. *She played with me for six weeks, to a succession of overflowing houses.* Nothing could exceed the enthusiasm with which this most amiable creature was received everywhere. "Clara Fisher" was the name given to everything it could possibly be applied to: ships, steamboats, racehorses, mint-juleps, and negro babies. Charles Fisher established a newspaper in New-York, called the "Spirit of the Times," and, to secure popularity to it and himself, advertised it as "*edited by C. J. B. Fisher, brother to the celebrated Clara Fisher.*" A hack proprietor started an omnibus, and, of course, called it the "*Clara Fisher;*" and another had another, called "*the celebrated Clara Fisher;*" and another yet, determined not to be outdone, named his "*Brother to the celebrated Clara Fisher!*" But anything so overdone was not likely to last, in her evanescent profession. She married Mæder, a very pleasing composer and talented musician; and though no diminution could be discovered, by the calm observer, in her intrinsic merit, the charm was broken, and she only now, as *Clara Fisher,* in remembrance lives.

Washington City could then only boast of a very small theatre, in a very out-of-the-way situation, and used by Warren and Wood as a sort of summer retreat for their company; where the disciples of Isaac Walton, with old Jefferson at their head, might indulge their fishing propensities, without having them interfered with by either rehearsals or study.

Now Miss Fisher had so turned the heads of the public in Baltimore, that I thought it a safe experiment to try if she couldn't turn the heads of the government, then in session, and I hired the theatre for an optional number of nights. "There is nothing like getting up an excitement," Pelby used to say. I immediately set a swarm of carpenters at work to bang out the backs of the boxes and extend the seats into the lobbies, which, in all the theatres built since the awful loss of life by the Richmond fire, were ridiculously large in proportion to the space allotted to the audience. As the house had seldom or ever been full, small as it was, my preparing it to hold twice the number which had ever tried to get in appeared somewhat extraordinary. Mashing down thin partitions, in an open space, plastered into a ceiling, is a most conspicuously dusty and noisy operation, and attracted, as I wished, numerous inquiries—the doors being all thrown open—and my people were instructed simply to say, that "*the house wasn't half large enough to accommodate the crowds which would throng to see Clara Fisher.*" The plan succeeded to a nicety. Never had there been such a scramble for places before in the capital—I mean in the theatre. At the end of two days every seat was secured for the whole of her engagement.

On the afternoon of the first performance I got a note from John Quincy Adams, then the President, requiring a certain box for that evening, directed to "*Mr. Manager of the Theatre;*" and I sent a reply, regretting that he couldn't have it till five nights afterward, directed to "*Mr. Manager of the United States.*" I was afterward told that the kind old man was highly amused by the response.

CHAPTER XI.

"*Quince.* Have you sent to Bottom's house? Is he come home yet?
"*Starveling.* He cannot be heard of. Out of doubt he is transported.
"*Flute.* If he comes not, then the play is marr'd; it goes not forward, doth it?
"*Quince.* It is not possible. You have not a man in all Athens able to discharge Pyramus but he."
Midsummer Night's Dream.

In consequence of the extraordinary success which had attended the temporary alteration of the Walnut-street Circus, the proprietors were easily persuaded to convert it into a permanent theatre. A lease on my own terms was granted for ten years. To my experience was left the general detail of the improvements, and the celebrated John Haviland was chosen as the architect, and the present Walnut-street Theatre was erected withinside the walls of the old building. Scarcely had the note of preparation been sounded, when an *entirely new theatre* was proposed to be built in Arch-street by some property-holders in that neighbourhood. Building theatres was supposed to be an excellent investment of capital at that time, and a good excuse for elderly, sedate, Quaker-bred gentlemen to take a peep at a play, or a look at what was going on behind the scenes in the character of a stockholder.

It had already been proved past a doubt to my mind and poor Warren's pocket, that Philadelphia would not or could not support more than one establishment of the sort; and *the one* the public would most probably select, in despite of my popularity, would most likely be the *new one*, and I began to tremble for the consequences. While I was wavering as to the course I should pursue, through the instrumentality of my friend Hamblin I received an offer from the proprietors of the Tremont Theatre at Boston to undertake its direction for forty weeks, for the sum of four thousand five hundred dollars, which, after duly weighing all the consequences, prudence, and the persuasion of my friends, induced me to accept. And that I did *I have most heartily regretted ever since.*

It was then late in June, and I instantly set off for Boston. Nearly all the proprietors there were my personal friends, and they readily agreed to take off my hands such engagements as I had entered into—among them Miss Stannard, Hallam, and Smith—and all other stipulations which I suggested were readily agreed to; and with two thousand dollars in cash to bind the bargain, I returned to Philadelphia.

As I passed through Providence, on my way to Boston, I had promised Arthur Keene that I would give him notice of the exact day I would return, that he might advertise me to appear for his benefit.

He was a sweet, untaught singer, in the style of Paddy Webb, an Irishman by birth, and overflowing with fun and *national modesty.* He made his first appearance in America at the Park, in Henry Bertram. A duet, his portion of which is sung behind the scenes, with the exception of the last line, was to introduce him to the audience. The air is very pretty, and the words, as I have ever heard them, very innocent, at any rate:

"List, love, 'tis ay—ay—I,
    Rum tum ti di-i-ay;
    Where art thou, rum tum?"

Then he should rush on, and, embracing Miss Mannering, most energetically sing,

"I'm here, I'm here!"

but, unfortunately, forgetting, in the anxiety of the moment, that there was a threshold to the folding doors of the flat, his toe caught the impediment, and with the tune in his throat, he came sprawling down the stage on his face, close to the foot lights; in an instant he was on his feet, and, at the very top of his *fal-setto*, shouted,

"I'm here, I'm here!"

and he probably got a more joyous reception than he would have done under the usual circumstances.

I left Boston in the mail-stage, after a jolly supper, at one in the morning, and arrived at Providence, Rhode Island, in time for rehearsal, the same day. The weather was excruciatingly hot, as hot weather always is in high latitudes when it is hot, and after dinner I determined to take my lost share of sleep. I took a file of papers, that most efficacious lullaby, from the reading-room, and finding a mattress thrown in the corner of a balcony, where all the air Providence could bestow appeared to flutter, I arranged a *siesta.* When I awoke it was dusk, and after repairing my toilet, I set off for the theatre, all my companions being there, though I only had to play Crack, in the last piece. As I passed through the bar I inquired of a servant sweeping it out, "What is the time?"

"About four, sir," said he.

"About four!" said I: "about eight, more likely," and on I walked.

The shops were all closed, and everything appeared particularly quiet; but the steady habits of Providence I was prepared for by long report, and, therefore, its appearance was not extraordinary. The carriers hanging the evening papers on the knobs of the doors, or insinuating them underneath, were the only human beings I met with on my way to the theatre, which, to my astonishment, I found closed and quiet. A thought flashed across my mind— Could it be possible? I made an inquiry of a milkman, and found, to my amazement, that it was not *to-night,* but *to-morrow morning.*

To return to the hotel and make an explanation I knew full well would be at the expense of remaining to perform that night; so I sneaked on board the Connecticut steamboat, which was to take me to New-York, leaving my baggage behind. My old friend Captain Bunker met me with astonishment; he had been at the play, and fully described the consternation I had occasioned. The theatre had been crowded, and after every room in the Franklin Hotel had been searched, and every conceivable place in the city, it had been unanimously agreed that, in walking to the theatre after dark, that I had walked off one of the docks, and already a reward had been offered *for the recovery of my body.* But that my business was too urgent for me to spare the time, I would have delivered myself up, for the joke's sake, and claimed the ten dollars; but as it was, I got Bunker to keep my secret, and laid perdue in the ladies' cabin till the boat was off, and took the news of my supposed untimely end, to personally contradict it at New-York and Philadelphia.

So popular was I at that time with the proprietors of the Walnut-street, that I had as much trouble in getting rid of the lease as most persons would have had in getting one granted. It was opened in the fall with an excellent but most extravagant company, under the direction of William Rufus Blake and Inslee, the latter having made a supposed fortune as keeper of the almshouse, and the former only wanting one to be fully considered one of the best fellows in the world.

Nearly the whole company had been selected for the Tremont prior to my engagement, and Booth had been appointed stage-manager for a month. And it was whimsical enough, in ignorance of my having the whole control, his offering me a situation for the season, of fifty dollars a week. I thanked him, and did not tell him then why I declined the offer.

The arrangements at the Tremont Theatre were both costly and injudicious; and therefore, though the season was a brilliant one, it was most unprofitable. Booth received one hundred dollars for each night's performance; and Hamblin, for twenty or twenty-four, the same terms. On one occasion, the "*direction*" wished in some other way to occupy one of his nights; and they not only paid him the one hundred dollars for his *supposed* playing, but gave him another hundred for *not playing*; or, in other words, they gave him two hundred dollars to be kind enough *not to perform at all for one night only.*

He was on a visit to my house during his sojourn at Boston; and while amusing himself with my children, during a leisure morning, made the discovery that my dear boy Samuel was perfect, both in the words and music of Crack, in the Turnpike Gate, and could give an excellent imitation of his father in that character. After dinner we had a full rehearsal. The pianoforte was put in requisition, and Hamblin and myself played the off-parts by turns. I confess I thought he was extremely clever—what father would not? Hamblin was in ecstasies of admiration, and Sam's talent furnished food for a chat in my room at the theatre that evening; and Dana, the principal of the committee of management, pertinently said,

"Now, Cowell, if *you* were to have the profits of your benefit," which was then advertised, "you would let your son play for it."

This legitimate Yankee suspicion, of course, I had no better means of removing than by letting Sam perform. He was delighted at the novelty, and no farther instructed than by a usual rehearsal; he made his first appearance *three nights afterward.* Whatever he may be now, he was a very little boy, even for his age, in 1829; and he certainly eclipsed anything in the way of juvenile prodigies which I had ever seen—and so an overflowing house said too. But from long experience of the consequences in after life of forcing precocious talent, *I never urged him to learn a line.* For some two or three years following he played and sung such parts and comic songs as he thought proper, for his own amusement and my emolument; but in the course of that time he never studied more than six characters—Crack, Chip, Matty Marvellous, Bombastes—I forget the other—and one of the Dromios; and his impersonation of me *was me*, at the small end of a telescope. He chose, when it was time to choose, the stage for his profession, and is now an admitted favourite in the Edinburgh Theatre: no small boast at his age, for there the drama is considered one of the

mental endowments of that refined and critical portion of Great Britain. And his uncle, William Murray, the manager, who, when a mere boy, was intrusted by his sister's husband, Henry Siddons, with the direction of the National Theatre, has been for years universally admitted as the most finished disciplinarian now remaining to uphold the good old school.

I was most heartily rejoiced when this engagement of mine terminated. The gentlemen composing the committee of arrangements for the proprietors, all with separate tastes and interests—some, but few, influenced by the probable loss and profit to themselves; others by the *he* or *she* actor they wished to patronise; some for the sake of seeing a play acted as they would like to see it—would beg me to give them "some good casting." One of these actually proposed, that to support James Wallack, who was to do Macbeth, that Hamblin should play Banquo—all well enough—and Booth Macduff! to Wallack!!

"No!" said Booth, "I'll not play Macduff to Wallack, but I'll tell you what I will do—I'll play either Fleance or Seyton!"

Hackett took the Chatham Theatre the following spring, and I was engaged as his principal comedian. For so long a time having been encumbered with the toils of management, for myself or others, a plain, well-paid stock engagement was a delicious change. But it did not last long; for, after a month or so, the business not continuing very profitable, some reduction of wages, or some mercantile arrangement of Hackett's, which I will not explain, being proposed, I *backed out.* My experience taught me, that when a manager asks you to take a *little less* one week, he will expect you to take nothing the next, and be perfectly satisfied. So I went *home* to Philadelphia. There I found my own-made theatre, the Walnut-street, under the management of Messrs. Edmunds, S. Chapman, and Green, on a commonwealth principle. Edmunds had been a clerk of mine, recommended to me by Cooper as a starving countryman of ours, with a large family, great honesty, and a good handwriting. Out of several proposals which he made me, which he had learned in my school, I accepted a sort of stock engagement for two weeks, to receive no salary, but the *whole receipts* of my last night, in the shape of a benefit, as payment; by which I cleared twelve hundred dollars.

John Boyd, of Baltimore, the Christopher North of South-street, and the laughter-loving and mirth-provoking Wildy, who cannot possibly have a higher caste in this world's estimation than by being acknowledged as the grandfather of the benevolent order of Odd Fellowship in the United States, had built an amphitheatre on some property that they and others owned on Front-street. Wildy and Boyd had both made me an offer of the establishment, which I foolishly declined accepting, and Blanchard became the lessee, and cleared, the first season, at least fifteen thousand dollars. I was engaged there for five consecutive nights—the sixth to be my benefit—on my favourite terms, receiving the whole receipts. I merely played six farce parts, and got nine hundred dollars by the job.

This establishment was burned down while occupied by Cooke's company; and the destruction of property and unoffending animal life on that occasion is too dreadful to speak of. It is now rebuilt by the same spirited and liberal proprietors; and, with its complete and substantial appointments, either for a theatre or a circus, is by far the most perfect building for such purposes now in the United States.

A fat-faced gentleman, buttoned up to the chin, with a queer hat and a lisp, called upon me at Barnum's, and introduced himself as Mr. Flynn, manager of the theatre at Annapolis, the *capital of Maryland*, the authority of *Boz* to the contrary notwithstanding, who bestows that honour upon Baltimore. He offered me half the receipts of his theatre there per night, for three nights, explaining that it would hold one hundred dollars. I accepted the proposal on having good security for the payment, which, in a very business-like manner, he immediately gave. I was to commence the engagement on the Monday following; and at dark on Saturday night I arrived at that very pretty little oldfashioned city. I must stop one instant here to say that the graveyard, with a few innocent sheep nibbling the short grass, and giving intensity to the repose of the romantic spot, would almost tempt anybody to be buried " quick" there. There is one grave where an Irish blacksmith is de-composed, with the iron anvil on which he worked for years for a tombstone: and a simple tablet " *To the memory of a good woman;*" only think of having " dust to dust" shovelled on you just there !

The hotel I found entirely deserted, with the exception of a negro, who was asleep outside the latticed portion of the bar-room. I had not been there an instant when I heard the chorus of the old Lincolnshire ditty I had introduced to this country :

> " Oh ! 'tis my delight of a shiny night,
> In the season of the year. Now, then !"

and in walked Booth—for 'twas he, followed by a clever young printer, by the name of Augustus Richardson, who afterward married Sam Chapman's widow, and a gentleman called Franciscus, whom I saw the other day at New-Orleans, and who didn't sow his *wild oats* with such good taste.

" Why, hallo!" said Booth, " what are you doing here, Cowell?"

I, like a true Englishman, answered by asking the same question.

" Why," said Booth, " I am engaged for three nights and a benefit by Flynn; I open here on Monday."

" So do I," said I, " and have the same nights."

" I am to get half the receipts," said he.

" So am I," said I.

" But I have it all signed and sealed, and Gwynn is security for the payment," said he.

" Exactly the same case with me," said I.

The fact is, Flynn had engaged us both on precisely the same terms, and as he explained to me, not having the slightest reliance on Booth's promise to be there, he had engaged me to save him from the anger of the audience if Booth should disappoint them; and was good-humouredly prepared to give *us all* between us. And it was with some difficulty—for, where money is concerned, Booth has sometimes a queer method in his madness—that he was induced to agree to take one third a piece all round.

But this chapter is getting to be something too much of this, and I have a journey before me to " *The Far West.*"

——◆——

CHAPTER XII.

" In no country, and in no stage of society, has the drama ever existed (to my knowledge) in a ruder state than that in which this company presented it."—*The Doctor.*

I AM not surprised that savages, when left to their own discretion to choose a God, should so frequently select the sun as the object of their adoration; for, in his absence, even the Alleghany Mountains may be crossed, and Nature receive no homage for her wonders.

It was one o'clock in the morning, at the latter end of November, that my dear boy Sam and myself left Baltimore in a stage-coach and a snow-storm; and in three days and two nights, through mud and mire, we arrived, as if by miracle, at Wheeling, Virginia, where we fortunately found a little steamboat, called the Potomac, ready to start for Cincinnati. The Ohio River is notorious for being twelve hundred miles long, but as nothing is said about its width, to my imagination it proved sadly out of proportion; it happened to be a low stage of water, which then I knew nothing about; and I was disappointed in not finding it wider than the Delaware, and not half so picturesque. The French christened it *La Belle Rivière*, but a Frenchman's opinion should never be taken where the beauties of Nature are concerned, unless they are fit to be cooked. John Randolph went to the other extreme, but was nearer the truth, when he described it as a paltry, nonsensical stream, dried up one half of the year, and frozen up the other. Winter had just taken Autumn in his rude embrace, and the country on either side looked wild and dreary, though divested of romance.

> " There stood the faded trees in grief,
> As various as their clouded leaf;
> With all the hues of sunset skies
> Were stamp'd the maple's mourning dies;
> In meeker sorrow in the vale,
> The gentle ash was drooping pale ;
> Brown-sear'd, the walnut rear'd its head,
> The oak display'd a lifeless red,
> And grouping bass and white-wood hoar
> Sadly their yellow honours bore."

Habitations were " few and far between," and then only a miserable log hut in the midst of " a clearing" of, perhaps, a dozen acres; the trunks of the fine old trees still standing, though burned to the core; and this evidence of their violent death adding artificial desolation to the naturally dreary landscape. At a wood-pile you would sometimes see a group of dirty, " loose, unattired" women and children,

> .... " With a sad, leaden, downward cast,"

destroying at a glance all your visions of primitive simplicity or rural felicity. These " early settlers," by a strange chain of thought, put me in mind of Paradise Lost and " Adam's first green breeches;" and I could not help but agree with Butler, that

> " The whole world, without art and dress,
> Would be but one great wilderness,
> And mankind but a savage herd,
> For all that Nature has conferr'd ;
> She does but rough-hew and design,
> Leaves art to polish and refine."

Cincinnati in 1829 was a very different place from what it is now, but even then it wore a most imposing appearance : thanks to the clear-headed, adventurous Yankees, who, axe in hand, cut through the pathless forests, undismayed by toil and defying danger, until they found a spot, rough-hewn and designed by Nature as the site for future ages to enthrone the pride of the Ohio Valley, the " Queen City of the West." We put up at the hotel near the landing, kept by Captain Cromwell, and in his little way quite as despotic as his namesake, the poor apology for a king; for after dinner—an operation which was performed by his boarders in three minutes at farthest—myself and two acquaintances I had formed on the road drew towards the fire, and commenced smoking our cigars.

"You can't smoke here," said Captain Cromwell. And we instantly pleaded ignorance of his rules, though they might be thought a little fastidious after our scramble for dinner, and threw our cigars in the fire.

"And you can't sit here," said Captain Cromwell. "If you want to sit, you must sit in the bar; and if you want to smoke, you can smoke in the bar."

Slapping his hand on the table, after the manner of his ancestor dismissing the Long Parliament; and into the bar we went, where a playbill on the wall announced that the " School for Scandal" was to be performed that evening for "the benefit of Mr. Anderson." I was making some inquiries of the barkeeper about the theatre, when a man about my own age and size, very shabby, very dirty, and very deaf, introduced himself as Alexander Drake, the manager, curled his right hand round his ear, and, in a courteous whisper, invited me to "take something." He was a kind, familiar, light-hearted creature, told me, with apparent glee, that he was over head and ears in debt to the company and everybody else; that that night he had given the use of the theatre, and the performers had tendered their services, t* an old actor who expected a "meeting of his creditors;" but that he had been obliged to close the theatre for the simple reason that it wasn't *fashionable!* What an abominable affliction have these ephemeral four syllables proved to the young and otherwise unfettered country of which I am now writing! Could the wrinkled outlaws of crippled monarchies find no other chain to goad the neck and bow the head of independence,

" Wandering mid woods and forests wild,"

than the introduction of fashionable atrocities to make the thoughtless laugh, the thinking grieve?

The manager gave me an invitation to witness the performance; and after a pleasant chat—for he was a delightful companion—and "taking something" till the time for commencing, excused himself for being obliged to leave, in consequence of having to "study Charles Surface, who went on in the third act." If he had never played the part before, he had an extraordinary "swallow;" for he was perfect, and performed it much better than I have often seen it done by those who consider such characters their line of business; and he was a *low comedian* and an *excellent one*, which may probably account for the unfitness of his dress: he wore white trousers of that peculiar cut you sometimes see frisk round the stage in what is called a sailor's hornpipe, and, being very short, exposed a pair of boots on which Day and Martin had never deigned to shine; no gloves, a round hat, and the same blue coat and brass buttons I had already been introduced to, buttoned up to the top. His wife was the Lady Teazle; a very fine looking woman, and plenty of her. I was not then accustomed to the peculiar *twang* in the pronunciation of the west end of the United States, which, in consequence, sounded uncouth and unlady-Teazle-like to me; for though Sir Peter particularly boasts

that he has chosen a wife " bred altogether in the country," he didn't mean, I suppose, the Western country; but, at any rate, she got great applause; everybody seemed very much pleased with her, and she seemed very much pleased with herself. Mrs. Drake has been very successful as a star since the time I speak of; she is one out of six or seven ladies who have by turns been called "*the Mrs. Siddons of America;*" but what for, for the life of me I never could find out; but as the baptizers, in all probability, never saw THE *Mrs. Siddons*, they should stand excused for taking her name in vain. Baron Hackett's sister-in-law, Mrs. Sharpe, was so christened; but that must have been an oversight; for she is an *English* lady, the daughter of Old Le Sugg, well known thirty years ago as an eccentric itinerant, and said to have been the preceptor of Matthews in the art and mystery of imitating Punch and Judy.

Raymond was the Joseph, a man nearly as big as " Big Scott," and would not now be mentioned here, if he had not drowned himself because some one said Parsons (another big one) was a better actor! Foolish fellow,

" How poor are they who have not patience !"

if he had waited a little longer he would have had the Western country heavy business all to himself; for, when theatricals began to decline in that hemisphere, Parsons turned Methodist, and joined the church. But whether he was disappointed in the profits attending his new profession, or that the groans his performance elicited were not understood at first to mean approval, and he fancied he had made a failure, I know not, but the offer of a star engagement induced him to return to the stage. And had he played the hypocrite, and got it understood that he was still a follower of the church, though, from necessity, an actor, he might have proved an attraction; but he was honest for once, and took the other extreme, selected Doctor Cantwell for one of his characters, and insulted common sense by his attempting to throw odium on the professors of religion; and to the credit of the supporters of the drama be it said, he played to empty benches. He is now, I understand, regularly engaged as a saint, and playing little business to Maffit.

It must not be understood that I wish to convey an idea that an actor cannot be a religious man, and even a capable and devout teacher of Christianity; but then his previous life should be strongly marked (like poor Conway's) with the attributes of piety, kindness of heart, and charity to all men; and Parsons, I'm afraid, if weighed in such a scale, like many other *parsons*, would be " found wanting."

At the end of the play, a tall, scrambling-looking man with a sepulchral falsetto voice, sung " *Giles Scroggin's Ghost,*" and I recognised him at once as an old acquaintance. While I was manager of the circus I called in one evening at the Park during the performance of " Bombastes Furioso," and was greatly amused at the eccentricities of one of the supernumeraries, and the more so, as I could plainly see it annoyed Hilson and Barnes. Simpson was with me, and we had a hearty laugh at the expense of the comedians, for they were all in the bill, and this man, *without a name*, was the only person the audience appeared to notice; and the next day Simpson told me that Hilson, Barnes, and Placide had made a formal complaint against this extemporaneous jester, and insisted on his not being again employed. His name, I found, was Rice, and not long after he

to his own profit and the wonder and delight of all admirers of intellectual agility. The theatre was a small brick building, well designed, but wretchedly dark and disgustingly dirty, and, with the exception of the beneficiary and the persons I have named, the performance was quite in keeping. I don't know if it was considered a *fashionable* house. There were about a hundred persons present, and I observed a majority of the ladies wore a little strip of silver cord or lace round their heads, an innocent remnant of national finery, I presume, and very generally worn by the Swiss and German peasants, who then constituted a large portion of the population.

Old Drake had been a strolling manager in the West of England, and some years before had brought to this country a large family of children, all educated to sing, dance, fight combats, paint scenes, play the fiddle, and everything else; and by wandering through the then wilderness, and giving entertainments at the numerous small towns which were daily ejecting the forest, he had made money by their combined exertions in that primitive dramatic way. But this portion of the Union had in a very few years outgrown even his boys and girls, and the march of improvement had marched rather beyond the point of his experience.

A few farms within a mile or two of each other had become, as if by magic, flourishing villages, then large towns and now magnificent cities, the stumps of the firmly-rooted fine old oaks still disputing inch by inch the paving of the well-built streets. A *full-grown*, enlightened population, kept pouring in from the older States, accompanied by the million skilful artisans who had been starving midst the crowd of equal talent in their native countries, and whom Great Britain and the Continent of Europe could so gladly spare.

New towns must have new theatres, sometimes even before they have new churches, and Frankfort, Lexington, Louisville, and Cincinnati had been so adorned for several years, and which now constituted the present circuit. Alexander Drake had been intrusted by his father with this branch of the concern, and had got in debt and got on the *limits*, and could not move out of the state till relieved by the insolvent law; and Old Drake was at Frankfort, Kentucky, waiting for this company, to open the theatre there, and they could not move for want of funds.

Poor *Aleck* so feelingly described his painful situation, that though there was very little probability that I should make money under the existing circumstances, with the remote hope of giving him some assistance, I agreed to play a few nights, to share with him after one hundred and thirty dollars, a sum very unlikely to be ever received, but to have half the amount of two houses for the services of myself and son, which, in all probability, would cover my expenses, and give me time to form a better judgment of this new country. But, strange to say, our business averaged over two hundred dollars, and both the benefits were crowded to overflowing.

There is no class of persons in the world who so ostentatiously exhibit their estate as the players. I speak of the majority. See them in prosperity with

their coat is always made in the extreme of the most ridiculous fashion then in vogue, and, that it may be useful on the stage, generally of a lighter blue, or green, or brown, than is usually worn; pantaloons of some peculiar colour—blotting-paper is a favourite tint—and a hat, either very little, very big, or very something, very unlike what would be seen on any head but an actor's; but when either garment is unseamed and seated, and the brim of the hat bowed off, every rent speaks with a "dumb mouth" of abject beggary, when a homely garment, though threadbare, if it did not conceal the poverty, would still shield the wearer from ridicule and contempt. The ladies, bless them, always dress beautifully when they can; but 'tis melancholy to meet them when they cannot, with lace veils and flannel petticoats, artificial flowers and feathers, with worsted stockings and muddy shoes. I shall neither mention names nor particularly describe the party I saw the first morning I went to rehearsal huddled round the fire, in what was called the green-room. In one corner, on the floor, was a pallet-bed and some stage properties, evidently used to make shift to cook with, such as tin cups and dishes, a brass breastplate, and an iron helmet half full of boiled potatoes, which, I was informed, was the domestic paraphernalia of the housekeeper and ladies'-dresser. She was a sort of half Indian, half Meg-Merrilies-looking creature, very busily employed in roasting coffee on a sheet of thunder, and stirring it round with one of Macbeth's daggers, for "on the blade and dudgeon, gouts" of rose-pink still remained.

I soon got acquainted with the ladies and gentlemen; Rice I found a very unassuming, modest young man, little dreaming then that he was destined to astonish the Duchess of St. Alban's, or anybody else; he had a queer hat, very much pointed down before and behind, and very much cocked on one side. I perched myself on a throne-chair, by the side of Mrs. Drake, who was seated next the fire, on a bass drum. I found her a most joyous, affable creature, full of conundrums and good nature; she made some capital jokes about her peculiar position; martial music—sounds by distance made more sweet; and an excellent rhyme to drum, which I am very sorry I have forgotten.

When a manager ceases to pay, he soon ceases to have any authority; the rehearsals, therefore, did not deserve the name; the distribution of the characters the performers settled among themselves, and said as much of them as suited their convenience; but they were all very civil, and apparently anxious to attend to my interests, and the audience was esily pleased. Sam made a prodigious hit; from ten to twenty dollars, and sometimes much more, would be thrown on the stage during his comic singing: a tribute of admiration not at all uncommon in those days in the South and West. At Louisville, one night, seven half-eagles were sprinkled amid the shower of silver which always accompanied his African Melodies. Loose change is not so plentiful in those days.

CHAPTER XIII.

> " The aspiring youth that fired the Ephesian dome
> Outlives in fame the pious fool that raised it."
>
> *Richard the Third.*

THE profits arising from our engagement had been distributed among the performers, and they had set off for Kentucky; and Drake had had an excellent benefit, for which we had played gratuitously.

It was now suggested by some of the *first people*, that if Mrs. Drake could obtain our services, and give an entertainment in any place but the theatre, she might be certain that all the *fashionables*, who wished particularly to see my son, would attend, and so give their aid towards relieving the manager of part of the encumbrances their want of patronage had occasioned. I consented to sing a song, and Sam had no objection to singing a dozen, and a *Grand Olio* was concocted. Mr. and Mrs. Drake were to act Sir Peter and Lady Teazle's, and Sir Adam and Lady Constant's detached scenes; Aleck to sing Kitty Clover, Gregory Redtail, Love and Sausages, and half a hundred more *fashionable* comic songs; and Mrs. Drake to deliver "O'Conner's Child," the "Scolding Wife," and half a hundred more *fashionable* recitations. I was to sing "Chit Chat for the Ladies," in the first part of the entertainment, and Sam to give his "Negro Melodies" with a white face, in the second; and a violin and violoncello were to constitute the orchestra. Tosso was the leader, a gifted musician, who played *familiar airs divinely;* but, being blind, his accompaniments to strange melodies had to run after the voice in a pretty frolicking manner, more for his own amusement than any assistance he gave to the singer.

Now this hotch-potch was supposed to be more attractive for a *fashionable* audience than the same actors would be in a wholesome play and farce, with the assistance of the company, and the advantages of scenery and dress. Pshaw! After due preparation, a night was chosen by Mr. Drake's principal patroness, when it was positively ascertained there would not be a tea-party of any consequence in the whole city, and the place of exhibition Mrs. Trollope's Bazar.

This is a very singular affair: built of brick in a by-street turning out of Broadway, so that, fortunately, its nonsensical appearance don't actually interfere with the good taste displayed in the simply elegant buildings just round the corner.

For what the original inventor intended this structure, Heaven only knows; in my time it has undergone a dozen alterations, at least, to endeavour to make it fit for something; but its first plan was so curiously contrived, that every effort Yankee ingenuity could suggest to make it useful has successively failed. It no doubt cost a vast sum of money to erect. These fancy buildings, which highly-imaginative ladies sometimes conceive, however clearly described, are very incomprehensible to the artists in bricks and mortar taught only to work by rule, even though the instructions may be assisted with prints in perspective to copy " *something like that little bit*" of the exterior of the Harem, or " this little bit" of the Pavilion at Brighton. But Mrs. Trollope's zeal to improve the taste of this young common-sense population, whom she intended, and fully expected, would ultimately look up to her with awe and admiration, nerved her with patience to surmount all the tortures of pulling down and building up, till she at length succeed-

ed in getting a roof with a tin-basin-shaped dome, and a large gilt crescent on the top, of the oddest-looking building that ever was invented. The interior, no doubt, was an after consideration. Two half-circular stairways met at the top of six or seven steps, which led to an entrance wide enough for two persons to pass in conveniently at the same time, into a large dingy-looking room : this was the *Bazar*. I am speaking of it as I saw it for the first time. There was a sort of long counter on either side, and some empty shelves here and there against the walls. On the left hand, near the door, an elderly lady in spectacles was sitting behind a little lot of *dry goods*, knitting either suspenders or garters; and at the farther end of the room a very melancholy-looking man was employed in reading, behind his share of the counter, I suppose. He put his book down as we advanced and stood up, as much as to say, "What do you want to buy ?" I glanced at his stock in trade. There were a few pieces, or, rather, remnants of calico and Kentucky jean, the ends unrolled and fastened to the ceiling, some ribands in the usual pasteboard box, and the cover upside down by the side of it, filled with papers of pins, and needles, and cotton balls; whether he had just *started in business*, or was about *closing the concern*, it was impossible to guess, so I bought a paper of pins and asked the question.

" I have only been here a week, sir," said he, dolefully, "and, with the exception of the socks I sold that young gentleman this morning, you are the only one as 'as bought anything since I opened." Sam had been to market, in consequence of the absence of the washerwoman, and had found out "this queer-looking place," as he justly called it.

" Then you don't find it answer ?" said I.

" Oh dear, no, sir—very far from it," he replied: "nothing answers that's rational in this outlandish country, as Mrs. Trollope says; I wish, with all my art, I'd never seen it."

" You are an Englishman, are you not ?" said I.

" Yes, sir, eaven be praised; and you is too," he continued, with a very knowing look. " I remember you at the Adelphi; I took the gallery tickets there."

" Pray, had I the pleasure of your acquaintance in London ?" I inquired, respectfully.

" Oh no, sir, but I knowed you was the same as I knowed there as soon as I seen the playbill. But I was very intimate with John Reeve," he continued, with much importance. " It was him as recommended me to Rodwell; he was clerk in the same ouse as I was in afore he turned a hactor—Mr. ——, the ozheer in Cheapside : I used to weave stockins in the front cellar at the hairy winder."

" I understand," said I: " a sort of living sign."

" Why," he replied, with a look as if he didn't approve of my interpretation, "it's rather confinin', to be sure; but one gets good wages, and with what I earned by keeping door at night, it's a plaguy sight better than setting all day in this rum concern, and getting nothing but your wickles."

" And is that all you get for your services ?" I asked.

" Why, you see," said he, in a confidential under-tone of voice, " the old woman thinks this ere will be a great go one of these days; but she can't get the Yankees to believe in it, and they won't rent the stands; so any of her own country as apply, she furnishes 'em with a few things, and gives 'em half the profits and a cold cut, and a cup o' tea, to try and get the place into notice. But I think it's all in my eye," he continued, with a cunning wink; "she'll never be able to *melerate* the manners of the Mericans, as she calls it: d'ye see them 'ere spitboxes?" pointing to a row filled with clean sawdust, on the outside of the counter. "Well, she can't begin to persuade 'em to make use on 'em; they will squirt there backer on one side, which teazes the old woman half to death."

It was in a room of similar dimensions to this that the aristocratic exhibition took place. At the extreme end there was a raised platform; this was permanent, and the apartment intended by the founder of the building as the forum, in which the mischievous outpourings of any wandering fanatic, whose solemn yet impotent efforts to overthrow the institutions and annihilate the creeds of the older country might here, on the fresh bosom of this newly-planted world, ingraft the poison of their mildewed minds, disguised in all the demoniacal decorations of our language,

> "And sweet religion make
> A rhapsody of words."

A green baize curtain was fastened from the ceiling across the middle of the platform, to form *the stage* and *behind the scenes*, where we were huddled together, with two chairs between us, before the audience arrived; there being only one door to get in or out at, this was our only resource, or to parade through the fashionables when time to commence. When they did come they came all together, Mr. and Mrs. Trollope, with their family, leading the way, and amounting to about thirty in all, laughing and talking very happily, accompanied by Tosso and the bass, with some plaintive Irish melodies. Drake interrupted this only expression of hilarity during the time I was sitting perdue behind the baize by ringing a little bell, and a minute passed in shuffling of feet and legs of chairs—all was breathless silence. Another tingle-dingle, and Mrs. Drake appeared, her majestic form and white satin train, which Drake had spread out and placed on the floor at its full extent, as she gracefully glided through a slit in the baize, taking possession entirely of the stage. Three queen-like courtesies to the right, the left, and centre, which was entirely vacant, with the exception of the doorkeeper, who stood a little in advance of his station cutting and shuffling the few tickets he had received in his hands, and with which he gave a wh-r-r-rup! which formed the only response to the courtesies. The fact is, it was not fashionable to take notice of anything; but a very loud sneeze, which a young lady favoured me with during the third verse of my song, caused a whispering titter; and the one that usually follows, being interfered with by a friend or pocket-handkerchief, went the wrong way, and the very odd kind of noise it assumed caused a general laugh, during which I finished my song, and made my escape through the slit.

The first part over, Mrs. Trollope invited me to the refreshment-room. Most of the gentlemen I had been acquainted with before, and many of the ladies I had had the pleasure of an introduction to, and among them the beautiful, blushing young creature, who made some innocent apologies for the cold in her head. Mrs. Trollope gave fifty reasons why at least fifty more of her

friends, and the first people in the city, were not there; but in an after acquaintance with the character of the inhabitants, I found that her having anything do with it made it a wonder there were any there at all, her philosophical mode of going to heaven being objectionable to a large portion of the American population.

She appeared delighted at this new appliance of her property.

"I always told Mr. Trollope," said she, with great glee, "that I should make a fortune by this building, after all. A series of entertainments of this kind must become fashionable in time. My friend, Mrs. Drake, is exactly of my way of thinking: we must prevail on you and your dear little boy to remain with us for a week or two longer."

"That will be impossible, madam," I replied. "And I have been too long accustomed to a regular theatre to be of any use in a performance of this description."

"Oh! I beg your pardon," said she, quickly; "the ladies are all delighted with your song—you must sing us another or two. And as to a *regular* theatre, just step this way, and I'll show you what I intend to do."

And away the bustling little lady went, and I at her heels.

"Now you see, Mr. Cowell, I'll have the dais enlarged, and made on a declivity; and then I'll have beautiful scenes painted in oil colours, so that they can be washed every morning and kept clean. I have a wonderfully talented French painter, whom I brought with me, but the people here don't appreciate him, and this will help to bring him into notice. And then I'll have a hole cut here," describing a square on the floor with her toe; "and then a geometrical staircase for the *artistes* to ascend perpendicularly," twirling round and round her finger, "instead of having to walk through the audience part of the area. Or," said she, after a pause, "I'll tell you what will be as well, and not so costly. I'll have some canvass nailed along the ceiling, on this side, to form a passage to lead to the stage; Mr. Hervien can paint it like damask, with a large gold border, and it would have a fine effect!"

Fortunately, a farther description of contemplated alterations was interrupted by one of her little ladies, as she appropriately called her daughters, who came in a hurry to inform her that the fashionables had eaten up all the cakes, and she trotted off to supply the deficiency; and I, recollecting the "one or two more" songs I might be expected to sing, whispered to Sam to follow me as soon as possible, and was sneaking quietly down stairs, when I was met by my friend Rogers. He then kept a dry-goods store, but formerly was of the firm of Rogers and Page, of Philadelphia, who had been my tailors for years.

"Why, hallo! Cowell," said he, "you are not going. The ladies have commissioned me to get you to sing them another song."

"Oh! certainly," said I; "with great pleasure. I shall be back in an instant."

I knew it was useless to refuse; everybody knows that tailors will never take no for an answer, even when they dun you for their bill; so, following the example of their customers, *I lied*. But fearing that his perseverance might induce him even to follow me to my hotel, I took shelter in a tavern at the corner of Market-street and Broadway; had a chat with Jemmy Gibson, then the proprietor, and sipped gin-and-water till the lights were extinguished in Mrs. Trollope's turret, and the show and all danger over.

Cincinnati bore the character of a very bad theatrical town at that time; but even in the sketch I have given, I have shown, I think, good cause why nothing else could be expected. But the first season I was acting-manager for Caldwell, though we had a temporary theatre, a more elegant and discerning audience could not be met with in the United States; and we had really fashionable, and, what was better, crowded houses every night.

The next morning we started for Kentucky.

CHAPTER XIV.

> " This is some fellow
> Who, having been praised for bluntness, doth affect
> A saucy roughness, and constrains the garb
> Quite from his nature. He cannot flatter, he !"
> *King Lear.*

THE regular theatre at Louisville, an excellent brick building, belonging to old Drake, was closed; but a cattle shed or stable had been appropriated to that purpose, and fitted up as a temporary stage. The yard adjoining, with the board fence heightened and covered with some old canvass, supported by scaffold poles to form the roof, and rough seats on an ascent to the back, and capable of holding about two hundred persons, constituted the audience part of the establishment, the lower benches nearest the stage being dignified by the name of *boxes*, and the upper, nearest the ceiling, the *pit*. Here I found a strolling company on a *sharing scheme*, at the head of which was N. M. Ludlow. Nothing I had ever seen in the way of theatricals could be likened to this deplorable party. At Cincinnati I thought it was as wretched a specimen as it well could be anywhere; but there it was really a theatre, and the company composed of much unexperienced talent: Rice and Mrs. George Rowe, for instance, and Drake and his accomplished wife, were capable of holding the first rank in the drama *in any theatre*; but here there was not one redeeming point. Who they all were, or what has become of them, Heaven only knows; I don't remember to have met with any of them since, with the exception of the manager and his lady. Hamblin had just concluded an engagement here; and after as formal a negotiation as if it had been the Park Theatre, we entered into an agreement for a few nights, I think to receive forty per cent. after one hundred dollars for six or seven performances, and half of the whole receipts at each benefit. We played to crowded houses.

The strict financial correctness, with the diligence and skill displayed by Ludlow in conducting this " poverty-struck" concern, is above all praise, and gained for him the confidence of Caldwell, who shortly after engaged him as his agent to manage a branch of his company at St. Louis and other places. This responsible though subordinate position he was well qualified to maintain, and with the powerful advantages of Caldwell's name and purse to support the respectability of the establishment, no matter if successful or not, his " official capacity" gained for him both friends and reputation. Three or four years afterward he went into management again on his own account with some success, and ultimately formed a partnership with Sol.

Smith—a very worthy fellow, somewhat overcharged with caricature fun, which is tolerated on the stage more for old acquaintance' sake in that part of the Union where he has been long known and respected, than for any other reason common sense could give. He had also been a strolling manager through some small towns in Alabama and Georgia, by which he had realized a reputed handsome property. At that short-lived time when what went for money was intrinsically of little or no value, and, of course, most plentiful, a splendid theatre was built and leased to them at St. Louis; and the profits of their first season was immense, for, receiving only money at par, or specie, and disbursing the depreciated paper then generally in circulation, their opportunities for a profitable *exchange* were alone worth a little fortune. But in a theatrical point of view only, the requisites that can make a few tattered actors in a room or stable profitable or respectable, are qualifications but ill calculated to exalt or maintain what should be the state of the *legitimate drama*. And now that Caldwell will no longer serve as a check or an example, the perfect prostration of the profession at the South and West may be considered as certain. I have just heard that they have leased the Mobile Theatre, as well as that *they call* the St. Charles at New-Orleans.

Anderson, who made his exit from Cincinnati as soon as his benefit was over, I again met here. He is an Englishman of good family, and married Jefferson's eldest daughter. Endowed with much natural and acquired talent, he can be a most agreeable companion, but so eccentric is his disposition, that his own and other's miseries are his only jokes : he will tell of a child having been run over, or something equally shocking, with a smile of satisfaction ; and a piece of good luck to himself or any of his friends, with a most melancholy countenance. Determined to be wretched and prostrate himself, he glories in meeting mankind in the same situation ; and the theatrical society he found at Louisville appeared to actually intoxicate him with delight. His extreme disagreeableness was most amusing to me, and he was a constant visiter at my room at Langhorne's, then considered the principal hotel. Some five years ago, when everybody who did not care where they went, went to Texas, he went too; and among the numbers I have known who have tried the experiment of making a living in that experimental country, he is the only one I ever knew return without either person or apparel being the worse for the trip; everybody else appeared as if they had slept in their hats all the while they were there; but he was water proof in hat and heart, and was the same as ever; and, according to his own account, he had literally lived all through the cholera on mushrooms of his own gathering. To his experience I left the selection of a boat for New-Orleans, as, in consequence of procuring two passengers, he explained that the captain would take him for less than the usual charge, or, in all probability, " *chalk his hat*," and he chose the Helen M'Gregor, Tyson, master, on these favourable terms.

A few days after we became intimate, by way of giving a business-like responsibility to our connexion, he became the borrower of a " V," as he called it, alias five dollars, which trifling obligation he soon increased to an " X ;" but, unfortunately, my not being in the humour a day or two after to add another V to his Roman numerals, " my offence was rank," and he left me, highly incensed at my ungentlemanlike conduct; and though we travelled on the same boat, he did not even condescend to look at me, much less to speak, and I lost the gratification of his sarcastic pleasantries, for which there was such a glorious scope in the variegated party who constituted our companions. The morning after my arrival in New-Orleans, before I left my bed, a yellow woman with a cup of coffee announced a gentleman: I opened my eyes to see Mr. Anderson toss with an air of dignity on the coverlet ten silver dollars, and then coming to my side, thrust forth his hand, and said, "Now, sir, I'm out of your debt—shall we be friends again ?"

I, of course, said *yes*, but urged that he would not inconvenience himself by an immediate payment.

"Sir!" said he, pompously, "take the vile trash, and never name the subject. I was partly wrong, and you mistook your man."

I *laced* my coffee; he mixed himself some brandy-and-water; he has never asked to borrow, and I have never offered to lend, and I have had the pleasure of his acquaintance ever since, and he is still the same; his well-merited, continual poverty serving to make his high sense of honour the more conspicuous.

As an actor, he is highly respectable in all he undertakes; and a little bit of him now and then is so delicious in a green-room, that wherever I am employed, and have influence with the management, Anderson is sure of an engagement.

Jemmy Bland's reply, in Shakspeare's play, describes him to a nicety:

"Who is this Coriolanus ?"

"Who is he ?" said Jemmy, not knowing what he ought to say: "why, he's a fellow who is always going about grumbling, and making everybody uncomfortable."

———◆———

CHAPTER XV.

"Oh, won't you—oh, won't you
Go along with me
Away down the river,
Through Kentucky ?"—*Western Ballad.*

THE floating palaces which now navigate the Western waters, bear as little likeness to the style of vessels then in use, as the manners and characters of the majority of passengers you met with then, resemble the travellers who now assemble in the magnificent saloons of the present day, where all the etiquette and decorum is observed of a *table d'hôte* at a well-appointed hotel.

A sketch of *what is* will serve, by contrast, the better to convey an idea of *what was* considered a first-rate class of boat in 1829. In speaking of the Western steamers of the present day, I shall only allude to that portion of the vessel appropriated to the passengers, and that must not be considered as identical, but *an average description;* the *Missouri,* the *Harry of the West,* and twenty others, I could name as far exceeding, in many instances, the portrait I shall draw. The saloon, or principal chamber, extends nearly the whole length of the boat, on the upper deck, over the machinery and steerage, as it is called—where comfortable accommodations are provided for the deck-hands and deck-passengers — terminating forward with large glazed doors opening on a covered space called the boiler-deck, and aft by the ladies' cabin, with which it communicates by folding doors, which are generally left open in warm weather, in the daytime. The whole is lighted from above by a continuous skylight, round the side of a *long oval,* which looks as if it had been cut out from the ceiling, and lifted some two feet above it perpendicularly, and there supported by framed glass. On either side of this carpeted and splendidly-furnished apartment are ranged the state-rooms, the doors ornamented with Venitian or cut-glass windows, and assisting, by their long line of perspective, the general effect. These small chambers usually contain two berths, *never more,* which always look as if you were the first person who had ever slept in them— with curtains, moscheto-bars, toilet stands, drawers, chairs, carpets, and all the elegant necessaries of a cosey bedroom. Another door leads to the guard, or piazza, protected with a railing on the side, and covered overhead; and this forms a promenade all round the boat, and joins the boiler-deck, where you can lounge with your cigar, and view with wonder, perhaps with regret, if your nature is picturesque, the hourly interference of untiring man with the solitude of the long-remembered wilderness.

The ladies are even more carefully provided for; there is usually one, and often two grand pianofortes in their apartment; which I should consider a positive nuisance if obliged to hear them tickled to death by young beginners and nurse-maids amusing themselves by making believe to keep the children quiet; but, Heaven be praised, there is plenty of room to get out of the way, this area being usually from eighty to two hundred feet in length. In many of the larger boats double state-rooms are provided for families, and young married people who are afraid to sleep by themselves, with *four-post* bedsteads, and other *on-shore* arrangements—such as are to be found at the St. Charles's Exchange, or Barnum's Hotel, or, what is better still, *at home.*

Now the Helen M'Gregor was a very different affair, but in her day her reputation was as high as anybody's or boat's. It was at night, and in December, raining and making believe to snow, when I arrived on board at Shipping Port, some two miles below Louisville; the boat being very heavily laden, and drawing too much water to get over the falls, and the canal was not then finished — a most beautiful piece of work, by-the-by; the excavation being made in the solid limestone rock, gave it the appearance of an enormous empty marble bath. She was crowded with passengers: perhaps a hundred in the cabin, and at least that number *upon deck;* for at that time the steerage occupied the space now allotted to the saloon, and was filled to overflowing with men, women, and children, chiefly Irish and German labourers, with their families, in dirty dishabille. This *man-pen* was furnished with a stove, for warmth and domestic cooking, and two large, empty shelves, one above the other, all round, boarded up outside about four feet high. These served for sleeping-places for those who had bedding, or those who were obliged to *plank it;* the remaining space above these roosts was only protected from the weather by tattered canvass curtains between the pillars which supported the hurricane-deck, alias the roof, which was spread over with a multitude of cabbages, making sourkrout of themselves as fast as possible, and at least fifty coops of fighting cocks, each in a separate apartment, with a hole in the front for his head to come through; and their continual notes of defiance, mixed up with the squalling and squeaking of women and children, and the boisterous mirth or vehement quarrelling of the men, in all kinds of languages, altogether kicked up a rumpus that drowned even the noise of the engine, which then was only separated from the cabin by a thin partition. By-the-by, all our old poets speak of "the cock, that is the herald of the morn," as if he did *not* crow in the night! but only at the approach of day, and in the daytime. I know little about rural felicity in my own country; but here, in America, the cocks crow whenever they think proper, *and always all night long*, particularly on board a steamboat, because there you are more likely to take notice of the annoyance.

The cabin was on the lower deck, immediately abaft the boilers, with a small partition at the stern set apart for the females. At the time I speak of, there were very few resident American merchants at New-Orleans at all, and those few generally left their families *at home* in the North and therefore the presence of woman—

> " Creature in whom excell'd
> Whatever can to sight or thought be form'd,
> Holy, divine, good, amiable, or sweet !"

was no restraint on naturally barbarous man, and, consequently, "a trip down the river" was then an uncontrolled yearly opportunity for the young merchants and their clerks *to go it with a perfect looseness*, mixed up indiscriminately with "a sort of vagabonds" of all nations, who then made New-Orleans their "*jumping-off place*," till Texas fortunately offered superior inducements, and there war and disease have bravely thinned the hordes of

> " Rascals, runaways, and base lackey peasants,
> Whom their o'er-cloy'd countries vomit forth
> To desperate venture and assured destruction."

All moral and social restraint was placed in the shade—*there Jack was as good as his master*—and never was Republicanism more practically republicanized than it was during the twelve days of confinement I passed on board this high-pressure prison.

Some such a party I presume it was that Mrs. Trollope met with, which she, *no doubt innocently*, but ignorantly, gives as a specimen of the "*domestic manners of the Americans.*" Poor old lady, what a mess she made of it!

There were no *state-rooms*, no *wash-room*, nor even a *social-hall;* and, therefore, on the *guard*—within two inches of the level of the river, and about two feet wide, with nothing to prevent your falling overboard if your foot slipped, or "*was a little swipey*"—you made your toilet, with a good chunk of yellow soap on a stool, to which two tin basins were chained, and alongside a barrel of water. The cabin contained thirty-two berths; and the two next the door Anderson had secured for myself and my dear boy. In the daytime these were piled up with the surplus mattresses and blankets, which, at night, were spread close together on the floor, and under and on the dining-tables, for so many of the remainder of the passengers as were fortunate enough to have precedence even in this luxury, after the berths were disposed of. The remainder of the party sat up, drinking, smoking, playing cards, or grumbling at not being able to find a single horizontal space, under cover, large enough to stretch their weary limbs on; perhaps changing the scene of their discontent by going on shore at a wood-pile, and putting their eyes out by standing in the smoke of the signal-fire, to defend themselves from the bloodthirsty attacks of a million of moschetoes.

Fortunately, the weather was most delightful, for the season of the year, and Sam and I passed most of our time on the hurricane-deck, among the cabbages, *leaving their fragrance behind;* and the chicken-cocks, with Sam and the echoes, all imitating one another. Your arrival at the mouth of the Ohio is visibly announced by the sudden and extraordinary discoloration of the water, which gives you notice the moment you pass the threshold of the great Mississippi. From childhood familiar with all the wonders of the ocean, a mental comparison with it and this gigantic river was natural to me, on first making its acquaintance; and I confess it claimed a formidable share of the awe and admiration I had hitherto considered only due, as far as water was concerned, to my old associate. Call it the Missouri—which I wish it had been called—and it measures 4490 miles in length! and if the Mississippi, 2910, and passes through more than twenty degrees of latitude!

What a pity that that microscopic observer of *nature on two legs*, the immense Dickens, should so soon have made up his mind that it wasn't fit either to taste or talk of!

> " Oh ! think what tales he'd have to tell"

if he, instead of *taking the wrong pig by the ear,* had taken a trip or two up the Missouri with my worthy friend Captain Dennis, of the Thames, or had had the useless experience

> " *Of wandering youths like me.*"

The Upper Mississippi, as it is called—God send that every friend I have on earth could behold *for even once* the stupendous wonders through which a portion of the navigable part of the Upper Mississippi rolls along—though *the stream itself* might wander through the world, and be likened to a hundred others, or pass unnoticed; but when it joins the Missouri, or, more fitly speaking, when the Missouri takes possession of its course, its pure and placid character is gone forever. A Bath-brick finely pulverized and stirred up in a pailful of spring water may give a conceived resemblance of its colour and consistency; and this appearance it maintains, with an interminable and never-ceasing rush, for the remainder of its journey, of more than thirteen hundred miles.

Well was it named "*The Father of Waters*," for even when the "crystal pavement," for a winter month or two, suspends a portion of its navigation,

> " The whole imprison'd river growls below,"

embracing in its mad career the thousands of miles of waters emptied into it by the Illinois, the Ohio, the Arkansas, the Red River, and the innumerable smaller streams, all aiding to increase its power. And in return, the mighty tyrant overwhelms on the instant their transparent interference, and carries with it, in its turgid course, its mountain-stained identity, even for miles, into the Gulf of Mexico! till, in continuous struggles for the mastery, it fades away, in oil-like circles, round and round the deep, dark blue of the old Atlantic.

Who the ladies were on board, I know not: none were ever seen with the exception of Fanny Wright; and her notorious anti-matrimonial propensities, at that time, hardly gave her a claim to come under that denomination. As soon as our breakfast was over, which occupied an hour and a half or more, the double row of tables, the extreme length of the cabin, consisting of a common mahogany one at each end, and the intermediate space filled up by a pile of shutters laid side by side, and supported by trestles, had to be three or four times provided with venison, wild ducks, geese, and turkies, and all the luxuries of this o'ertceming country, and there called common food. This operation ended, the *original Fanny* would take her station at a small table, near the door of the ladies' cabin, and sit and write or read till late at night, with the exception of the time for meals, and an hour or two of exercise upon the guard; and the moment she made her appearance there, without form or show of ceremony, it was respectfully deserted by the men till her promenade was over. The Americans are naturally the most unostentatiously gallant people in the world. An Englishman will make a long apology for not doing what he should have done, and said nothing about it; and a Frenchman will upset a glass of *parfait l'amour* in a lady's lap, by dancing over a tea-stand to hand her a *bon-bon*, in an attitude!

Among the men were some most intelligent and entertaining companions. A day or two formed us all into little knots or parties; and I was a member of a most delightful one, among whom was gladly admitted, for his good-humour and originality, the proprietor of the fighting cocks. He was a young man, but had evidently taken so many liberties with Time, that he, in return, had honoured him with many conspicuous marks of early favour, and milk-white hairs began to dispute with his untrimned auburn locks the shading of his open, manly brow.

He took a great fancy to my dear boy, and, in consequence, I was high in his favour and confidence, and he insisted on telling me a portion of his history. His grandfather was a man of great wealth in the *Old Dominion*, and a distinguished member of her councils. His father, born to inherit his certain share of the property, began to spend it before he actually came in possession of his fortune, married early in life, and lost his wife in giving birth to this only son; and living night and day full gallop, died of literal old age at forty-five.

"The night he died," said my young friend, putting a *deck* of marble-backed cards into his pocket, with which he had just satisfactorily concluded a game at *old sledge*, "the night he died, my father called me to the side of his bed. 'Washington,' said he, taking my hand in his, which felt as cold and clammy as a dead fish, 'Washington, you'll never be able to pay off the mortgage on the property, and you'll be left without a dollar.' I said nothing; it was of no use. 'Here, take my keys,' said he, 'and go to the escritoir, and in the right-hand little drawer you'll find—but no matter, bring the drawer and all.' I did as I was told. 'Now,' said he, picking out the apparatus, 'send the boy to get a chicken, and I'll show you something I paid too dearly for the learning—and that's just it,' said the old man, with a deep sigh; 'if my father had left me nothing else, I should not now leave my boy in poverty.' I couldn't speak, for I saw the old man rub his hand across his eyes, so I kept on waxing the silk as he had directed. The boy had brought the bird—a perfect picture—he didn't touch the feathers; he had learned me all that, and how to hold a chicken, when I wasn't bigger than your boy Sam, but the *heeling* was the grand secret. The old gentleman then trimmed and sawed the spur, and spit upon the buckskin, telling me, all the time, to look on and mind what he was doing; but he was so feeble the little exertion was too much, and he got quite exhausted, and I made the boy take the cock, while I supported father. When he got through, 'There,' said he, triumphantly, with a kind of squeaking chuckle, '*that's the way to gaff a chicken! that will beat the world!*' and fell back upon his pillow. He made the boy jump when he said, *that's the way to gaff a chicken!* and the steel jerked through the nigger's hand—the blood spirted out upon the sheet; and as I turned to sop it up, father's eyes were full upon me, *but yet he didn't look.* 'Father,' I said, softly, and waited, but he didn't speak: 'Father!' I put my ear close to his open mouth: 'Father,' I said again, but he didn't answer—the old gentleman was dead. *But he had showed me how to gaff a chicken-cock.*"

Playing at cards was the chief amusement at night, and my skill only extending to a homely game at *whist*, I was more frequently a looker on than a participator. My friend Washington was an adept at all short gambling games; and one that I don't remember to have seen played since, and which he boasted of having been the inventor of, of course he was particularly expert at. It appeared a game of chance, as simple as tossing up a dollar. Two only played at it, and three cards were singly dealt to each, of the same value as at whist, and a trump turned up; and the opponent to the dealer might order it to be turned down, and then make it another suit more agreeable to his hand, or play it as it was. Of course, the great point in favour of the opponent to the dealer was to know if he held *any* trumps, and *how many* he had. For some time luck seemed to be greatly in favour of my chicken friend, and the bets were doubled—trebled, and he gave me a knowing, triumphant look, while glancing at his *pile*. But suddenly there came a sad reverse of fortune.

Sitting by was an apparently uninterested looker-on like myself, peering over my friend's hand, and marking, by his fingers stretched upon the table, the number of trumps he held. The eagle eye of the Virginian soon detected the villany, and taking out his hunting-knife—it was before Bowie christened them—began paring his nails with well-acted indifference, as if entirely absorbed in the game, and laid it quietly on the table without its sheath. The next hand dealt him one trump, and the spy placed his fore-finger on the table, which my friend instantly chopped off!

"Hallo! stranger, what are you about?" shouted the dismembered gentleman. "You have cut off one of my fingers."

"I know it," said old Virginia, coolly; "and if I had had more trumps, you would have had less fingers."

This was considered an excellent practical joke, and we all took a drink together, and I lent the wounded a handkerchief to bind up his hand, which I reminded him last fall, at Gallatin races, that he had forgotten to return.

A lieutenant in the navy, on his way to Pensacola to join his ship, was one of our boatmates, and belonged to the *flooring committee*—so all were called who had to sleep on it. Two ardent devotees at *seven-up*, finding no better place late at night, while he was fast asleep coiled away in his cloak, squatted on either side of him, and made his shoulder their table.

The continual *tip, tap*, as the cards were played by each upon his back, rather aided his seaman-like repose; but an energetic *slap* by one of the combatants at being "*High, by thunder!*" awakened him, and looking up, one of the players, slightly urging down his head, said, in a confidential whisper,

"Hold on a minute, stranger; the game's just out—I've only two to go—have twelve for game in my own hand, and *have got the Jack*."

He, of course, accommodated them, and when the game was out, he found they had been keeping the run of it *with chalk tallied on his stand-up collar*.

One night, while I was getting instructed in the mysteries of *uker*, and Sam was amusing himself by building houses with the surplus cards at the corner of the table, close by us was a party playing *poker*. This was then exclusively a high-gambling Western game, founded on *brag*, invented, as it is said, by Henry Clay when a youth; and if so, very humanely, for either to win or lose, you are much sooner relieved of all anxiety than by the older operation.

For the sake of the uninformed, who had better know no more about it than I shall tell them, I must endeavour to describe the game when played with twenty-five cards only, and by four persons.

The aces are the highest denomination; then the kings, queens, Jacks, and tens; the smaller cards are not used; those I have named are all dealt out, and carefully concealed from one another; old players pack them in their hands, and peep at them as if they were afraid to trust even themselves to look. The four aces, with any other card, *cannot be beat*. Four kings, with an ace, *cannot be beat*, because then no one can have *four aces;* and four queens, or Jacks, or tens, with an ace, are all inferior hands to the kings, when so attended. But holding the cards I have instanced seldom occurs when they are *fairly dealt;* and three aces, for example, or three kings, with any two of the other cards, or four queens, or Jacks or tens, is called *a full*, and with an ace, though not *invincible*, are considered *very good* bragging hands. The dealer makes the game, or value of the beginning bet, and called *the anti*—in this instance it was a dollar—and then everybody stakes the same amount, and says, "*I'm up*."

It was a foggy, wretched night. Our bell was kept tolling to warn other boats of our whereabout or to entreat direction to a landing by a fire on the shore. Suddenly a most tremendous concussion, as if all-powerful Nature had shut his hand upon us, and crushed us all to atoms, upset our cards and calculations, and a general rush was made, over chairs and tables, towards the doors. I found myself, on the flash of returning thought, with my dear boy in my embrace, and Fanny Wright sitting very affectionately close at my side, with her eyes wide open, in silent astonishment, as much as to say, "Have you any idea what they are going to do next?" and her book still in her hand. The cabin was entirely cleared, or, rather, all the passengers were huddled together at the entrances, with the exception of one of the *poker* players; a gentleman in green spectacles, a gold guard-chain, long and thick enough to moor a dog, and a brilliant diamond breastpin: he was, apparently, quietly shuffling and cutting the *poker-deck* for his own amusement. In less time than I am telling it, the swarm came laughing back, with broken sentences of what they *thought* had happened, in which *snags, sawyers, bolts blown out*, and *boilers burst*, were most conspicuous. But all the harm the *fracas* caused was fright; the boat, in rounding to a wood-pile, had run on the point of an island, and was high and dry among the first year's growth of cotton-wood, which seems to guaranty a never-ending supply of fuel to feed this peculiar navigation, which alone can combat with the unceasing, serpentine, tempestuous current of the *I-will-have-my-own-way*, glorious Mississippi.

The hubbub formed a good excuse to end our game, which my stupidity had made desirable long before, and I took a chair beside the poker-players, who, urged by the gentleman with the diamond pin, again resumed their seats. It was his turn to deal, and when he ended, he did not lift his cards, but sat watching quietly the countenances of the others. The man on his left hand bet ten dollars; a young lawyer, son to the then Mayor of Pittsburgh, who little dreamed of what his boy was about, who had hardly recovered his shock, bet ten more; at that time, fortunately for him, he was unconscious of the real value of his hand, and, consequently, did not betray by his manner, as greenhorns mostly do, his *certainty of winning*. My chicken friend bet that ten dollars and *five hundred dollars better!*

"I must see that," said Green Spectacles, who now took up his hand, with "*I am sure to win*" trembling at his fingers' ends; for you couldn't see his eyes through his glasses: he paused a moment in disappointed astonishment, and sighed "*I pass*," and threw his cards upon the table. The left-hand man bet "*that five hundred dollars and one thousand dollars better!*"

The young lawyer, who had had time to calculate the power of his hand—*four kings and an ace—it could not be beat!* but still he hesitated at the impossibility, as if he thought it could—looked at the money staked, and then his hand again, and, lingeringly, put his wallet on the table, and *called*. The left-hand man had four *queens*, with an ace; and Washington, the four *Jacks*, with an ace.

"Did you ever see the like on't?" said he, good-humouredly, as he pushed the money towards the lawyer, who, very agreeably astonished, pocketed his *two thousand and twenty-three dollars clear!*

The truth was, the cards had been *put up*, or *stocked*, as it is called, by the guard-chain-man while the party were off their guard, or, rather, on the guard of the boat in the fog, inquiring if the boiler had burst; but the excitement of the time had caused him to make a slight mistake in the distribution of the hand; and young "Six-and-eight-pence" got the one he had intended for himself. He was one of many who followed card playing for a living, a very common occupation at that time in that section of the country, but not properly coming under the denomination of the gentleman-sportsman, who alone depends on his superior skill. But in that pursuit, as in all others, *even among the players*, some black-sheep and black-legs will creep in, as in the present instance.

After the actors, there is no class of persons so misrepresented and abused behind their backs as the professional gamblers, as they are called; especially by those who sit down to bet against them every night without their wives and families knowing anything about it, and who would think it most praiseworthy *to cheat them* out of every dollar they had, *if they knew how.* As in my trade, the depraved and dishonourable are selected as the sample of all. But the majority are men too frequently born under similar circumstances with my good-hearted friend Washington, and left without any other resource but the speed of a horse, or the courage of a cock, to obtain wealth, in a world where to be rich is considered of too much importance. My way of life has for years thrown me much in their society, in steamboats and hotels, and as a general body, for kindness of heart, liberality, and sincerity of friendship—*out of their line of business*—they cannot be excelled by any other set of men who make making money their only mental occupation.

And now, wicked reader, go on shore with me at Natchez " under the hill," on a Sunday morning, where our jovial captain, Tyson, *tied up* his boat for the day, for the sake of his passengers' enjoying a *spree.* He was of the race, which miscalled refinement has almost made extinct, who would take the grand mogul or a giant by the nape of his neck and pitch him overboard, to wriggle a minute and then be sucked under the Mississippi, if he did not .behave himself; and take a poor woman and her babes as passengers, and nurse, feed, blanket, and physic them all for nothing, and provide them with employment, or put money in their pockets till they found some way of living, all in the same breath. He and Captain Shrieve were selected by the government to combat with the Red River *Raft,* and there they have met with their match. But, now I think of it, you must be tired of this steamboat trip, so we'll pass Natchez by, and land at New-Orleans.

CHAPTER XVI.

" Sister of joy ! thou art the child who wearest
Thy mother's dying smile, tender and sweet ;
Thy mother Autumn, for whose grave thou bearest
Fresh flowers, and beams like flowers, with gentle feet,
Disturbing not the leaves which are her winding-sheet."
Revolt of Islam.

Shelley's beautiful thought applies, in its fullest force, to New-Orleans, even in December; for there " Winter's savage train" is literal-'ly left out of the calendar, and a long summer meets in luxurious greenness an early spring.

There had been a formidable rise, and the river was in all its glory ; overtaking the uprooted, " unmanufactured produce of the forest," and running on its own-made hill, actually above the land on either side, which gave us an opportunity, not to be enjoyed at a low stage of water, of viewing the magnificent homesteads of the planters on the *coast.*

It was a dark and drizzly evening when we arrived at New-Orleans, and landed at the foot of Poydrass-street, then close to the Levée, and before a wharf was built in the upper faubourg, now the Second Municipality, and parcel of the city. Captain Still, a harmless teacher of music, but who had been an actor, and honestly earned his warlike title by being so often advertised for all the *Captains,* " *with a song,*" was my conductor to the Camp-street Theatre. At the time I speak of, an experienced pilot, *with a lantern,* could scarcely save you, in rainy weather, from being knee-deep in mud in wading to the *Banquette,* then only *curbed* by the old timbers of a broken-up flat-boat, doomed by the impedi-

mental current of the river never again to reach the quiet spot where it was launched,

" Amid the obsolete prolixity of trees."

I have seen two mules with a dray sink in a mudhole, in the now well-paved Camp-street, and struggle for an hour, till hauled out by ropes, with only their ears and noses above the mire to assure you they were there!

The enterprising, great Caldwell—"*great will I call him*"—for who but he, chained down by a profession which all the world is ever willing to degrade, would, or could, have first attempted to raise the standard of the American drama in the outskirts of a city then governed by the refugees of France and Spain, and the immediate inheritors of all their national prejudices; and speaking—that apparently insurmountable obstacle to his pursuit—a different language? But he was undismayed, and built the *brave old Camp*: one of the prettiest of theatres, and better adapted to that peculiar climate, and character of the theatrical patrons, than any I have ever seen. Caldwell's energies were not alone confined behind the scenes; his prophesying was listened to by the wealthy and intelligent Americans, and his example followed in buying and improving property in the immediate neighbourhood; and it is now admitted by all that he is the actual founder of the *Second* Municipality, as it is called, but really *first* in everything ; its churches, hotels, squares, and well-paved, expansive streets leaving the old city " away down the river," literally *out of town.* With his own hard-earned, handsome fortune, in 1836 he raised a temple to the drama on a spot where, a few years before, a swamp had been, far excelling in extent and magnificence any building of the kind on this continent, and comparing with advantage with any in the older world. At the time I speak of the Camp was the only building in the city lighted with gas, manufactured on the premises, and superintended by an intelligent Scotchman named Allen ; and thus practically educated, by experimenting with an apparatus not much larger than a cooking-stove, Caldwell ultimately introduced that best of all police to the whole city, and became the president of the New-Orleans Gas-light and Banking Company. The destruction of the " Temple" by fire on Sunday evening, the 13th of March, 1842, with property to the enormous amount of half a million of dollars, prostrated, in all probability, his dramatic fortunes forever. But his energetic nature is still unconsumed, and, as an able member in the councils of his adopted city, he still promises long to continue to witness and aid her increasing prosperity.

Hamblin I found just concluding an engagement, at the termination of which I entered into a most successful one for " *a few nights,*" which, to the advantage of all parties, was renewed from week to week, till the " springtime of the year" found me parting with regret from a host of new-found friends. The company, taken collectively, was the best by far on the continent, the gentlemanly though austere nature of Caldwell ensuring to all kindred spirits a lasting and profitable employ under his liberal government. Richard Russell was his acting manager, with whom I formed a friendship which ended with my paying the mournful ceremony of holding the corner of his pall. Miss Placide, Mrs. Rowe and her husband, Hernizen, Field, Old Gray, all, too, are gone; and others, which any eulogium of mine to their memory would but painfully disturb the slumbering recollections of their numerous lamenting friends.

Mrs. Russell and her charming daughter are still ornaments to the stage, the widow paying the highest tribute of respect in her power to her husband's memory, *by still retaining his name.* The daughter married my worthy friend, George Percy Farren, and she is now, and has been for some years, the principal attraction of Ludlow and Smith's company; the expression of sincere regret at her yearly departure from St. Louis obliterated, in turn, by the smiles which always welcome her at New-Orleans. The *amiable woman* and the *talented actress* were never more happily blended than when nature selected her as the model for both. Every one who knows her loves her, the endearing freshness of childhood still remaining to adorn the well-borne duties of the wife and mother.

It was my intention to have returned to the North again by the river, and, of course, I gave the Helen M'Gregor the preference as a conveyance; but, unfortunately, or, rather, fortunately, I missed my passage. I arrived at the Levée with my dear boy and baggage just five minutes after the boat had started, and at Memphis her boiler burst, and an extraordinary number of passengers were blown into eternity as she shoved off from the landing. "It had been so with us, had we been there;" but "those who are born to be"—"*the proverb is something musty.*" And in the good little ship Talma, Captain Dennis—who now sails a vessel large enough to take her as a cabin passenger—after a boisterous passage of twenty-eight days, we arrived at New-York.

◆

CHAPTER XVII.

"What need'st thou run so many miles about,
When thou may'st tell thy tale the nearest way?"
SHAKSPEARE's Richard III.

My then "sweet home" was at Philadelphia, where we were joyfully welcomed the following day. That summer poor Charles Gilfert died, and Hackett and Hamblin became the lessees of the Bowery, at which I was engaged. But as my early acquaintance, Hamblin, whom I had ever considered as a brother, properly expressed it, "friendship has nothing to do with business;" and as I was unreasonable enough to believe that it should, our theatrical connexions terminated forever at the end of *three nights.*

Russell had taken the Tremont Theatre, and I engaged with Caldwell as his acting manager at New-Orleans for the coming season, broke up my establishment at the *North*, as we Southern gentlemem call all places where the ice grows, determining to make the *Far West* my home for the future.

Willard employed me to conduct the Richmond Theatre for him for a month, where Caldwell and young Kean were to play a few nights, on their way to New-Orleans; and that job ended, I made my route through Virginia over the mountains, by the way of Charlottesville and the Sulphur Springs, to meet the Ohio River once more at Guyandotte.

"Memory, the bequest of the past to the present and the future," urges me to linger in *recollection* of this most wondrous country; but it is not german to the character of this book to do so—that is, *if this book has any character at all*—and I must therefore pass it by, as other travellers have done, for I know of none who have ever noticed it!

That year I bought a pretty little farm of one hundred acres in Whitewater township, Hamilton county, Ohio, eighteen miles northwest from Cincinnati, and seven due south from the estate of General Harrison, then clerk of the County Court; a most amiable and kind-hearted neighbour, he then as little dreaming as I did that in ten years from that time he would be the most enthusiastically popular President of the United States ever known, "*for a little month.*" What a queer world it is! He might, in all probability, have lived there for many years, but for this over-excitement that was heaped upon him, honoured as the defender of his country in her determination to maintain the position she had achieved, and pointed out in his calm old age as a model for the American farmer in the peaceful valley of the Miami.

To compare small things with large, I meant, and had a right to believe then, that there I should pass the remainder of my days, making my profession, during the winter months, a profitable pastime. But it was not to be. When Caldwell built his Dramatic Temple in 1836, I once more joined his standard for the season, and was hailed as New-Orleans knows how to welcome back a favourite; but, in the midst of our splendid career, I was unexpectedly laid on a bed of sickness for four long months; and to Doctor Carey, who tended my flickering chance of life with all the devotedly intense anxiety a timid child bestows upon an almost exhausted taper, left between it and darkness, I am indebted for being able now to say, I here, for the sake of others, throw a veil of oblivion over my theatrical life, which individually I should wish to lift. For what gate leading through life is so strongly barred, even by virtue and religion—putting out of the question our compelled business in the world, which sometimes leaves it open—where *poverty, disease,* and *death* does not unhinge the doors, and, in one or all these shapes, take possession of our chimney-corner, and drown in unearned wretchedness the brightness of our domestic hearth? *I have endured the tortures of all these, in their most terrific forms;* but I am "one, in suffering all, that suffers nothing" *in appearance;* an iron constitution has upheld what, in a fragile one, would have been sympathized with as a sensitive mind; and my *uncountable* number of friends in the United States—I shake hands with twenty-five thousand at least every year—will bear me out in the assertion, that during the varieties of fortune they have known me to struggle with, "*Old Joe Cowell*" has always seemed the same. But, *my dear wicked reader!*—"so must I call you now," for we should by this time be on very familiar terms—I have not achieved this boasted reputation from apathy for the miseries I have endured: no; but from the self-satisfactory triumph between *myself* and my *nature,* of proving my power to conceal them. And I have often gone to a theatre, and made an audience, you included, "die with laughing," when I have felt my heart broken into such little pieces, that I have expected to see the fragments leaking out through the darns in the funny stockings I was wearing for Crack.

The nature of my task, as I have already observed, prevents me from giving even a sketch

96

of the beautiful "Crescent City," as she now is; but to me she must ever be most dear, as the depository of one unlettered tomb, on which I never

> "Shall have length of days enough
> To rain upon remembrance with mine eyes."

CHAPTER XVIII.

'It is time to close what I have to say of myself; one never gets anything by egotisms, which is a species of indiscretion that the public hardly ever excuses, even when we are forced upon them."—J. J. ROUSSEAU.

FROM the little experience I have gained while making this book, I firmly believe that the main difficulties an author has to encounter, in any work of the same ephemeral character, is to skilfully arrange a *beginning* and an *end*. A well-chosen text often entreats listening for a prosing sermon, and "many a dull play has been saved by a good epilogue." In choosing a book, too, of this class, the first and last chapters are all that are ever consulted; and, in many instances, all that are ever read. But I am deprived of the many advantages which fiction could so easily furnish, to dazzle and disarm criticism, and secure applause at the close of this performance, in consequence of being tied down by a plain, matter-of-fact narrative, and must, therefore, against my will, put an end to my *theatrical life*, in the same uninteresting, insipid manner in which it actually occurred. The remaining chapters will therefore contain as brief a detail as possible of the circumstances attending my last engagement, which may be considered as a very favourable picture of the dramatic world as it now exists in the United States.

CHAPTER XIX.

"In another room we found comedians shut up for having made the world laugh. Said they, 'If by chance some equivocal words have impressed the spectators with evil thoughts, was it not rather their fault than ours?'
"'Oh!' said the devil to me, 'if they had done no more than that, they should scarcely have come here; but think of their lost time, knaveries, and secret crimes! No, it is not the comedy which damns the players; it is what passes behind the scenes.'"—QUIVEDO'S Vision of Hell.

AFTER the destruction of the St. Charles, John Greene and myself took a lease from Caldwell of the Nashville Theatre, which we opened in April and closed in July, 1842. Our company was highly creditable on and off the stage, and we realized all we expected in that beautiful little city, *with the exception of money.* Mr. Buckstone and Mrs. Fitzwilliam were our chief attractions, with the single exception of Martin Van Buren; he very kindly visited the theatre one evening, and it was filled to overflowing. I should like to have engaged him, on his *"own terms,"* for the season. But Buckstone and the joyous Fanny were not so successful; their best house amounted to two hundred and eleven dollars, and their worst to thirty-eight; and we paid them half the gross proceeds!!

The American, and the "Old Camp," then used as an auction mart, were both burned down —by design, no doubt—during the summer; and every effort Caldwell could exert to restore the *Temple* had totally failed, leaving New-Orleans without any theatre saving the French Opera-house. The proprietors at length agreed to re-build the American, which was offered to Caldwell and accepted; and the day he signed the contract, his man of business, worthy George Holland, sent me an offer in his name. When I arrived in New-Orleans, in October, a very few minutes' conversation with my friend Caldwell gave me reason to believe it would be more to my interest to take an engagement for the winter at Mobile, if at that late period I could obtain one. The next morning I crossed the lake, and succeeded. The theatre there, Caldwell, who is the proprietor, had leased for the season to Messrs. De Vandel and Dumas. The former is *"president pro tem."* of the Gas Company, and the latter a celebrated restaurateur, who, having made a supposed fortune by keeping an eating-house and opening oysters, thought to easily increase it by opening a theatre. Charles Fisher, who is *"secretary to the Gas Company,"* was employed by the *"president pro tem."* to select the performers, his knowledge and experience in theatrical matters being as notorious as that he is *"brother to the celebrated Clara Fisher."* Now he being very desirous of proving his friendship for the Jefferson family, engaged all the immediate descendants of the *"old man"* now alive, and as many of the collateral branches as were in want of situations. Mrs. Richardson had been in Mobile the season before, and therefore she was the nucleus around whom was clustered her two sisters and their husbands, Messrs. Mackenzie and Wright; her brother, Mr. Joseph Jefferson, and his two very clever children, and her niece, Mrs. Germon, and the good man who gave her that name. The whole company, in consequence, were literally in the family way, with the exception of Jemmy Thorne and myself, Mrs. Stewart, Morton, and Hodges and his lady; so that when poor Joe Jefferson died of the yellow fever, which he did on the 24th of November, the theatre had to be closed for two nights, for without the assistance of the chief mourners we could not make a performance. By-the-by, it should have been said before, that the *"president pro tem."* had backed out, and Jules Dumas became the *"sole lessee;"* but, unfortunately for him, the *"secretary"* had made the selection before he or his stage-manager had any control.

Dumas was a Frenchman born, and, while a mere child, had been thrown headlong into the world's vortex, and had struggled round and round in every possible capacity where shrewdness and industry were all the capital required, to make money, till at last he got a little out of his depth, as the manager of the Mobile Theatre. His dramatic education had been obtained by being employed for a short time by the Ravels, as a sort of prompter and interpreter, and having kept the saloons with great success. But even in the intricate conduct of a theatre, his superior talent for finance saved him from the pecuniary embarrassments which, in all probability, would have prostrated an American or an Englishman, surrounded by the same encumbrances. Well schooled, by *saloon experience*, in the modern propensities of dramatic life off the stage, immediately opposite the theatre he had a snug, quiet, well-appointed drinking-room, where backgammon, dominoes, and other inducements to conviviality might be comfortably indulged in, with the advantage of *unlimited credit at the bar*. And behind the scenes, contrary to the usual fastidious rules in most well-regulated establishments, a servant was ready to procure, at a moment's notice, anything required, from a bottle of Champagne down to a gin-cocktail. Consequently, a large portion of each salary—sometimes all—was paid in liquor to most of the gentlemen (*including myself*) beforehand; and the balance, if any, it was in his power to retain as a forfeit, should any one be imprudent enough to take a drop too much. And by this very ingenious, tariff-like system, each actor was liable to a heavy tax upon his income, without feeling or considering that he was putting his earnings again into the pocket of the manager.

The taste and moral wants of the audience were quite as carefully provided for. Next to the tavern he erected a spacious assembly-room, where, two or three times a week, as policy dictated, a ball was given, where "ladies that have their toes unplagued with corns" could dance, and drink iced-punch, and sip hot coffee free of all expense; and gentlemen in character or without character, or disguised in any way, even in liquor, or in "happy masks that kiss fair ladies' brows," by paying only one dollar for a ticket, could jig away a harmless night to the ear-piercing noise of a negro band, and fancy themselves in heaven or Wapping, Paris or a lunatic asylum, without any extra charge. It was a glorious relaxation from the perils of the sea and toils of cotton sampling for the jolly Yankee captains and honest deacons' sons, whose early days had passed unknowing such enjoyments. The master of the ceremonies was a sleek-haired downeaster, from some place "*where the sun rises*"—he was a delicious character—a study for Dan Marble—he looked so particularly out of his natural element, dancing in his hat—I mean, with his hat on—his coat out at elbows, and a large diamond breastpin. It was a delightful place for fun or philosophy. I had a free admission, and was there every night.

Hodges, one of the very best *educated tenor singers* on the continent, but too lazy to assert the fact, had, from some cause or other, been appointed by Dumas stage-manager, an office which nature, habit, and inexperience rendered him more unfit to sustain than any other man of the same high respectability in the Union. He said to me, seriously, and in a business-like manner, one night, in the office,

"Cowell, have you ever played the comic part in the Apostate?"

Of course I said, "Yes, often. But there are two comic parts," said I, "Pescara and Malec. Now if Thorne will do one, I'll do the other."

Unfortunately, the *stars*—Kirby and Jones—had named these characters for themselves, or I believe he would have cast the play as I dictated. Whatever talent his good lady possessed, was entirely obscured by her transcendent personal charms—the beautiful Miss Nelson will no doubt be recollected, as the "divine perfection of a woman" who played with some success during Fawcett's stage-management at Covent Garden. Now this lady, and Mrs. Stewart, and Mrs. Richardson, were all engaged for the same line of business. Mrs. Stewart and Mrs. Richardson were both powerful favourites with the audience, and the stage-manager very naturally believed his wife was a much better actress than either of them, and, by placing her continually and favourably before the public, hoped, in time, to get them to think as he did; but she couldn't play everything; Mrs. Richardson was, therefore, kept full in sight, but Mrs. Stewart was scarcely seen or heard of. Dumas was easily convinced of the folly of paying three ladies for doing what two were made sufficient to perform, and determined to get rid of one of them; but, unfortunately, made an imprudent selection.

A long part was sent to Mrs. Stewart, which, as was expected, she refused, or said she couldn't learn in the short time required, and a forfeit of a week's salary was the consequence; which, being resisted, ended in a discharge. She sued for the amount, and gained her suit: the next week the same course was repeated, with the same result. It was then agreed, mutually, to have the matter settled by arbitration. Some gentlemen of high standing were chosen on both sides; and they decided in favour of the lady, awarding her her salary and a benefit, according to the contract, which, they agreed, had not been violated on her part; but with this verdict Dumas very impolitically refused to comply.

Mrs. Stewart, though not actually born in Mobile—very few people are born in Moble who can possibly avoid it — was, from a residence there since childhood, held in the respect of a most estimable citizen. The regard demanded by her exemplary conduct as a daughter, wife, and mother, perhaps, might cause her actual talent to be a little overrated; but on the honest, unmolested exercise of that talent depended, not only her own support—now a widow—but that of an aged parent and her two orphan children; the course Dumas had pursued was, therefore, justly considered an insult to public opinion, in selecting, as a victim to his untheatrical arrangements, a lady so conspicuously entitled to moral consideration and support. A most delicious row was the consequence; and it so fell out, that it occurred on the very night that Hackett had advertised that he would prove to the whole critical world—or, at any rate, as large a portion of it as might be found in Mobile—that *Kean* knew nothing at all about the character of Richard the Third, and *Cook* but very little ; but that he, after long study and research, had arrived at the genuine, historical, and Shaksperian meaning of the part, and, on that occasion, would so delineate it.

The house was filled as soon as the doors were opened, for most of the audience rushed in without paying, made a prodigious noise, broke some benches and gas-fixings, and demanded a *free benefit* for Mrs. Stewart, and *the whole of her salary to be paid for the ten weeks*—the period of her engagement—all which Dumas was *obliged to agree to*. The mayor made a speech, and the row was over; and Hackett was left to deliver himself of his great conception. Under the circumstances, a fair judgment couldn't be formed. The little I saw of it I thought was very odd, and very original, and reminded me very much of his unique manner of performing Rip Van Winkle.

CHAPTER XX.

"The best thing in him
Is his complexion ; and faster than his tongue
Did give offence, his eye did heal it up.
He is not tall, yet for his years he's tall ;
His leg is but so so, and yet 'tis well ;
There was a pretty redness in his lip,
A little riper and more lusty red
Than that mix'd in his cheek ; 'twas but the difference
Between the constant red and mingled damask."
As You Like It.

HACKETT may be more properly called a successful *dramatic merchant* than an actor. He started in business with a very small lot of goods, to be sure, but their variety was suitable to many markets; and, with great tact and shrewdness, he made everybody believe they could not be obtained at any other shop.

Rochefoucault says, "The only good copies are those which expose the ridiculousness of bad originals." But, be that as it may, with an imitation of poor old Barnes that amounted to identity, he made

" The two Dromios one in 'semblance,"

and gained, without farther study or struggle, a reputation, which many, with industry and talent, have wasted a lifetime in endeavouring to attain. His profits were enormous. Barnes went with him everywhere, caricaturing himself, to increase the effect. When this attraction began to flag, who but Hackett would have thought of using Colman's excellent but seldom-acted play of "Who wants a Guinea?" as a vehicle for introducing such a sketch of humanity as Solomon Swap? And though whittling a stick and cheating a man out of a watch are not very complimentary characteristics to select for a Yankee portrait, they were highly relished by the audience, from being better understood than Solomon Gundy's unpractical jokes and broken French. Hill and Marble put in their very superior claims to delineations of that description, which interfered greatly with the original inventor; but Hackett had an unapproachable resource in his ancestral dialect, and in Rip Van Winkle he could securely say, " *You can't come it, judge!*"

When Kean was driven from the stage, reeking with criminality in public opinion, Hackett undertook to play Richard the Third in imitation of him, the high reputation he had gained as a mimic giving warranty of a skilful likeness. Now here was an excellent opportunity given to the curiously virtuous to admire the secondhand *mental beauties* of Kean, portrayed by a gentleman of unquestionable private worth and moral deportment, without having their nicer feelings shocked by the actual presence of the depraved original. This must be admitted to have been a clear-headed mercantile conception, but, strange to say, it didn't answer. I so advertised him at Baltimore sixteen years ago; but it failed to attract a house, in the first place, and the larger portion of those who did come went away before the exhibition was half over. In fact, Hackett, from the first, looked upon the drama as an easy means of acquiring wealth with very scanty materials, if properly managed, and he has realized the justness of his calculation. He still holds a high place in dramatic estimation; though he thought it necessary, the winter before the last, at New-Orleans, to rouse up public attention by a long ancestral and heraldic *exposé*, which occupied half the columns of a short-lived newspaper there, to prove that, though he condescended to conduct himself like a plain, honest, well-disposed Republican player, he was, for all that, *a real baron!* And I'll bear witness that *"that is a fact;"* for some six years ago, in order to remove the possibility of any doubt or quibble on the subject that might arise hereafter, he actually imported his *ancestor, with the title, and Dutch dialect*—a most gentlemanly man, and a very ingenious gunsmith, with red and white mustache. He died of the yellow fever, and was buried at New-Orleans in the summer of 1839 or 1840, and therefore Hackett is now the *last of*

the barons of that ilk, Bulwer's novel to the contrary notwithstanding. By-the-by, Hackett, if you have not read the book I allude to, do; you will find an excellent hint for a new conception of Richard there.

Connor was another star: a very gentleman-like specimen of well-dressed mediocrity; not good enough in anything to be bad *by comparison with himself* in anything. He possesses an excellent wardrobe, and knows so well how to use it, that, in consequence, he often looks the character he intends to represent so excellently, that I have frequently felt sorry he was obliged to say anything about it. Richelieu is one of the parts I allude to. I am told he plays it in imitation of Forrest; but I can't believe it; he reminds me very strongly of Blanchard, of the Coburgh's manner of tottering about after he was changed, by a slap of Harlequin's bat, to the "lean and slippered Pantaloon."

Connor has his ancestors too. Some few years since, at St. Louis, the papers made it to be understood that he had great expectancies from a rich uncle. They didn't say if the old gentleman was a baron or not, but went on to explain that the nephew considered emolument a secondary matter, and was merely acting for his own amusement: an excellent way, by-the-by, of accounting for his style. *It took.* He got great applause, and was driven about and drenched with Champagne by all the first *young* dry-goods and grocery men in the city—they have all taken the benefit of the Bankrupt Act since—and they made him a great house. But on his return, a few months afterward, the same paper, by way of variety, I imagine, hinted at *"pecuniary embarrassments," " domestic claims on his income," " disappointments:"* his uncle wouldn't die, I suppose; or else he had, "and made no sign" in his favour; in short, the truth leaked out that he was "an honest, exceeding poor man," and could lay claim to the negative virtue of supporting an aged mother; and the corks ceased to pop, and the benefit was a comparative failure.

To secure a bumper this time (in Mobile), it was advertised that *a splendid silver cup would be presented to him by a committee of gentlemen, who had long admired his public virtue and private talent.*

It answered so well, that on my night I got a committee of gentlemen to take a fancy to my public and private virtue, and present me with a splendid *tin* cup. Connor had the best house; but when it is taken into consideration that his *silver cup* must have cost from eight to ten dollars, and I only gave six bits for my *tin pot*, I guess, in the end, we were about even.

Mrs. Sefton, the very best general actress on the continent, adorned the theatre through a long engagement; and Miss Mary Anne Lee, "*the celebrated American danseuse,*" and Joe Field, with some pleasant new farces, proved a refreshing relief. The audience were in ecstasies at her attainments, and the press declared she was quite equal to Ellsler. I am no judge of dancing, and I never saw Ellsler; but I hope it's the fact; for her father was a worthy creature, and a great favourite of mine, and I have known her to be a very good little girl ever since she was dancing in her mother's arms, and I am oldfashioned enough to have a strong prejudice in favour of old acquaintances.

Dan. Marble, that most irresistibly comic soul, came with his bundle of fun. He possesses that extraordinary arbitrary power of making you laugh whether you like it or not: no matter if

99

you have the toothache, the headache, or the heartache; the cool, quiet, deliberate *nonsense, if you please*, with which he surrounds you, as if he didn't mean to do it, would make you laugh at a funeral. In my opinion, he is a much superior actor than he himself, or the public in general, believe him to be. It is an abstract portion of nature, to be sure; but so perfect, so pure, that if you are not even acquainted with the source from whence the picture is drawn, you can swear that it is a likeness. The pieces which he carries on his shoulders are generally sad trash; but if he could get Buckstone, or some of these dramatic *tacticians*, to prepare two or three for him, and go to London, if he did not make a powerful impression, I will resign all claim to any judgment in such matters.

The management, no doubt, must have looked at some future point of policy when they engaged *Ludlow and Smith as stars at Mobile!* Not both together; that would have been too much to expect; neither do they shine to advantage in the same sphere. They each have a favourite round of characters; but, strange to say, very nearly the same round of characters are the favourites with each. In their own theatres, this is very amicably arranged between them. In the first place, Sol. Smith has given up the entire range of high tragedy to Ludlow, with the exceptions of Hecate and the High-priest in Pizzaro; he also retains The Three Singles, another bit of tragedy; but, as a set-off, Ludlow is permitted to play Baron Willinghurst, which he makes equally melancholy, six or eight times in every season; and as he has to keep looking like Ludlow, and change his dress seven times, it may be justly considered a fair equivalent. Puff, in the "Critic," they do turn and turn about. Sol. plays Darby, and Ludlow, Nipperkin; and they both amuse themselves with the Lying Valet occasionally. Now Smith came first; and, not satisfied with playing all his own pets, took a touch at one of his partner's, *Frederic Baron Willinghurst.* I don't want to kick up a row between them, but I decidedly think myself it was taking rather an unfair advantage of Ludlow. They are both remarkably good-looking men; but Ludlow, as the saying is, is no chicken, and though he is most abstemious in his habits, particularly in eating, he is getting a little clumsy for light comedy, especially about the legs. What a change a few years will make in a man! I remember him a perfect *he-sylph* in appearance. Now Smith still retains his figure, and the same fine, frank, joyous, elegant, yet playful deportment that he ever had. But, then, he is extremely particular about his personal appearance on or off the stage. I don't believe he either pads or laces, but he might be suspected of doing both; proud of his hair, his nails—I mean his fingernails—and when he laughs, you can count every tooth he has in his head. Now, knowing his superior advantage over Ludlow, and that his engagement would commence immediately after his was concluded, and that Ludlow *must play Baron Willinghurst or die,* his forestalling him in that part, I say it again, was very unkind. Of course, I did not see Smith play the Baron; but I saw him dressed for the first scene. His coat was a little too short in the sleeves, to be sure; but that could not be said of the tail; and it was very Revolutionary in its general character; white trousers, which had been badly packed; a very suspicious-looking hat; and a pair of highlows without strings.

Well, as arranged by the sapient management, Ludlow followed, with the Lying Valet, Doctor Pangloss, She Stoops to Conquer, cut down to the *Humours of Young Marlow*; Nipperkin, the Duke in the Honeymoon; and on my benefit night he requested me to let him play *Baron Willinghurst*, and, as I wanted something to give time for me to change my dress, I consented, but suggested that any of his other farce parts would be better, as Smith had already played the Baron.

"Smith played the Baron!" said he. "Psh-a-a-a-w!"

I wish I could write down his face at that moment.

"Smith played the Baron! Pshaw!" and he looked as if he had swallowed a bad oyster. "Smith played it? Then that's the very reason why I wish to do it myself."

And I hadn't the heart to refuse him, though I knew it would keep money out of the house.

Young Vandenhoff, an infinitely better actor than his father was at the same age, played to empty benches for a few nights; and Sinclair was mixed up with Sol. Smith, so that it was hard to tell who kept the money out of the house, but he proved to the few who did hear him the feeble power Time, in his case, has had over

"Linked sweetness long drawn out."

But the great incident of the season was the first appearance, on any stage, of Mr. Charles Fisher, in the character of Dazzle, in London Assurance. Gifted with a refined taste and great literary acquirements, and his whole life having been passed in intimate association with theatricals, it was unthinkingly supposed, in consequence, that he would present a more than usually brilliant display of histrionic talent. A large audience was assembled on the occasion, but not so large as might have been expected under the circumstances, when, in addition to the high claims on public favour of the fair beneficiary, for whom he had gallantly volunteered his services, it is remembered that Mr. Fisher has been a resident of Mobile for some years, both summer and winter, and universally known and respected. In proof of his great popularity, among other honorary distinctions may be named, that he is a Mason, Odd Fellow, corresponding secretary for the Jockey Club, full private in the volunteer artillery, a fireman, a cowbellian, the founder, and a member for life of the Can't-get-away Club, and, as I have before stated, making a living as secretary to the Gas Company. Now all this should, at any rate, have produced a full house, *but it did not.* I staked half an eagle to a sovereign with Joe Field, that there would be six hundred dollars, and I lost my American gold.

Suffering from great nervous embarrassment, and his natural timidity increased by the knowledge of how much was expected of him by the overwrought anticipations of his friends, who had long looked up to him as the sole dramatic oracle for the State of Alabama, he became perfectly bewildered, and certainly did make a sad mess of poor Dazzle. No allowance was made for stage fright. A highly-finished, experienced performance was fully expected from a critic

"Whose lash was torture, and whose praise was fame;"

and his devotees were actually angry with him because he was not himself all that he had explained to them, in print and private, a good player ought to be. But I see no reason why he

100

might not, with a little practice, make a star at any rate, if he wouldn't answer for a regular actor. He has excellent requisites for the kind of parts which assimilate with that he made choice of for his *début*. An immense point in his favour is his extremely youthful appearance, for which he is chiefly indebted to his fine pink complexion, resembling the Jack of Hearts; with the same large, soft, washed-out-blue-looking eye, and not unlike him in figure when dressed in regimentals, if Jack wore a *bustle*. When diamonds are trumps at a game at *uker*, I always think of Charley, if I happen to have *the left bower guarded*.

A Mr. Kirby, and Mr. G. W. Jones, "*the celebrated delineator of American sailors*," two more stars, twinkled through a week or two; but if I was to devote a page in giving a description of their talent, it is probable by the time that page is in print they will have ceased to shine, and the reader would then wonder who I was talking about.

A strong Frenchman—*I won't remember his name*—proved the strongest attraction of the season. His benefit was an overflow! while poor John Barton, the Shaksperian scholar, the innocently eccentric companion *for a gentleman*, whose talent, wrestling with infirmity, claimed the respect his private worth demanded from all who knew him, took, no doubt, his farewell forever of an American audience, and lost money by his!

------◆------

CHAPTER XXI.

Any scrap of Locke's *poetical* description of modern discoveries in the moon, which may live in the memory of the reader, will be very applicable to the subject most prominent in this chapter.—THE AUTHOR.

ALL the engagements terminated at the end of twenty weeks, which closed the season; but a few members of the company with small salaries, who could afford to accept one third, or even half of their former income, or, to speak plainly, who could not afford to go without any income at all, commenced a new campaign under the management of Mrs. Richardson, instead of Mr. Hodges. Madame Vestris, I believe, was the first to set this fashion of petticoat government, which has been followed, with various claims to popularity in this country, by Miss Cushman, Miss Maywood, Miss Virginia Monier, Miss Clarendon, Mrs. Sefton, and now Mrs. Richardson, I am grieved to say, lent her name to eke out the very small demands on public favour of only half a company, only half paid.

I had a right to a benefit during the twenty weeks, but the season had been so monopolized by sometimes two and three stars at a time, that I had to continue a week longer for a vacant night, and as in all probability I made my last appearance on that occasion, I'll reprint the bill.

"MOBILE THEATRE,

Under the management of Mrs. Richardson.

FAREWELL BENEFIT

OF

MR. J O E C O W E L L,

Prior to his departure for some place, but where, He don't know, nor will anybody care.

At the close of the performance, of course Mr. Cowell will be *called out*, but if not, he will *go out*, and have a *splendid wreath* thrown to him from a corner of the second tier, and be addressed from the stage-box by one of a committee of gentlemen who have long admired his *private worth* and *public services*, and be presented with

An elegant Tin Cup;

to which he will make an extemporaneous reply, *prepared for the occasion*, after the manner of other distinguished artists.

Among the many luxuries that could be named for both mind and body, such as old wine, old books, and old boots, might be mentioned old plays; but old Joe Cowell being desirous to please everybody, though he may *lose his ass into the bargain*, has made a selection of one about his own age; two, born within his recollection, and another that never saw "the light of other days" till now, called

JOE SHORT.

Now Joe Cowell having the *Assurance*—not London — but of many friends, that they intend to *Meddle* in his favour on this occasion, begs in a *Courtley* manner not to *Dazzle*, but inform the public that his benefit will take place on Friday evening, April 7th, 1843, when he hopes it will not be considered *Pert* his recommending the patrons of the drama to keep *Cool* and *Harkaway* to the theatre, and have the *Grace* to give him a *Spanker*.

The performance will commence with the first and second acts of

LONDON ASSURANCE.

Sir Harcourt Courtley -	Mr. Bridges.
Dazzle - - - - - -	Mr. Ludlow.
Meddle - - - - - -	Mr. Cowell.
Max Harkaway - - -	Mr. Germon.
Charles Courtley - -	Mr. Morton.
Grace Harkaway - -	Mrs. Mackenzie.
Pert - - - - - - -	Mrs. Germon.

After which,

Not a Star, but a real Comet,

from somewheres so far away down east that his childhood was passed in breaking day with brickbats, will appear and sing

The Pizen Sarpient.

By particular desire,

OF AGE TO-MORROW.

In which Mr. Ludlow will personate Seven Characters!!

Maria, with a favourite song, Mrs. Richardson.

To be followed by a new farce called

JOE SHORT.

Principal characters by Mr. Cowell, Mr. Anderton, Mr. Wright, Mrs. Mackenzie, Mrs. Wright, and Mrs. Germon.

To conclude with the

WIDOW'S VICTIM.

Jeremiah Clip, *with his inimitable imitations* -	Mr. Cowell.
Jenny - - - - - -	Mrs. Richardson.
The Widow - - - -	Mrs. Mackenzie.

The Splendid Tin Cup!

will be exhibited on the day of performance, and a deposite at George Cullum's made at the bar by the committee, for Cowell's friends to drink to his *success in a bumper!*"

The resident population of Mobile is too refined in taste, and too well acquainted with how
the drama ought to be conducted, to visit the
theatre at all, unless very superior attraction be
offered; and at this season of the year all strangers are moving homeward as fast as they can,
with the exception of the new members of the
Can't-get-away Club, and, poor fellows, their play-
going days were passed long ago. Now setting
at defiance all these disadvantages, the steward
of the steamboat Southerner, who had so far the
advantage of Dumas that he had a taste for
acting as well as managing, opened a new establishment in a large room over the Corinthian
—a splendid grogshop—and called it the *American Theatre*.

Mr. and Mrs. Hodges, Sinclair, and Jemmy
Thorne were engaged as stars; there were none
but stars employed, I believe, including the steward, who, unfortunately, indulged himself by giving *his conception* of Richard the Third, and got
hissed so heartily that he advertised his retirement
from dramatic life at the end of the week; and
in the same paper I saw that "the American
Theatre was, *for the future*," to be under the
management of the pretty young woman who
played Grace Harkaway originally, and so very
badly, at the Park.

To effectively compete with such an opposition, Doctor Lardner was engaged at *the* theatre
to deliver a course of astronomical lectures, and,
in excellent taste, Mr. George Holland to exhibit his magnificent *Optical Illusions on the same
evenings!*

For some time past a horde of locomotive
penny-magazine men had been scattering their
real and pretended knowledge about the country,
dignified by the name of lectures, till, like every
bubble fashion indiscriminately inflates, the
practice had become most ridiculously distend-
ed. Of course, the more inexplicable the subject of dissertation, the more attractive; and,
therefore, every description of mysterious humbuggery had been administered, and greedily
swallowed, and followed, though decency might
be set at defiance under the influence of *exhilarating gas*, or common sense prostrated by *experimental Mesmerism*. This imbecile mania produced some little good, at any rate. It had opened an unexpected path for a few scientific men,
with a small share of worldly tact, and *expensive*
families, to find a ready money-market for their
hitherto unsaleable philosophical attainments.
The doctor was one of these; and very judi-
ciously took the moon by the horns, by way of
a bold beginning, and without much danger of
the numerous intellectual itinerant quacks presuming to intrude with him

"Into the heaven of heavens!"

A very fashionable audience attended his first
lecture. The upper portion of the theatre was
kept closed on the occasion, and very prudently,
too, for I certainly think the gods would never
have sat quietly and patiently for an hour and a
half to hear their old acquaintance, the moon,
abused like a pickpocket. All that portion of
her early history which we usually learn in the
nursery—so simple, and yet so wonderful—was
most agreeable to hear repeated with *a bit of the
brogue;* but *devil a bit of the blarny* was used to
describe her, now that she is found out to be a
hard, ill-formed, chaotic lump of disagreeableness,
" without one good quality under heaven."
The doctor is such a notoriously gallant man,

too, that one would have thought her grammat-
ical sex would have protected her from the rude
and familiar manner in which he spoke of her
behind her back, as if she were

"Base and unlustrous as the smoky light
That's fed with stinking tallow."

And, after setting the only beauty he allowed
her to possess (and that a borrowed one) at defiance, with his proposed *Drummond Pharos*, he
must have the Irish impudence of Daniel O'Con-
nell himself if ever he looked her in the face
again. And her inhabitants, too, *if she has any*,
according to his account, are the most unpleasant people on earth—neither able to walk, talk,
smell, see, hear, touch, taste, nor do anything
like other respectable persons. In short, as Butler says of some other lecturer, more than a
century and a half ago,

"Her secrets understood so clear,
That some believed he had been there;
Told what her d'meter t'an inch is,
And proved that she's not made of green cheese."

In fact, destroying, in very commonplace prose,
half the charm of Moore's poetry; and, indeed,
everybody's poetry; and what is worse, and
cruel, annihilating, with these scientific imaginings, the *childish hope* (if you please) of the poor
shipwrecked mariner, who cheats despair with
the innocent reliance on the moon's change to
bring relief, while clinging to life, "with one
plank between him and destruction." But, seriously, if all Doctor Lardner said that night is
really true, and any one believed that it was,

"A *sadder* and a wiser man
He rose the morrow morn."

George Holland's exhibition followed. He is
a man after my own heart, and thinks, with old
John Ford,

"Far better 'tis
To *bless the sun*, than reason why he shines."

His magic lantern was wisely introduced between the first and second parts of the lunatic
harangue, and the audience seemed to express
their sense of the pleasing relief by their frequent approbation. This was as it should be;
this was delightful; it disturbed no innocently
happy belief, but brought back, in all its freshness, the days of our childhood—the Christmas
holydays, the evening at home, the hoarse music of the grinding organ, and the cry of the
shivering Italian "*Gallantee show!*" indistinctly
heard through the pattering rain. The joyous
preparation for its reception—the screen put
round the blazing fire, the large table-cloth forked against the wall, and the homely, moral fun,
never to be forgotten, of *pull devil! pull baker!*

But, when you come to think of it, what a
strange combination to form a fashionable entertainment in this lecturing age, in a playhouse, instead of the sterling comedy, supported
by the educated, good old actor, "all of the old-
en time!" The doctor labouring with scientific
enthusiasm to make you look with philosophic
apathy, instead of awe and admiration, on one
of the *most conspicuous wonders in nature;* and
Holland, with his show, demanding you to be
once more a child, to enable you to express delight at his *little trifles in art*.

As I wandered through Orange Grove, on my
way to my solitary lodgings, I looked up at

"Mine own loved light,"

and could not help but regret that *Locke's* description of her had so soon been found out to

102

be a *hoax*. What glorious playhouse lectures *he could have made!* "with new scenery, machinery, dresses, and decorations;" much more agreeable to listen to, and quite as easy to believe, as Dr. Lardner's learned suppositions.

The next day I went to New-Orleans. As I had predicted before the building was completed, Caldwell had been unable to maintain the American; his system is too legitimate for these degenerate days. At the end of a month he published a manly valedictory, and bade farewell to management forever. Dinneford, who had achieved some unenviable notoriety as a *theatrical speculator* at New-York, some how or another became the lessee. His career, as might have been expected, was of very short duration. Mrs. Sefton now had the control: the company was small, but her superior talent and experienced energy made it respectably effective. I looked in only for an instant. Connor was toddling about as Richelieu, and Rowly Marks, a distinguished member of the Synagogue, with an extraordinary large emblem of Christianity tied round his middle, toddling after him as "*Jo-o-zeph.*"

Ludlow and Smith had managed to scrape together some bricks and mortar, and built a small, unpretending affair, in one corner of the ruins of the Temple, and called it the St. Charles. The interior is very neat and pretty. The night I was there, Colonel Richard M. Johnson, the ex-Vice-president of the United States, *had also* honoured the theatre with his presence, but there was a very slim house, notwithstanding—very few ladies; and a *Quadroon* ball happening on the same evening, at which, it was ridiculously hinted, it was the intention of the colonel to attend, accounted for the absence of that portion of the audience.

On the day that the fanatic, Miller, said the world would end, I took my departure from the Balize — which is more like the last end of it than any place that can be imagined — in the brig Orchilla, bound to Baltimore, with her hold full of pork, and a deck-load of molasses and blue-bottle flies.

THE END.